...nd Vernon lives and writes in Somerset, where ... lso runs his own marquee company. After ...uating from university he trained as an operatic ...r, and for a short time pursued that career, ...re opting for a more settled country life. He is ...ied, with three sons. Previous books include ...*in the East*, a biography of Jiddu Krishnamurti, ...the novel, *A Dark Enchantment*.

005038425 2

Also by Roland Vernon

A DARK ENCHANTMENT

and published by Black Swan

THE MAESTRO'S VOICE

Roland Vernon

BLACK SWAN

TRANSWORLD PUBLISHERS
61–63 Uxbridge Road, London W5 5SA
A Random House Group Company
www.rbooks.co.uk

THE MAESTRO'S VOICE
A BLACK SWAN BOOK: 9780552775526

First publication in Great Britain
Black Swan edition published 2010

Addresses for Random House Group Ltd companies outside the UK
can be found at: www.randomhouse.co.uk
The Random House Group Ltd Reg. No. 954009

The Random House Group Limited supports The Forest Stewardship
Council (FSC), the leading international forest certification organisation.
All our titles that are printed on Greenpeace approved FSC certified
paper carry the FSC logo. Our paper procurement policy can be
found at www.rbooks.co.uk/environment

Mixed Sources
Product group from well-managed
forests and other controlled sources
www.fsc.org Cert no. TT-COC-2139
© 1996 Forest Stewardship Council
FSC

Typeset in 11/13pt Giovanni Book by
Kestrel Data, Exeter, Devon.
Printed in the UK by
CPI Cox & Wyman, Reading, RG1 8EX.

2 4 6 8 10 9 7 5 3 1

For my very special Benny

THE MAESTRO'S VOICE

PART ONE

At the high point of the crisis, Campobello had a dialogue with the non entity.

Is this it? Is this the moment when I die?
Have you got anything to say for yourself?
Let me go back.
Why should I?
Time is running out. Quickly. Please let me go back.
You people go on about time. Why can't you accept that time is your enemy? Time is at the heart of your tragedy. You think that by measuring everything you'll be safer, but I'm afraid life doesn't fit into neat little squares. We'll touch on this again before I let you go.
Let me go? So you mean you're going to let me go back?
Believe me. You won't want to.
But I do.
Only because that is all you know. I ask again. Why should I let you go back?
Because I serve a purpose in the world. Because millions of people love me, and my work is not complete. Isn't that enough? And I've been a Christian man. I've given money to the Church, I'll remind you.
Ah yes, the Church. Very quaint.
You would pour scorn on the Church?

11

Not scorn, no no. People need a way to reach the water. Animals were made stupid so they just crawl to a riverbank if they're thirsty. But man was made upright, intelligent, crafty. He needs to have a cup. He fashioned the Church to be a cup of sorts, I suppose, and very picturesque it is too.

Picturesque! How dare you?

Oh come on! Don't be pompous. Cups can come in all shapes and sizes, big ones, small ones, gold ones, china ones. The point is this: once a man has tasted the water, what need should he have of a cup? If he can jump into the spring pool and immerse himself in the good water, why should he remember the cup that gave him the first tiny taste?

I don't know what you're talking about.

Of course you don't.

What is the water?

Nothing.

You're talking in riddles. What's this business about water? Hurry!

I'm just calling it water in the way you might call me a person. But it's no thing in particular.

What is the water, then?

You don't need to ask.

I need to know. I'm dying here. Please tell me. What is the water?

I am. I am. And you are my son.

I don't believe you.

I don't want you to believe. I want you to know.

I can't understand what you're on about. This is it. I'm dying.

[*A timeless interval.*]

Time is slipping back to you, so it's time to be on your way.

12

Don't send me back.

Aha.

The water is so good. Don't let me go.

Don't send me back. Please.

You've had a taste. You can bear me with you.

Why must I go back?

You know why: to put your house in order.

Of course. You've said it a million times. I'm sorry, I forgot.

There's no need for apologies. You know what to do, don't you?
I will be with you.

I know what to do. But don't send me back.

I know how you feel. When you've done what needs to be done, we'll see about what happens next. Now, you know where to start?

Of course. We've been through this a thousand times.

That's maybe how it feels.

Will you have me back?

Time is returning.

I can feel it. Everything was smooth and clear before, and now there are ugly shapes moulding through. Thinking puts a heavy grid across the world.

Nicely put.

There's no way out, is there?

No.

In which case – I'm ready.

Chapter 1

The great tenor Rocco Campobello lay unconscious on the slab. His arms rested by his sides, his palms splayed open. The little coral amulet he carried with him at all times for protection against the evil eye, the *mal'occhio*, had fallen to the floor. Life was draining from his body but there was not the slightest trace of suffering in his face. Quite the opposite. He looked like a slumbering monk consumed by the ecstasy of prayer: helpless, sickly pale, in receipt of divine whisperings. The slight, involuntary smile that warmed his half-open mouth seemed touched with the feather of an angel.

But his mystical rapture must have been fed either by an illusion or by a source cosmically removed from the present scene, because the contrast between his tranquillity and the surrounding bustle could scarcely have been more pronounced. All around the prostrate tenor's yielding form a team of men and women toiled urgently, their darting eyes betraying a sense of contained panic that the bland uniformity of their hygiene masks could not conceal. They comprised one of the finest collections of surgeons and operating theatre technicians that New York could boast, brought together at lightning speed and short notice on a Saturday night from different reaches of the city. And yet, despite their earnest labour and abundant experience, few of those in attendance could help but reflect on the career-defining significance of what they had assembled to accomplish; and few could stop themselves stealing a look from time to time at the face of the man beneath their lamp, as a child might glance at a much-prized present before turning to sleep on Christmas night, again and just once again, to check it was still there in the corner of his room.

He was not as corpulent as most of them remembered from the famous photographs, having lost so much weight in recent months, but he was still a big man, by any standards. He had the frame of one born for labour, but not the muscle system to go with it: as if fortune had spared him the hardships for which nature, after generations of breeding, had predisposed him. His arms and chest were consequently rather pale and flabby, which seemed slightly incongruous beneath the broad, tanned face, and the powerful brow with its high forehead that shone like polished brass.

A map print peninsula of dried blood spread from the corner of his mouth, turning most of one cheek the colour of beetroot. This was the residue left after the coughing fit he had suffered earlier in the evening, right in the middle of his concert recital. He had been in severe pain from the start of the performance and had done what he could to conceal it, but when his mouth suddenly filled with blood he could not even get to the wings in time, and retched it all up on to the stage in front of a horror-stricken audience.

Presiding over this medical crisis team was the eminent

16

Dr Jonah D. Goldblatt, who had been compelled to cut short a dinner engagement with the mayor in order to attend. An iron wool beard protruded beneath the taut muslin of his mask, through which his heavy breathing – rhythmically metered bear grunts – offered a kind of bestial counterpoint to the slice and tinkle of steel surgical instruments at work. He, alone amongst the company, seemed unaffected by the celebrity of his patient, and went about his craft expertly, without distraction, as if his fingers danced to a choreography set prepared and rehearsed weeks in advance.

The deep incision had been made and the abdomen clamped apart when a door on the far side of the theatre opened. A nervous young man entered and approached Dr Goldblatt cautiously.

'I'm sorry, sir,' he half whispered, looking like a guilty dog anticipating rebuke, 'Mrs Campobello asks me to ask you if it's absolutely necessary that you, that you,' he pointed to the wound and flinched, 'that you cut through her husband's rib.'

Goldblatt breathed heavily through his mask. 'Get this person out,' he said in a central European bass.

'Yes, sir, of course, sir,' said the man, raising both hands in grateful surrender and backing away.

'You can tell her it is a choice of the rib or the man,' Goldblatt added quietly.

'Sir?'

'A four-inch section of one, maybe even two ribs may have to be removed if we are to get a clear route to this abscess.' Goldblatt's glistening fingers reached for the fine-toothed saw on the trolley beside him.

*   *   *

17

Molly Campobello meanwhile paced impatiently across the floor of the room adjacent to the theatre, drawing heavily on her cigarette and muttering soundless curses as she exhaled the smoke. One or two members of the hospital staff had already noticed her agitation, and, assuming that it was rooted in concern for her husband's welfare, had tendered quiet words of consolation and refreshments, but their good intentions were met with steely indifference. Molly's vexation would not be ameliorated by warm drinks or the attentions of skivvies; and she couldn't even be bothered to scold them for their impertinence. Unable to contain her impatience any longer, she had strode into the hospital's admissions office and instructed a reluctant clerk to take a message personally to the surgeon; and, such was the force of her personality, neither the unfortunate young man nor anyone in his path dared refuse her. His cowed response, when he arrived back in the waiting room a few seconds later, ignited a blaze of white heat in her eyes.

'Who does the man think he is?' she spat. 'It's not just anyone he's got in there. Does he know who he's operating on?'

The clerk looked to the floor. 'I'm sure Dr Goldblatt knows it's Mr Campobello,' he said.

'Oh, for heaven's sake!' said Molly and turned away in disgust, allowing the man to return to the refuge of his office.

If Dr Goldblatt now went ahead and removed parts of her husband's ribs, as he appeared to be insisting upon, it would put the tenor out of action for weeks, if not months. Which would as good as whitewash the remainder of the year's engagements, instigate a flood of media speculation about the singer's future, and poleaxe every detail of Molly's carefully orchestrated calendar for the foreseeable future. It was quite simply an intolerable situation. She puffed a cloud of spent smoke into the air with exasperation.

Half an hour later she was still digesting the unhappy prognosis, when she heard cries from the operating theatre next door, followed by a muffled bang, feet running, and a man shouting instructions. Alarm flashed across her face. She stubbed out the cigarette under the toe of her shoe and, steadying her heavy string of pearls with one hand, ran over to the connecting door. What she saw, on entering, instantly anaesthetized her fury.

An intense stench of putrefaction had filled the room, something so disarmingly offensive that Molly immediately brought a scented wrist to her nose. An appalling mess and confusion seemed to have overrun the former orderliness of the scene. One or two of the nursing staff had retreated back against the wall, hands over their masks, their aprons soiled; others hurried to and fro with bowls and cloths. Dr Goldblatt, assisted by two doctors, stood firm over Campobello, elbows raised, grappling an instrument that was connected to the patient's ribcage by a length of flexible hose. And everywhere – over the surgeon's clothes, the trolley of instruments, the floor, and even, in one or two places, the walls themselves – were the splattered deposits of a fluid that had exploded from her husband's body. Campobello himself lay open-armed and motionless in the midst of the frenzy, oblivious to it all, the same restful smile fixed to his lips; and by some peculiar muscular reflex his eyelids had worked themselves open, though they were sightless and he was still unconscious. Nevertheless, it was eerie to see him apparently witnessing the horror, the theatre staff's shock, the peculiar device attached to his innards, and the effect of whatever internal rupture had caused the fetid expulsion.

Molly pressed her palms to her lips, frozen to the spot, and Dr Goldblatt shot her a look. Her complaints were stifled, and a sudden redness came to her eyes; but it was not because of disgust at the sight, nor because of pity for the frail shell of her husband lying there, so close to death, though that feeling was certainly present in some remote locker of her mind. No, the immediate paralysis that afflicted her was more personal. She understood suddenly that this crisis would entail more than just the scrambling of her precious social diary; more, too, than the inconvenience of an invalid husband; or even widowhood. The realization that was being so brutally and unexpectedly forced upon her was more simple, and unarguable. Her youth had come to an end. There were no more ways to delay it, no deviations or clever little back streets. She had arrived at the line at last and it was time to cross. The great Campobello was felled, and she would be henceforth nothing but an old woman. Until this moment she had never quite admitted the degree to which her prospects and self-esteem were so tightly intertwined with the welfare of her husband's career, but that was now humiliatingly plain.

Within the hour, Campobello's long-time personal assistant and secretary, Pietro Boldoni, had appeared on the steps of the hospital to address the press corps and the swelling crowd of fans awaiting information. Boldoni was neat and dapper, with a flower in his lapel, silver-topped cane in hand and homburg hat slightly atilt. 'I

20

am pleased to be able to tell you,' he began, in accented English, while the cameras flashed, and between each phrase of the prepared statement that followed, his nose twitched with a delicate sniff.

Minutes later, his guardedly positive announcement concluded, he skipped with a dancer's grace back up the steps to rejoin the select group keeping vigil outside his employer's bedroom. Although some of the crowd refused to be moved on, the reporters instantly dispersed, scattering off in different directions like loosened spokes from a spinning-wheel, to offices, waiting cars, to telephones or telegraph offices.

Mrs Campobello had left as soon as she realized the immediate crisis had been averted. She had slipped out of the hospital's back entrance where her car awaited her, and returned unnoticed to her apartment. Boldoni had caught her just in time, and called out to her departing, mink-clad figure that he would be prepared, of course, to attend day and night without rest, should it in any way assist his Maestro's recovery or ease his peace of mind. His expression of loyalty was met with a withering look from Molly, and she swept out of the hospital, entourage in tow. Molly did not try to hide her disdain for Pietro Boldoni, and, for his part, Boldoni would neither accept her condescension nor submit to being treated like an ignorant orderly. He was too long-standing an ally and confidant of his Maestro to be classed as a mere domestic. Though never openly disrespectful, he made it clear to Molly that his allegiance and obedience belonged to her husband alone, and that it would be counter to her interests to make an enemy of him. A state of undeclared war therefore existed between the two of them which occasionally found expression in sharp skirmishes.

*

When all that could be done was done, the man at the centre of it all drifted back into consciousness; which meant that he gradually felt the miracle retreat and slip away.

He became aware of time again, and the boundless view of his resting mind's eye began to close in on all sides. East, west, north and south converged. It was agony to feel paradise shrink around him as his mind submitted to the regulation of thought.

Limitation reasserted itself and limitless possibility diminished. It was a familiar world he was re-entering but so very unwelcome.

*

The staff at the hospital, assuming that he would be confused and in pain, took care to ensure that he would be greeted with a calm scene when he came round. He was aware of nurses tiptoeing up to him every so often, and he was aware of Pietro Boldoni entering the room, placing the precious coral amulet in his palm and squeezing his fist around it.

He ignored them all for the time being because he wanted to cling to the retreating bliss; but he felt the presence of monsters in his mind; they had arrived in force and encamped around his defences. They lit their fires, laid siege, beat their drums, and began their dance of war. He knew he had no choice but to gird up.

*

The inevitable moment arrived and he crossed back over. His mind became alert, his thinking sharp. A spasm gripped his brow. A sweat arose on his body and he backed away from the slipway of oblivion. The threshold of paradise had become the brink of a hellish chasm, and he was staring down into the raging pit. He cowered there amidst the ruins, orphaned, wounded. Through the devastation he lamented that his fall from grace could be so quick and simple, just the flip of a coin.

He shivered violently and took a sharp breath. His hand was being squeezed and he heard Pietro Boldoni's reassuring whispers. That hand, those whispers were his mooring in the tempest, and as the winds calmed and the seas stilled they were still there, pulling him through. His eyes rested, unblinking, on the sharp and perfect features of his assistant.

'Maestro,' said Boldoni quietly. 'Maestro, can you hear me?'

'Yes, Pietro. Perfectly.'

'Thank God.' There were tears in Pietro's eyes. 'Is there anything you want?'

A slight smile worked itself on to Campobello's mouth. 'You won't believe me,' he muttered.

Encouraged, Pietro smiled back. 'Try me.'

'I'd like you to help me tidy up my house. Get it in order.'

Pietro blinked, hesitated a moment, and then replied, 'We have people to do that.'

'That's not what I mean.'

'What then?'

Campobello was silent.

'Ask anything of me, Maestro.'

Campobello hesitated before answering. 'Shave my head.'

23

This did surprise Pietro but he didn't show it. 'I can arrange that. Is there a reason?'

Campobello closed his eyes. He was exhausted after the distance he had travelled. It was all over, now, once and for all. Over.

Chapter 2

*From tapes of an interview with veteran Hollywood musicals
tenor and former matinée idol Franco Steel, at his home in
Santa Barbara, California, June 1986.*

Interviewer: OK, forget the legend, forget the scratchy old
records that no one can hear properly anyway, forget
the clichés – did the guy really compare favourably
with the big stars of modern times, the Pavarottis, the
Domingos?

Steel: I've been asked this question so many times before.
Well (*laughs*), I guess everyone'll think I'm biased. After
all, I owe him everything. For those of us who remember
that time, there was no comparison with the modern
era.

You see, back then there was nothing that came within a million miles of opera, no pop music, no rock and
roll, no TV. Especially in Italy. Every town had its opera
house, everyone came to the shows, brought their own
food, their kids, sang along with the famous tunes.

When the phonograph took off, and then the wireless,
opera was fashionable the world over, what the world
wanted to hear.

And Campobello was the first big star of the recorded

era, available to any householder for a couple of bucks in the privacy of a humble front room. All of a sudden gramophones – or phonographs they were called – were everywhere, and that's how Campobello literally became a *household* name.

During his career he made around four hundred recordings. He was the first artist to sell over a million records, and earned himself more than three million dollars in royalties alone, and that was quite a sum in those days. This was show business on a giant scale.

So, by 1926 he's the biggest entertainer in the world. And a master of his craft. It's like – what's a fair comparison? – like an idol of pop music rolled together with a top crooner rolled together with a great classical virtuoso; say, Elvis Presley, Sinatra and Yehudi Menuhin in one man. I don't exaggerate.

To me, aged eighteen in the mid-1920s, this man was a god, especially because he originally comes from my own town, Naples.

But to get back to your question: you ask me how he compares with the big guys of today, because you can't judge from the old records.

(*Pauses*)

(*To himself*) How can I put this so you'll understand?

(*Pauses*)

There's never been anyone who could do it all like him. Power, characterization, lyricism, drama, *legato*. He was a master of every department, you might say.

(*Pauses*)

Very occasionally – and I mean once, maybe twice – I've heard a voice with equivalent intrinsic beauty. Gigli at his best, maybe. Or the young Bjorling, certainly. But you'd have to go somewhere else for barnstorming bits: maybe to Corelli, or del Monaco. For top notes you could try Lauri-Volpi, and you just mentioned Pavarotti. But Campobello had all these things. In abundance. And when you listened to him you felt as if you were hearing something complete in *every* way. A flawless performance, and I don't use the phrase lightly. No one in my business would. And when he put on a costume he *became* the guy that he was acting. Terrifyingly, at times. Sent a shiver down your spine. He did his work. It's well documented. What I'd give to have just an ounce of his professional – whad'ya call it? – dedication.

Interviewer: We've all heard the stories, I'm sure, about how that professionalism came at a price. Colleagues said he was impossible to work with, made life difficult for everyone else backstage.

Steel: Is that so?

Interviewer: That he was dictatorial, self-centred.

Steel: Maybe that was before I met him.

Interviewer: He could be obsessive.

Steel: He was a perfectionist.

Interviewer: They say—

Steel: Look, say what you want. Maybe. Show business is show business. It's a lot worse in the movies, let me tell you. But not when I knew him. The man I knew . . . he was not at all like that. He was . . . well . . . (*Pauses*) . . . Sorry, I'm sorry, can we stop for a moment?

Interviewer: Sure.

Interview paused.

Steel (*resumes*): Some will say I'm a sentimental old man. They'll pull out the old 78s, compare them to their new digital CD whatnot, and go away laughing, but . . .

(*Pauses*)

Here's an interesting point: before Campobello there were many beautiful tenors, lots of styles, different types of voices. None of them sounded like Campobello at all. And yet after he came along, and ever since, almost every great tenor is in some way reminiscent of Rocco Campobello.

Now, what does that tell us? Well, the birth of the recording industry had something to do with it. Campobello, being the first major recorded artist, became the prototype tenor for the future. His style was the blueprint.

But it wasn't just the recordings.

A new kind of music was being born at the end of the last century, pithy and dramatic. The *verismo* style, it was called, and it needed a big chesty sound, more muscular, with thrilling long top notes and full-blooded passion. The orchestras were bigger, the scores thicker, and a different type of tenor voice was needed. Campobello owned *just that voice*, or at least, he turned his voice into that type, maybe forced it a bit too much, who knows? And so yes, he was the man of the moment, the first of the modern era. We're still in his debt.

Interviewer: So you're saying that all tenors who came after are just imitators of Rocco Campobello?

Steel: Pale ones at that. (*Laughs*)

Interviewer: You included?

Steel (*laughing*): Me especially. But I could never be the real thing. My voice was always too small to sing in the opera house proper. But I tried to sound like him on film. Don't forget – I had to act Campobello in the movie. I had to be him!

Interviewer: Of course. In *The King of Song*. That must have been a challenge, considering you actually knew the man in person. And as everyone knows, *The King of Song* went on to become one of the most successful screen musicals of that or any period, and you were nominated for an Oscar in 1955. But just how true a portrayal of Campobello does the movie present?

Steel: It was all nonsense of course.

Interviewer: Really?

Steel: Of course. What d'you expect? Showbiz and real life are never the same. Movie audiences wouldn't have wanted to see what really happened. Neither would some of the people still living when the movie was made. Though the true story would have made a hell of a show. But too dark, too dark.

Interviewer: Are you saying that the true facts about Campobello have been covered up?

(*Pause*)

Interviewer: There has always been a certain amount of speculation about the circumstances of his death.

Steel (*to himself*): So I've heard.

Interviewer: What's that?

Steel: Nothing.

Interviewer: His widow is on record as having said at the

time that the movie was as near the truth as could have been shown.

Steel (*laughs*): She would never say a thing like that. What nonsense.

Interviewer: But here it is: (*consults a book*) from Molly Campobello's memoir, *Never Ending Sunshine*—

Steel: Oh, Molly, well, yes, of course.

Interviewer: His widow.

Steel: Yep.

Interviewer: Mrs Campobello says—

Steel: I know what Mrs Campobello said. Well, that's good. I'm happy she was so pleased with the picture. Shall we move on? It was all a long time ago. No point in stirring up old grievances.

Interviewer: Grievances regarding Mrs Campobello?

Steel: May she rest in peace. Let's move on.

Chapter 3

Villa Rosalba, Naples, September 1926

Two middle-aged men were lounging idly in the shade beside one of the Doric columns that supported the Campobellos' first floor balcony. One was Signor Pozzo, the chauffeur, a veteran in his trade, a man whose passion for mechanics made him one of the first to risk the leap from driving carriages to driving automobiles, the best decision he ever took. The other was Taddeo, a local man hired to be the great tenor's physical double; and they had both thrown their jackets aside because of the heat.

The garden that stretched between them and the main gates of the compound was a scene of quiet, rather gentle, but well marshalled industry. Anything more vigorous would have been asphyxiating for the staff, now that the sun had risen so high in the sky. Groundsmen watered young lemon trees, a barefoot boy with dusty, cracked toes pushed a roller mower across the immaculate grass, and a pair of pretty dark-skinned chambermaids with white aprons crunched in step along the gravel path, carrying piles of clean linen back to the house from the laundry. Aside from the delicate measured noises made by these servants, the only other sound to break the morning air was the monotonous rasping of the cicadas, together with the occasional cry of a seagull wheeling in the sky above.

Suddenly, from inside the villa, came the violent thud of a door slammed in anger, and the two men in shirtsleeves paused from chatting and looked at one another. Their faces expressed mild shock, but also a touch of shared complacency, as if the noise fulfilled some joint prediction they had earlier made together. The hollow crash came from deep indoors, but it caused the sun-scorched outside walls of the Villa Rosalba to tremble at its impact, as if in sympathy with the building's inner fabric. Faint particles of sand trickled out of an arid crack in the ochre plaster up above, just at the point where the breast of a low-relief iron swan was pegged to the wall. Higher up, almost out of view, the same swan's neck, head and beak formed part of an ornate upper storey balustrade. Neither Pozzo nor Taddeo had ever been invited to set foot up there. It was not their place to be received in so Olympian a realm as the upstairs terrace.

This deep veranda, supported by its heavy classical colonnade, protruded from the villa on the garden side, forming a large vaulted portico through which cars would pass in order to drop people at the house's front entrance. During the summer, the shade beneath this massive stone construction offered a welcome shelter from the sun's blaze – hence the two men's presence there as they awaited their call to duty.

Taddeo, the double, puffed his cheeks and shook his head when he heard the bang. An actor by trade, he had worked with modest success at Naples' smaller theatres ever since leaving school, but had arrived at a stage of life when there just did not seem to be many roles left for him. He was too old and fat to take on the male leads, and had never had a flair for comedy. This clandestine job for Campobello had come at just the right time, and he had been in it for six weeks now, ever since the great tenor had come back to convalesce in the city of his birth. Nevertheless, Taddeo did not entirely understand what was going on here. Something was wrong, and it wasn't just Campobello's illness. There was an unsettling atmosphere in the house, an impermanence, as if its homeliness had been purchased and contrived overnight, to give an impression from the outset of settled domesticity; but it had no more substance than a stage set, and felt as if it might be taken apart, flat-packed and shipped out again in an afternoon, leaving not a trace of itself behind. Taddeo couldn't quite put his finger on it, and supposed it was none of his business anyway, but such artificiality didn't sit well with him. Which was ironic, he mused, considering that his whole professional life was dedicated to the craft of artifice. He was masquerading as somebody else, setting out to deceive and quite literally mislead. When he was with Pozzo, he liked to pretend a degree of exasperation with the job, and the two of them would share a grumble together, but the truth was: Taddeo wouldn't change places with anyone in the world. He felt privileged to resemble the Maestro so closely, almost as if the likeness implied that he shared, to a degree, his employer's manifold great gifts. He enjoyed learning how to act the part, the pay was generous, and the glamour of it all still made him tingle when he lay in bed at night.

But questions niggled at Taddeo and made him uneasy. Why, for example, after reporting here daily for all this time, had he still not set eyes on the great man in person? Mrs Campobello, who more often than not greeted him in the morning with a minimum of courtesy and a face of thunder, offered no explanation. And why had no official statement about the tenor's condition or recovery been put out yet? Above all, why did Campobello need a double sent off on a random mission to nowhere almost every day? Such an elaborate hoax, such extreme trickery – what was he hiding from, behind the walls of the grand villa?

'*Per carità*. Here we go again,' said Pozzo, at the sound of the slamming door. He feigned the same baffled exasperation as Taddeo, but Pozzo knew more than he let on, and gloried in the privilege of that knowledge. As chauffeur he was included in the small circle of those privy to the Maestro's twin secrets: he knew about the bizarre transformation in the tenor's appearance, and he knew about the great man's frequent jaunts to the heart of the city under cover of darkness. It certainly was not Pozzo's place to ask questions, but he was proud to be part of the select band that had knowledge of these confidential matters, limited though it was, and was quietly pleased, of course, that he knew more than Taddeo. The two men's relationship was not as congenial as it appeared. It irked Pozzo that he had to act the deferential servant with the double when they were out on jobs – had to touch his cap and hold the car door open for him. He suspected that all the finery and play-acting was going to Taddeo's head, and that the fat oaf was getting ideas above his station. If Pozzo had but known that he and Taddeo would one day share a common destiny, side by side, in a moment of mind-splitting violence, he might have felt more tolerant of the old salt, who wasn't so bad after all;

and he might have made the effort to forge some kind of comradely bond.

'Maybe it's the doctors this time,' said Pozzo.

'What do you mean?' asked Taddeo, cocking an eyebrow and looking down his nose at the smaller man.

'The doctors. Those two smug overpaid brothers. Maybe they're the ones who've annoyed her this time. If it's bad news they'll get a lashing.'

'Lambs to the slaughter,' added Taddeo with a smile. 'Serve them right for being so pleased with themselves. Ponces.'

'They can afford to be. They're top of the pile. Only the best clients. Even Mussolini was taken to see them when he last came to Naples.'

'What was wrong with him?' sneered Taddeo condescendingly. 'I thought he was supposed to be indestructible.'

'He hurt his knee when he fell over in front of all the dock workers. Don't you remember it in the papers? He's always falling over or breaking things.' Pozzo checked his watch and looked up at the sun, wincing. 'It's getting late, and hot. They'll be out soon. You ready?'

'*Meno male*,' sighed Taddeo, lowering himself majestically to pick up his bowler hat and cane from a stool beside the villa's front entrance, 'as ready as ever.' He was a large man, unusually broad and tall for a Neapolitan, but that was one of the prerequisites for the job. The rest of his act he had learnt from studying newsreel clips, obtained specially for his benefit by Mr Boldoni. By now he felt he had got Campobello's stately manner and swaggering elegance down to a T. Even the peculiar little limp that seemed to afflict the tenor in public yet disappeared mysteriously whenever he was on stage.

Indoors and up above, Molly Campobello walked briskly down the corridor away from the landward balcony under which the two men were idling. She had a sheet of paper in her hand, and the silk of her stole fluttered a trail behind her. She was heading towards the broad, sun-drenched terrace that overlooked the sea, on the other side of the building. When she arrived, she walked straight across to the far balustrade, screwed the paper into her fist, and tossed it over the edge. It caught the breeze, but for all the determination of her hurl, floated aimlessly like a leaf over to the left before dropping lightly into the sea.

Be gone with you, damned note! thought Molly, as she observed it being tossed around on the little waves beneath. And damned be those that sent you! How dare they preach to her, those tight-lipped sexless matrons. The Committee of the Women's Auxiliary of the Episcopal Church, the notepaper had announced in heavy print, had come to the conclusion that Molly Whittaker Campobello's influence was detrimental to the morals of young American girls. And the reason they gave: Mrs Campobello's much-chronicled adherence to fashion – particularly the fashion that encouraged knee-high skirts ('for the first time in the history of mankind'), bare arms and shoulders, and the abandonment of corsets. The latter was a heinous crime indeed, the letter droned, because contemporary dancing demanded that a girl should 'bounce continuously'. The committee therefore felt bound to ask Mrs Campobello, because of her high public profile, not merely to restrain her hitherto unfettered devotion to fashion, but to present herself as a model of upright living and clean behaviour. The implication being – thought Molly, as the crushed letter disappeared beneath the oars of a passing fisherman's dinghy – that I am currently judged dirty by these self-righteous women. And oh, won't Father just glory in that? She could picture his handsome Anglo-Saxon brow right now, and hear his voice clear as day: 'What did you all expect? She marries a peasant, she consorts with Jews and homosexuals, emigrates to the whorehouse of Europe, and now she's demonized for corrupting the young. My girl was lost to me years ago!'

Henry Burdett Whittaker had been a widower ever since his only child was an infant, and had spent thirty-four years of his adult life – up until the announcement of her engagement – in undisguised adoration of his daughter. A once distinguished Union Army soldier, he had succeeded to the family's Maryland estates, whereupon wealth and age had tarnished his natural tendency towards liberal politics and turned him into an increasingly reactionary, if beneficent, landowner. However, his worship of Molly – whom he still regarded as his own little belle with golden ringlets, and for whom no governess, no pony, and certainly no suitor was ever good enough – remained undiminished. And that despite her preference for city living, her extravagance, her penchant for smoking, and – perhaps worst – the bobbed hair. He could overlook everything until the day when she announced, at the age of thirty-four, that she was to be engaged to the opera singer Rocco Campobello.

Mr Whittaker, though well-spoken, affluent and widely respected, was not a man of culture. He had certainly never set foot in an opera house, and claimed, with something like pride, that he had met only one Italian person in his life. That his beloved daughter should be abandoning him was bad enough; that she was marrying a low-born entertainer with a foreign accent, who wore ostentatious clothes and carried with him a fortune amassed within a mere decade, stretched Henry Whittaker's fading liberalism beyond its bounds. And why had the upstart not come in person to declare his intentions? 'He's a very busy man,' was Molly's ill-advised reply, though she tried to sweeten it with a dimpled smile, 'and, Papa, it's a long way from New York.' Tact had never been among her talents.

At first, Molly attempted in vain to convince her father that she had made the right decision. In a reversal of roles, she now showered him with presents, became a Mary Pickford of girlish devotion, and sent him tender letters in scented envelopes. In the end, she played what she thought would be her trump card and announced that a grandchild would melt his angry heart. But the thrill of her pregnancy failed to raise even a nod of approval from her father, and after the agony of losing the baby just a few weeks in, she decided never to play the sentimental family card again. As it happened, there were no further pregnancies, and the will to attempt them eventually dried up. Never one to linger in the realm of failure, she quickly pasted over that hole in her life and moved on, so that nowadays it seemed not just absurd, but faintly repulsive to her that she had come so close to being lumbered with children. Her priorities had changed, or a change had been forced upon her, but the result was the same: regrets she would have none, the past was done, and all that was saccharine in her nature had turned sour. Instead, she became free to pursue a life of her choosing; free to concentrate on keeping her arms slender, on perfecting the craft of society networking, and on spreading the good news of her own beauty.

And so her father suffered in silence when he saw glamorous photographs of his daughter in all the magazines, when he read articles about her appearances at every significant event in the social calendar, receptions, conventions, handing out prizes, launching ships, dining with the President; and when he heard ever more dazzling reports of her husband's unparalleled triumphs. Never did he deign to listen to Rocco's recordings, even though he had been sent every one. His heart may have been broken, but he held the pieces together with unforgiving resentment.

The lad passing below Molly in the fishing boat stopped rowing and waved energetically across the water at her; she tutted but managed to manufacture a smile and raised her hand slightly. Mustn't overdo it, she reminded herself, or the wretch will come back for more. Everyone knew where they lived, every common little labourer, every street urchin. Some were even prepared to row this far out just to catch a glimpse of them. It was one of the downsides of having a house on the waterfront. One couldn't put a fence up in the sea.

She looked across the immense bay towards the distant sweep of Mount Vesuvius. A trail of smoke drifted inland from the pale blue volcano's summit. Nearer, the gargantuan sand-coloured structure of the Castel dell'Ovo jutted aggressively out to sea on the end of its slender causeway. Such a celebrated vista, but she could not begin to engage with its beauty. She lamented, in a sense, that circumstances had hardened her heart, because twenty years ago she might have wept at the view, and at the privilege of being able to live in a house like this. The Villa Rosalba had the most stunning position in Naples, perched on a prominent rock that jutted out from the Posillipo coastline, a few miles from the main city. To the rear, facing inland, they were surrounded by a couple of acres of private park, protected by tall spreading cedars, with gates and fences that were constantly patrolled, and so, aside from the views, they benefited from a welcome degree of privacy.

Signor Graziani had organized the house and so much else for them, and she was grateful to him for it, she supposed. He was clearly a powerful and wealthy old man, and apparently full of good intentions for Rocco, but she always wondered whether his sickly sweet words were genuine. They did not seem grounded in real friendship, and, if he was as fond and caring as he claimed to be, where had he been all this time? She had barely heard his name mentioned by Rocco in five years (but that did not count for much; there was much in her husband's life that he did not share with her). There was just something about Signor Graziani's persistent concern, and the too frequent telephone calls he would make to her personally, that was a little irksome, to say the least. She always made the effort to sound pleased to hear his voice, because, in the face of all his apparent kindness, it would be rude not to do so, but she was far from convinced that she liked the old man.

Molly's fury about the letter began to subside and was replaced with a familiar dull lethargy, the kind that always ushered in the spectre that had been haunting her these past months. What now is left for me? she asked herself for the thousandth time, and the same, predictable answer came to mind: a lonely and gradual descent towards decrepitude. The fear was never far from her thoughts. She had even begun to convince herself that her body was deteriorating. She became aware of a tiredness in her step as she climbed the stairs and noticed that one of her toes was being misshapen by what could only be called a bunion, another irritating reminder that the clock of life refused to be rewound, even for her. If Rocco were to decide to retire from singing, she might as well say goodbye to everything that made life worth living. She could already hear the daggers of her enemies and society rivals drawing to cut her memory to shreds.

Last winter's season at the Metropolitan Opera, the world's premier house, had been a disaster, and largely because of her husband. The Met's reputation nowadays hinged on the perennial appearances of its foremost star, Rocco Campobello; but out of twenty-three scheduled engagements, her husband had been able to fulfil only seven. And then came the terrible night of the collapse: his much-anticipated recital at the Carnegie Hall. She could not help wondering why he hadn't pulled out of it earlier if he had been in such pain. A cancellation would have been damaging, certainly, but preferable to the gruesome spectacle he had served up in its place. And in front of such an audience! Everyone who was anyone was there that night.

Not for the first time Molly reviewed her options, and not for the first time came to the same conclusion: no, she could never leave him. That would truly spell the end for her. She was barely clinging to respectability as it was – this morning's letter had kindly reminded her of that. If her interest in fashion were controversial enough to close a hundred drawing rooms to her, then a divorce would surely close ten thousand. And anyway, she was less enthralled nowadays by the independent life that had once seemed so attractive. She no longer cared if she was drowned in the swamp of her husband's success. Wasn't that why she had chosen Rocco in the first place? She wanted to share his eminence.

When they had married, she had told herself that love would come in time; their glamorous life would melt away any obstacles in its path. But Rocco had never doted on her in the way her father had, did not care to delight her with gifts and surprises, and, as time went by, the slight amusement he had once derived from her company turned dreary pale. He grew ever more remote and egocentric, and as each childless year chased ever more vigorously on the heels of the one before, she began to feel that their lives were passing by with a depressing momentum. Like two felled trees, they seemed to be floating separately downstream towards the sawmill, occasionally snaring themselves in thickets, sometimes riding the rapids, sometimes crushed together alongside other trunks, damming the river and causing minor local floods. They were heading vaguely towards a shared destiny, but only occasionally brushed into each other along the way. For the most part the one had not a clue about the ups and downs of the other's life.

Her thoughts returned to the present, but that brought little comfort. If only those damned doctors would hurry up and finish with her wretched husband – deal with his insane fantasy and find out what was going on in his throat – she'd be able to sit down with a drink. It was nearly midday, for God's sake.

As if in answer to her vexed thoughts, a maid met her at the terrace door, bobbed a curtsey and announced that the Doctors Florio awaited her in the morning room with their report. 'At last,' muttered Molly to herself, and swept past the girl down the corridor, leaving an atmosphere of citrus scent in her wake.

The eminent Florio brothers rose as one when Molly Campobello entered the room, but with a little wave she bade them return to their seats. She did not approach close enough to make a shaking of hands feasible, but folded her arms to get straight to the point. These quacks might be big shots in a backwater like Naples, she thought, but if they didn't prove themselves in a hundred and eighty seconds flat they'd be out of here and she'd have her own doctor on the next boat from New York. Molly was only tolerating their contribution so as not to offend Signor Graziani, who, again, had taken it upon himself to hire them. She thought it best to play along with the old man for the time being, not least because he seemed to have the entire city at his beck and call; but the sooner this charade with local doctors was over, the better.

'So, gentlemen. Tell me your news.'

Marco Florio, the smaller, elder and mildly more extrovert of the two serious-looking brothers, took a step forward, quickly brushed the tip of his moustache with his index finger, and spoke in measured, rather polished English. 'Signora, we have examined Maestro Campobello and wish to report that our findings show there is no obvious physical evidence for concern.'

'You concur, then, with Dr Goldblatt's latest report?' she said bluntly.

The Florio brothers cast a glance at one another. 'We

43

have not had the privilege of seeing Dr Goldblatt's report. Is it in your possession?'

'Is it in my possession?' Molly's eyes flashed. 'You people,' she said to herself in exasperation, placing a hand to her brow. 'Why should I carry around doctors' files? Has nobody given you the report? Did Signor Boldoni not have it?'

Marco Florio looked down and coughed. 'I have not heard about this report,' he muttered, but before Molly could retort, his brother, Andrea, raised his chin to interrupt: 'We have made a thorough examination. The pain has quite subsided, we believe the fluid in the pleural cavity, the subphrenic abscess, was successfully drained and there is no evidence of further accumulation.'

Molly held back from snapping further at them. 'Well, that's good news, I suppose,' she said, 'as far as it goes. What about the bleeding in his throat?' At this question the doctors looked on more comfortable ground, and Marco Florio began to relate his findings in the rehearsed manner in which he had earlier begun. 'The haemorrhage in the throat was an entirely separate affliction, but perhaps exacerbated by the Maestro's intercostal condition.'

'Oh yes? Please explain.'

'We find that Signor Campobello's larynx has been drawn down to an unusual – perhaps unnatural – degree. Virtually into the thorax.' The last sentence he announced with particular triumph, as if he were already anticipating the widespread fame that his discovery would earn him.

'Meaning?' asked Molly flatly.

Florio senior continued, 'Signor Campobello has for several years artificially attempted to deepen and augment the area above his glottis, raising his epiglottis—'

'and drawing apart the ventricle bands,' said his brother, pincing his fingers in an illustrative gesture, while Marco cut in: 'Over-stimulating the laryngeal depressors, particularly the indirect depressors,'

'the sternohyoideus and omohyoideus,'

'relaxing the anterior elevator between tongue bone and shield cartilage,'

'the thyreohyoideus.'

'My heavens, gentlemen,' said Molly without enthusiasm. 'I had no idea you were so well informed about the voice. Could you please put it more plainly?'

'The violent means employed by your husband in order to enlarge and darken his natural timbre—'

'In simple terms,' interrupted Andrea Florio, 'his method of singing may have led to a chronic deterioration of his voice. There are scars of multiple nodules on his cords. Thankfully, the resting has done him good. He appears to be nearly fully recovered.'

'Has permanent damage been done?'

'We believe not. The bleeding in his throat turned out to be a blessing, of course. It drew the surgeon's attention to the more pressing complaint of the abscess, and may therefore have saved the Maestro's life.'

'And so. Will he be able to sing again?'

'There is nothing to suggest otherwise. Though he should take care not to accept as many engagements as he has done in the past. If he is sensible, and does not strain the larynx or attempt to depress it artificially any further, he should continue to sing at his best – though less frequently – for another ten years. Or more.'

Molly sighed, lowered her chin and smiled graciously.

'Thank you, gentlemen. I apologize if earlier I under-estimated you. It would appear that you may indeed be qualified to attend my husband.' But if this last remark was intended to mollify the learned brothers, it was not met with the gratitude that she might have expected. Instead, both doctors tensed and looked at the floor; but she was not bothered by that. 'I'm sure you must be very busy and have more important things to do than stand here talking to me.' She stretched for a little bell on the side table. 'Mr Boldoni will pass me your full report as soon as you have time to write it.' A maid with wide, nervous eyes had appeared at the bell's summons, and led the way for the doctors along the corridor to the front door.

While Molly, left alone upstairs, decided that this better news called for immediate champagne, the chauffeur Pozzo was arranging for the doctors' car to be driven up to the entrance portico. He nodded at Taddeo to indicate that they would themselves be departing in a moment, in order to decoy any potentially curious observers, so that his master would be free to leave for a quick incognito bathe at the Posillipo Lido. Not that anyone would recognize him. The portly Taddeo represented how the world liked to picture Rocco Campobello: huge and confident, with immaculately oiled hair, jaw thrust out and up like a battleship's prow. The stooped wraith who now occupied the palazzo's east wing apartment would never in a hundred years be mistaken for the legendary tenor. So long as the Maestro's face was kept hidden, Pozzo believed, his identity would remain safe.

Chapter 4

A little earlier in the morning, before the doctors' visit, in the east wing of the palazzo, a procedure – a ritual, almost – took place that would have struck an uninitiated observer as bizarre, if not in some way perverse; and because of its peculiarity, only a select few were allowed near the area. Indeed, if Molly herself had attempted to reach her husband's private quarters in this part of the house (though she never came out of her own suite earlier than 10.30a.m.), she would have found the door securely locked. Only Pietro Boldoni was permitted to attend; he and a succession of elderly, shabby men who were being summoned one by one into the study.

It was dead quiet in the vestibule outside Campobello's private wing, and a man waited there, sitting on a chair with his head bowed. He looked up when he heard the click of the apartment door open, and watched another man shuffle out, wide-eyed, having just completed his interview. A butler indicated that the departing man should make his way down the back stairs, and out of the villa by a side entrance; meanwhile, the new interviewee was asked to stand, and then ushered into the apartment. He wore shoes that were split in several places, but no socks.

As far as Boldoni was concerned, this newcomer's

identity was an irrelevance. He was a nobody, born and bred, and would probably vanish quite soon from living memory as if he had never existed. He was lucky even to have reached this age. He, and the others who had come to the Campobellos' house that morning, hailed from one of the most downtrodden, ignorant and destitute communities on the European mainland: they were dwellers of the Naples slums, folk descended from war, oppression, crime, disease and famine. It defied belief, Pietro Boldoni thought, as he led the man into the study, that, despite the centuries of misery, these people continued to breed with such prodigality. They were insignificant specks of humanity. In purely historical terms, Boldoni believed, the most noteworthy event in this man's life was just about to occur, because in the next few minutes he was to have an encounter, of sorts, with an individual who genuinely ranked amongst the history-makers of his generation; and this moment would be the closest the decrepit visitor would come to being able to leave his mark, however faint, on the chronicles of his time.

Boldoni glanced at the pocket notebook in his hand. This would be the twenty-third. There were six more coming tomorrow, four lined up for the day after, but thereafter his employer had decided to pause for a few days before resuming the search. So far nothing of substance had been gleaned except some largely irrelevant fragments: slight memories, hearsay, wishful thinking for the most part. One or two of the old men had concocted bits of nonsense in the hope of getting a bigger tip or being called back for a second hearing, but it was fairly obvious who was spinning tales. One of them had them all fooled, and the Maestro ordered scouts out to investigate the truth of his claims. They pursued what turned out to be false trails all around the region of Via Pisanelli, the Quartiere di San Lorenzo, right down to the Girolamini church and the Via dei Tribunali. Nothing came of it. For the most part the people they questioned were scared into keeping their mouths shut. History had taught them that men who talked too much were more likely to end up lying in a back alley with their throats slit, or worse. *Omertà*, the code of virile silence, which usually meant pretending ignorance for the sake of honour or fear, was the safest and wisest course in a city where life was cheap.

Before opening the study door, Boldoni turned to look at the newly arrived man and smiled reassuringly. 'There's really nothing to be afraid of,' he said. 'There's nothing sinister about this. You may find it rather odd in here, but don't worry. The Maestro prefers not to be seen, and will not say anything. I shall ask questions on his behalf, but be assured, though you won't set eyes on him, he is there, listening to every word. You should feel honoured.'

'Yes, *commendatore*. An honour,' the man muttered, looking down at the cap he clasped to his navel.

'Good,' smiled Boldoni, then opened the door and led the way in.

The shutters were closed and curtains drawn. The room was lit by a few lamps, and it was as if night had fallen, except for the furnace-like heat, which was ameliorated only by a ceiling fan that kept the warm air moving. Across the middle of the room, leaving only enough space at the edge for a man to pass through from one side to the other, was a high screen of purple silk fabric, set within a mahogany frame. It stood on polished brass castors, raising it a few inches from the floorboards. There was a single circular hole in the centre of the silk, a few feet from the ground, about half an inch in diameter. A solitary chair was positioned about four yards from the screen, to which Boldoni now directed the visitor, asking him politely to sit. The man glanced to the bottom of the dividing screen: a pair of patent leather black shoes were clearly visible through the gap. There was someone sitting directly on the other side. He flinched when he became aware of an eye observing him through the hole.

Pietro Boldoni arranged some papers in his hands, wedged his pince-nez into place, and let out a little cough, in the manner of a consultant doctor or lawyer about to address one of his clients. Just before he did so, he disappeared behind the screen and there was the sound of whispering before he re-emerged, pen in hand. He then sat himself at a compact bureau to one side.

'Signor . . .' he consulted a piece of paper, 'Signor Ventori. This won't take long. You live in the area of the Via Vicaria Vecchia, but were born in the Via Anticaglia, in approximately 1860. Is this the case?'

'Yes, sir. But the year . . .' He shrugged apologetically and looked back at the eye through the hole.

'No matter. First, do you remember meeting any person from the Campobello family in your youth?'

'Me, sir? No. But my father was friends with Giancarlo Campobello, who I think was the Maestro's cousin. But much older than me.'

'And so you do not remember Rocco Campobello. By name or reputation?'

'Not until afterwards.' He laughed. 'And then we all remembered him. Our boy. From our streets.'

'Indeed,' replied Boldoni. 'Did you know anyone who sang in the church choir of Santa Maria Regina Coeli, close to where your family lived?'

'No, sir. My mother's brother was a curate at San Domenico and so that was our church.'

'And did you therefore never come across the choir-master of Santa Maria Regina Coeli, an organist by the name of de Luca, Carmine de Luca?'

'I heard of him. Everyone wanted to be in his choir after Campobello made it big. After he'd left Naples, I mean. Every boy who wanted to be a star, like the Maestro, wanted to be in de Luca's choir. And so it was the best choir in the *quartiere*, maybe in the city. But I never met de Luca. I saw him a few times. Funny little man. He died, you know.'

'Indeed,' said Boldoni again, gathering his first sheaf of papers into a neat pile and reaching for the next. 'Were you ever aware of any resentment directed at Signor Campobello?'

'What, sir?'

'Resentment. Idle gossip. Perhaps fed by jealousy, or a feeling of – let's say – injustice.'

'*Sul serio?*' he asked, opening his palms in surprise. 'Oh no, sir. Everyone is proud of the Maestro.'

'Good.' Boldoni treated the answer as if it were a foregone conclusion and turned to his next sheet of paper. 'Now I want to ask you about some people. Names you may remember from your childhood. Their families, even.' He spoke slowly and quite loudly, as if to a roomful of children. 'I am going to read from my list here, and you will tell me if any of the names rings a bell for you. And please do not be afraid to speak up. We wish only to find old friends. Are you ready?'

'Yes, sir.'

Boldoni examined the first sheet of paper, took the lid from his pen and began to read out a succession of names from his list, ticking with the scratchy nib as he went. 'Raffaele, Giuseppe; Antonini, Achille; Consiglio, Angelo; Bastianini, Antonio . . .' Of course, there were only a few names on the list that had any significance for his employer, and they were deliberately disguised in the midst of all the others – which were invented – so as to dilute the interviewees' fear or catch them off their guard. 'Fratelli, Aurelio; Ceccarelli, Fernando; Silvio, Frederico . . .' The man shook his head or answered 'no' to almost every name. Occasionally he would raise a finger in the air, holding the recitation suspended for a moment, trying to remember something, or he would mutter that he knew someone, maybe, who knew someone, but nothing of any substance.

Then, suddenly, from the other side of the screen, came the sound of a man clearing his throat and the purple fabric billowed fractionally. Boldoni stood up and moved behind the screen. There was more whispering before he came back and sat down again at the desk. He resumed, as if nothing had occurred, and said, without looking up, 'Tomassini, Gabriele.'

'Sir?'

Now Boldoni looked up at the man, but with no expression whatever. 'Do you remember someone by the name of Gabriele Tomassini?'

'A singer?'

'Perhaps. You know this man?'

'No, *commendatore*.'

Boldoni inclined his head. 'But you seemed to remember something.'

'Maybe not, sir.'

The shoes visible beneath the screen shifted back some inches.

'Who did you know with this name? And what makes you think he was a singer?' asked Boldoni quietly. The man looked down. 'I will give you five lire for this,' Boldoni added. The man looked up again.

'Well, sir, I didn't know him myself. My brother once worked with a man called Gabriele Tomassini. I think that was his name. At the opera.'

'At the opera?' For the first time Boldoni's eyes betrayed a flash of animation.

'They were cleaners or something. At the opera house.'

'I thought you said he was a singer.'

'He said he was. He always wanted to be a singer. So do plenty of other guys. But he was just a cleaner. An odd-job man.'

'At the Teatro San Carlo?'

'No, the Teatro Bellini. That's all I know. It was a long time ago.'

'And your brother? He would know more?'

'My brother died ten years ago.'

'Do you know anyone else who might have information on this Tomassini? Family? Other cleaners from the theatre? Women? Singers?'

'No, sir, *niente*. Nothing.' A silence followed, during which Boldoni scribbled some notes, but he was stopped short by another slight cough which summoned him back to the other side of the screen again. After a moment he reappeared and faced the man on the chair.

'Please stand,' said Boldoni ceremoniously, and the man obeyed, a slight fear descending on his face. There was a rustling sound behind the screen, and the shoes disappeared from sight. Then came a voice, lightly shaded, quite high in pitch, smooth and bell-like.

'*Paesano.* Can you hear me?' The accent was Neapolitan, similar to the man's own, but fresher, less guttural.

'Yes, Maestro,' said the man, cap squeezed tight between fingers, awestruck.

'This is a matter of great importance to me,' continued the voice. 'If you can tell me anything about this man, this Gabriele Tomassini, you will earn my friendship.'

The man's eyes filled with tears. 'Maestro?' he uttered. 'Do you speak to me?'

'I am asking you to do me this kind favour. There will be money, as well.'

'Maestro, your friendship is worth more than a thousand lire,' said the man to the hole in the purple silk screen. The tears brimmed over and splashed on to his leathery cheeks.

'And so you will help me?'

'In any way I can, Maestro. Ask, and all I have I shall give.' A ray of morning sunlight pierced through a crack in the shutters, found its way between the curtains and illuminated his face, which was caught between utter joy and despair. A visitation from the archangel would hardly have affected him as much as this; to be thus addressed by one so supreme, to be thus called to service. He felt as if he were in church, and made as if to lower himself on one knee, to express his meek compliance, but was gently brought to his feet by the timely intercession of Boldoni.

Chapter 5

For the first part of their drive from the Villa Rosalba back to Don Graziani's house, the doctors Florio sat in silence, looking out of their respective windows. There wasn't anything to say just yet because they were pre-occupied with the same thought: how uncomfortable it was that matters had got this far.

For years they had found no reason to complain about their close association with old man Graziani, because they had benefited royally from it. They had become the most prosperous and influential medical professionals in Naples, they had their own clinic, enjoyed preferential tax concessions, and had the support of the most powerful legal firms in town – which rendered them, to all intents and purposes, flameproof before the law. They also had access to a network of street thugs, available to them at the drop of a hat, which they preferred not to use, but it was important to flex muscle every now and then, to deter other medical practices in the city from entertaining the notion that they could compete with the Florios' exclusivity. Yes, Don Graziani's wide influence had served them well; but there had, of course, been a price to pay for this pact with the devil.

It had begun eleven years before, when Andrea Florio had been working late at the hospital. A young man had been brought in from the streets during the night with a gunshot wound. After Andrea had succeeded – against the odds – in stemming the flow of blood and bringing the patient to a stable condition, he was asked, by the man who had brought the lad in, to step out into the lobby for a quiet word. There, Andrea was introduced to another person: a small, middle-aged man, who observed him with almost scientific inquisitiveness through a pair of bottle-lens glasses. He had a goatee and wore rather shabby clothes; a kind of unprepossessing back-room clerk, Andrea remembered thinking, with slender fingers, rather dull eyes, and a smile that had to be urged on to his face because it would not arise naturally. This nondescript little man went about his business in an assured manner, and appeared to carry considerable authority. It dawned on Andrea that a degree of respect was called for, though the man did not demand it, but behaved very properly, with old-fashioned courtesy.

Then he came to the point, and an air of menace was suddenly there, though unarticulated. The injured boy, he said, was not a relative, but one of his workers who had got himself into an ugly situation. It would be best for all if the police were not informed about the incident. In return, the man promised, holding out a hand and introducing himself as Emilio Graziani, Andrea would never have cause to regret having lent a helping hand. It would be regarded as a personal favour, something that would bind them together, almost like family.

Andrea Florio knew exactly what was being intimated, and suspected that a refusal might have unpleasant consequences. There was effectively no choice, and so he suggested a plan: he could fudge the paperwork, include the wounded young man in the muddled ledgers of all those maimed and shot-up servicemen being brought in daily from the front. He could even have military shells and identity tags ready to show the police if they started snooping; it would be fairly straightforward. Because of the war, men were dying every day in the hospital, or moving out, or changing wards, and the record-keeping was a shambles. No one would notice. Graziani once more forced a smile on to his face. He wanted to show that he liked what he heard, and nodded his approval. This was a doctor he could do business with.

After that, the Florio brothers were introduced to a network of men of varied type and profession: lawyers, shopkeepers, restaurateurs, a university professor, even a priest and a policeman, all of whom, the doctors were told, they should now consider their associates, their family. Marco was decidedly more hesitant about the arrangement than his brother, but was quickly convinced by its benefits. The Florios' reputation rose meteorically, swiftly followed by their fees, and then, as a natural consequence, their personal tastes. Once in a while, they were called upon to deal with a situation for Don Graziani, usually involving bullet or knife wounds; occasionally it would be something more subtle, like ensuring a favoured young man would achieve high grades at the city's medical college, or helping to obtain a supply of restricted drugs – some benign, others not.

They had grown accustomed to the routine, the balance of give and take; but this recent business was altogether different. Campobello was just too big a name. His welfare was close to the hearts of millions. If anything unfortunate were to happen, it would become a *cause célèbre*, to be chewed over by doctors and detective bureaux across the globe, for years to come. The Florios' role would be microscopically, almost gleefully, investigated. And despite Graziani's reassurances that his son in New York had everything in place to douse any potential flames, the doctors knew there would be no protection if something serious – or the worst – were to occur. And so they sat in silence as they drove along the coast from Posillipo towards the city, both of them contemplating the awkwardness of what had arisen these past few weeks.

As their driver negotiated the sharp bend around the headland at Mergellina, Marco Florio leant forward to close the glass partition.

'Prize bitch,' he said.

'We just have to put up with her,' replied Andrea. 'The old man says she has to be kept sweet. We need her on our side. Priority.'

'I know, I know,' said Marco impatiently. He turned to look out of the window, but something still niggled at him and he could hold it back no longer. 'We should tell the old man what we really think. We're the only doctors he'll listen to. We shouldn't pretend. It's just not worth the risk.'

'He knows the facts. And he doesn't want anything done about it. That's it, as far as we're concerned.'

'Well, is it?' Marco was jittery. 'It'll be *we* who get it in the teeth if something happens to Campobello. Why can't we press the point? He's pushed himself off the edge. His voice and his body. He should go to Rome, where they've got the equipment, the facilities, and have those lungs properly seen to. The man needs to be X-rayed, first and foremost.'

'We have his American X-rays.'

'Out of date. And why weren't we given the American report?'

'The old man has his reasons. But we do have the X-rays, and the evidence they show is enough to keep everyone quiet for the moment. Most particularly, *her*.'

'That's irrelevant,' said Marco. 'We can't make a sensible diagnosis about that abscess unless we can get Campobello to Rome and have new X-rays made. But we're not allowed to suggest it in case it upsets the old man's plans, and therefore we're lying to her when we tell her he's going to be back on stage again in a few months. I don't like it. This isn't some back alley melon merchant who's neglected to pay his debt. This is Rocco Campobello, for God's sake.'

'The old man thinks it's a risk worth taking. For the moment. I'm as uncomfortable as you, but we've got to be realists. You know what he's capable of doing, if he suspects we're not watertight.'

'Don't I just,' muttered Marco, turning to the window again.

'In which case, you'd do well to keep your thoughts to yourself. And don't tar me with your brush.'

'You know what I mean,' answered Marco. 'It's as well to have it out between us.' He leant over to close the window next to him as they were approaching the Santa Lucia seafront. By this time of day the stench of rotting fish entrails and mountains of discarded mussel shells would be high indeed, and an unwelcome intrusion in the car. 'Quite apart from the man's physical health,' Marco continued, 'what about the state of his mind? He's completely away with the fairies.'

'Not our problem,' answered Andrea. 'We just stick to what we know about.'

'But what if he goes completely loopy? We—'

'Don't even whisper it,' shot back Andrea. He had had enough of this loose talk. 'If word about that got out – it doesn't bear thinking about. Just zip up.' After a pause, he felt a little bad about having snapped at his brother, and added, 'The idle mind is the devil's playground. Campobello needs to focus on something, to get him back on the rails.'

'Maybe Graziani should find him a mistress,' smiled Marco. 'Some plump local girl with big tits. Teach that skinny bitch of a wife a lesson!'

Both brothers laughed at the thought of Molly's discomfiture, but Marco's face soon fell back into an expression of thoughtful anxiety. Their invitation to attend Campobello had of course been an honour, one they expected and duly received, but they had not entirely been looking forward to the period of treatment. They had met him once before, though he clearly had not the slightest recollection of it, and at the time, some eight years ago, they had not formed a particularly favourable impression.

They had been visiting New York, where the old man's son, Bruno Graziani, held sway in his own Lower East Side fiefdom, and where the doctor brothers were entertained like kings, dining at the best restaurants, meeting the most beautiful girls, and, to crown it all, presented to a man Bruno described as his great friend, Rocco Campobello, after one of the tenor's performances at the Met. The opera had been sensational. Verdi's *Il Trovatore*. The Florio brothers sat through it spellbound and literally open-mouthed at Campobello's portrayal of the romantic warrior Manrico. For such restrained and socially self-conscious individuals, the doctors behaved with near dizzy enthusiasm, leaping to their feet and yelling their support as Manrico held on to his top C for an inordinately long call to arms, just before the interval.

Backstage, the tenor was decidedly less heroic than his stage persona. Loud and bullish, with his costume shirt unlaced to the navel, he beckoned all and sundry from the corridor outside to come into the dressing room, telling them not to be shy. He barely glanced at the Florios when he was introduced, being far more preoccupied with a list of requirements he was spouting at the obliging Signor Boldoni, who quietly nodded, and with a minimum of response, calmly noted them in a little pocketbook. Campobello's list ranged from demanding a different carpet in his dressing room, to sending a letter of complaint about the quality of the wine he had been served at dinner the previous night. He was sweating heavily; the stage paint dripped down his forehead, forming tinted rivulets on his neck, and perspiration boiled up beneath the hairs on his broad chest. The Florio brothers made no more impression on him that night than the damp sponge used to clean make-up from his face.

'It seems his brush with death may have changed him altogether,' mused Marco. 'And who are these men he's having brought to the house every day? What's that all about?'

'We can only guess. The old man's not too concerned. Says we should just let him get on with it, if it keeps him happy. Anything to get him back on track.'

'Is it so important?' said Marco at last, as they neared Don Graziani's house in the Via Fiorelli. 'Is it so important that he sings again? Why not leave him in peace? What's at stake for the old man?'

'I don't know, I don't know,' tutted Andrea despairingly as he climbed out of the car. 'They say Graziani loves him like a son, but it must be all about money, and lots of it. Otherwise they wouldn't be going to such extremes. Bruno's coming over to look after the situation. It must be important.'

'Yes, well,' added Marco, 'Bruno needs to get out of New York, we all know that. To let his little bit of trouble simmer down. It'll be interesting when he gets here. Bruno will want to do things his own way. I've got to tell you, I'm not looking forward to it one bit.'

'Don't you worry. I'll take care of it,' concluded Andrea as they walked up the front steps of the house. A small crowd of shoeless boys instantly materialized around them, as if from thin air, holding their palms out for loose change, their enterprise entirely flawed by the undisguised mockery of their manner – not that the doctors had any intention of digging into their pockets for street scum like this. If Mussolini would actually get on and do what he barked on about endlessly, he'd have boys like this marshalled into squads and uniforms put on their backs. The upstart leader might be a cocky little martinet, but some of his ideas were sound – though this was an opinion the Florios did not dare to share with any member of Don Graziani's circle.

The begging boys scattered as quickly as they had assembled at the approach of two heavy-set men who were keeping watch outside the door to which the Florios were bound, a door which now opened without them even having to knock. The doctors glanced at each other for a second, then removed their hats and went in.

Chapter 6

Pietro Boldoni asked Pozzo to stop the car and drop him off at the corner of the university, on the busy Corso Umberto Primo. This broad new avenue had been constructed just a few years before, part of an ambitious plan to renovate and modernize Naples. It slashed the old dockside map of the city in two, providing an artery of fresh air, affluence and commerce through the heart of what was previously a disease-ridden slum quarter. The impoverished former residents of these waterfront districts had not been helped by the grandiose building plans, of course, merely driven like rats into the already overcrowded slums deeper inland.

Boldoni stepped back from the edge of the pavement when he noticed a tram rattling towards him from the left, and was buffeted by people rushing to reach it as it slowed to a stop. People in a hurry, pavements heaving, commerce thriving, he thought approvingly, and watched Pozzo's Lancia join the jam of large black cars inching their way slowly down towards the resplendent Piazza Municipio. He liked the tangy smell of motor fumes in a throbbing metropolis. It spoke of prosperity.

The new Corso was flanked with grand civic palazzo blocks, painted golden, with ample stucco ornamentation. A little fussy but nonetheless dignified and impressive, thought Boldoni. He noted admiringly the muscular statues labouring interminably beneath the weight of upper storey balconies, and thought this avenue had a more Parisian or Viennese feel to it than older parts of the city, which showed that Naples was gradually assimilating the atmosphere of northern Italy and Europe in general. No bad thing, he reflected. The sooner Italy's regional divisions were healed and cultural diversity eradicated, the better for the modern state as a whole.

Boldoni was unashamedly patriotic, a man for whom loyalty to a higher cause was the grandest expression of human nobility. The dominant cause of his life, naturally, was the well-being and supremacy of his Maestro, but his loyalties extended with almost equivalent fervour to the theory of Italian nationhood and devotion to his monarch. He quietly considered himself something of a soldier, in the sense that he admired order and conviction demonstrated through service; he had even thought about enlisting during the Great War, but decided fairly quickly that the Maestro should come first, and, besides, combativeness was alien to him. The strength of a country should be articulated through the benefits it affords its citizens, he mused, not the whetting of sabres. He believed modern Italy would thrive by an iron unity of north and south, led by a man of vision in alliance with a benign, fatherly king and a strong central executive in Rome. Like the glorious days of the ancient empire, but preferably without the warfare. He smiled to himself for falling so unapologetically into one of the great propagandist clichés of the time. Well, why not? he conceded. Why not allow ourselves a bit of harmless, nation-building rhetoric? Italy hadn't had it so good in years. He was pleased to be back in his homeland after so long in New York. He felt invigorated by the scent of virile ambition in the air. Decisiveness was a fine masculine virtue and Mussolini seemed unafraid to grasp the nettle.

Pickering did not agree, of course, but Wallace Pickering, master pianist and répétiteur, was not one to overstate his disagreement. He would just let his nonchalant scepticism be known through tuts and sighs, together with an occasional comment of wry resignation, uttered in his broadest Yorkshire. How could Pickering possibly understand the miracle of Italy's regeneration? thought Boldoni. Brought up in a remote moorland village – cheeks permanently stung by icy winds, clothes smelling of damp sheep fleece – the short and tubby Pickering was about as far from the imperial Roman ideal as was possible. And far too from the Florentine model of Renaissance polymath accomplishment, which had always been Boldoni's own holy grail. Nevertheless, when the question of their move to Italy arose, Pickering had acquiesced without complaint. He went along with the Maestro's wishes, not because he had reached an age when he lacked the drive to seek out a new path, nor because he had been Campobello's coach and accompanist for twenty-one years and there would never be another job to compare with it (both of which were true), but because he simply did not care about the outer circumstances of his life.

His and Boldoni's work alongside the great tenor took them all over the world, but it was Boldoni who had to look after the minor administrative tasks of their lives. Pickering's attempts at organization were unutterably disastrous. He had twice forgotten to pack a suitcase before embarking across the Atlantic, and once travelled halfway by train to St Petersburg before being heard to mutter, after noticing something out of the window, 'I'll be damned. I thought we were going to Monte Carlo.' By the same token, he was oblivious to all the inconveniences of travel and hotel living. This greatly amused Boldoni, who would tease that the humble-born Yorkshireman had been numbed by the hardships of his youth. He would quote the story of the Princess and the Pea in reverse: you could tell a peasant by his uncomplaining acceptance of discomforts. But Boldoni knew it wasn't really true. Pickering was just wholly, almost eccentrically, wrapped up in his craft. The music – its metre, style and every nuance of its interpretation – was his entire world, and there was no one else who could get to the heart of a vocal score with such insight. It was a standing joke that Pickering understood the music better than the composers who'd written it, and he was therefore an irreplaceable component in the Campobello household. Indeed, no one would question that Pickering was essential to the maintenance of that most precious and supreme commodity upon which all their fortunes depended and towards which so many eyes across the world were now expectantly and anxiously turned: the Maestro's voice.

Boldoni took the little card from his breast pocket. It was not a very long walk from here through the lofty-walled passages and stairways to the address he had been given. He decided to refresh himself first with a glass of chilled lemon water, which he bought from a rather opulent mahogany street stall, before turning right into the Piazza Bovio, and climbing up some steps into an arched alleyway on the far side. Within a few paces he had left the atmosphere of a prosperous modern city and entered the bowels of the earth.

Everything here lay in shadow, visibility being instantly quartered by the meagre allowance of sunlight that found its way down between the rooftops high above. The murkiness of this netherworld combined with other elements to create a setting of deprivation that was almost theatrical in the way it assaulted the senses. Boldoni would have preferred to walk through with a handkerchief held to his face, but did not want to offend the many diminutive and dark-skinned people who were milling around. Most of them paused in whatever they were doing, to stare at the affluently dressed gentleman passing through. Young men watched with studied nonchalance, arms crossed, from under the peaks of their caps; children – some without clothes from the waist down – hurried enquiringly in his footsteps, their shoeless feet padding lightly over the flagstone filth; tired young housewives with desolate, empty faces – too young to be mothers, Boldoni hoped – stood in doorways, some still in their nightclothes, silently smoking cigarettes. Older women with grey hair tied tightly back from their faces followed his progress from upstairs, sometimes two of them to a window, while higher up, other women called across from their balconies to neighbouring blocks or pulled in washing from the many lines that spanned the alley.

At ground level, a stagnant smell drifted from the doorways of countless windowless homes and merged with the scent of the drains, spreading into every darkened nook, even rising to blaspheme against the smooth-cheeked perfection of a Madonna in a wall shrine. The smell's consistency was a stale mélange of destitution: a month's worth of casually discarded garbage, a thousand daily portions of shit, gallons of urine trickling down open sewers, all of it blended sensuously and tangibly with simmering tomato, fried garlic and pasta vapours from the hundreds of stoves. And the interminable burbling sound of compressed living, with its shrieks and jagged edges bouncing harshly off the grey medieval walls in a constricted acoustic. There was nowhere for it to go: the noise, the air, the gloom and the stench, even the people; trapped here together, a closed environment, removed from the world of open horizons.

The immensely high tenement blocks, that almost seemed to sway above Boldoni as he stepped quickly along, were separated by the slenderest of gaps, which, higher up might have disappeared altogether had not their inward inclination been forced apart at various stages in history by the insertion of an occasional stone arch. Thus crudely held in check, these crowded buildings kept to their ancient foundations, constructed on the very street grid used once by the Romans, who, in their turn, had inherited it from ancient Greek colonizers. If the noble ancients could only see what had happened to this place, thought Boldoni as he emerged at the far end of the alleys into the brightness of a busy piazza; these very streets where even Virgil had once promenaded. How appalled they would be at the level to which their descendants had sunk. The modern state would have to do something about it, he thought, and that gave him added justification to nip quickly into a church. He checked his watch, remembering that he had concealed its gold chain in a waistcoat pocket before passing through the slum. He still had time, and so crossed the piazza and made for the broad stairway of San Domenico Maggiore.

It was not a delicate sensibility that led him to pause for a moment's refuge in this richly gilded and marbled sanctuary, but a genuine impulse to seize the opportunity to reiterate his devotion, something he would do whenever he could. And there were a couple of particular pleas he wanted just now to put before the Lord.

Once inside, he glanced around the cavernous nave for a suitable place to settle himself. The aesthetic in these Naples churches, the palatial opulence and wild ornamentation, was not entirely to Boldoni's taste. A Florentine to the core of his being, he was more attracted to Albertian symmetry and measured proportion than to the excesses of this southern baroque. He looked at the dazzling trickery of the sculptures here – stone angels that seemed unsupported, floating above the altar, gossamer pages of a marble book seeming to flutter in a breeze – and felt almost insulted. There was no call for this sort of cheating. He had no need of cunning theatricality in order to secure his faith. Illusion was useful for artists, he granted, because that was their business, but deceit was not a tool to be used in arguing the existence of God. And the dense population of statuary in these churches, forever restless and open-mouthed, twisting upwards, almost dancing their way to paradise, struck Boldoni as just too noisy; it was more like an overcrowded *festa* than a place of solemn worship. It lacked appropriate severity.

He knelt down in a little side chapel, its floor paved with the smoothed-down effigies of armoured knights, whose hands were poised for eternity on the hilts of their old swords. There was a neat altar before him, within which was displayed, behind glass and nestled comfortably on a red velvet pad, the shrunken remains of some female saint hitherto unknown to him. Wispy strings of hair, bleached colourless by the years, still clung to her blackened skull, flattened down beneath an embroidered satin headdress, while spherical rosary beads gleamed in loops around her twig-like fingers. On the walls of the chapel a series of old frescos depicted scenes in her life – her youthful receipt of spiritual ecstasy, when abundant golden hair still curled around her shoulders, followed by her rejection of a wealthy home and family, her giving all to the poor, the usual story of good works, ending with a starkly pious deathbed scene showing the prostrate saint surrounded by a gaggle of identically clad nuns at prayer. It was difficult to relate the painted legend to the shrunken cadaver in its miniature cassock behind the glass. But Pietro Boldoni had no doubt that she emanated love and grace, and this was a peaceful corner; here he could quietly say his prayers, undisturbed by passing worshippers who might pause to kiss the altar cloth, or cross themselves, before departing to resume their lives on the frantic streets outside.

First of all he whispered his way through his usual litany, the familiar words rolling from his lips with liturgical fluency: he prayed for Rocco Campobello, the Almighty's beloved son, asking forgiveness for the Maestro's neglect of divine intercourse, but, as ever, guaranteeing that, despite such negligence, the Maestro led a good and Christian life, brought hope and joy to millions, and revealed the Lord's glory through the immeasurable splendour of his voice. And then, as if concluding with a seasonal addendum to the habitual rite, he begged for the Maestro's recovery and a happy solution to the quest that currently devoured him.

His murmurs ceased as he mused in half-prayer about the interview he was about to attend. Campobello had been shaken out of his reverie by this one. He seemed to believe that this Signor Ventori held the key. Something the man had said, or the way he said it – though Boldoni himself hadn't noticed anything particularly sensational – had galvanized Campobello into believing that his hook had at last found a bite. Boldoni prayed that something might come of it, but could not suppress a heavy sense of pessimism, especially in view of the previous empty leads he had pursued. He would not allow his hopes to die, and squeezed his hands together in a final intense prayer to the Almighty, that, whatever the outcome of this latest trail, his Maestro would be let down gently, because if he were to fall uncushioned, the subsequent fractures might be irreparable – an unthinkable prospect which made Boldoni tighten his mouth and shake his head where he knelt, for all his soldierly resilience.

Rising to his feet with a few last words, as always, for the health and happiness of Wallace Pickering, he crossed himself, stooped to touch his lips to the top of the withered saint's altar, and made his way out to the piazza.

The address written on the card was now just a short walk away, and within minutes he was there, standing in another narrow slum alley in front of a massive arched entrance. It was cut from coarse grey rock, and at its apex was a keystone emblazoned with an ancient, indecipherable coat of arms. This was a sign that some distant historical personage of considerable means had been resident in the building, but other than the decaying crest above the entrance all sign of the affluence he had enjoyed here had long since vanished.

Sidestepping deep old wheel ruts in the flagstones, Boldoni passed through the darkened interior of the arch to an inner courtyard. This might once have been the noble family's shaded *cortile*, planted with lemon trees, perhaps with a decorated well at its centre and an elegant open stairway leading to chambers on the upper floors. But nowadays it was home to an entire community, every room of the ground floor providing lodging for a three-generation family; likewise upstairs, on all four sides of the courtyard, up as far as the attic rooms beneath the roof timbers, which were too hot for daytime occupation. Because of the heat and overcrowding, most of the residents had come outdoors, either into the yard, or on to crumbling balconies above, or even into the street, where several were now sleeping on the pavement after the sweltering restlessness of the night indoors.

Boldoni was bewildered by the sheer quantity of people crushed into the courtyard, with their tables, chairs, livestock and carpets, the swathes of laundry draped on every level, the ranks upon ranks of flowerpots dripping from balconies, and the babbling activity. He wondered how many clans were represented in the compound, and how closely intertwined the blood ties between households. Was it inbreeding, rather than just generations of impoverishment, that seemed to have stunted their growth and distorted their brown leathery faces? For a moment he was too distracted by the peculiar, Brueghelesque inquisitiveness of the expressions all around him to notice Signor Ventori, the man who had visited Campobello's palazzo a few days before, standing by his side, nodding and smiling. A tug at his sleeve brought the man to his attention.

'Ah. So you're here,' said Boldoni. 'This is the place, I take it?'

'Yes, *commendatore*,' said Ventori. 'The men are waiting for you upstairs.'

'Men? Previously you mentioned only one.'

'No, sir, three men, three men.'

Boldoni sighed. He did not want these people to think that by outnumbering they could intimidate him. 'Very well. Lead the way, then.' But Signor Ventori was not quite ready to move on, because several of his family and neighbours had gathered around; for them, a visit from so distinguished a gentleman was a significant occurrence. Boldoni was a sight indeed, with his spotlessly laundered and stiffened collar that pressed up into his jawbone, his black silk tie and pearl-buttoned canvas spats. News of his connection to Maestro Campobello had of course preceded him, and before long he was crowded in by people of both genders and all ages, none of whom stood much higher than his shoulders. They gawped at him, studying the details of his garments with frowning curiosity, and quietly tilted their heads this way and that, assessing his face. They reminded Boldoni forcibly of apes at the zoo, but he felt as though he were the caged exhibit. A man of less imperturbable mettle might at this point have taken fright and fled, but Boldoni tapped his stick on the stone floor and peremptorily snapped at Ventori, 'Enough of this. Take me to the men.'

Ventori, who above all wanted to please, waved the crowd away with shouts of '*Va via! Passaggio!*' and scowled at them all for their impertinence. The two men then proceeded through a silent and needling ocean of stares towards a stairwell on the far side of the courtyard. To ascend, they had to pick their way through a group of girls, all about ten years old, who were playing on the steps, with a crèche of babies in their care. They were giggling and shrieking with joy at one another, and Boldoni wondered at what point in the lives of these unfortunate folk the realization of misery would descend. These infants had obviously not yet understood, and for all the scars on their feet and tangles in their hair seemed as happy as any children he knew anywhere in the world. Their paradise would be short-lived, he imagined, but the memory of it might at least sweeten the hardships of adulthood.

On reaching the third floor, Ventori pointed the way to a closed door. Ever a stickler for manners, Boldoni rapped twice on it, and waited for a reply before turning the handle and entering.

The room was small and contained the bare essentials for subsistence living. A bed took up much of the space, but there was also a plain table, with six chairs, a wardrobe, and a cooking stove. A single window opened on to an inner ventilation shaft which scores of other apartment windows overlooked, all of them wide open because of the heat. The cacophony of life within the tenements was amplified in the resonance of the shaft, as if by a giant soundbox, and noticing Boldoni's flicker of a frown at the racket, Ventori hurried over to close the window.

Three men were waiting. No introduction was offered and Boldoni did not ask for one, neither did he let the men think that he might be observing the surroundings with judgement or distaste, but without hesitation he removed his hat and took his place in a businesslike manner at the table.

Opposite sat a middle-aged man in a tatty, ill-matching suit, who leant forward on his elbows across the table with the earnestness of a corporate chairman. Next to him was a considerably older man with no teeth, wearing braces, and leaning back on his chair, apparently detached from the proceedings, almost smiling, a walking stick laid across his lap. Over to the side, resting against the windowsill that looked over the ventilation shaft and observing Boldoni with large, intense eyes, was the third person, a young man, no more than eighteen years old. Boldoni noticed the thickness of his hair, oiled and swept back like a great black mane, and the flawless complexion of his skin. The boy had stepped straight out of a Caravaggio canvas, and possessed a quality of languor that seemed almost to beg debauchery of the sort celebrated by that lawless painter. Boldoni immediately glanced away, furious with himself for having nearly dropped his guard.

If he had expected from these men the sort of fawning obsequiousness displayed by Ventori, he was mistaken. All three regarded him with suspicion, and so Boldoni paused to allow them an opportunity to voice their minds – a privilege they failed to take, at least not in the brief time allowed by Boldoni, who was keen to keep the agenda crisp and compact.

'Allow me to make matters clear. I have agreed with Signor Ventori that a sum of five hundred lire will be payable for information leading to one Gabriele Tomassini, or to his close family, or to proven information of what fate may have befallen him. In the event that the evidence supplied turns out to be false, or if for whatever reason the man to whom we are directed is not the person we seek, the agreement between us will be null and void. Are we clear about this?'

The middle-aged man opposite raised his chin to reply, 'Let us see the money.'

'You don't think I'd be fool enough to walk here with that amount in my pocket? Let me hear what you have to say, and, assuming I am convinced that we have a definite lead, you can send Signor Ventori to the house in Posillipo later today to pick up half the sum.' Noting the perplexed look on the face of the man, Boldoni softened his tone and allowed them the smallest hint of a smile. 'The remainder will be paid when we are satisfied with the result. I give you my personal guarantee.' When no response came, he lowered his brow and spoke more seriously again. 'These are my terms. What is your answer?'

The man opposite now leant back in his chair. 'We do not want trouble,' he said quietly.

'Trouble? What do you mean?'

'We can help the Maestro, but we don't want to get involved with Don Graziani. È pericoloso.' Boldoni now relaxed a little. Far from trying to intimidate him, these men were afraid.

'Signor Graziani has nothing to do with this, you have my word. There's nothing to be frightened of.'

'They say Campobello is under Graziani's protection. They say the two of them meet together every day, that Don Graziani has saved his life and they are partners.' Boldoni, for whom such an idea was a personal affront, hid his offence and replied calmly. 'That is an exaggeration. They are just friends. Old friends. And, yes, they have business connections, but, as you know, many people in Naples have dealings of one sort or another with the Graziani family.' He continued with deliberate emphasis, 'This matter, however, has nothing whatever to do with Signor Graziani.' The man opposite tightened his eyes to squeeze out another assurance. 'Or any of his associates,' added Boldoni.

The man considered for a moment and then raised his chin. 'Tell us, in that case, *dica*: why does the Maestro want to know about Gabriele Tomassini?'

Boldoni artfully concealed a flicker of discomfort. 'It is a personal matter, something between the two men, but there is nothing to worry about.' They seemed unconvinced. 'See it more as a matter of sentiment. A nostalgic journey into the past, if you will. That is all.' There was no need for him to elaborate on this simple explanation because the man opposite nodded as if satisfied, and signalled across the room to the boy, who, as if briefed in advance, went straight to retrieve an orange from a cupboard, put it on a plate and brought it over to Boldoni with a knife and a glass of water. A princely gift indeed from such impoverished folk, thought Boldoni, regarding the size and ripeness of the fruit; but it would not do to play into the hands of these people, and he refused the orange, smiling directly at the boy to compensate on a personal level for what might appear an unfriendly response.

'We can arrange a meeting. At a tavern,' the man said, while his ancient neighbour still stared aimlessly around the room, occasionally licking the toothless edges of his collapsed mouth.

'Give me the time and the address,' replied Boldoni, sitting upright and removing a fountain pen and notebook from his breast pocket. But the man waved his hand to slow him down.

'*Piano, piano.* In time. First, our terms. Half the money at the meeting in the tavern. The other half after the introduction.'

'Introduction? To whom?'

The man paused. 'To the person who will give you the answers you want.'

'But the tavern? Will we be meeting this person there?'

'No. The tavern is the first step. To make sure we all know where we stand. And to make sure he is alone.'

'What's that supposed to mean?' Boldoni said quickly.

'Signor Campobello must come alone to talk to us, and we will take matters from there.'

'That's a preposterous suggestion,' Boldoni said quietly, tapping the top of his pen in time with his consonants. 'The Maestro could not possibly go to a public tavern on his own. He would be mobbed. And he is also unwell, you must know that. He barely ever leaves the house.'

'He has been seen often in his car,' said the man. 'They say he looks healthy.'

Boldoni upheld this demonstration of how successful their use of decoys had been, and conceded, 'From time to time. And we must give thanks to God that He has seen fit to restore the Maestro's strength. But the strain of this would be too much.'

'We can ensure his safety, you need not fear. And as for the strain – does he want to find something or does he not? If it's too much of a strain, then come back in a month. Or two, or three. We can wait.'

'That is almost impertinent.'

The man leant forward over his elbow and fixed Boldoni with his eyes, while the old man next to him chomped his jaws and stared at the ceiling, hands still resting on the stick. '*Senti*. Listen. Those are our terms. Accept them or go.'

Boldoni glanced at the boy by the windowsill. His eyes were on fire, though he said nothing. 'I will put it to Signor Campobello,' Boldoni concluded, putting away his pen. 'But there will, of course, be no money until the Maestro is convinced that this is a genuine lead.'

'And it will be six hundred lire, not five.'

Boldoni flared inwardly at the presumptuousness of this, but knew that to Campobello the sums were trivial. If only they knew. The Maestro would happily have offered six thousand just for a shred of what they seemed to promise.

'Very well,' Boldoni said, and pulled a cigarette out of a silver case. He lit it, drew deep and exhaled, sending a cloud of smoke into the face of the man opposite, something he had not intended to do, and he hoped would not be interpreted in the wrong way. Just then, the old man leant across the table and held out his hand to Boldoni, nodding his head encouragingly in the direction of the cigarette case. '*Sigaretta?*' asked Boldoni, and pulled one out for him. But the old man shook his finger in the air, gestured more emphatically, and held out his palm once more. 'This?' asked Boldoni, holding up the silver cigarette case. The man nodded, and with a sigh Boldoni sat up and handed it across the table.

'*Bella*,' said the old man in a high-pitched voice, pulling the case to his face with both hands as if to sniff it.

'Please,' said Boldoni, 'keep it.' The old man accepted the gift without the smallest gesture of surprise, placing

it on his lap beside the stick with the single word, '*Grazie*.'
Boldoni supposed this kind of exchange was normal in
such a situation, and, keen to uphold his façade as an
experienced back-alley negotiator, moved quickly on to
conclude the details of the proposed meeting.

Chapter 7

Wallace Pickering looked uncomfortable by the time he reached the music room. He was sweating and out of breath as he closed the door behind him and hurried over to open up the Steinway. Although it was horribly muggy in the room and a cool sea breeze was just a window's latch away, he was too preoccupied to notice, and did not even bother to remove his unseasonal tweed jacket before getting to work.

Drawing up the piano stool so that it grated noisily and left a mark on the polished parquet, he snatched up an opera score that he had earlier left on a side shelf, placed it on the piano's music stand, and then pulled a second score out of his briefcase, one he had just succeeded in borrowing for the day from the Teatro San Carlo's archive library. It was of an obscure and rarely performed opera by a Neapolitan composer, and for some years Pickering had just had a hunch about something in it. He was determined that today he would find out for sure.

Fingers of both hands wriggling in anticipation of action, he turned to the first score: a famous opera by an equally famous composer, and began to play a wonderfully lush and sweeping section of music from the third act: a well-known expansive quartet for the four protagonists at a critical moment in the drama.

Finishing with an improvised tiddlypom in the same key, Pickering now opened the rare edition from the library, at the place where he had earlier left a bookmark, and began to play an excerpt from this one. 'Well, I'll be damned,' he muttered to himself, finally letting his hands drop from the keys on to his thighs. 'The cheeky so-and-so.' He stayed like that for a moment, beady eyes blinking through his glasses, darting from one score to the other and back again. His hunch had been right. The unknown opera had been shamelessly pillaged, the prize in this case being one of the juiciest, most pimple-raising moments in the whole operatic repertoire, known to everyone through the fame of a completely different composer's work.

The door to the room opened without warning, and a tall man in a collarless linen shirt came in.

Pickering glanced up just for an instant but seemed more interested in the two scores. He shook his head and tutted, as if genuinely disappointed by his discovery. 'I've found another one,' he said without raising his eyes.

'I could hear you were up to something.' The man walked towards the piano. His hair was cropped to the scalp, a short bristle mat peppered with silver and edged by two receding arcs above a powerful high forehead. Hardly any dark hair remained in his short beard, which was unusually white for a man of his age.

'Italians are all the same,' said Pickering. 'Wouldn't trust them as far as I could throw them.' He closed both scores with a scornful tut. The man had arrived by his side and gave Pickering a slightly weary smile.

'An English composer would never plagiarize?'

'Not to my knowledge,' replied Pickering, refusing to

be drawn by the humour. 'But I can't answer for every single Englishman. I dare say there are one or two unwholesome types in London. But you fellows duck and dive on a daily basis, as a matter of course. It's as if all Italians take pride in winning by dishonourable means.'

The other man's smile widened, though the creases on his brow seemed immune to the lighter mood and would not ease. He glanced around the room, looking for something.

Pickering spread his rather pudgy hands flat on the closed lid of the piano in front of him. 'May I make so bold as to ask the great Campobello how he is feeling this morning?'

'You'd have to find him first. They say he's gone missing. A terrible tragedy.'

'Aren't we a bundle of laughs today?'

The man did not reply, but went over to open wide the window, securing it on an outside hook, and felt the relief of the breeze wash over his broad tanned face and scalp.

'Are we here to work?' Pickering asked.

'No.'

'No. Thought as much. Are we here to talk, then?'

'Maybe. If you have something interesting to say.'

'How about this?' Pickering came back quickly, still deadpan. 'You look better. Something's happened, hasn't it?' The improvement in Rocco Campobello's appearance was indeed striking, and any observer other than Wallace Pickering would probably have commented on it more promptly and enthusiastically. A heavy strain still racked his face, his eyes seemed to have deepened and darkened, and his neck moved too freely in a collar that was now a size too large; but he was at least venturing out of his apartment from time to time, and changing from his nightclothes.

Campobello walked over to an armchair, sat down heavily, crossed his legs and laid his head back, observing the ceiling. 'Thank you,' he eventually sighed. 'You also look nice today.'

Pickering ignored the remark. 'Would you like to talk, or are you going to leave and let me get on with doing something more productive?'

Campobello rested his head back and turned to look at his accompanist. He had known Pickering since his first London season, nearly a quarter of a century before, when Rocco had been the youngest tenor in history to make his debut on the stage of Covent Garden. Pickering had been a resident coach at the opera house, in his mid-thirties at the time, although he'd looked much older. Stuffy, detached from worldliness, and mildly misogynistic, in the manner of a long-cocooned Oxbridge academic, the pianist had adopted, even as a young man, the demeanour of late middle age, something he wore like a heavy suit cut from dull, unfashionable fabric. Having for many years seemed old before his time, he did not nowadays look particularly different than when he had agreed to become Campobello's full-time accompanist and coach, all those years ago. A little more girth, and the unruly curls of his head had turned sandy grey instead of mouse, but his vigour remained untarnished, as did the nimble skill of his fingers.

'Yes, something has happened,' said Campobello. 'Don't pretend you haven't heard,' he added wryly, glancing sideways at his accompanist. 'Pietro has told you.'

'So you're going to tell us all about it now? About

time. What's so important about this man, this Gabriele Tomassini?'

'Someone I used to know.'

'Obviously. And?'

'My best friend as a child.'

'Very touching,' said Pickering. 'And? Why is it so important to find him?'

'Unfinished business,' said Campobello and yawned.

'Unfinished business? Is that it? There's a lot of unfinished business about at the moment. Next winter's season at the Met, the following spring in Monte Carlo, summer at Buenos Aires, a week at La Scala, then the Met again, not to mention all the concerts peppered about, eight roles, ninety-three stage performances and thirty-two recitals in a twelve-month period, booked, confirmed and sold out. That's unfinished business for you. What about your public? What are you going to tell them?'

Rocco raised his eyebrows and returned his gaze to the ceiling. Age had dampened neither the acerbity of Pickering's wit nor his needling insistence on unattainably high standards. But this time Campobello was not smiling. '*Force majeure*,' he replied. 'People will just have to understand. Besides, there are other tenors. Let them have the engagements.'

'They're not you.'

'They're good. A new generation.'

'How would you know? You haven't heard any.'

'I am told.'

'Enough nonsense.' Pickering pursed his lips. 'What are you trying to say?'

'It's over, Wallace.'

Pickering did not answer immediately, but looked

down to his lap and readjusted the glasses on the bridge of his nose.

'And why, may I ask, do you say that?'

'Everything has changed.'

'Go on.'

'It's as if a veil has been lifted.'

'Load of old fiddle!'

Campobello smiled. 'Maybe. But it's over, I say. The singer has gone.'

Pickering kept a straight face. 'Gone.'

'That's right.'

'Is this your idea of humour? You don't seem very gone to me.' As ever with Pickering, it was difficult to know whether he was innocently confused or just irritated.

'I am here, of course, but the Maestro, his voice, and everything that was part of that whole nonsense, has departed. And not too soon.'

'You have a gift from God.'

'You think something as petty as a sweet voice has got anything to do with God?'

'So they say,' Pickering answered sombrely.

'Well, they haven't seen what I've seen.'

'So we're on first name terms with God now, are we?'

'A man's voice has no more significance in creation than a leaf or a snowflake. And anyway, if I had been Chinese my voice would not be thought nice at all. It's all just a game, a man-made game. Nothing to do with God, I assure you.'

Pickering elected to ignore the little speech. 'Before burning your boats once and for all, we should try it out. See what shape the voice is in.'

'You're missing the point.'

'Pray enlighten me then, Maestro.'

Campobello looked at Pickering, who was observing him with expectant curiosity, eyes blinking donnishly, from the piano stool. How would any of them understand? He sighed. 'All right, I'll say this as simply as I can. Peasant to peasant.'

'I beg your pardon?'

Rocco smiled. 'You know what I mean.'

'There haven't been peasants in England since the time of King George.'

'Isn't the king at the moment called George?'

'I'm talking about George the fourth.'

'All right. Just hear me out.' He paused to collect his thoughts. 'I have at last come to know the man that I really am. And I hope it's not too late.'

Pickering nodded sagely. 'You've seen a light. Is that what you're trying to say?'

'Exactly. Rather like that. Like a light.'

Pickering stopped nodding and looked at him straight. 'This sort of thing happens to men of your age, you know. It passes.'

Campobello smiled again. He got up from the armchair, went over to the mantelpiece and took a cigarette from a silver box. A gust from the sea rocked the window behind him and foiled his first attempt to light it. The gurgling of a motor launch on the bay's water rumbled in and out of earshot. 'I've been told I'm too thin,' he said, stroking the sides of his abdomen as he caught a reflection of himself in a mirror, 'I've lost fifty pounds.' He struck a second match and lit his cigarette.

'Well, whoever told you that doesn't know poppy-cock,' said Pickering. 'You were too fat before, that's all.'

'Don Graziani tells me to eat more. And to shave my

87

beard. He says that tenors have not had beards since the days of Tamagno and de Reszke at the beginning of the century.'

'Verdi wrote his operas for men with beards, that's why he had one. Look at you!' Pickering held out his hand in a rare demonstration of feeling, but could not find the words to accompany the gesture. He gave up with a tut, and opened the keyboard. Campobello laid a hand on the little Yorkshireman's shoulder. Leaning down, he said quietly, 'Be careful, Wallace. Anyone might think you were about to flatter me. It's not like you.'

'Well, sometimes we're driven to extreme measures,' replied Pickering, shaking the hand off his shoulder and striking a chord. 'Sing me a scale.'

'No.'

'Just one.' He played an exaggeratedly florid arpeggio by way of introduction. 'Nothing difficult. D major, downwards.'

'No.'

'One, two—' Pickering encouraged, but the tenor remained silent. The sustained chord, held there with the pedal down, began to fade into a nondescript harmonic mush until Pickering finally released his fingers from the keys and let the pedal rise, killing the sound. The two men looked at each other in silence for a moment, until, from somewhere in the villa, there came the noise of a distant crash, as if a vase or dish had been dropped on flagstones. Campobello blinked.

'I don't want you to worry about your future, Wallace,' he said. 'You'll have everything you ever need.'

Pickering was overcome by a dozen or so furious responses that sprang to mind, but all he could manage was a half-spluttered laugh. 'Me? I've already got more than I need for another three lives. It's not me you want to be thinking about.'

'And Pietro,' continued Campobello, 'because the time will come when I will no longer—'

'That's enough for now,' interrupted Pickering. 'No more doom and gloom. You run along, if you like. I've got work to do.' There were tears in his eyes as he fiddled clumsily with the pages of the scores in front of him.

'What we have done together cannot be undone,' said Campobello, again touching him on the shoulder. 'We've made our contribution, and it's been a good one. We've done our share.'

'Away with you,' Pickering responded. Just at that moment Campobello's face flinched and he heaved slightly to one side, putting a hand to his flank. He turned away from the piano, trying to conceal the reflex, but Pickering had noticed. 'Still hurting, then?'

'It comes and it goes.'

'I thought the doctors said you were clear.'

'Maybe it is getting better.'

'Have you told the doctors you're still in pain?'

Campobello dragged on his cigarette but did not answer.

'No. I didn't think so,' continued Pickering. 'But I don't suppose it would make a lot of difference if you had. Those doctors say only what Mr Graziani tells them to say.'

'Don't be too harsh on Don Graziani,' admonished Campobello gently. 'He's been very kind to me, to us all.'

'And he's got reason to be. He's been trying to get his claws back into you for years. Ever since you left the Jupiter

Company and started making records for Columbia. In other words, ever since he stopped getting his slice on all your recordings.'

'You don't have to remind me.'

'Why do you put up with him?'

'Because we go back a long way. Yes, even before I met you.'

'Just be careful, that's all I'm saying. Get another doctor's advice.'

'Don't worry about Don Graziani. There's not a card in his pack I haven't seen a hundred times before.'

A look of slight disgust tugged the corners of Pickering's mouth and he nodded towards Campobello's hand. 'You'd be better off without the cigarettes,' he said.

'They help my lower register.'

'Your lower register's the best I've ever known. And anyway, what does that matter now, if you're not going to sing?'

'Are you always going to lecture me?' said Campobello. 'Even when we're old men sitting in bath chairs watching singers at the opera young enough to be our grandchildren.'

'Which reminds me,' said Pickering, raising his spectacles to wipe aside an errant tear that had escaped his lower eyelid, 'I saw the director of the San Carlo this morning. They're all counting on you coming to the opening night of *Andrea Chénier* in three weeks' time. There'll be fancy politicians and whatnot there as well. They're giving you pride of place in the royal box.'

'Yes, yes, I know.'

'Will you go?'

'We'll see.'

'The director's very keen. I think he wants to show

you off. He's retiring soon. Do you know who they're appointing to take over?'

'Don Graziani has ideas on the subject,' Campobello said wearily.

'If you do go, you'll be recognized in the street from then on, of course.'

'I cannot hide away for ever.'

'Glad to hear you say so,' said Pickering, 'it's a first step.' When Campobello did not respond to this, Pickering added, 'You don't have to throw the baby out with the bathwater, you know. It's only natural you should feel the way you do right now. You nearly died.'

'A part of me did die,' said Campobello, suddenly earnest, and Pickering cleared his throat rather awkwardly. He never felt comfortable in heart-to-heart chats, and so began to spread a few chords on the keyboard in order to dilute the import of Rocco's pregnant statement.

'Wallace.'

Pickering's hands were now sweeping up and down the keyboard as he attempted to ignore Campobello.

'Wallace,' repeated the tenor with no more force or urgency than before, but his very restraint compelled Pickering to pause. 'Can I count on you, Wallace? To support me. You and Pietro?'

Pickering looked at him wide-eyed. Again, it was impossible to know if he was in shock, or sympathy, or had taken offence. 'Need you ask?' he said. 'You know where I stand. If the voice is there, I'll move heaven and hell to get it back to work. But if something serious is up, you won't find me forcing the issue. You can have the best mill in the land, but you won't ever make wool without sheep. Sounds to me your sheep's lost out in a storm on the moor somewhere. We'll find him and bring him back by and by. No need to hurry.' He finished rather flatly and did not look up from the piano stool, but started to sway from side to side, as his torrid improvisations took flight and modulated towards a new and brighter key.

Chapter 8

There was thunder out in the bay that night, but as yet no downpour, and the crickets were at their business full pelt under cover of darkness in the garden bushes below. Rocco Campobello could hear them as he lay naked on a reclining wicker chaise in front of his bedroom's open French window. Splintered moonlight bobbed restlessly on the sea far to the left, while a more steady luminescence entered through the window and defined the curves of his resting body. The fragment of pink coral – which had once belonged to his father, and which Rocco had carried as protection against the evil eye since boyhood – hung on a slender golden chain around his neck.

The room was unlit, the ceiling fan off. Although nearly midnight, it was still warm enough to bring pinpricks of perspiration to the surface of his skin, thousands of them, and this gave his abdomen a slight sheen in the half-darkness. The heat in this town was different from heat anywhere else in the world, and it brought back the old days with frightening immediacy. It was by no means the hottest place Rocco ever been to, but the closeness here had an oppressiveness of its own. In Naples, the heat felt somehow tainted, as if it carried with it an old scent, nurtured in these streets and alleys by centuries of despair. Yes, it was just like a smell, he

93

thought, though without flavour. He recalled it well, and rather liked it, in a perverse way, for all its fermented decay and unwholesomeness.

Positioned neatly on various tables around the room where he was lying was a collection of photographs in silver frames. Their monochrome images were reduced to mere shadows in the dim light, silent and ghostly shapes, like indistinct memories, which is what they were fast becoming. Each showed a picture of Rocco Campobello in a different costume: thirty years of triumphant appearances, stage personifications that people said had reinvented opera, shaking the industry to its core. Aside from the odd cry of disapproval from the old guard, the overwhelming consensus was that Campobello had raised the threshold of excellence in the art of musical drama. Before Campobello, dramatic credibility was neither expected nor attempted. A tenor protagonist would square himself rotundly centre stage, raise an arm, regardless of plot or character, and deliver his piece with concert finesse, before taking an elegant bow and acknowledging his audience with a gracious smile. But Campobello changed all that. Some called it cinematic realism, others said he had democratized opera, but all agreed that the effect was electrifying. Now people came to the opera to feel the very tears wrung from a lover's despairing heart; they wanted to hear the anguished sob of pain in his tone, to feel the prick of vengeance rise and boil in his veins.

The faintly visible spectres in frames around the room were memorials to these landmark interpretations, but Rocco looked at them now in the way a contented family man might glance over impassioned love letters he had written as a youngster: the fever of it all seemed not exactly misplaced, but quaintly irrelevant. That time was past, its contours levelled, its mercurial ups and downs mere distracting recollections. His father had always said there would come a time when the fever of life would begin to calm. He said that it even happened to the great emperors and generals of ancient times, who would turn quite soft towards the end of their lives, and hunger just to trail their fingers through the soil of home, the ground ploughed by their forbears. It was odd how his father's words sprang so easily to mind nowadays, how they were always there, like little polished bells strung across the threshold which tinkled every time he passed, having previously been absent and forgotten for so many years.

Rocco sipped a cold drink and observed his own perspiring body, the softness of it, its spongy vulnerability. A trace of the miracle was still with him and it was like a grace beyond words. He felt as if he had stepped clean from a hardened old shell, and it was oddly chilly and unfamiliar, here, in the outside world – frightening, in a way – but he was free at last of the old shell's daily chafing. Over the years the shell had become more important than the man inside, had become all that mattered. He had been turned into a monument, because the Voice, his sovereign, had demanded monumentality. They had all made a plinth for him, to raise him above common men and turn him into an object of veneration.

Molly had had to share the plinth, for better or worse, standing slightly to one side, a pretty but minor adjunct; not a role she particularly relished, but it was the Maestro and the Voice she had wanted to marry, so eagerly, so childishly. After their first meeting in Chicago, Campobello had been to her like a cake on a baker's shelf: she would not rest until she could take him home with her.

For all her waywardness and the deep roots of bitterness between them, Rocco could not help but feel a little sorry for her now. He looked back on it all with weary detachment. Molly could not have realized when they got married that there would never be room for love within the Voice's matrix. Its nature was selfish and inconsiderate. How could fragile love ever take root in such a wasteland? Rocco had known, but he did nothing to deter Molly, and so the blame was his, in a way, as it was in so many other ways. Of course the Voice would rule their married lives with brutal tyranny, as it had ruled his life from the start. It hadn't been long before Molly had felt the need to beat a secret path through to some kind of refuge. She had chosen her path years ago, following the obvious and easiest routes away from her troubles, like a mountain brook that tumbles into the clear-cut contours and gullies of a falling landscape. Men slipped easily into her stream from time to time, and she never had the resistance to block them out. There could be no route back up the mountain now, after so sheer and rocky a descent.

The thunder rolled and echoed distantly again, like groans of pain from an ailing giant of the spheres. Around the harbour other people were listening, and there were twinges of fear at the sound. Despite the rationale of modern times and the triumph of science, the deities and myths of bygone times retained a shred of menace, and the thought of their celestial malaise still struck dread into the hearts of simple men.

Campobello felt the tug of an ache behind his rib – no spasm or sharpness, just a sombre reminder, lest he should forget, that time was no longer an open-ended account and that there were matters to settle. He ran a palm around the top of his cranium, through the short bristle, and reaped a harvest of sweat on his hand. An eight-inch vertical scar, pink and sensitive to the touch, slashed a line from his navel up towards the inverted V of his ribcage. It was a beautiful mark, almost holy for Rocco, like a saint's stigmata, because through its sweet pain it reminded him of the poisons' release. Both poisons. The stuff from the abscess had been drained from here but that was only part of it. The real poison, the infection that had all but consumed him, had been a disease of character.

He recalled with absolute clarity watching the operation from somewhere above the table, and wondering what all the fuss was about. It wouldn't have happened like that in the old days. Like when his father's grandfather – a true Campanese giant, who could labour for three men – had been crushed beneath his donkey. The animal had stumbled on the path from his quarry, carrying six great cut stones on its back. The big man's friends just stayed by his side and stroked his hair until he breathed his last. That was how things were in the old days. But not for his great-grandson, Rocco Campobello. How they had toiled to bring him back from the dead, and he had watched it all from somewhere above, bemused. He witnessed the voluptuous ease with which his skin seemed to blossom open at the knife's slice, saw the orange rubber tubing inserted in the wound, and the poison at last beginning to gurgle obediently out of his abdomen.

And then the dialogue began and he was utterly spellbound by it. It turned into an argument, quite heated, and he had tried to labour his point against an

97

unbending adversary, but the outcome was strangely predetermined, of course. He was being sent back to put his house in order. The simple words were etched into his memory, though he had not much idea what they meant. At the time he didn't even care because the flavour of paradise was thick with him, but he soon knew what he had to do, where he had to start.

The light in the bedroom was now growing dull as clouds began to slide across the harbour sky and veil the moon. Campobello's chest and arms were covered with a light spread of hair, his pale feet crossed, genitals slumped to one side. Salvation now seemed like a dim and distant light leading him through the night storm. He lay back on the soft feathered cushions of his chaise and shut his eyes. His right hand reached up to the piece of forked coral hanging at his neck, and he stroked its curve with an old familiarity. He could remember that evening at the docks, of course. So long ago, almost beyond reach. He recalled perfectly the light of that day fading and the stars appearing in the sky. That had been the start of it all.

The crickets outside the window, as if forewarned of stormy times ahead, suddenly stopped their tuneless rasping and scuttled away for cover before the first drops of rain began to fall. The moon was now hidden behind a dense blanket of cloud, and darkness consumed the room. Before long, a peppering of rain had begun.

Chapter 9

Naples, 1894

Thirty-two years before. One afternoon when they were both seventeen. It had been raining then as well, and heavily. That was why they were running so fast through the streets. It wasn't because they were short of time before their appointment with the choirmaster – they had at least a couple of hours to spare; nor was it because the rain was cold – in fact it was quite refreshing after the recent hot spell. There was just something about the heavy downpour that made them want to run, and run as fast as their legs would carry them, even if it meant crashing through the herd of goats that was ambling down the street, even if it meant buffeting the arm of the blind barrel organ grinder and sending his meagre collection of coins spinning into the air. Gabriele was the faster of the two because he was thin and wiry. Rocco, by contrast, was the heaviest boy of his age in the district, outsize in every direction, with puffy red cheeks, long arms and clumsy ways. Some neighbours teased him about it and called him an oaf. He was an easy target because he was self-conscious and a little too earnest; but kinder elders took pity on him and would pat his big round shoulders, reassuring him that his size would stand him in good stead in his job. His father should be proud to have a boy with such unusually broad hands and fingers, they said. There would be few blacksmiths in the city with such natural endowments. God had smiled on the Campobello family at last, after all their terrible misfortunes.

'Stop!' called Gabriele, and Rocco bent over double to get his breath back. 'I'm going to get some water.'

'Ferrata?' said Rocco with surprise, looking up and seeing the distinctive earthenware jars of Santa Lucia iron-rich water on the pavement. They were shaped like gigantic bosoms, with air release valves for nipples. 'Expensive.'

'So what?' said Gabriele, who was not in the least out of breath. 'We're going to be rich. And it's all starting today.'

'You hope.'

'I know. Do you want some?'

'No,' replied Rocco, who had spotted a spaghetti vendor firing up his charcoal burner for a customer. 'If we're spending, I'm having some of that.'

The vendor noticed him and pulled a face of haughty disgust. *'Co' sbruffo, o senza sbruffo?'* he scowled at Rocco, his voice dry and rasping through overuse.

'Con,' replied Rocco, meaning that he had opted for the tomato sauce as well – a real extravagance. The vendor piled the spaghetti into a newspaper boat, sucked a ladle-ful of warmed sauce into his own cheeks and then, to get an even spread, sprayed the contents of his mouth over the pasta before handing it over to the eager boy; but not before taking payment – he knew what these lads could be like, even the ones with money in their pockets.

It was still raining while they had their snack – in the end they shared the spaghetti and water between them. They were too busy eating to talk, and watched in silence the cartloads of stone and rubble being towed by donkeys this way and that along the quayside. The destruction and rebuilding of various quarters of old Naples had been under way ever since they could remember, and they would not think to question the sight of yet another street being ripped apart. More interesting was the army of young women that stood around the remains of a demolished building nearby, picking out stones that might be suitable for recycling – Roman, medieval, it made no odds – as their forebears had done since ancient times. Gabriele eyed them with a greedy smile because their skirts were tucked up higher than would generally have been thought respectable. The normal boundaries of decorum were suspended for women doing manual labour.

'Come on,' said Gabriele, setting off again while Rocco stuffed his last mouthfuls away, 'I can't wait to see what it's like down under.'

'*Vengo, vengo.* What's the hurry?' spluttered Rocco, and started after him as best he could.

The heavy squall was beginning to ease now, and beggars with twisted spines and lopped-off limbs were dragging themselves back from filthy nooks into the sunshine, where it was easier to impede passers-by. Drenched lines of washing that hadn't been rescued in time before the deluge hung heavily between and around the buildings, dripping abundantly on people in the streets below.

The boys darted out into the broad thoroughfare of Via Medina, where Gabriele, seeing an opportunity, hopped on to the back of a horse-drawn omnibus. He ducked down to hide himself from the driver, but then had to jump off when he noticed Rocco standing in the middle of the street some way behind, holding out his hands in exasperation.

'*Va bene*,' called Gabriele with the condescension of a natural and frequent victor, 'we'll walk the rest of the way.'

They were on their way to meet Pepe, one of the last of the city's infamous *pozzari*, keepers of the wells. Before the great cholera epidemic of 1884, fresh water had been supplied and distributed to all parts of Naples by a vast network of underground cisterns and aqueducts, which dated back to ancient times. The flow was maintained and managed by a team of professional well-men, *pozzari*, who were something between petty engineers and slaves of the darkness. They had to be small and agile enough to squeeze through the tiniest underground shafts and passages, and were archetypally mud-encrusted, bad tempered and wily. To ease the misery of their dank, subterranean labour, the *pozzari* traditionally demanded hefty tips from owners of private wells and even from churches, or anyone who wanted a decent supply of water to his tank. Because of the distinctive hoods they wore they were associated in popular legend with the *monaciello*, or little monk, a character from children's bedtime stories, who would creep from a hole in the ground and steal mischievously into homes under cover of night.

There weren't many *pozzari* left now. It was discovered that one of the main causes of the great cholera epidemic had been contaminated sewage seeping through the porous rock to the underground water reservoirs. Almost overnight the old cisterns, wells and aqueducts, together with their legendary keepers, were abandoned. Many of the *pozzari* had died in the epidemic anyway, and most of the others slowly shrivelled up with rheumatism, but Pepe was still relatively robust, and one of the few men alive who held the secrets of that pitch black, subterranean labyrinth, above which the bustling city of Naples heaved.

The boys found him sitting in the street on a stool, being shaved. He was no more than five feet tall, but had the face of a Roman warrior: thin, hardened cheeks, an eagle's nose and a crescent scar on his chin. His eyes flashed towards them as the barber took a large glass marble from his pocket and popped it into Pepe's cheek to get a smooth finish for the razor.

'Hello, Pepe,' said Gabriele. 'You see, we're on time.'

'Eh, he's too fat,' said the *pozzaro*, pointing at Rocco, his words distorted by the protrusion in his cheek.

'Please, Pepe,' pleaded Gabriele, 'there must be some wells wide enough.'

'Eh. *Zitti*! Sshh.' He pointed at the barber, who closed his eyes and raised his eyebrows, as if to assure them of his discretion. It was against the law for anyone to enter the underground cisterns, most of which had long been sealed.

'*Mi dispiace*,' said Gabriele.

'Eh,' came the acid voice of Pepe again. 'How much have you got?'

'Twenty *centesimi*. We've saved it up.'

'Ya, ya, ya,' Pepe gave a poisoned laugh and almost spat with scorn. Meanwhile, the barber dextrously lopped the marble from one of the old *pozzaro*'s cheeks to the other. 'You'll have to do better than that.'

103

Gabriele, who had actually accumulated nearly fifteen lire from serenading jobs (the romance market was quite lucrative in springtime), at last agreed to part with half a lira for the privilege of being shown a secret route down and around the underworld; and, after a deal of cajoling, Pepe agreed to let Rocco come with them for a further ten *centesimi*, though they would have to choose their shafts carefully because of his size.

'Who is the oaf, anyway?' asked Pepe, leading the way towards an alley in the San Lorenzo district.

'He's a singer, like me,' said Gabriele, skipping to keep up with Pepe's brisk little pace. 'We want to see what our voices sound like down there.'

'Eh. Just make sure the whole thing doesn't fall on you. Too much noise and you'll be crushed to death. It's happened before, you know!' This was Pepe's idea of a good joke, and for half a minute or more his dry 'heh, heh, heh' echoed off the walls of the little lanes down which they scurried.

They arrived at a shabby archway whose plaster had crumbled to reveal coarse brickwork beneath; multiple coatings of dog piss stained and glazed the basalt coigns at pavement level. Passing through the arch, Pepe led them into a *cortile* and on beyond, to a smaller, abandoned courtyard, no more than a ventilation quadrant between hopelessly decayed blocks of *fondaci* apartments. There, in the centre, was a square iron plate on rusted hinges.

'If you come here without telling me first,' said Pepe, narrowing one eye and looking devilishly up at the boys, who were taller than him, 'I'll kill you both. In your beds. *Capisci?*' Rocco and Gabriele nodded solemnly, but could not entirely suppress a giggle, at which Pepe waved a hand in the air with a disgusted, 'Pah!' before opening the lid and taking a little oil wick from his pocket. Holding the lighted wick between his teeth, he slid with an easy familiarity into the narrow mouth of the well, his feet finding the small cut-away niches that had been used for centuries by *pozzari* to descend into their underground kingdom. 'Make sure you hold on with at least one hand and one foot. One mistake and you're dead – and anyone underneath you, so wait until I've got to the bottom. It's thirty yards, so I'll be a while.'

The boys watched in awe for what seemed an age as the tiny light from the wick diminished to nothingness. Scared that something might have happened to Pepe, they called out, but were quickly greeted with a snakelike 'sshhh!' that hissed up the shaft as if he were just there beside them. They then noticed more light below and realized that Pepe must have lit some lanterns, which would help them find their footing. 'What are you waiting for, idiots?' rasped the subdued voice of the *pozzaro*, and the two friends began their climb down.

Pepe had illuminated the passage at the bottom by putting a flame to several earthenware oil lamps which stood in chiselled out wall niches. 'I'll go in front and light the way. Don't come too close or you might not see where you're putting your feet. Look!' He held out his wick to the right and they saw, a couple of paces away, another well shaft vanishing vertically down into the bedrock. Pepe seemed highly amused at the thought of the boys slipping to their death, and they could hear his dry giggles echoing in front of them as he walked ahead, lighting lamps on alternate sides of the narrow passage as he went.

The gradient sloped downward and the height of the

passage became shallower as they progressed, so that soon they had to duck in order to avoid scraping their heads against the rock. They were aware of several side passages turning off along the way, some of them wider and higher, but Pepe would not deviate from his chosen tunnel, even though at one point it became too slender for them to walk through forwards, and they had to shuffle sideways on.

'It's because he wants to scare us,' whispered Gabriele to Rocco. 'Don't give him the satisfaction.' But Rocco was hardly aware of his friend's words, nor of Pepe's taunts. His eyes were wide open with awe at the cold and silent underworld that lay beneath the crowded city he knew so well.

They came at last into a large cavern whose walls pitched gently up towards an unseen apex in the darkness above them. The circular ground area, which stretched several yards across, was sectioned into two neat halves, one of which fell away precipitously to form a deep black pool, into which drops from high up were plopping at regular intervals. There were several passages radiating off from the chamber, but Pepe made his way purpose-fully towards the tiniest one on the far side. They would have to crawl.

'Why can't we just stay here?' asked Gabriele, who was looking a little uncomfortable. 'This will do.'

'If you like,' replied Pepe, 'but from here on you're on your own.' He took out a stick of chalk and marked the tunnel from which they had just emerged, then gave Gabriele the chalk, a spare wick and a few matches. 'If you decide to go further, make sure you mark the walls so you can find your way back. Or else—' and he began to snigger again. 'Anyway, from now on, I don't know you.

I never met you before in my life. If anything happens to you, it's your fault.' And he turned to go.

'How far do the tunnels go?' asked Rocco, his mellow high voice resonating in the great chamber.

'All over the city. Down to Posillipo and further. The other way towards Ercolano, everywhere. They say if you go inland far enough you can find yourselves in the church catacombs under Capodimonte,' he grinned, 'and see all the skulls and bones.'

'Are there any other big chambers like this, nearby?' asked Rocco.

Turning to go, Pepe growled back, 'Plenty. And much bigger. It's a whole city down here. Anyway, what do you take me for? A fucking tour guide? Eh!' He spat at the ground with disgust and walked away into the darkness. For some while they heard his footsteps, and then, a couple of minutes later, a distant clang as the iron lid at the top fell shut.

'Come on,' said Rocco, eyes shining in the flickering light, 'let's go in further. This way.' He pointed to one of the passages that led away from the chamber.

'Why?' asked Gabriele. 'This cave will do fine. Listen.' And he let ring the exuberantly climactic last line of a song, 'La donna è mobile', hanging on to the final high B flat for longer than normal, to prove his point. '*Meraviglioso!*' he concluded, hugely satisfied with his performance. 'You try.'

'In a minute. Let's just go a bit deeper in.'

Gabriele looked alarmed, but quashed his reticence so as not to seem cowardly. '*Va bene*. You take a lamp, I'll bring the chalk.' Rocco disappeared into the tunnel that he had chosen and hurried onwards. 'Not so fast!' Gabriele called more than once, carefully marking the

107

walls where his friend took turnings. 'Where are you going, anyway?'

'This way,' Rocco called back as he veered off and downhill on a new and seemingly reckless trail. He paused for a moment for Gabriele to catch up. 'This one's wide and straight. The ancient Greeks built all this. Using slaves they brought back from wars. Can you imagine that? How many of them died digging out all of this? And we're the only ones in the world who know about it right now!'

'How do you know all this stuff? You always know so much stuff,' said Gabriele, but Rocco barely heard, because he had begun running along the downward gradient, hardly able to see more than a yard in front of him. The discrepancy in their physical fitness was now more than compensated for by Gabriele's sluggish reluctance, with the result that the gap between them widened. All of a sudden, Gabriele found himself in pitch blackness and came to an abrupt stop. He heard his friend's voice cry out from some way ahead, 'Oh my God!'

Gabriele paused, dead still, before venturing, 'Rocco? What's up? Are you there?'

'I'm here,' came a quiet reply, and then Gabriele saw the needle prick of light from the oil lamp ahead of him. 'Take a look at this,' said Rocco.

They had arrived at a chamber so vast that, even after exploring twenty tentative paces across to where a stream cut along a neat, straight aqueduct, they could not see the extent of its width. 'Do you think the stream still carries the disease?' whispered Rocco, as if the place demanded a kind of hushed respect. Talking too openly about evil things might raise a demon from the depths. He looked with awe up into the blackness above.

'Better not touch the water, just in case,' said Gabriele.

'My mother's killer. And my sisters'. Weird.' His eyes were wide and reflected the flame of the wick in his hands.

'Don't think about it.'

'All right, then,' said Rocco, turning back to him, 'let's sing. You first.'

'No, you first,' said Gabriele. 'It's your turn.'

'You've got a bigger voice.'

'So what?'

'I might learn something from you.'

'You've got a teacher already.' Gabriele sneered at the thought. 'What's she like, anyway, this Signora Signorelli?'

'Strict. She hits me with a stick,' said Rocco.

'What for?'

'If I do something wrong. Or if I talk like a commoner.'

'You are a commoner,' laughed Gabriele.

'But she wants to turn me into something else.'

Gabriele scoffed, 'You can't change who you are.' He sat down on the smooth stone ground. 'Anyway, I don't need lessons. I've got it here.' He beat a fist hard against his chest. 'I feel like God when I sing.'

'Maybe I haven't got what you've got,' said Rocco.

'You're wasting your money with the old Signora.'

'If I can't pay, she teaches for free. I think it's helping my voice. Perhaps you should go and see her.'

'For free, eh?' Gabriele looked at Rocco and raised his eyebrows. 'She must think a lot of you.'

'She's still a bitch,' muttered Rocco. 'I hate her.'

'Then why do you go?'

'Because I'm beginning to hit the top notes.'

'Does she realize you hate her?'

'Of course not. I pretend to be the perfect pupil.'

'*Ruffiano!* So what does she make you do?'

'Lots of exercises. Breathing,' he put a hand to his diaphragm, 'and vowels – forever vowels – the shape of the mouth, opening everything up for the breath, making my throat sort of . . .'

'Sort of what?'

'Longer.'

Gabriele grimaced through his smile. 'What?'

'You know, pulling everything down in here.' He gripped his larynx between thumb and forefinger. 'To make it rounder, darker. Difficult to explain.'

Gabriele wasn't convinced. 'Let's hear, then. We'll see if it's working. Sing me what you're going to sing for Signor de Luca this afternoon. Have you decided?'

Rocco moved a few paces away from his friend, and let out a couple of short, sharp tenor barks into the black dome above. The sound echoed miraculously, seeming to amplify itself without any extra effort on his part. The boys looked at each other and laughed. Rocco put a fist to his mouth, closed his eyes, then looked up with a slight frown.

'Very professional!' Gabriele clapped from where he sat cross-legged, but Rocco took no notice, and began, in a restrained *mezzo piano*, the opening bars 'Cujus Animam' from Rossini's *Stabat Mater*. On hearing the first few notes, Gabriele was about to interject playfully that it was an ambitious choice for a choirboy's audition, but stopped before saying anything, listening instead to the noticeable change in his friend's voice. Rocco's brows were knotted, his forehead slightly lowered. He had worked on his mouth shape, as Signora Signorelli had taught him, and now dropped his jaw in a way that

110

allowed his upper face to remain relaxed as he sang, front teeth showing slightly beneath his top lip. It gave his formerly rather thin and nasal sound a greater depth and freedom. One hand stretched out and up in front of him as he curled high to the final top D flat, holding on to it for a respectable few seconds, the strain showing on his face, before descending down the closing cadenza with studied grace. He came to a stop and let his head fall gently forwards. There was a still moment during which neither of them spoke or moved, and the humour seemed to have drained from Gabriele's face.

'You're good,' said Gabriele.

Rocco came out of his reverie and looked up. 'It's the cave.'

'I know. But you've changed. And it's bigger. Whatever she's doing for you seems to be working. I'm going to have to watch my back.' Now he smiled.

'*Davvero!* You'll see. I'll be better than you soon!' said Rocco, a comment which drew a mock glare from Gabriele. 'Come on. Your turn now.'

Gabriele, eager to test the acoustic, needed no more persuasion. He sang a more modest aria, a well-known one by one of the famous classical Italian songwriters of the eighteenth century. His tenor voice was distinctly stronger and more polished than Rocco's, with a quick, pulsing, muscular vibrato and a ringing buzz in the lower tones. Gabriele had always been more mature in body, and had first started sprouting bristle on his chin when he was only twelve; just a year later he boasted of his first sexual conquest, and even contemplated eloping with a pretty girl in the next street.

'Yah,' Gabriele concluded with satisfaction and slapped his hands, 'this is a good place for a sing. If de Luca could hear us down here, he'd make us principal tenors just like that. How long have we got, anyway?' Both boys had rather forgotten about the time, but agreed that they were safe. They had planned to meet Signor de Luca, choirmaster at Santa Maria Regina Coeli, at two o'clock, and neither of them underestimated the significance of the meeting. News that the maverick choirmaster would be recruiting junior probationers, in order to expand his already famous little choir, had reached them a few days ago, and they had wasted no time in arranging an audition. Successful candidates would not only earn themselves a small salary, but would get new clothes, shoes and an education at the church's orphanage, the Ospedale.

'If we do well he might let us live at the Ospedale,' said Rocco.

'Why would you want that?'

'We could dedicate ourselves completely to studying. No distractions. And we'd be noticed. All those rich men who give money to charity. They go to the Ospedale all the time, looking for new ways to spend their cash. If they like the way we sing they could help us get on. Sponsor us.'

Gabriele looked at Rocco with surprise. 'You've thought it all out,' he said. 'Is that what you want? To be some rich man's pet?'

'If it means I can get to sing at the opera. And if it means I don't have to hammer metal all my life.'

'You'd break your papa's heart. Who will look after him when he's old?'

'I'll send him money.'

Gabriele looked down. 'And what if you don't make any?'

'*Porco!* You were the one who said we're going to be rich!' protested Rocco, suddenly indignant.

'I know,' Gabriele replied quietly. 'We can dream. But we're talking about your father. He's a good man. And he hasn't got your mother to comfort him any more. Nor your sisters. You know how proud he is of you.'

Rocco pursed his lips. 'That's too bad,' he murmured. 'I have my life, too.'

Gabriele shook his head and scratched his scalp, yawning. 'Anyway. Not for me,' he said. 'I don't want to live at the Ospedale. No women there.'

Rocco looked up at his handsome friend, who had now got to his feet and was stretching. 'Are girls everything to you?'

'Of course. Isn't it the same with you?'

'Maybe,' said Rocco without much conviction, and turned away. 'Who is it now? Chiara? You've fallen for that pretty little Chiara Santangelo, haven't you?'

'Chiara Santangelo! CHIARA SANTANGELO!' yelled Gabriele in a huge operatic tone that rang like a cathedral bell around the massive hollow of the stone chamber. 'What a woman! She's already sixteen. In a year's time they'll be looking for a husband for her. I'd better put in my bid. *Chi s'aiuta Dio l'aiuta!* God helps those who help themselves.'

Rocco sniggered. 'With four brothers, all of them sharing the same bed, you wonder what used goods her husband will find on the wedding night.' At this both boys began to laugh so loudly that they had to calm themselves for fear of the roof collapsing, as Pepe had warned. Anyway, it was time to go. The precious wick was burning low.

Rocco opened the outside lid of the well just a crack, so

that he could scan the courtyard before emerging from the depths into open air. Gabriele clearly felt relieved to be back in the real world, but the catacomb experience had pepped him up, and he walked off in the direction of Santa Maria Regina Coeli with a confident spring in his step. There was something almost lordly in the way he called to various acquaintances along the route, as if he needed to share the zest he felt at the prospect of what was in store. At one point he stopped so that his friend Gino, the *maruzzaro*, who sold snails, could give him one of the little beasts, boiled in water flavoured by fish heads, parsley and chervil. Surprisingly, Rocco refused a mouthful. He seemed preoccupied and oblivious to his surroundings. He even ignored buoyant little Gianetta, the old nutcase who meandered cheerfully around all day wearing colourful hooped stockings and jabbering non-stop greetings to all and sundry. She waddled up to pat him on the back, squeaking with joy, and her bristly chin wiggled like a puppet's while she chatted; but Rocco walked on regardless, frowning at the ground.

'Don't tell me you're frightened?' said Gabriele, taking his hand and swinging it as they neared the church. 'You've always had nerves of steel.'

'I don't know what frightened means,' Rocco replied, under his breath. 'I'm just saving myself.'

'Well don't let it get you down. Tonight we'll be celebrating!'

Passing through the iron-studded doors of the church, the boys breathed deep the familiar ecclesiastical cleanliness within, and made their way towards the sacristy at the rear. Their reflections flitted across the mottled purples and greens of the polished marble floor, while the sound of their steps echoed around the calm span of the nave.

Gabriele peeped tentatively through the open sacristy door and smiled. Choirmaster de Luca was a short balding man in a cassock, with the build of a diminutive but shapely wine barrel. He had one pencil between his teeth and was annotating pages of sheet music on the table with another, but did not look up, even when Gabriele coughed to attract his attention.

'Signor de Luca?'

'Yes, yes, yes, I know you're there,' said the choirmaster through the pencil, still without turning to face them. 'Just come in and wait until I'm ready.' The boys shuffled obediently forward and stood rather sheepishly against a pair of gilt-encrusted pillars, hands crossed in front of them. Thus they remained for another ten minutes while de Luca completed his task. He was marking the scores, warbling fragments of melody in a voice heavily distorted by vibrato, and occasionally conducting silent bars of music into the empty space in front of him. When the job was complete, he gathered up the music, removed his spectacles and leant back to observe the boys, one at a time, from head to toe. They had each borrowed a pair of laceless shoes for the occasion but hadn't given much thought to the rest of their appearance, and now regretted it as the little man scrutinized them.

'I hope you sing better than you look,' said de Luca. When they made no response he raised his eyebrows and added, 'Or is that not what you're here for?'

'Sir?' said Gabriele, looking and sounding more imbecilic than he was. De Luca sighed, and continued with exaggerated clarity: 'Have you come for an audition?'

'Yes sir, yes sir. An audition,' replied Gabriele nodding enthusiastically.

'Well, you don't seem to have any music with you. Most of the others brought something with them to sing.'

'Others?' asked Gabriele, his face falling. 'Have there been others?'

'About thirty or forty. This is one of the best choirs in the city, you know. We have a reputation. Word gets about.'

'We know, sir, we know.'

'How many tenors do you need?' ventured Rocco.

'Only one more,' answered the choirmaster. 'Maybe two, if one of the boys I've heard doesn't shape up a bit. You've got to be quick. The keen ones are quick.' Noticing the devastation on their faces, his mouth softened into something like a smile and he gave the slightest of winks, from which the boys drew oceans of reassurance. 'I've seen you here before, haven't I? You sit quite near and listen a lot. I've noticed.'

'Every Sunday,' said Gabriele. 'Sometimes twice.'

'Let's have a listen, shall we?'

De Luca led the way towards the organ which was housed above a cluster of classical columns in an elegant oval-shaped loft. Rocco was instructed to work the organ's bellows, while Gabriele was given first chance. The piece he had chosen was well known enough for de Luca not to require music in order to accompany him, and though his delivery of it was neither as confident nor as resonant as it had been in the cavern, Gabriele seemed quietly pleased with his own performance when he stood down to swap places with Rocco.

De Luca almost laughed when he heard what Rocco wanted to sing, but again began the introduction without

116

the assistance of a score. Rocco took up the opening line and one or two heads that were bent in prayer turned in the direction of the organ loft. Rossini's 'Cujus Animam', although masquerading as sacred, was in fact a shameless showpiece for the operatic tenor, and there were worshippers in Santa Maria Regina Coeli that day who considered their prayers in some way tainted by the profanity of the music they heard.

Rocco began pleasantly enough, with an elegant accommodation of the first high A flat, and at this he noticed de Luca's head tilt to one side, eyebrows raised. But as he progressed, he started to force the tone. His fists were clenched and he gave his all, but the sound, with added weight, came across thinner and reedier than Gabriele's. When he reached the extended uphill crescendo of 'et tremebat, cum videbat', the veins stood out around the sinews of his neck, and at the climax of the phrase 'nati poenas', the sound was tight and strangled. He began to repeat the phrase, as the score demands, but found to his surprise that the organ accompaniment had broken off. He stopped singing mid-phrase and turned to look at de Luca.

'That's quite enough,' said the choirmaster softly as the echo of the strained high note began to subside. 'I don't think so. The first one – what's your name?'

'Gabriele Tomassini.'

'Yes, we'll try you out. In fact one of my tenors has got a cold and I need someone to sing the Pergolesi solo tomorrow morning. If you can learn it, and if you sing it properly, the job's yours.' Gabriele's eyes were on fire and he went down on one knee. 'None of that,' said de Luca, flicking him away with his fingertips.

'*Grazie, signor, grazie,*' Gabriele was repeating.

117

'Yes, well, we'll see how you do. Now run along, and tidy yourself up before tomorrow. I want you here an hour before mass so we can run through it.' De Luca was gathering up his things when Gabriele reached out and touched the sleeve of his cassock to stop him.

'Sir?' he said.

'Yes, what is it?'

'Sir. I cannot sing for you unless you have Rocco as well.'

'What's this?' replied de Luca, momentarily confused. 'Who?'

'Rocco. Rocco Campobello, sir, my friend here. Let me share the solo with him tomorrow. We both know it already. We'll take half each.'

'Don't push your luck, lad. I've told you: I only need one tenor.'

'You can pay us half and half,' pleaded Gabriele.

'Pay you?' puffed de Luca. 'Who do you think you are? I'm doing you a favour here.'

'*Mi dispiace*, signor,' grovelled Gabriele, 'forgive me.'

'There'll be no talk of pay until you prove what you can do when the heat is on.'

'Yes, sir, sorry, we understand. But just this one time. Try Rocco. He was nervous just now. He's a good singer, I promise.' Rocco looked at his friend with surprise, and detected the faintest wisp of a smile as Gabriele glanced quickly sideways at him. In that split-second smile, which in years to come he would try to wipe from his memory, was contained everything that was most intimate, affectionate and noble about their friendship. In that smile was the essence of camaraderie, loyalty and an almost bashful love for one another.

Hope seemed to be slipping away as de Luca shook

his head and made for the stairway down; and so Rocco spoke out for himself. 'Signora Signorelli will vouch for me, sir,' he said. At this de Luca stopped on the top stair and half turned back.

'What did you say?'

'Signora Signorelli. She is my teacher. And her brother, Don Sebastiano, likes my singing. And he is the prefect of—'

'I know who Don Sebastiano is, you cheeky little blighter. And Signora Signorelli. So she teaches you? How can you afford that?'

'She teaches me for free, sir.'

De Luca looked intrigued. 'Does she indeed? I've never heard of that before. She must think a lot of you.' He pointed a finger at Rocco and gave him a serious look. 'I can check all this, you know. If you're lying—'

'I never lie, sir,' interrupted Rocco, his eyes wide with defiant innocence. 'And I would sooner fall dead in this church tomorrow morning than let you down in the solo. Give me the chance, sir, and I will sing to make the angels smile.'

At the novelty of this outburst de Luca gave a little laugh that was almost nervous and scratched the back of his head. Gabriele was looking at his friend with awe.

'Well, you're certainly passionate, I'll give you that,' said de Luca. 'But you're trying much too hard with your singing. Your voice isn't ready. How old are you?'

'Eighteen,' said Rocco. It was a lie he had told many people, including his teacher, because he did not want to be held back by his age.

'Well you're far too young to sing "Cujus Animam". I'm surprised Signora Signorelli allows it.'

119

'She doesn't, sir. I chose it. She would be angry if she knew I'd sung it for you.'

'And quite right, too. A larynx does not mature overnight, you know. It takes years of gentle practice, guidance and simple growing up. I've seen plenty go down the pan because they think too much of themselves too young. Especially tenors. You don't want to damage yourself, do you?'

'No I do not, sir, and I'll do exactly as you say. I want to learn.'

De Luca sighed. 'All right. You're in. Both of you. Eight o'clock tomorrow morning. Prompt. If you're late, I'll have your private bits for breakfast.' The boys smiled, both at the news and the implied profanity. 'We'll try you for three months' probation. Come along to the Ospedale on Monday and we'll sort out some clothes for you. And your timetable.'

Gabriele's mouth opened in surprise. 'Is that it?'

'What do you mean?'

'Don't we need to see the priests? Or something?'

De Luca chuckled and started to descend the stairs. 'Don't you worry about the priests. They'll do what I say.' Gabriele followed after him, turning to wink with joy at his friend. 'You know how to say the right things,' he whispered to Rocco. 'That Signorelli thing. The whole speech. You cunning devil, you!'

The boys made their way as quickly as possible back to the Quartiere di San Lorenzo so that they could break the news to Rocco's father. They were hungry again, and Rocco, in particular, needed to fuel himself up before heading down to the quayside for his evening work. His employer was expecting him there by five o'clock at the latest, to paste a hundred or more death announcements on walls all over the parish. Rocco would be busy until at least eight, and would then have to meet up with Gabriele to practise the Pergolesi. It was standard church repertoire, a favourite at Santa Maria Regina Coeli, and they both knew it well enough by heart.

The streets to the north and south of the arrow-straight Via dei Tribunali, in the heart of old Naples, were laid out in a rectilinear pattern that predated almost any surviving civic plan in Europe west of Athens, though the boys knew nothing of this. Rocco had, however, heard an explanation for why this rigid grid was corrupted in one place, along Via Pisanelli, the very street where he lived. Here, the geometric regularity of the lanes gave way to a curve, forming something of an oval of buildings, which legend told was once the site of the city's Roman amphitheatre. Indeed, a powerful ancient archway still spanned the street, just down from the Campobello home, leading off from the oval, and here decaying plaster and stonework revealed unmistakable traces of Roman bricks buried deep in the fabric of the building. Rocco had grown up in the knowledge of this historical curiosity, and often liked to imagine the ghosts of vast crowds just yards away from where he slept, their roars and applause, the trumpets, soldiers, banners. There was even talk of hidden tunnels beneath their street, where slaves, prisoners and wild beasts had been kept chained in cells by the imperial rulers.

'Hey, Rocco!' It was Stefania, who lived two doors down, standing there beside the open drain with two dripping buckets in her hands. She had been pouring away her family's toilet slops when she'd seen the boys coming down the street, and her sharply observant eyes had noticed something new in the way they walked. Nothing ever escaped Stefania. It was said that she could tell when a woman was pregnant even within hours of the baby's conception – a power of intuition that had raised more than a few eyebrows, and once even led to an investigation by the local parish priest. Fortunately for Stefania he was a good-natured old salt and just advised her to keep her head down and not go making pronouncements all over the place. People liked to find someone to blame if things started to go mysteriously wrong in the neighbourhood, he said, and made the sign of the cross over her kneeling form. Now she called across to Rocco Campobello. 'Rocco boy! What've you been up to? You look as pleased with yourself as a Frenchie king.' She did not really know the provenance of the expression she'd used, but it was an old jibe that had its roots in the time when Bourbon monarchs sat on the throne of Naples.

'And so he should,' called Gabriele gleefully. 'You are looking at the new tenors of the Santa Maria Regina Coeli choir!' Rocco instantly scolded Gabriele into silence. 'Zitti! Not until I've told Papa, idiot.' He had become almost unbearably tense on the walk home. Gabriele was surprised that the happy outcome of the audition hadn't cheered him up. 'You shouldn't take it all so seriously,' he muttered back. 'Your Papa will be proud of you.'

'You don't understand,' replied Rocco. 'It's all so easy for you.'

'Well, well, well,' called Stefania, leaning back, hands on hips, as they approached. 'Don't let your new fame go to your heads.' Her eyes met Rocco's when he came level but something she saw there caused a flicker of a frown to dent her humour, enough to put paid to any further teasing. And so she said no more, but picked up her buckets and went back indoors. Gabriele winked a farewell to his buddy, pointing his finger from across the road as a silent reminder of their rendezvous later in the evening.

Rocco arrived at number 20 Via Pisanelli, on the ancient curve of the road, to see the blacksmith's anvil and hammers left out on the cobbles unattended. Enrico Campobello's work stove, which he had to operate out in the street, had clearly been abandoned for some while; unused animal dung bricks – the staple fuel – lay stacked beside it, there was only spent ash within, and the bellows rested inert on the cobbles. It was unlike Enrico to leave his post for more than a few minutes. He was known to be one of the hardest workers in the parish, and for that reason was never short of clients. His fortunes had been thrown upside down, like so many others, ten years previously when his wife and three daughters had all succumbed in a matter of weeks to cholera. But unlike many other blighted widowers in the district, whose lives had fallen apart and who were reduced to grief-stricken inertia, Enrico had battled on, redoubling his efforts in the face of adversity. Uncomplainingly, he shouldered the responsibility of his rather bewildered youngest child – who several times himself appeared to be coming down with the fatal symptoms – and also took care of his own elder sister, Maria Anna: a monstrously built maid in her fifties, cursed with a minor mental condition that was enough to ensure she would never find a husband. It was Maria Anna who now blocked the small arched doorway of the family home, squinting with unintentional disgust at the two boys as they approached.

'Where's Papa?' asked Rocco curtly.

'Indoors,' she replied, still squinting, her lip curled into a kind of snarl. 'He stopped at lunch for the day. What's wrong with you?'

'At lunch? He said he'd have to work like a dog to get the Bellalucca estate work done on time. All those railings! They're nothing like finished.'

'The *pazzariello*'s here,' Maria Anna added by way of explanation, shuffling aside from the doorway as Rocco approached. The *pazzariello* was a kind of professional spirit deterrent, or exorcist, who provided a necessary community service, visiting households in rotation to expel harmful occult influences. His antics centred around a primitive dance, accompanied by a drummer and piper, during which he would lash wildly with a stick, and sprinkle the place with blessed water. If a home contained more than one room, which was rare, he could charge a higher fee.

'What's he doing here?' said Rocco, impatiently. 'He's not due until November.'

'It's the new *pazzariello*, the son,' Maria Anna muttered. 'The old man died last year, and his son's changed everything.'

Rocco stooped to pass through into the low barrel-vaulted interior, but found the exorcist and his musicians blocking his path; having completed their task, they were making for the exit. It was dark inside, the only natural light coming from the doorway, but he saw his father's broad silhouette following behind them. Everyone looked pleased at the outcome. The *pazzariello* nodded a smile at Rocco who did not return the pleasantry but turned instead to look at his father.

'Everything's fine,' said Enrico as the men departed.

'They found nothing bad. Same as last year, God be praised.'

'What did you expect?' said Rocco.

'You can never be sure about these things. Spirits travel. Some day—'

'How much do these fellows charge you?'

'That's my business.'

'Gabriele said the going rate is ten lire. What a waste of money! Those frauds are raking it in!'

'Hold your tongue!' his father said quickly, but not so much to reprimand his son as to prevent the awakening of any latent evil in the air.

'I'm sorry, Papa,' said Rocco, 'I mean no disrespect. I just don't believe in any of that.'

'You can think what you please,' added Enrico gently, 'but there's no point in saying reckless things. Just in case.' He ushered his son into the tiny windowless room that was their home, and put an arm around his shoulders. 'You left this behind today.' He opened his palm to reveal the coral amulet that Rocco usually wore around his neck.

'I know,' said Rocco with a note of genuine remorse, despite his apparent scorn for superstition.

'I hope nothing bad has happened today as a result?' His father was smiling.

'Nothing yet. Actually, everything's gone well. Couldn't be better.'

'Don't speak too soon. The devil can hide his work in a candy. Put it back round your neck quickly. We don't want your fortune to start going downhill from today. Just when you've grown into such a fine young man.' He ruffled his son's hair. 'I should get back to work. Are you going to give me a hand?'

'I'd like to help, Papa, but I've got to go and do the pasting down at the docks. I gave my word. If I don't turn up I'll lose the job.'

'That's all right. Of course you must go.'

Rocco watched the retreating figure of the big man, who now sighed quietly to himself as he turned his mind to the workload ahead. He had hours of heavy labour to accomplish before he could drag his anvil and tools back under cover for the night, and he would surely have to be up a few hours later, before dawn, to start again. And it would be heavy toil tomorrow, and the day after. From time to time Enrico would smash a fingernail or brand himself accidentally but there would be no respite from the work that needed to be done; nor any caring feminine hand to soothe and comfort him. It had been the same since before Rocco could remember, and thus it was likely to remain, through thick and thin. The possibility of retirement was never mentioned.

Perhaps because of the accumulated tension of the day, Rocco felt tears spring to his eyes as he watched his Papa shuffle away to work; and he took a step towards him – this man who had been his guardian, friend, nursemaid and confidant ever since the great blackness had swallowed their home. His friends' fathers were wastrels to a man, Gabriele's included: good for nothing except boiling up cupfuls of slugs harvested from the cobbles when it rained, or waiting at the Porta Capuana for carts to come in from the fields, so they could scavenge the odd onion as it fell off. But his own Papa was a mighty engine of dependability. After a lifetime in this city, where starvation and disease were rife, Rocco could swear with his hand on his heart that he had never once gone hungry, a boast which few of his acquaintances could make.

'Papa,' he said, and Enrico turned with surprise to see his son rooted to the spot, unable to articulate his feelings, as his eyes welled up.

'What's the matter, my boy?' Enrico opened his muscular arms and took the boy in an embrace. 'Tell your old man what's up.'

'Papa,' repeated Rocco more quietly, 'I'm sorry, Papa.'

'Sorry about what?' Enrico asked soothingly, still holding him tight. 'It's all right. Tell me what's happened.'

There was a long pause, during which he gave his son time to recover his composure.

Rocco pulled away, wiped his eyes, and said, 'Something's happened today.' He brought his voice under control, sniffed heavily and swallowed, as if doing away with the loose mucus would force his feelings into retreat. It seemed to work. 'Something's happened,' he repeated, 'and everything's going to be different from now on.'

Enrico waited for an explanation, but none came. 'Are you going to tell me?'

'I . . . I don't want to.'

'Because you're frightened of what I'll say?'

'I'm frightened of disappointing you.'

'You could never disappoint me,' said Enrico and kissed him on the cheek. 'But you can wait until you're ready. We've got all our lives. We'll have to find lots of things to talk about when we're stuck next to each other at the forge all day.' It was a throwaway joke, but its effect on Rocco was acute. He wrenched himself apart from his father.

'I don't want to be a blacksmith, Papa,' he said, his

former caution being replaced with a note of defiance. 'I'm going to be an opera singer. I went to sing today for Signor de Luca. He's going to let me join the choir.'

Enrico looked at him, a little baffled by the assertive tone. 'Well, that's good,' he said. 'It's a good choir. But don't burn your boats just yet. Singing in a church choir is a long way from making a living in opera. You've got a good job as a blacksmith ready and waiting for you.' He meant the advice well, but Rocco took a step backwards, tensing.

'Are you going to stop me?'

'Just give yourself some time to think about it. You're always so impulsive.'

Rocco did not reply, but stared back at his father. His anger could not voice itself but it was present in his eyes.

'Look,' went on Enrico, 'I'm not criticizing you, I just want you to have a good future. Remember, I've seen a lot of hardship, I know what it's like.' He smiled and put a hand on Rocco's shoulder. 'Sometimes, maybe, you should remember that your old Papa knows you better than you know yourself.'

Rocco recoiled furiously from his father's touch, but still said nothing.

'Come here, my boy.'

'No!' cried Rocco, backing off.

Enrico stood up. He'd had enough of this nonsense and his expression turned stern. 'You don't know how lucky you are,' he said.

'Do I have to thank you for the rest of my life?' answered Rocco, shocked at his own impertinence. It was the first time he had ever spoken to his father in this way.

Enrico looked with disbelief. 'Of course not. I don't

want your thanks. What makes you think such a thing?'
But Rocco could say no more, and fled the house,
ashamed at the tears that now streamed down his face.

Down at the docks, a few hours later, Rocco rested after
finishing his pasting work. There were fewer notices
than usual, which was good, he supposed, for the people
who might otherwise have died that week, but less
good for himself, because he was paid for each named
individual's batch. The black-edged posters, with their
solemn words of memorial and funeral details, were still
wet on the harbourside street walls as he leant back to
observe the hulks of anchored ships at their moorings.
Despite the almost medieval squalor of the city, Naples
still had one of the most important and dynamic ports in
Europe, and a colossal tonnage of trade passed through
its waters every day of the week. It was an artery to
the world beyond, and the incessant coming and going
of foreign visitors, sailors, tourists and merchants kept
alive a sense that the people of Naples were connected
to a world beyond that flat sea horizon which almost all
of them – except those who chose to emigrate – would
never cross. It fuelled Rocco's dream of a greater fortune
that awaited him.

He resented Gabriele for having it so easy. There were
no expectations put upon him, and every day for him
was like a game, to be played out for as much fun and
pleasure as could be gained from it. The result was that
Gabriele did not even care much about the future. Yes,
he had a plan to sing at the opera, but he also had a plan
to screw Chiara Santangelo, and a plan to sail his own
yacht one day into New York harbour. They were all just
playful dreams for Gabriele, and that was probably why

he was so relaxed and happy all the time. Which could also explain why he was such a good singer, thought Rocco. Gabriele didn't weigh everything down with doubts, didn't give a second thought to theories and methods, and certainly never felt roused to shout at his own father.

Just next to Rocco, groups of boys were diving off the quay with happy shrieks, searching for coins on the seabed next to the ships' hulls. They were not put off by the sludgy water, nor the tankfuls of sewage that were freely released from the ships nearby, but turned their enterprise into a playful competition of diving skills, leaping upside down and somersaulting into the depths. Near to where they frolicked, seafood peddlers were packing up their business for the day and returning wicker baskets of shellfish to the dirty water to keep them fresh for the next day's trade. Rocco remained where he stood for a long while, until boys and vendors had given up their activities and all vanished into the gloom. The *mozzonari* were now the only others at large, lighting their lanterns and silently scouring the harbour's pavements for cigarette ends which they would dissect and reassemble in new papers so that they could sell them as a cheap alternative to the real thing.

Rocco remained on the same spot long after the time he had arranged to meet Gabriele. The horizon stretched before him as the last of the sunset dimmed in the west. The sea's distinction from the sky was discernible now only as the point at which lights from distant night fishing boats were superseded by stars. Rocco felt small before the potentiality of the openness; and it was in that quiet moment, humbled by the vastness of the bay, that a decision fell to him, without the need to reach or stretch.

In fact, he was surprised at how so fatal a conclusion could be achieved with so little exertion or discomfort on his part: his father and his past life would henceforth be nothing but an impediment, and must be shunned. It was clear as day. He must become like an emigrant, steer a new course and leave it all behind without looking back.

He would cajole Choirmaster de Luca. The boys' dormitory at the Ospedale would not be so bad. From now on, the choir, his studies, de Luca and Signora Signorelli would provide the fuel to stoke his engine and churn him forwards, across these waters, away from his past and this place for ever.

The pounding of his heart felt sharp and violent and rang in his ears like the strike of the blacksmith's hammer. His thoughts splintered off wildly in all directions, like sparks flying decoratively around the anvil when his father worked at night. The uninvited image of Enrico toiling in the dark brought a furious oath to Rocco's lips: as God was his witness, he would never become a blacksmith; and the vow was no sooner sealed than he was aware of a great celebratory uproar inside his head, throats raised in triumphant cheering. He smiled to himself at the apparent endorsement of his life-changing decision; but his smile faded when the cackles did not seem to let up. He felt frail and lonely suddenly, while the gales of laughter continued to crow within him, and he reached into his shirt to touch the amulet that hung around his neck. It was there, and it was warm, as ever; all would surely be well.

Chapter 10

1926

The vast Galleria Umberto I, in the heart of town, where Don Emilio Graziani had arranged to meet Molly Campobello, was more than a grand shopping arcade. It was a metropolitan monument dedicated to the gods of leisure and affluence, and had been constructed just thirty years before on the scale of a giant glass-domed cathedral. Like its ecclesiastical counterparts, it was laid out in a cross plan, but instead of hushed shrines and tombs along its length, the Galleria Umberto was crammed with humming shops and cafés. There was no more fashionable and bustling destination for the higher ranks of society, whether they came to shop, dine, visit the cinema or merely promenade beneath the cavernous span of its glazed roof.

Don Graziani liked to arrive at his appointments fifteen minutes early, even if, as in this case, it meant sitting alone at a cafeteria, in full view of the public, sipping coffees (he would order one after the other). Quite a number of those who now passed by recognized the diminutive old man whose notoriously sad, empty eyes were enlarged by the thick lenses of his spectacles. Some looked briskly away and quickened their pace;

others raised their hats self-consciously or paused to pay their respects; a few just gawped from a safe distance until shooed on by one of several granite-faced men who would materialize from the shadow of a nearby pillar or arch.

Don Graziani's bodyguards had no choice but to accept their employer's reckless penchant for parading himself in public places, because they understood that the boss could not cower in the shadows like a sewer rat. It would only do his reputation good to be seen sauntering about the city's centre, flagrantly defying his opponents' whispered threats. So long as the chief maintained a show of power, his traditional enemies on the streets would keep their vendettas buried, albeit in shallow pits. Because enemies there were, official and otherwise, and they had a habit of multiplying like flies on faeces when they sensed a tremor of weakness. The Prime Minister's pledge to bring about the dawn of a new era of law and order had caused more than a flicker of concern for the likes of Don Graziani, whose interests and local networks were, to say the least, not always in tune with the dictates of a central executive. The government threat was real enough. A restaurant in town, in which Don Graziani was known to have a small financial interest, had last month been sacked by thugs, rumoured to be party *squadristi*; and one or two members of the wider Graziani clan had endured recent brushes with the tax authorities: minor incursions, warnings, perhaps, but unthinkable even a year ago.

Not many of the people who spotted the deliberately unostentatious little man at the café that morning realized that, behind those doleful, magnified eyes, Don Graziani's mind was alive as a snake pit, with plans and imaginary manoeuvres. The truth was that his future hung by a thread, and he was under no illusion about it. The news that his son, Bruno, had managed to mess everything up in New York and was having to return to Naples made matters worse. Tired as he was, Graziani was being compelled to postpone retirement in order to step in himself and put things right.

He was not related to Rocco Campobello, although the tenor had always called him *zio* – uncle – a title that sat comfortably with them both, bridging the territories of familiarity and respect. Graziani had helped Rocco in the early days, and, though discreet in public about their old bond, he had always made his fondness for the tenor plain to those within his inner circle. Of course, his apparently sentimental attachment to Campobello was not entirely fuelled by avuncular affection. Graziani was too shrewd a player to ignore the great benefits to be reaped from a lifelong investment in so stellar a protégé, and from the very beginning had allied his own interests in some form or other to the fortunes of his adopted nephew. That was how it had all started, and that was at the heart of his present strategy, now, in this hour of crisis.

The roots of the story led back to a golden time, nearly thirty years earlier, when they had truly been close. The lad who would one day become the Great Campobello was then a fresh-faced stripling, and Graziani had navigated him step by step along a perilous early career path, sidestepping the hazards, probing the labyrinths of possibility for short cuts, and trampling over the ruins of failed competitors. He had smoothed the young tenor's way with favours too many to recall: he had paid the claques, ensuring Rocco healthy applause while rivals were mobbed; he introduced the boy to impresarios, prepared the ground for auditions, wined and dined grandees from opera companies all over Italy, manipulated newspaper editors, and encouraged complimentary reviews. He had proved his friendship time and again; and then, to cap it all, he had introduced Campobello to Walter Fleming, legendary recording engineer and talent scout of the Jupiter Company. The hurried series of records that had ensued from that first meeting more than twenty-five years ago established Campobello almost overnight as a worldwide phenomenon, in the wake of which it seemed entirely judicious to the young tenor at the time that he had been persuaded to sign a contract, beforehand, guaranteeing, to Emilio Graziani, thirty per cent of royalties received on all recordings for the Jupiter Company, in perpetuity. What did it matter if the contract was so clearly stacked against the singer that it made every witness in the room, including the elderly public notary, raise his eyebrows with surprise? Rocco trusted Don Graziani, without whom, after all, he would probably have had no career at all.

Time, however, had apparently dampened Campobello's appreciation of the terms, and in a sudden, almost defiant act, five years ago, he had brought the agreement to an end by abandoning the Jupiter Company in favour of its younger rival, Columbia. The move sent shock waves through the recording industry, as singers' contracts were instantly reviewed in order to forestall a mass emigration between companies. Campobello protested that his reasons were purely artistic, but Don Graziani had it on good authority that the move had been advised by the tenor's assistant, Pietro Boldoni. It stank of that queer valet's filthy, conspiratorial mind. The man might as well have declared himself Graziani's foe on a public billboard. A way would have to be devised sooner or later to counter, perhaps even punish, the posturing little pansy. Bruno Graziani, on the spot in New York, had suggested dealing with Boldoni there and then, to put an end to any further dissension, but Graziani was not convinced. He chose instead to sit it out. The right opportunity to bring his old protégé back to the family fold would arise sooner or later.

The news that Campobello had collapsed on stage at the Carnegie Hall was just the opportunity Graziani had been waiting for. It did not come completely out of the blue. The string of cancelled appearances throughout the latter half of the year had already alerted Graziani, so that when word of the actual cataclysm came through, he was not entirely unprepared. The ailing singer's subsequent decision to return and convalesce in Naples had delivered him straight into his old benefactor's hands.

Much would hinge on Graziani forging an effective alliance with the wife, Molly, and he was surprised that his work on her had progressed so pleasantly thus far. His dealings with her in the past had been cool, to say the least. He had been against the marriage from the start. When news of it was first announced, he had felt a stab of jealous resentment that the boy he had coddled and cultivated from near childhood had gone public with such an important decision without even consulting his old *zio* first; and so Graziani did little to befriend the new bride, suspecting that a glamorous, extravagant socialite would serve only to corrupt the steely ambition that had marked Campobello out amongst his rivals. But, as it transpired, Graziani had had no cause to lose sleep, and was never compelled to drive a wedge into the marriage. The couple appeared to have done that themselves.

Don Graziani nodded an acknowledgement to the Bishop who stopped briefly by his table, in the company of two chaplains, to say good morning, and as the clergymen swept away down the length of the Galleria, Graziani checked his watch. She was five minutes late, but that was to be expected. Women like Molly Campobello liked to appear indifferent to the petty social constraints of common folk; she would see it as a privilege of her class and gender to demonstrate a disdain for punctuality. It was not the same with men like himself, he reflected, for whom meticulous efficiency was an indication of a clear and purposeful mind; but he would always be one step ahead of Molly. He had her pinned, and that was how he wanted it to remain.

Whether or not he liked Molly was an irrelevance. He had long since ceased to evaluate human beings according to qualities that he might find attractive or otherwise, but instead measured them by their usefulness to his enterprise, which in the case of Mrs Campobello was considerable at present. She alone, amongst the tenor's inner circle, would be a mouthpiece for Graziani's interests. She would apply pressure where it was needed, and, just as importantly, would report back any developments direct from the Villa Rosalba. It was not docility that would make Molly so compliant an ally, he suspected, but hunger – a hunger that was plain to see and easy to sharpen. Graziani was schooled in the craft of manipulating another person's frustrations, amongst which greed was his speciality. He had a nose for the dark, fertile soil of self-interest, knew where and when to plant the seed of avarice, and made the cultivation of its subsequent twisted, ugly plant appear like a gift of friendship.

Molly got out of the Lancia by the arched portico of the Teatro San Carlo. A pair of dapper young men wearing boaters paused on the kerb to observe the hem of her shift ride above the knee as she negotiated the step down from the car, and they made no effort to conceal their interest even after she'd noticed them. It was a glare from the chauffeur, Pozzo, that persuaded them to move on, grudgingly.

Although already late for Signor Graziani, Molly decided she would dally for a little longer before crossing the busy road to the steps of the Galleria Umberto. She did enjoy promenading through the opera house's charming portico, where tatty little scribes with spectacles and battered top hats sat at fold-up desks to pen letters for the illiterate, and girls in bright dresses sold trinkets to protect against evil spirits. Molly was charmed by the blend of ignorance and superstition that seemed to characterize the simple Neapolitan mind. One moment these people would invoke the aid of the Madonna or a saint, while the next they would curse the object of their prayer and invest in a protective necklace as a more reliable guard against ill fortune. Molly meandered along the cobbled way, smiling at the picturesqueness of it all. She could not deny that she was really rather happy this morning.

Her husband's sudden change of heart had left her feeling better about being in Naples than at any time since her arrival. Until a week ago the Villa Rosalba, despite its great beauty, had been a place of dark confinement for her. Its isolation made her feel in some way contaminated, and she could not drum up the enthusiasm to venture beyond its quarantined precincts. The inescapable scent of cleanliness and polish indoors clung in her nose like the antiseptic scrub on prison walls. Everything that others might consider pretty she regarded as tainted, and all the while it seemed to her that the tatty remnants of her life were draining away before her eyes. And then, out of the blue, Rocco had begun to emerge from his apartment, and would meander across to the main part of the house, smiling or calling a soft greeting to Molly if he happened to see her. He even chose to sit and talk occasionally. The first time this happened, she had waited tensely in her chair, jaw tight, head and eyes locked sideways, prepared for battle. She steeled herself to parry and repulse the inevitable stream of lightly voiced, egotistic dictates that would mark Rocco's return to form; but in the event he nonplussed her by saying almost nothing about himself. Instead, he asked about her well-being, listened to her cautious replies and expressed a concern that she should begin to enjoy her new life in Italy.

He had been like this for several days now, and she dared to hope that her earlier fears about the future might have been grounded in a delusion. She had already tasted the bitter pill, of course, and was not fool enough to think that the disappearance of her youth could be put on hold because of Rocco's change of heart; but was it not possible, in the light of his recent pleasantness, that he might re-emerge a better husband, resume his career, and grow old alongside her, bestowing dignity on them both? Perhaps he had become wise after his brush with death; they might even discover a new love, of sorts, to warm and comfort them in their declining years. No sooner had this happy thought arisen than it was marred

139

by the smallest chisel-cut of a doubt. The cynic within her questioned how she could shift with such ease from hopelessness to sunny optimism. Did it not say more about the hungry and desperate state of her mind than the potential for real change? It was an uncomfortable question, but she could not altogether gloss over it.

She entered the Galleria and turned her thoughts to the matter in hand. In view of the new and more settled state of affairs at the Villa Rosalba, she had come to find Signor Graziani's friendship rather burdensome. His daily telephone calls and prying questions, together with his persistent reminders that she cajole her husband into a commitment to start working again, had begun to irritate her, so that when she spotted his rather bent little figure sitting in front of an empty coffee cup at the cafeteria, she regretted not having sent her excuses earlier and cancelled the meeting. For all his supposed kindness, she found that his solemn, bottle-eyed distance rather dulled her spirits. Now that he had helped them to settle in, she rather wished he could just go away, or at least turn up only occasionally, for the odd celebration or Sunday lunch, like the doting old relative he purported to be.

Molly approached the table and was conscious of a slight frisson passing through the people around her, a mixture of glances, and an almost indiscernible parting of the waves, as shoppers and promenaders became aware that she was heading into Graziani's company.

He was dressed tattily, as ever, which also rather irritated Molly. Here was a man wealthy and influential enough, she was told, to have anything he desired in the province, and yet he opted to present himself in shabby suits that sagged at the shoulders and old shirts whose collars were frayed to the lining. She concealed her disdain, but decided not to allow herself to be manipulated by so charmless a creature. Beneath it all, he was probably just one more of those who would work his way into her husband's circle in order to further his own ends. Her life with Rocco had been full of such people, and she felt she knew how to deal with them.

She held out a hand with an expression of measured joy, and greeted him in Italian, which she knew would charm him. He responded with an extravagantly gallant sentence in the same language, which both of them knew she wouldn't understand, but that was part of the game and they both let out a little laugh. He kissed her hand, called the waiter and ordered a small coffee for Molly along with yet another double for himself.

After a few vapid and predictable compliments about her appearance and general well-being, the forced smile fell from Graziani's face and he resumed his mournful glances around the Galleria, tapping his fingers on the table as if waiting for something more interesting to come along. Molly knew it was just his manner, but she found it off-putting. It made his former courtesy seem so insincere. She shifted uneasily towards the edge of her seat to take refuge in a sip of coffee, but just at the moment when the silence between them reached a point of unsustainable awkwardness, Don Graziani turned to her and said, 'And the staff? The house? Is everything exactly as you want it?'

'Perfectly so,' responded Molly.

'Anything you need, you must tell me. Anything at all.'

'You've been so very kind.'

Graziani acknowledged her gratitude with a silent

shrug as if to minimize the scale of his generosity, and fell silent once more. Again, Molly hurriedly searched her thoughts for something to say, but before she had the chance, he had begun again. 'I am glad to hear that your husband is feeling so much better. You must be very relieved.'

'You've heard?'

'Of course. You did not mention it, but . . . word travels.'

'Well, yes, I am delighted.'

'You believe he is recovered?'

'He's certainly turned a corner. It's wonderful to see him smiling again.'

'Perhaps I can come for a visit. He has been receiving people, I hear.'

'Not friends. He has seen no one socially. But I'm sure he will make allowance for you. He speaks so warmly of you.'

'That's kind. And so,' Graziani put his hand flat on the table, 'he has talked about when he intends to sing again?'

'He has not talked about it,' replied Molly, raising her chin in slight defiance. Why should the old man charge so bullishly into such sensitive territory with so little warning? 'And, as a matter of fact, I don't want to press him about it. Perhaps he is not ready.'

'Not ready?' Graziani's eyebrows rose above the heavy black frames of his spectacles.

'No. There's no cause for alarm. The rest is doing him good. He has quite changed, and for the better.'

'What?'

'We should allow him to settle.'

'This is what you think?'

142

'Why not? He seems so happy. As if he's shed a burden.'

'Forgive me, signora,' Graziani's voice had a grain of contempt, 'but I had understood you were keen to see him return to his career as soon as possible.'

Molly leant forward. Her tone became more urgent and intimate. 'Of course that is what I want. But we must be grateful for small things right now. Until last week he wasn't talking to anyone. Except Boldoni. Now he's warm, he's relaxed, and he's affectionate. The change is miraculous. The rest is doing him good. Maybe it's right that he should wait a little longer.'

'A little longer? We do not have a little longer. Time waits for no man, and . . .' Graziani allowed his sentence to evaporate, looking at her expectantly.

Molly smiled and moved her fingers to rest on his arm. Mild flirtation and a personal touch could work miracles. 'I think he is very happy to be back home in Naples,' she said warmly. 'He wants to spend a little time finding old friends and remembering his childhood.'

'Why should he want to remember those days?' said Graziani hotly, removing his arm. 'Has he lost his mind completely?'

Molly frowned. 'It's not unusual to feel nostalgic. Perhaps there are matters he'd like to sort out.'

'What sort of matters?'

'I don't know exactly what they are. Regrets, maybe. He has mentioned some people from the past, people he had allowed himself to forget.'

'Who?' Graziani flicked his hand at a pigeon that had flapped down on to the table to investigate potential pickings. As it flew away, Molly tried again to lighten the mood. Her smile was almost playfully conspiratorial.

'Would you like to know what I think? I think he may be feeling just a teeny little bit of guilt about something in his past.'

'Guilt,' repeated Don Graziani under his breath, and the word seemed to hook his attention in the same way that a fragment of carrion at the roadside catches the interest of a circling vulture. But he said nothing more and so Molly went on, 'I think he may feel that all his fame and fortune have led him to forget about where he came from and the people he was once close to. We should just allow him his pause, let him make peace with himself, or find whatever he's searching for, and wait until he feels well enough to begin again.'

'So,' Graziani sighed, 'the illness is in the mind. The Florio brothers tell me his body is fully recovered.'

'Perhaps, but . . . they've been very attentive, and we all so appreciate your organizing their visits. But . . .'

'Yes?' he sighed wearily, and the whisper of exasperation in his tone gave Molly the courage to speak her mind.

'Well,' she said, 'Signor Boldoni believes that Rocco is still having pains. And he recommends we seek the advice of another doctor. A specialist. Perhaps in Rome, where he can have more tests done.'

'Boldoni knows better than my doctors?'

'Of course not, but he seems to have persuaded Rocco. Perhaps it's not such a bad idea to have another opinion. After all, there is not the appropriate equipment in Naples for a thorough examination.'

Graziani looked at her coldly. 'Do you understand what is at stake?'

'Of course,' replied Molly. 'I, more than anyone.'

'The world will not wait for ever. There are good

young tenors who want nothing more than to snatch Campobello's crown. The sums of money at stake are huge.'

'I am aware of that,' said Molly looking down, piqued that so distasteful a subject as finance should have to be raised; a gentleman would have known better. 'I merely think it would be in everybody's interests if—'

'Excuse me, signora,' the Don interrupted, leaning forward and raising a teaspoon from his saucer to add emphasis to what he was about to say. 'You should know that I have a plan that will put your husband on top of the world again.'

'Oh yes?' she raised her eyebrows. 'What plan is that?'

'A single day of recordings. That is all it will take.'

'Recordings?'

'An afternoon's work. That might do it, for a start.'

'I don't understand,' replied Molly. 'Why should a few more records make any difference when he has made so many?'

'Because, my dear signora,' and there was nothing warm in his smile as he craned ever closer to her, lowering his voice, 'because a revolution in the technology of sound has presented us with an opportunity that might come only once in a generation. The entire music industry is about to be transformed. Have you not heard? The electronic microphone has arrived in the recording studio.'

Science was not amongst Molly's interests, but this kind of news had not entirely escaped her, though she had not really considered its significance. 'I have heard mention of it,' she said.

Graziani raised his hands rather theatrically in the air,

fingers splayed. 'Rocco Campobello, the most marketable voice in the record business, is yet to be captured by the new technology. All his past recordings – yes, they have made history, in fact, some would say they have given rise to the record industry itself – but they are suddenly out of date. Overnight! Singing into a cone horn! Pah! Laughable.' He swept his hand through the air with disgust. 'Compared to the new method, the old ones sound like . . . like trying to look at a fresh egg through a bed of straw. You know what I am saying?'

'Well, there is a little hissing,' conceded Molly.

'A *little*?'

'And the voices do sound rather distant, I suppose. I'm no expert, and I've never thought that records do justice to the singers. But—'

'Exactly!' interrupted Graziani. 'But a new collection of the great operatic arias, recorded through the electronic microphone, with full orchestra in a large hall, would put the greatest singer in the world at the head of the new generation, leading, as he did at the start of commercial recording, back in the early days. It is what everyone wants, what everyone is ready and willing to pay a lot of money for.' He paused fractionally to give his next statement greater emphasis, and then said with a flourish, 'The Great Campobello must return to the Jupiter Company as soon as can be arranged.'

Molly knew a little about her husband's defection to Columbia some years before, but was unaware of the contractual arrangement with the Grazianis. She was therefore ignorant of the extent to which her husband's return to Jupiter would benefit his old patron, or indeed salvage the Graziani clan as a whole in the stormy times that lay ahead. She was also far from convinced by the old man's argument. The accumulation of further wealth, though never unwelcome, was neither her, nor Rocco's, chief priority at the moment. She tried to sound reasonable as she made her point. 'I believe, in the first instance, we should strive to restore the Maestro's strength, and usher him back into society. Thereafter it would be very pleasant indeed if he were to resume his programme of engagements. But I doubt he would want an immediate return to a very commercial undertaking.'

'He must be told to take control of himself,' Graziani insisted, now not even attempting to hide his irritation, 'and make plans to return without delay. I can arrange for the director of the San Carlo opera to come and visit him, tomorrow, if necessary, to discuss when he can appear on stage. And I can make appropriate announcements to the press.'

'I do not think Rocco would agree to any of this,' said Molly, her mettle rising. She would not be bullied.

'It is time I spoke to him in person about the matter,' snapped Graziani. 'We have wasted all these weeks.'

Molly turned the fine profile of her face away and looked down, her heavily painted eyelashes blinking. 'You will have to contend with Signor Boldoni as well,' she said.

'Boldoni again?'

'And Mr Pickering.' At this, Graziani leant back and tutted a heavy 'pah!' into the air. Unperturbed, Molly continued, 'For all his shortcomings, Mr Pickering is an expert in matters musical, and he seems to think the peace and quiet is doing Rocco good. He and Boldoni are of one mind about this. They are quite determined.'

'What can we expect from men such as them?' snarled Graziani, and for the first time seemed to smile naturally.

'Their type will always avoid a fight. At the first sign of danger they run for shelter with their tails down like frightened dogs.'

Molly had no great affection for Pietro Boldoni, but was taken aback by Graziani's vituperation; she allowed herself to be distracted by a commotion at the far end of the Galleria. A procession of about forty children, marching in column, six abreast, shoulder to shoulder, was making its way down the length of the arcade, preceded by an indifferently tuned brass band and a trio of teenage officials. The children, all boys aged about ten, were dressed in black shirts and shorts, with wide white belts and little black pillbox hats strapped beneath their chins. They marched in step, faces glaring with concentration and swinging their arms determinedly, much to the delight of bystanders, some of whom must have been their parents. When the troop reached the centre of the Galleria, right beneath the glass dome, the older boy at their head, who held aloft a banner bearing an image of the Roman *fasci* bundle of sticks, called out a command, and they juddered to a less than tidy halt. Molly noticed that a small reception party had assembled there to inspect them, in the middle of which was a tall man with a trim moustache, also dressed in black and sporting a black necktie, who was clearly the main attraction. He stood, smiling, hands tucked statesmanlike behind his back, while a short poem was declaimed in a fierce manner by the flag-bearer. The tall man and everyone else standing around clapped their hands in appreciation.

'How charming,' said Molly, clapping lightly a couple of times. 'Who is that man? He seems very distinguished.'

148

'It is Pompeo Tedeschi,' replied Graziani, checking his watch, 'a thug who thinks he can be a politician. He used to be in charge of the local *squadristi*, and would happily arrange for his master's enemies to be beaten up and left to die in ditches. As a reward he was appointed top party official in Naples a couple of years ago. The power has gone to his head, and now that Mussolini has tightened his grip on everything and everyone, Tedeschi feels he is the unofficial king of the city. He even thinks he can teach the children right from wrong.'

'Oh, but those little boys look so smart. And don't they march beautifully?'

Graziani did not answer, but summoned one of his bodyguards with a gesture of the hand.

The makeshift band struck up a new tune; it was 'Giovinezza', a song that had become so popular in recent months amongst party enthusiasts that there were some who recommended it should replace the national anthem. As the tune plomped into full swing and the beaming crowd began to clap in time, Tedeschi stretched out his arm and raised a palm in solemn salute, and the column of children marched past him down one of the Galleria's transepts. The ceremony over, people began to circulate around the arcade once more, and Molly turned back to Graziani. Their differences still hung in the air, but before she could decide how best to deal with the situation, Graziani had risen stiffly to his feet and a slight warmth returned to the cold grey of his distended irises.

'Signora,' he said, and held out an arm for her to take, 'allow me to accompany you to a very special place. There is something I would like you to see.'

'Of course,' said Molly, springing to her feet, delighted

149

that the atmosphere had eased. Graziani silently signalled instructions to his attendants, pointing in various directions with a quivering index finger. The men leapt into action: one disappeared to summon the cars, another went to find the head waiter, while a third and fourth walked ahead, clearing a passage for their employer's progress to the Galleria's arched exit. Graziani went through the motions of taking out his wallet for the cafeteria's owner, who was bowing obsequiously, but payment was of course refused and no further offer was made. Molly took the old man's arm, and they made their way out of the arcade through a small crowd of bystanders who had paused in their various activities to observe them passing. A pretty child with fat cheeks, her hair in tight bunches, walked forward and blocked Graziani's path, staring up at him for attention; but Graziani noticed only inasmuch as he was compelled to sidestep the obstacle, and continued on past the child without giving her a second thought.

Once in the car, they drove away from the seafront up the long straight gradient of the Via Toledo. It was hot, the shops were tumultuously busy and the pavements heaved with people. Molly's earlier buoyancy had been punctured by the dispute with Graziani, so that, despite the sunshine and the dynamism of the scene around her, she could not engage with its charm as she had before entering the Galleria.

Off to the left, a grid of long, high-walled residential alleys flashed past them at regular intervals, each of which led back from the main thoroughfare like a darkened tunnel towards a distant flight of steps at its far end. As the driver negotiated his way carefully around a large railed fountain in the centre of the street, Molly noticed a clan of lepers taking a rest from begging to recuperate in a patch of shade on the kerb. Their bulbous fingerless hands knuckled the air like bears' paws, but they were chatting and sharing a joke as they carefully passed an earthenware water cup between them. Molly tried to feel pity for them, but found nothing but revulsion in her heart and silently willed the driver to move on quickly.

'Where are we heading?' she asked, looking away from the lepers.

'To a place that you must see. It is fascinating.'

'I'm intrigued,' she replied, but no further information was offered.

Higher up, they turned into a side street and pulled up outside an unusually stark chapel façade squeezed in between tenement blocks. Molly was directed by a pair of bodyguards to a small door to one side of the chapel's sealed main entrance. Inside the building, they were intercepted by a rather vexed sacristan in a stained cassock, who was clearly peeved that a party of visitors had trespassed unannounced into his fiefdom; but a quick glance at Don Graziani silenced his complaint before it was voiced. Another word from one of the bodyguards sent him scuttling from the chapel, whereupon the door of the building was locked from the inside.

It was an austere and ancient little basilica, its thick, unevenly plastered walls punctuated high up with tiny windows that slanted thin shafts of sunlight down to a flagstoned floor. Graziani pointed to a small doorway at the far side of the nave, and led the way towards it, tapping his walking stick on the flags as he progressed. The door opened on a narrow spiral stairway that led down beneath the chapel floor, and Graziani sent his men down in advance with an order to light candles.

While they waited, Graziani said to Molly, 'I used to come here as a boy.'

'Oh really?' she replied, expecting an elaboration, but none was forthcoming.

As soon as the candles were lit, they squeezed single file down the old stairwell, their shoulders brushing against the pale masonry wall.

They came out into the flickering half-light of an old crypt, its roof vaulted with narrow red bricks, each no thicker than a slice of bread. 'There was a Roman temple on this site,' said Graziani.

'How thrilling,' replied Molly, relieved that this might be no more than a well-meant sightseeing trip. She clutched her bare upper arms for warmth and peered into the darkness as her eyes adjusted themselves. It was then that she noticed the deep stone shelves on either side, from floor to ceiling, as if made for cool storage. Each contained an embalmed corpse, still dressed in faded funeral clothes, its face uncovered. Many were monks, but there were ordinary people as well – civilians, soldiers, men, women, children, even babies. Their jaws hung open, stretching the grey parchment of their cheeks so that their faces were for ever trapped in a final moment of terror. Some had rotted through to the bone, others looked unnervingly fresh, but in each case the hollows of the eyes, bereft of soft tissue, bore witness to a lonely and silent oblivion.

Don Graziani led the way forwards, glancing to left and right as if wordlessly greeting familiar old acquaintances. Between each horizontal shelved niche, an upright corpse had been positioned, shrunken to the bones within its clothes, head tilting forwards. Molly followed nervously, clenching her teeth.

'The first body to be placed in this vault was a Dominican monk in the sixteenth century,' said Graziani. 'He's over there somewhere, but there is not much left of him. By about a hundred years ago this had become the most fashionable and expensive place in the city to be buried. People left large sums of money to reserve themselves a place, and special instructions about how they should be dressed. Come, there's one man in particular I would like to show you. My own grandfather knew him well, as it happens.'

His step gained pace, as if fired by boyish enthusiasm, as he made his way to the corpse of a gentleman sus-pended upright, dressed in a dusty black frock coat and patent leather shoes. Its head was tilted, as if locked in a state of perpetual query.

'Here we are,' said Graziani, smiling up at the cadaver, while Molly came to a stop behind his shoulder. 'This is Don Giuseppe Goldoni, a wealthy banker once, but now, as you see,' he held out his hand as if introducing Molly to a friend, 'not much at all.' He seemed amused. 'Poor man, he died quite young, about forty-five, and his family were left with nothing.'

Molly swallowed and calmed her voice before saying, 'Why so?'

'He had enemies, they say. He was killed. At night, on a street corner, more than one hundred years ago. And soon after his death his entire fortune disappeared. Fortunately for him, he had already paid for his in-terment, but his wife and children died in poverty. Come, see this.' He stepped closer, stretched out his fingers and began to fumble with the corpse's clothing, pulling at the shirt where it was tucked into the faded black trouser top. 'We used to look at this when we were boys,' he said puckishly, and in order to use both hands, passed his stick to one of the bodyguards standing nearby, who looked uncertain as he stepped forward to take it. 'Here,' continued Graziani with one final tug at the clothing; it made the body tip slightly forwards and a small cloud of dust descended on Molly's hair. 'Look.' Reluctantly Molly craned forward and saw, where Graziani's fingers held up the hem of an under-vest, a small incision in the pale grey flesh near the man's navel. 'That was what did it,' he said. 'A single stab wound. Quite deep, but not a wide blade, as you can see for yourself. In the soft area beneath the ribs. Professional work. He bled to death where he lay. It would probably have taken . . .' he assessed the scar with an expert frown, 'forty-five minutes or so. No one would have listened to his cries for help. They would be too frightened to get involved.'

'Please!' said Molly, clutching at her mouth and turning away – a reaction that seemed to satisfy Graziani.

'All that money and power – gone, overnight. My grandfather would often tell the story. I think he wanted to teach us boys a lesson,' he added whimsically, 'about friendship, failed opportunities, and enemies.' He clicked his fingers at the bodyguard, indicating that the corpse's clothing should be rearranged, and turned to walk Molly back to the stairwell. 'I'm sorry, my dear, did you . . . ?' He did not finish, and Molly reconfigured her fractured demeanour.

'Not at all,' she said a little too hurriedly. 'I've just never seen anything like it before.'

'You see,' Graziani said, stopping her at the foot of the spiral steps and placing his hands together in front of him, 'this matter of your husband returning to his career. I care very much about it. I do hope you understand.' He put out a hand and held hers, which was still trembling. His touch was like tanned leather.

Molly had learnt at an early age to hide her feelings beneath a wide repertoire of artful disguises, according to the demands of the situation or encounter, but the present scene stretched her skills to their limit. Like a malign magician able to read the secret terrors of his victims, Don Graziani had isolated and gently probed her unutterable fear of death. She wondered how he could possibly have known, but the menace of his intent was clear as day. Suddenly, he was neither family friend nor even a meddling irritant. She did not care to think what might lie beyond his sinister implications, but her acquiescence was required, and in her current fragile state she felt compelled to lend it without hesitation. 'I will do whatever I can to help,' she said, to which Graziani replied quickly and almost tenderly, 'Of course you will. I never for a moment thought otherwise. Let us return to the warmth, shall we?' And they made their way back up into the slightly brighter atmosphere of the Romanesque chapel above.

Before emerging into the street once more, Graziani touched Molly's forearm. 'I have arranged for someone to help us in our endeavour,' he said.

'Oh yes?'

'He is a reporter, from America, by the name of MacSweeney, Brian MacSweeney. You may have heard of him?'

'I don't think so.'

Graziani flicked his hand airily. 'He writes about opera in the newspapers. Anyway, I have invited him to

Naples. He arrives with my son Bruno next week to write the story about Maestro Campobello's return to health, so that readers in America and all over the world will be prepared for the great event. I trust you will make Mr MacSweeney welcome when he arrives, and help him with any information he might need. Perhaps allow him into your home?'

'If that is what you wish,' said Molly.

'Good, very good. He has also asked to be present at the recording sessions.'

'The what?'

'The forthcoming recording sessions,' continued Graziani, with perhaps more relish than was strictly necessary. 'I may have forgotten to mention it to you when we were speaking earlier: Walter Fleming, of the Jupiter Company, is coming to Italy shortly. He has some engagement at the Vatican, and we thought it would be the perfect opportunity for the great Campobello to make his debut at the electronic microphone. I have invited Mr Fleming and his engineers to Naples.'

'I see.'

'Mr MacSweeney will make it all look very fine in the newspapers.'

'That's good,' replied Molly.

'You see, I have not been idle.' He raised his eyebrows at her, merrily.

'Clearly.'

'There are one or two minor contractual matters to sort out. We will talk to Mr Boldoni. Don't concern yourself about that side of things.'

'No.'

A few minutes later they were driving back down the Via Toledo in the direction of the Teatro San Carlo, where Molly's car and chauffeur awaited her return. Graziani now chatted easily, pointing out sights and giving advice about the best shops to visit. He was very different from the cold, brooding presence that had sat beside her on the journey out, some half an hour earlier. He had his driver stop the car right beside her Lancia, and insisted on climbing out to kiss her hand in a warm farewell.

Shortly afterwards, as Pozzo negotiated the sun-drenched angles of the Via Partenope that curved the seafront route back through Santa Lucia, he could not help but wonder what had happened to his headstrong employer. Glancing from time to time in the mirror he saw that her head was bowed and that every so often she would bury her face in her slender palms. He tutted to himself. This woman's life went from drama to drama, it seemed.

As it happened, Molly had not sunk into a state of despair. A practical woman above all, she was breathing deep into her hands, allowing the shock of what had happened to recede so that she could begin to plan her strategy. She would not set out to make an enemy of Rocco. The seed of hope she had so gratefully sensed these past few days was too precious to throw away; she would go as far as to say that her life depended on it. She must either come clean to him about Don Graziani's intent, and thereby risk potentially horrible consequences, or quietly hide the detail of her mission and work to achieve the old man's ambitions under the cloak of her and Rocco's newfound marital accord. The more she thought about it, the greater she recognized the appeal of the latter option. After all, the nasty old man did have a point, for all his disgusting manner. It would, indeed, be best for everyone if Campobello were to return to the stage, and, in the circumstances, why not a little sooner rather than later? If it required a bit of pressure to bring him there, so be it. It was a risk worth taking, and she would be up to the challenge.

Chapter 11

They met Campobello at the door of the tavern and put a drink and a pack of cards into his hands before saying anything. There was no fawning, none of the seemingly irresistible urge people usually had to lower their heads and grin like imbeciles as they made eye contact with him. These men looked him in the face no more than to acknowledge with a nod that he had come to the right place at the right time.

The cul-de-sac alley, where the tavern was located, looked little different in the dusk than it would have been fifty, or a hundred years before; and the same smell of decaying egg from the harbour had settled in there, as it did every evening, undisturbed by fresh air. A small crowd milled around the entrance of the building, men smoking, noisily exchanging pleasantries or remonstrating at one another with hand gestures; and so no one particularly noticed the small group into which the unusually tall stranger was now absorbed.

Once inside, he was navigated with jostles towards a table at the back of the large room, where a chair was indicated for his use. Master actor that he was, he needed little prompting, but shuffled the playing cards expertly between his fingers, glanced at the circle of men around the table and began to deal. The ceiling was low and the atmosphere close and hot, like the under-deck of an old warship. Noise burbled incessantly. A party of foreign sailors at a nearby table were stripped to the waist, their skin glistening with extravagant tattoos in the lamplight: images of sea monsters and voluptuously breasted Negresses, names of long-lost comrades or distant loved ones. A smell of spilt alcohol blended with the resinous scent of the pine barrels that lined the walls. A tang of scorched wick and hot candle wax hung in the air. There was neither electricity nor gas, and the light of naked flames danced on the walls.

The man who had received Campobello at the door – the same one who had sat opposite Boldoni in the back alley tenement some days earlier – pointed out a deficiency in the number of cards he had been dealt. 'We start with nine,' he grunted, and then introduced himself across the table as Filippo. He said that an old man seated next to him was his father – it was the one who had acquired Boldoni's silver cigarette case. Together with the others around the table they now began to play a popular Neapolitan card game, one which Campobello recalled soon enough.

Now that he was seated, his height was less obvious. A heavy cap covered his head down to the eyebrows, and the white beard prevented casual recognition. Not that anyone present in the tavern would have recognized him even without the disguise. A handful of iconic images of the great tenor were well known and would of course have been engraved in all their minds – the famous studio photograph of him as Canio in *Pagliacci*, perhaps – but they were years old, idealized and smoothed rather too clean. The waxed moustache and rakishly quiffed dark hair which he had famously sported in his youth were long gone. At best, the flesh and blood man who sat amongst them, with weary eyes and pockmarked cheeks, might have been judged teasingly reminiscent of the great man, in a haggard, swarthy kind of way. As it was, he sat hunched and inconspicuous, playing cards in the far reaches of the room, where the lantern light flickered dimly and heavy drinkers swayed on their chairs.

'In case you're at all worried,' Filippo muttered from behind his hand of cards, displaying a slight nervous twitch that made one of his eyes blink emphatically, 'I have men in position everywhere. The smallest problem and we'll have you out and away.'

'I'm not worried,' said Campobello. 'How long till I see Gabriele?'

Filippo looked up sharply. 'I didn't bring you here to meet Gabriele Tomassini. Didn't your man tell you that?'

'Why have we come here, then?'

'You'll see. Be patient.' His expression revealed the trace of an appeal that was almost compassionate in its sincerity, but his hesitancy implied a hidden snag.

Pietro Boldoni had done everything in his power to prevent Campobello going to the tavern in person. He had suggested reneging on the agreement altogether, sending a detachment of police to sort the idiots out and bring them all in for formal interrogation, or, as a last resort, deploying the double, Taddeo, to masquerade as Rocco. But Campobello would not hear of it, and put an end to any further discussion. He now tossed his stake of a few coins on to the table, rearranged the cards in his hand and began to sip a coarse local red from an earthenware cup. There was music at the front of the room, someone playing the mandolin and the beginnings of a song that

161

subsequently fell apart amidst cheers and laughter. It was then that a man came and stood by their table and nodded at Filippo.

'Eh, *paesano*, who's your friend?' asked the man, indicating Rocco. 'New here.'

'My daughter's wedding, don't you remember?' replied Filippo, his left eye twitching. 'This is my cousin Angelo, from Rome.' Rocco looked up from under his brows and tilted his head slightly, not so much in greeting as acknowledgement.

'Romans are ponces,' joked the man, with a hint of danger in his smile. 'But he looks like one of us!'

'*Davvero*. Can't change your blood,' muttered Filippo.

'He looks just like his Papa,' piped up Filippo's father from across the table, and smiled directly at Rocco. 'The spitting image, I'll swear.'

'Old men always say things like that,' the newcomer added, then patted Filippo on the shoulder and wandered away. Rocco was holding the old man's smile.

'You knew my father, didn't you?' he asked quietly.

'*Ma certo*. Everyone in the district knew Enrico the blacksmith. You were a lucky boy, to have such a father.' Rocco wanted to question him further, but a sharp look from Filippo held him in check.

'A double, and three royals,' Filippo now interjected, slapping some cards on the table, turning everyone's attention back to the game.

'Enough,' said Rocco, under his breath, but with a forcefulness that made Filippo look up at him. 'You have something to tell me. When and where am I going to see my man?'

'When the time is right. There's more to this, you see—'

'Tell me now, and I'll be the judge of when is and when's not the right time. Now,' and he laid his cards down prematurely, face up on the table. A couple of them were outstanding but the rest were hopeless. It was not a winning hand. In the distance the mandolin player had started to retune his instrument and several people at the front were calling 'sshhh' to the crowds behind. Rocco lowered his voice to a whisper. 'Tell me this. Does he at least know I am coming to see him?'

Filippo hesitated and looked uncomfortably at his cards, eventually gathering them into a neat pile and placing them to one side, out of play. 'Wait. Just a short while now.'

'Let him know,' came his father's fluty voice from across the table. 'It doesn't make any difference.'

'Know what?' said Rocco.

Filippo looked away, towards the front of the hall, where a young man had climbed a little platform. It was the handsome, fierce-eyed youth who had also been there when Boldoni had come to meet them. People at the front were cheering and whistling theatrically. 'Amedeo! Amedeo! Come on!'

'It's Amedeo,' Filippo enunciated to his father as if the old man were hard of hearing. 'He's going to sing. Do you want to go nearer?' The old man declined with a shake of his head.

'Know what?' repeated Rocco, and now Filippo looked quickly back at him, resigned.

'That he's dead, of course. Gabriele Tomassini died years ago.'

Rocco remained stock still and silent for a moment. His eyes flickered an inch or two to one side but instantly returned to stare straight into Filippo's. 'When? How?'

163

Filippo looked to one or two of the other men around the table, and after a couple of shrugs and suggestions from them, replied, 'Twelve. Maybe thirteen years ago.' The others pursed their lips and nodded. 'It happened at sea, in his boat. He worked at the opera, repairing, painting things, keeping the place tidy. But he also liked to build boats. Good with his hands. He took one too far out of the bay one day. The fishermen found his body trawled in their nets right down at Agropoli. Complete chance that they managed to trace it back to here. Took them six months, but that's another story.'

Rocco was still looking straight at him. 'Agropoli?' he asked, a huskiness now coming into his voice.

'That's right,' said Filippo. 'He must have gone way out to sea. God knows where he was heading.'

'New York, probably,' answered Rocco quietly, and turned his gaze downwards.

Filippo nodded with a faint smile. 'You knew him well, then.'

At the other end of the tavern, Amedeo was looking a little anxiously out at the audience while his accompanist on the mandolin began to play a melancholy prelude. The hall fell silent. It was in a minor key, and its phrases moved along with a pleasant lilt. 'Listen to the boy,' whispered Filippo. 'He's got a good voice. We'll talk after. I'm sorry.'

'I should go,' said Rocco.

Filippo put a hand on his arm. 'No. Not just yet. There's something else. You will want to know, I promise you.' His expression had that same sincerity of appeal. The old man opposite, still smiling, added his encouragement by signalling with an outstretched finger that they should simmer down and watch the boy. But Rocco was not so easily persuaded.

'Don't worry. You'll get your money,' he said, rising to his feet.

'It's not just about the money. You should stay.'

'Why?'

'Because I think you'd like to hear this boy.'

Rocco looked at him in disbelief. *'Per amor di Dio!* Do you have any idea how many letters I receive every day from people who want me to hear them singing? Do you think I'd fall for a trick like that?'

'Eh! Be quiet will you, big boy! Sit down,' called someone at Campobello, and a few heads turned: 'we want to listen.'

Filippo looked furiously at the man who had spoken, but then turned back to Rocco. 'It's not that,' he whispered urgently. 'I'm not trying to push the lad. It's just that he's Gabriele's boy. Amedeo is Gabriele Tomassini's son.'

Rocco remained where he stood while furtive tugs at his sleeve and repeated whispers advised that it would be best if he sat down. He looked at his chair as if it were an object whose purpose he had forgotten, but then came to, blinked, and lowered himself on to it. At that moment the singing began. It was a ballad Rocco knew well, had always known.

The other men seated there could not resist a glance at him while the song began to unwind. His expression was not in itself one of despair or abject disappointment, though these feelings were present at the periphery of his eyes. There was instead a hint of amused wonder in his face. His lips were ajar in what might have been the slenderest of smiles, as though he were distantly

165

incredulous at the injustice and slight absurdity of fate's having wrong-footed him like this.

The old melody filled the room, and its poignant bitter-sweetness silenced all voices other than the young singer's. Filippo, watching from the shadows, frowned and flicked his thumbs. He pulled his chair next to Campobello and whispered close to his ear.

'I didn't know Gabriele that well. There was a family connection. We went to the same village in the Campania every year for the Saint's Day feast. I didn't see him much towards the end, but I helped the widow and the boy. Otherwise they'd have been on the streets. Amedeo's a good lad, underneath it all. I managed to find him a job. Apprentice to a net-maker in Santa Lucia. The boy's got a chance now. Just as well,' Filippo continued, glancing quickly around the room, 'because he can make life difficult for the people trying to help him. I love him, but he can be trouble.' He said no more for the moment because the song was swelling to its climax. No one could fault the boy's singing, Filippo thought. Perhaps if the lad were to sing a bit more and argue less he would overcome his silly immature ways and make a decent future for himself.

Filippo's ruminations were brought to an abrupt close when he was distracted by a movement opposite him. Campobello had risen to his feet again. The song was coming to an end and Rocco was pushing his way to the front of the room through a throng of enthusiastic, cheering spectators. Filippo stood up to stop him but was too late. The sea of bodies had closed and the Maestro had vanished.

*   *   *

166

When Amedeo Tomassini stepped on to the platform to sing he felt his stomach fall away. He'd been told about the operatic giant who was sitting in a dark corner of the tavern, and the thought of it very nearly made him sick. He hid his fear and decided to trust his own voice. It was small, but it was free in his throat and agile, and had never let him down before. And so he sang his heart out, indulging himself, exaggerating the top notes and embellishing them, while the mandolinist kept time and looked on with admiration. The reception was tumultuous, and Amedeo nodded to the crowd modestly, taking a swig of wine from someone standing nearby.

Then, without warning, they were face to face. Amedeo knew it was him – more from the granite nobility of the face than familiarity with his features. They looked at each other without speaking. Those cheering and clapping nearby sensed something in the air and almost held their breath as the big man stretched out an arm to touch the boy on the shoulder.

'How about "A Vuchella"?' said Campobello quietly. 'We'll take a line each. You go first. *Va bene?*' and he turned to the mandolinist who nodded agreement. '*Ascoltami!*' Rocco announced to the crowd in his thickest Neapolitan accent. 'This is one you all know, a particular favourite of an old friend of mine.' And before Filippo could reach the front of the room and work out a way to intervene, the music had started up again, another gentle song in three-four.

'*Si, comm'a nusciorillo,*' began Amedeo's slightly tremulous *piano* voice, with Rocco's arm draped around his shoulder, and he sang the rest of the phrase with exquisite *legato*, finishing gently on the low E flat. Campobello took up the line, camouflaging the potential immensity of his voice, hiding the flesh of it so that only the nectar remained, making sure his tone dovetailed ingeniously with the light sweetness of the boy's. The audience hooted its appreciation of the newcomer's contribution and began to sway in time with the music. 'He can certainly sing, that cousin of yours,' said the man who had earlier questioned Filippo.

'Yes, not bad,' Filippo replied, 'we're a musical family,' and turned away to avoid further conversation. Amedeo had now taken up the line again as the ballad's middle section demanded a swell in volume, *'Dammillo e pigliatillo . . .'* and he reached the high F with as much sound as his femininely silver voice would allow, after which Rocco took over the phrase and led it to a minutely *pianissimo* climax, a high E flat, which he held for several seconds, allowing the sound to dwindle almost to nothing before falling to the B flat. Amedeo concluded the gentle song '. . . *nu poco pocorillo appassuliatella,'* and on the mandolinist's final chord, the hall exploded in applause.

Filippo fought his way through and grabbed Rocco by the arm. 'What do you think you are doing?' he whispered through the cheers, attempting to hide his agitation. 'Do you want to cause a riot? You could be killed.'

'It's all right,' replied Campobello and turned to smile at Amedeo. 'Let's go,' he said to the boy. 'I want to talk to you.'

'Ehi!' called out someone at the front. 'Stay there! We want more! Let's have another one from the new boy!'

'Who is he, anyway? Who's the stranger?' called someone else, and others joined in the questioning. 'He's with Filippo,' said the same man as before. 'It's his cousin from Rome. Or so he says!' At the implied deception several others hooted and jeered, while the shout for more music gained pace, the mandolinist joining in, calling for another song.

'It's not his cousin!' shouted a new voice from further back, and heads turned. It was Signor Ventori, forcing his way through. Although Filippo considered the man a buffoon, he had been compelled to include Ventori in the evening's arrangements because it was he who had been responsible for the initial meeting. But he had been instructed to keep his distance and keep his mouth shut, and had therefore gazed star-struck at Campobello from a different part of the room ever since his arrival. By now he had drunk amply and was losing his head in the excitement. Reaching the front of the crowd, he stretched out his arm and pointed straight at Rocco. 'It's not Filippo's cousin at all,' he yelled. 'Can't you see? It's Maestro Rocco Campobello! I arranged it all!'

Filippo looked at him in horror, but Rocco burst out laughing and others followed his lead. It wasn't a bad likeness, several said, draining their cups and stretching for a refill from the jug: they had found their own answer to the Great Campobello, here in their old tavern. What a hoot! 'No! It's true! It *is* the Maestro,' yelled Ventori, credibility sliding from under him as his insistent cries were swallowed up by ever greater howls of laughter. In the mayhem Filippo grasped Rocco by the hand, and told Amedeo to leave by a different door and meet them around the block. In a moment they were outside in the cooler air and, joined by Amedeo, climbed into the carriage that had been on standby all evening in case of an emergency. They clattered off into the obscurity of the alleys.

'That was too close. It was reckless,' said Filippo, taking

off his hat to cool his head. 'Why did you do a thing like that, Maestro?' But Rocco was consumed by private thought.

For a few minutes no one spoke, and then Campobello said, without turning to face Amedeo, 'You're engaging the head voice too low down in your register. We can get a good chest timbre going down there, blend it in with the head as you go up and it'll transform your sound.'

'Yes, Maestro,' replied Amedeo.

'The exact placement of your transition from chest to head is crucial. Everything hinges on it. That, and a smooth concealment of the transition.'

'Yes, Maestro.'

'But you've learnt the lesson that resonance has nothing to do with volume. You haven't damaged your voice yet. That's a good start.'

'Yes, Maestro.'

'But it's only a start. There's years of work there to be done. You don't want to sound like a suckling lamb all your life.'

'No, Maestro.'

'And no more of that "maestro" nonsense. You are my best friend's son. You call me *zio*, all right?'

'Yes, sir,' came the subdued reply. Rocco grunted, recognizing a needle prick of irony in what he had just said. He remembered clearly the jolt of embarrassed resentment he himself had felt when Don Graziani had asked him, more than thirty years ago, to call him *zio*. At the time, it was as if an unearned intimacy had been forced on him, and he now regretted being equally presumptuous with Amedeo. He turned to Filippo. 'Take me to the boy's home. I want to see Gabriele's home.'

Chapter 12

A little earlier, at the Villa Rosalba, Pietro Boldoni was sitting at a desk in his upstairs apartment, contemplating the Maestro's ill-advised escapade. He neither moved nor blinked while he sat there, and the silence of the room was punctuated only by the faintly lepidopterous flicker of the carriage clock ticking on the mantelpiece. Wallace Pickering was on his way to bed when he spotted Boldoni through the open study door. He stopped and asked if everything was all right, to which Boldoni replied in a curt monosyllable, and so Pickering let him be.

It was a full twenty minutes before Boldoni was disturbed again from his reverie, and this time it was a sharp knock on his door. The houseboy from downstairs was standing there.

'Signor,' said the boy, 'somebody has arrived to talk to you.'

'At this time of night?' Boldoni replied, checking his gold watch. 'It's a bit late. Who is it?'

'He didn't say, sir.'

'Why did the guards allow the car through? They have specific instructions about this kind of thing.' The boy shrugged, out of his depth. 'Well, take him into the morning room and I'll be down shortly.'

'He won't come in, sir. He wants to meet you at the porch. Straight away.'

When Boldoni descended to the hall and approached the open front door, one glance at the man and the car that awaited him confirmed his worst suspicions. 'Don Graziani sent you, did he not?' he said to the driver. 'Is that why the guards let you through?'

'This won't take long,' said the man, and held the car door open. 'We'll have you back home within the hour.'

Pietro knew that refusing was not an option, and so climbed into the back of the car. A short while later they arrived at the Grazianis' house, set just back from the fashionable Via Chiaia, and Boldoni was ushered to the entrance. He had resolved not to betray any anxiety, but an astute onlooker would have noticed something hunched about his shoulders as he walked up the steps to the house. His head hung with that look that all men have, innocent or guilty, when they mount a courtroom dock.

He was conducted into a small, sparsely furnished study. A large old photographic portrait of an elderly man, posing stiffly in his Sunday best, hung in a frame on one wall, but otherwise no decoration softened the austerity of the room. One shelf of books alone promised an insight into the minds of the house's occupants, but it was a slender promise, the books, for the most part, being long out-of-date Neapolitan gazetteers. A simple timber desk and chair, plain and chipped, stood on uncarpeted floorboards. Some would have said that the Grazianis' home lacked a woman's touch, there not having been a female resident there since Don Emilio's wife had died nearly two decades earlier; but to Pietro Boldoni, for whom femininity held no exclusive rights or mystique, the house in which he now stood merely revealed the aesthetic crudity of its inhabitants.

There were four men in the study: two bodyguards, Don Emilio Graziani, and a younger man, who occupied the chair behind the desk. He was slender and well-groomed, his dark hair neatly oiled, and looked rather too elegant and sophisticated to be at home in such spartan surroundings. It was Bruno Graziani, the old Don's son.

'Ah, Signor Boldoni,' said Don Emilio, and extended his hand. 'Very good of you to come. This won't take long, but I am not going to dally. I am too old to work at this time of night. I leave you in the hands of Bruno. He arrived only yesterday from New York.' As usual, the forced smile dropped from Don Graziani's face rather prematurely, and he walked from the room without another word.

Pietro waited for the door to close behind Don Graziani. He did not offer his hand to Bruno. 'To what does Naples owe the honour of your return?' he asked.

Bruno crossed his legs in his father's chair and the loose joints in the old wood creaked.

'Let us say,' he replied, 'that it's just a little too warm in New York at the moment.' He spoke Italian without the complete fluency of a native and almost seemed to affect a slight American accent.

'You may find it even hotter in Naples. Uncomfortably so.' Boldoni was not fooled. He had heard what had been happening in New York. It had been in the newspapers. Some veteran policeman had got Bruno in his sights, and publicly declared his mission to track him down once and for all. It was music to the ears of the other New York

173

families; they smelt blood and joined the fray to get the Grazianis out. The truth was that Bruno had been driven back to Naples like a rat to its hole.

Boldoni had known Bruno Graziani for many years. Back in the States there was hardly a department of Rocco Campobello's life in which Bruno had not demanded a stake, whether the benefit was financial, social or merely the satisfaction of curiosity, and the effect of his ever-present watchfulness had been oppressive. Boldoni never attempted to hide his disapproval of the seemingly unbreakable tie between his master and the Graziani clan, but had no choice but to tolerate it. On one occasion they had pushed him too far, and he came close to resigning from the Maestro's staff. It followed the discovery of a dead restaurateur in Brooklyn. The man had been found tied to a stove, his head simmering in a vat of home-made broth. A grass in the family implicated the Grazianis in the crime, and Pietro Boldoni had been pressurized to appear in court as a character witness. It contributed to Bruno's eventual acquittal, which meant that the unfortunate informer, the police's key witness, had to be speedily removed aboard the next ship to Italy. He was last seen arriving at the docks in Palermo, but never heard of thereafter. It was rumoured Bruno Graziani favoured the disembarkation hit because it was quick, clean and difficult to trace.

Bruno leant across the desk rather formally, placed a pair of spectacles on the bridge of his nose and picked up a fountain pen. 'I have no intention of insulting you by attempting to minimize the importance of the matter that I have brought you here to discuss. It is this ongoing nonsense of Campobello's recording contract with Columbia. We wish it to be cancelled and for him

174

to renegotiate a contract with the Jupiter Company. As before.'

Boldoni spluttered his response. 'How can you even think of such a thing? First of all, the Maestro has no plans whatever to make any recordings in the foreseeable future, and secondly, even if he did, there is not the slightest reason why he should want to revert to an arrangement that left him tens of thousands of dollars poorer every year.'

Bruno made a note on the piece of paper in front of him and then, after a moment, looked up and said quietly, 'Shall we waste time chatting or shall we get to the point?' Boldoni made no answer, and so Bruno continued, 'I'm sure you don't need me to outline the ways in which we could exert pressure to make you change your mind.'

'Don't you threaten me,' barked Pietro. 'Italy is not the same as it used to be. People like you don't have the same power any more. You might have been better off staying in New York.'

Bruno blinked behind his glasses but remained un-moved. 'You have a point, of sorts. Which is all the more reason for us to act quickly,' he said. 'No one knows for sure what the future holds for this country, but we must feather our nests for any eventuality.'

Boldoni took a step forward and leant over the desk. 'Have you any idea of the costs involved in breaking the contract with Columbia? This isn't some back-street deal with grocers and bakers. It'll take more than a smashed shop window.' The implied insult made no impression. 'We're talking about one of the most important and lucrative legal agreements in the whole entertainment industry.'

'That is my point, precisely,' answered Bruno.

Boldoni stood upright. 'What if we refuse?'

Bruno sighed. 'Too much talk. You are a practical man, Pietro. In fact, despite our differences, you and I do things in the same sort of way.'

'I think not.'

'Think what you like, but this situation will be resolved one way or another. There is an easy route or a less pleasant one. The choice is yours.'

'Are you threatening to kill me? Is that the bottom line?'

'If we had wanted you out of the way, we'd have done it years ago.' Bruno's eyes were cold. 'We don't want it to come to that.'

Pietro stiffened, blinking. 'What, then?'

Bruno removed his spectacles. 'There is the issue of Mr Pickering.'

Boldoni concealed the piercing anguish he felt at the mention of the name. 'What about him?' he said.

'We have been informed that Mr Pickering may not be exerting the right influence on Signor Campobello at the moment.'

'Informed by whom?'

'Sources.'

'Well, your sources don't know what they're talking about. Pickering is the only man who'll ever persuade the Maestro to sing again. When the time is right. But you cannot ignore the fact that Campobello narrowly escaped dying.'

'More than six months ago.'

'Nor can you force a man to do something against his will.'

'Be that as it may, we feel that unless this contract

176

business is sorted out, and unless the Maestro begins to prepare his voice for an electric recording session with Walter Fleming of the Jupiter Company in a month's time, we will have to insist that Mr Pickering considers retirement.'

'That would be as good as killing him. His work is his life.'

'Then let him get on with his work. Without delay. That is all we ask.'

'He will not retire. He won't just go.'

Bruno stood up and walked around the desk towards Pietro. He gave a quick nod to the guards, which was enough to inform them that they should leave the room, and when the door had closed behind them, he turned back to Boldoni. His face and eyes were not vacant, for they had purpose, but they were disconnected from the chain of emotional effect that in most people leads a path eventually to some level of human understanding, good or bad. Unfeeling was too kind a word to describe the distilled menace of his expression, because feeling was not just absent but denied.

'We have observed for some years your personal life,' he began. 'You cannot expect your tastes to have gone unnoticed.'

Boldoni looked up sharply. 'What are you talking about?'

'Do I need to spell it out?'

'How dare you intimidate me? What lies are you planning now?'

Bruno sighed. 'Enough of this. For years my father has tolerated your revolting – activities – only out of fondness for Campobello.'

'What activities?'

Bruno did not reply, but kept his eyes fixed on Boldoni, who at last caved and looked at the floor.

'I thought you might come to your senses,' continued Bruno. 'Let me tell you this, then: your disgusting secret is safe with us so long as you demonstrate your willingness to cooperate.'

'You would threaten me with this?' muttered Boldoni.

Bruno inclined his head. 'Speak up!'

'Tell me what you want me to do,' said Boldoni, looking up at him.

'I say you are safe, but if you decide to be headstrong and impede what is, after all, only an attempt to go back to what was a very good arrangement for us all until a few years ago, then we will have to take steps to – let us say – hang your filthy little private life out to dry. After that you wouldn't need us to finish you off. You'd most likely be lynched in the street within the week.'

Boldoni did not say anything. Bruno returned to the desk, picking up the spectacles and the fountain pen once again. He began to write, taking no further notice of Boldoni, who remained there, looking down at the floor. Finally, Bruno finished his paragraph, put the lid back on his pen and looked up with surprise.

'What are you waiting for?'

Boldoni looked up, slightly startled. 'What?'

'You piece of shit. Get out of my sight.'

'Yes,' said Boldoni quietly, 'I'll be on my way.'

Chapter 13

When Rocco Campobello arrived at the lower ground room that was Amedeo Tomassini's home, he had to stoop to avoid scraping his scalp. The lime painted plaster of its shallow vaulting was unforgiving, and it brought to mind an old image of his father bending down in exactly the same way. Enrico had been just as tall himself, and their home – not so far from here – had also been accessible only by going down a few brick steps from street level. The musty, cave-like interior here was reminiscent of the old place, and it was perhaps because of this that Rocco felt something comforting about it as he entered. The familiarity was enhanced by a benign scent in the air – spices cooking, cinnamon, he thought, with some ginger, a gentle mulling vapour that he would forever associate with this evening, this home, this encounter.

The room was dimly lit, but he could see through the candlelight the silhouette of a woman he knew must be Amedeo's mother. On being introduced she curtsied, shook his hand lightly, but otherwise made no great display of greeting. Rocco observed her closely, which made her look away. The full bloom of youth and beauty had abandoned her only recently, he could see, because the skin of her face still held a trace of softness. She had large eyes, a full chest and long hair bundled up with combs in the old-fashioned way. Her skirt was thick and pleated, covered by an apron, above which she wore a checked blouse, quite shabby and tailored closely at her waist, again in the old style. Filippo indicated that Rocco should take a seat at the table, and Amedeo concealed himself in a shadowed corner by the entrance.

For some minutes no one spoke, and Rocco was content to observe the woman moving quietly around the room. She did not seem perturbed by the unexpected visitor, but continued her chores as though nothing out of the ordinary had happened. She was kneading something with both hands in a porcelain bowl, and the close acoustic of the place meant that Rocco could hear the slip of its pasty texture between her fingers. He watched her in the half-light; the sway of her hips within the ample skirt, her arm stretching to a shelf for ingredients, the tilt of her head as she turned to look for something mislaid; and he felt transported to a distant time, but only the faintest images came to mind.

'Would you like some food?' Her question interrupted his thoughts and he looked up to see her cleaning her fingers with water from a china jug.

'Thank you. Yes,' replied Rocco, and watched as she sliced up the remains of a bread loaf. Giant splinters of crust cracked beneath the knife's cut and tumbled on to the table. She reached for some cheese and poured a few olives and some oil from a jar. 'Thank you,' he said again when the food was placed before him, along with a cup of wine.

She sat down next to him at the table, a candle between them, and watched as he ate in silence.

It was he who eventually spoke. 'Gabriele was my friend.'

'I know,' she replied.

'I'm sorry about his death.'

'It was a long time ago.'

He ate some more and then mopped up the olive oil with a chunk of bread wedged between his fingers. 'What was your name, before you married?' he asked, chewing the bread.

'Chiara Santangelo,' she replied and after a moment added, 'I met you.'

'Really?'

'With Gabriele. Once or twice.'

Rocco paused from chewing and stared into the darkness ahead of him, but then shook his head. 'I'm sorry. It's been so long.'

Chiara smiled for the first time and her face seemed to Rocco like the dawn sun. 'That's all right,' she said. 'You probably meet a lot of people.'

'I do,' said Rocco, also smiling, though behind the smile he concealed a sense of shame. How far had he strayed in all this time, and in pursuit of what? The comfortable warmth of this place made the wound of the lost years feel all the sharper. 'But I promise you this, Chiara. I will remember you now until my dying day.' At this she let out the smallest of laughs, stifled it with a hand to her mouth, and got back to her feet, taking away the board off which he had eaten. There was another long silence, and Rocco sipped from time to time at the cup of wine. She returned to her work and began to beat the contents of her bowl with a flat wooden paddle.

'Maestro.' It was Filippo. 'We should not be too long.

You never know. People from the tavern might be curious. Someone could arrive.'

'All right, all right,' said Rocco. 'Just give me some time with Signora Tomassini alone.' Filippo looked up sharply at Amedeo, who shrugged, still petrified with shyness. 'We are old friends,' said Rocco. 'Just a few minutes and then you can take me home.' The two others got to their feet, made their way to the door and closed it quietly behind them.

Chiara was examining the creamy substance in her basin, and dipped a hand in to test its consistency. Not entirely satisfied, she licked the white mixture off her finger and continued to whip.

After a pause, Rocco spoke. 'Do you have any other children?'

'No,' she answered rather too quickly.

'I was the only child as well. My sisters died in the cholera.'

'So many died,' said Chiara, arching her back to relieve an ache.

'Your lad has a fine voice, you know,' said Rocco. 'Of course you know. Like his father.'

'Different, though.'

'Different indeed. I want to help him. Will you let him come to me for lessons? We can start right away. Tomorrow. I'd like to see him every day.'

She smiled. 'He has a job,' she said, putting aside the wooden paddle and shaping her mixture into small balls between her palms. She laid each one in its own little square of white muslin.

'Making nets for the fishermen?'

'It's a good job.'

She seemed to be avoiding eye contact with him, and

so Rocco lowered his head to catch her line of sight. 'Signora, money is not a problem,' he said. 'I will look after you both.'

'Why should you do such a thing?'

'Because I want to. Because I need to. Gabriele was my friend.'

'There are people worse off than us.'

Rocco closed his eyes and sighed. 'Signora Tomassini, allow me to do this. From this day you are my responsibility.'

'Thank you,' she said almost inaudibly and without looking up again. She had started to tie together the corners of the muslin squares with pieces of string.

'I can offer the boy a good future, perhaps even a great one.'

'As a singer?'

'Yes, as a singer. Just as Gabriele wanted for himself. Just as Gabriele would have wanted for his son.'

'Like you?'

'In a way.'

'And has it been a good life for you?' One by one, she was reaching up to hang the muslin balls on small wooden pegs that stuck out from the wall. Milky drips fell from them to the floor, and she put a pan down to catch them.

Rocco hesitated. 'I've made my mistakes.'

'Everyone makes mistakes,' she said.

Rocco looked around the little room. 'Do you have any photographs of Gabriele?' She smiled and shook her head gently and he realized what an absurd question it was. These sort of people couldn't afford to have a photograph taken. 'Did he . . . did he ever talk about me?'

'From time to time.'

183

'What did he say?'

'Things about when you were boys.'

'Like what?'

She paused to reflect. 'This and that,' she said at last.

'Can't you tell me just one thing?'

She smiled. 'He said you were always the clever one.'

After another pause, Rocco ventured, 'Did he . . .' but stalled and began again, in a lower voice, 'I need to know if he ever spoke ill of me. Did he ever express resentment? Or anger?'

She thought for a moment, while he waited urgently for the reply. 'No,' she said.

'And you?' he went on. 'Aren't you going to ask me why I never came back? Why I never saw my best friend again? Or any of the others, Choirmaster de Luca . . . and . . .'

'I think people understood,' she said, and sat down next to him at the table again. 'You shouldn't fret about that.'

Her plain words struck at the heart of his demon, and he felt a sudden urge to rest his hand on top of hers, but resisted. 'I do fret, Chiara,' he said quietly, 'I do.'

Behind him the door opened and Filippo came in, followed by Amedeo. Rocco now rose to his feet and turned to the boy. 'Your mother agrees. So, can I expect you tomorrow? We'll start at eleven o'clock. Signor Pickering has been wanting to get his teeth into something for months. He can get his teeth into you.'

Filippo's eyes darted between Campobello and Chiara, and he asked what this was all about. Rocco explained, but Filippo seemed far from happy at what he heard, and asked for a quick word with the Maestro.

'What about his job, his apprenticeship?' he said when they were out in the street.

'He can forget about nets and fishing from now on,' said Rocco. 'I will pay him twice whatever he got from his master.'

'And in six months, or a year's time,' persisted Filippo, 'when you lose interest or go back to America?'

Rocco smiled. 'You don't need to worry. I will take care of everything.'

Filippo, feeling the ground slipping beneath him, changed tack. He moved in closer to Rocco and whispered, 'Maestro, it's not as straightforward as you think. Amedeo is not an easy lad. He gets into trouble. He will make life difficult for you, as he's made it difficult for his mother. And being close to you will . . . it will go to his head. All the fame, the money. It will end in disaster.'

'What sort of trouble?'

Filippo waved his hand through the air, impatiently. 'Political. Meetings at the docks, showing off silly opinions. He's got a good heart but he's easily led, and the police have got his name on their lists. If he doesn't go and find trouble, it will come calling soon enough. Maybe you don't know what it's like here nowadays. Ever since the disturbances of last year the authorities have come down hard on anyone they suspect of mischief. They break down doors in the night and leave streams of blood in the streets.'

'They won't break down my door.'

At this, Filippo stiffened slightly. 'Maybe not. But don't count on it. Things are changing every day.'

'Then I'll make sure the boy stays out of trouble.'

'I'm thinking about your welfare, as well, Maestro.'

185

But Rocco was not convinced. He put a hand on Filippo's shoulder. 'This boy is now my son. If it weren't for his mother I would have him in my own home, but I'm not going to take him away from her. I left home at about his age, and I know now that it was wrong.' Filippo conceded and bowed his head, after which Rocco led the way back indoors.

Amedeo was waiting nervously for them, but Rocco smiled and raised his eyebrows at him. 'Well? What do you think?' The boy stared back, his eyes darting back and forth with nervous energy. 'Would you prefer to think about it for a while?' asked Campobello. 'I don't want to rush you.'

For a moment he seemed incapable of a reply, and Filippo stepped in. 'Maybe leave it a few days,' he said quietly, and then, moving close in to the boy, added. 'It's a big decision.'

'No,' blurted Amedeo. 'I mean yes, Maestro, yes, yes, I will be there tomorrow at eleven.'

'Excellent,' said Rocco, darting a quick look at Filippo. 'I'll send my car to fetch you from the piazza,' and he kissed Amedeo on the cheek. 'And tomorrow we start to look for a new home for you both.'

'Signor,' called Chiara, stopping Rocco as he was about to walk towards the door.

'Yes?'

'I don't care about my house. I don't care about anything. But my son – if anything should happen to him . . . He is my whole life.'

Rocco walked back to her, took her hand and kissed it lightly. 'It is for that very reason that I will treasure him,' he said.

The carriage was waiting for him in the street outside,

but he insisted to Filippo that he did not want company, and would travel back to Posillipo alone.

It proved to be a noisy and bumpy journey. The wheels of the carriage were an ill-matched pair, a hasty piece of repair work, the driver said, following a traffic collision earlier in the week; and the horses' hooves made no allowance for the lateness of the hour, but clattered emphatically through the peaceful alleys.

The night air in the empty streets was close and still. As ever, the scent was inescapable, though less unpleasant than during the day, the edge of decay now replaced by a flat warmth, reminiscent of quarry dust. Campobello barely noticed the change, nor the racket of the hooves and the discomfort. He was closed to the world around him and his eyes were sealed tight. His thoughts were consumed by imaginary scenarios which refused to be brushed aside. One persistent image was huge – clear as a scene from a wide-screen movie. It showed Gabriele, in open sunshine, rowing out into the bay, dipping his oars gently in and out of the water, the slight splashing as he progressed, stroke by stroke, out, out and beyond, his eyes fixed on the horizon. He was smiling, too. Rocco shook his head in an attempt not only to dispel the picture, but to deny culpability for what he knew would be its eventual outcome.

Surely Gabriele was too experienced a seaman to have gone so far by mistake. Unless completely deranged, he must have gone out there on purpose. A question arose uncomfortably in Rocco's mind, and hovered there like a restless phantom. What despair had driven Gabriele to take his life in such a way? What hopelessness, what shattered dreams?

Chapter 14

Pietro Boldoni always felt better for starting the working day with a good walk, and most mornings by around eight o'clock he was taking a peppy promenade around the Villa Rosalba's gardens. Today was no different, and he had just walked past the villa's pleasant seafront terrace when he noticed, through the early morning haze, Taddeo, the tenor's double, being let in by the guards at the main gate. It was as good an opportunity as any to take the man aside and break the news, thought Boldoni – something he had been meaning to do for a couple of days, but with the matter of Bruno Graziani pressing on his mind had not yet got around to. He called out across the lawn for Taddeo to stop and wait for him.

Taddeo, as ever, was splendidly attired when he arrived for work, suit brushed, moustache trim, boater atilt. His dedication to the job had recently extended to a request that he be supplied with the Maestro's eau de Cologne – a costly brand, which Boldoni was persuaded to permit for the sake of authenticity, though Taddeo seemed to be getting through bottles of the stuff, certainly more quickly than the gentleman he emulated.

As Taddeo waited for Boldoni to approach, he struck a dignified pose, his portly frame resting on one leg, cane held at an angle, the other hand tucked neatly into the small of his back. An uninitiated eye would have placed Boldoni, scurrying across the grass, as hierarchically the junior of the two; but only up until they had begun their conversation, at which stage the flabbergasted reaction of the larger man would have quickly put paid to the illusion.

'I'm not saying that we no longer require your services,' said Boldoni, softening the impact of his opening remark, 'but that a few things are going to have to change – and change quickly – if you want to keep the job.'

'I'll do anything, signor,' spluttered Taddeo, stooping to pick up one of his silk gloves that had fallen into the dirt, in the process dislodging his boater. 'Anything at all.'

'I felt sure we could count on you,' said Boldoni, and indicated that they should proceed along the path. 'You may or may not have heard rumours that Maestro Campobello is planning a return to public life. He will shortly be attending a performance at the Teatro San Carlo, followed by a gala reception in the Palazzo Reale. Thereafter he intends to make more regular appearances.'

'*Bene*. That is good news,' said Taddeo cautiously.

'Indeed,' said Boldoni, 'and if anything it will make the necessity for employing a skilful double even more pressing than before.'

'Yes?' said Taddeo, wondering when the sting would come.

'But the simple fact is this: Maestro Campobello no longer looks the same as he did.'

'He . . . what?'

'No one blames you for not knowing. It has been kept private until now. But he has changed, and therefore anyone who wishes to impersonate him accurately will have to accommodate such changes as have taken place. All this –' he waved briefly at the double's attire, and then at his face, whereupon Taddeo raised his eyebrows, 'all this must go.'

'But how – how am I to know what to do?'

'If you want to keep the job –'

'I do, I do.'

'We will give you good instruction. You may come to the Maestro's apartment this afternoon. At two-thirty precisely. Present yourself to the houseboy, and he will bring you up. Then we'll run through the clothes you have to buy, the haircut –'

'Haircut?'

'Yes, the head will need to be shaved, I'm afraid.' Taddeo looked at him open-mouthed, while Boldoni scrutinized his face. 'And there will be a need for chalk, or some such substance. How well does your beard grow?'

'My beard?'

'Yes. The Maestro now wears a beard. And it is white, so we'll have to do something about that. But above all, there's the matter of the diet.'

'The what?'

'The diet. Maestro Campobello has lost fifty pounds in weight since he was last formally received in public, and obviously it will not do to have his double looking like –' once again his hand waved up and down the length of Taddeo, who waited for the forthcoming description with an anticipation of injury, 'it would be pointless,' continued Boldoni, changing tack, 'and counter to your professional standards, I'm sure, for you to embark on your job with anything less than complete . . . accuracy.' Marginally relieved at the choice of words, but still in shock, Taddeo nodded his agreement. 'Signor Campobello's private doctors, the Florio brothers, are at your service, should you require medical advice about how best and fastest to shed the weight,' concluded Boldoni, coming to a stop, 'but the general wisdom on such matters encourages a drastic reduction of food and alcohol consumed, together with increased exercise.'

'Yes, signor.'

'And we must act quickly.'

'*Certamente.* Quickly, yes.'

'I'm afraid I must insist on this. I will have some scales delivered to the staff rest room later today. Please be so kind as to weigh yourself and post a note of the figure in my pigeonhole by the pantry. I shall expect daily updates. We will review the effectiveness of whatever measures you have undertaken a fortnight from today. We have every faith in you, but I must be plain: your job depends on this. Good morning.'

'Good morning, signor.' And with that they parted company, Taddeo, his genteel poise shattered, walking towards Pozzo's lodge; while Boldoni, checking his watch, made his way towards the house.

At that moment, Wallace Pickering was waiting alone in the music room, a little earlier than instructed. He was seated on a simple wooden chair and held an old leather briefcase on his lap. When Campobello entered the room, Pickering neither stood up nor uttered a word of greeting.

Rocco took one look at his accompanist and sighed; then he picked up a chair from the other side of the room, placed it in front of Pickering and sat down, mirroring the pianist, their knees inches apart.

'So,' said Rocco, attempting to engage the other man's line of sight, 'you've had him for a few days now, I have let you get on without interfering. You must have come to some sort of conclusion.'

'He's a tenor, I'll grant you that.'

Rocco smiled. 'And?'

'And? And what made you decide to sing in public for the first time in six months, without so much as a hint that you might have changed your mind, after saying you were finished for good?'

'Amedeo told you?'

'He did.'

'Are you offended?'

'Don't be ridiculous. This isn't about me. You are not a twenty-five-year-old any more. You could put your voice back months by singing on an unexercised throat like that. Do you expect an athlete to go out and run a sprint after months of sitting in an armchair?'

'It was hardly a sprint,' said Rocco calmly. 'It was barely even singing, just a few lines of a ballad.'

'Why did you do it?'

'It felt right. You won't understand, because you don't want to.'

'You could try and explain.'

'I was back amongst my people. And there was my friend's son. The closest I've been to Gabriele for more than thirty years. It was good, I tell you. I felt like a real person for the first time in as long as I can remember, and the feeling's still with me. I've been given another chance, Wallace.'

Pickering was far from convinced. 'We've been to hell and back worrying about you, and now you're all fine and dandy, singing with the local yokels, and we're sitting here looking like bloomin' idiots.'

'I didn't plan it. And I'm sorry if it's upset you.'

At this Pickering popped like an overcooked casserole and rose to his feet, the briefcase falling from his lap, spilling its contents of musical manuscripts all over the floor. His face reddened, either with fury or with the effort of having to stoop to collect the music.

'Do I have to say it again? This is not about me.'

'Why are you so angry, then?'

'Because you could do untold damage to your voice.'

'It doesn't matter any more.'

'So that's the great Campobello's future from now on, is it? Back-street brothels and taverns, instead of La Scala and the Metropolitan?' He was on his hands and knees, collecting up the music in a haphazard way. 'Roll up, roll up, ye whores and drunks! The Maestro's dropped by for a singsong. You can all join in, if you like!' He turned on Rocco. 'When will you understand? Your voice is a rare and valuable commodity. You should not be allowed to make decisions about it on your own.'

'That is where we differ. I'd prefer to talk about Amedeo.'

'I wouldn't.'

'What do you think about him?'

'I've already told you,' replied Pickering. 'He's a tenor.'

Rocco was not deterred by the masterly understatement. 'Can you do something with him?'

The purple flush drained from Pickering's face and his eyes narrowed in concentration. He thought for quite a while before replying. 'Hard to say,' he finally said, easing his position enough to make Rocco press further.

'Give me an honest opinion. It means a lot to me.'

Reluctantly, grimacing almost, as though being forced

against his better judgement to skin a fruit before it was properly ripe, Pickering conceded, 'All right, yes, there is something there. But it's much too early to say, much, *much* too early, so don't go giving the lad ideas.'

Campobello smiled. 'I think so too.'

'But it would take years,' added Pickering deflatingly, 'and he'll never have the patience. And anyway, the voice is too small. Won't ever be enough for a big house.'

'Times are changing. We have the microphone, radio, the cinema. He might become a different sort of singer.'

'And who wants them?' muttered Pickering, making his way over to the grand piano. 'Now,' he said, 'I'm less interested in your so-called protégé than in you, so if you want to put things right, you can give me a couple of scales so's I can see what's going on in there.'

'You will be wasting your time.'

Pickering's eyes flashed. 'If you can sing your heart out for a bunch of beggars in the slums, you can do me the decency of giving an inch. You owe me that much.'

Rocco conceded with a sigh.

Boldoni was approaching the music room when he heard what was going on, and the sound stopped him in his tracks. Over the past few days he had heard Amedeo singing the same exercises on the other side of the same door, but this was wholly different, and there could be no mistaking it. It was the voice to which no other voice on earth could compare: the shining brassy timbre of it, filling out and ringing louder and rounder as it progressed, scale upon scale upwards. For Pietro, at this moment, the implication of the sound carried even greater resonance than the sound itself. It was more than just the Maestro's voice. It was sweet consolation from the Lord Almighty, the whispered response of God Himself, an answer to his daily, hourly, prayers. Profoundly moved, Pietro stood outside the door to listen, intending to wait until there was an appropriate pause before entering.

He was still there when Molly appeared, silhouetted against the window at the end of the corridor. She visibly stiffened when she saw Boldoni, and began to stalk purposefully towards him, but she suddenly became conscious of what was happening in the music room, and stopped to listen. For all their differences, and despite the years of hostile counter-manoeuvring, Boldoni and Molly now looked at one another with something like the understanding of co-conspirators. Hardly daring to breathe, as one exercise after another was accomplished with apparent ease, they registered a mutual cause.

'Did you know?' whispered Molly. Her face seemed gripped by a kind of ecstatic pain.

'I had no idea,' Pietro replied. Neither of them said anything else, nor sought to explain the urgency of their individual plight, but wordlessly, and with eyes ablaze, they acknowledged that from this moment, on a particular territory, they were allies, albeit unlikely ones, and that they had jointly sensed a trail of hope.

The singing stopped, and Boldoni turned the brass handle of the door, holding out his hand to usher Molly through. Pickering was sitting at the piano, head down and arms crossed, as they came in, but Rocco approached them with a smile. Molly ran over to him. Her face was now all innocent happiness. It was an expression that would occasionally surface if she was wrong-footed by a pleasant novelty. It made her cheeks glow like young apples, the corners of her mouth dimple and her eyes widen, bringing out the girl in her. She embraced her husband tightly, as she hadn't for some years, a show of affection that made Boldoni look away with a light cough.

Rocco withdrew slightly, but Molly, still gazing happily at him, asked, 'What are we supposed to make of this?'

'The singing? Nothing, really. Pickering and I were playing around.'

'It sounded more than that,' she persisted, almost hopping on the spot with excitement. 'How did it feel?'

'We were just experimenting,' Rocco replied, with a frown, and reached inside his jacket for a cigarette.

'It sounded marvellous to me,' Boldoni said, then glanced for a moment at Pickering, who still sat cross-armed and silent at the keyboard. 'Are you planning to do more?'

Molly answered for her husband. 'Of course he is. He will do a little more every day – isn't that right, my dear?'

Rocco did not entirely disregard the question, but answered with a shrug as he lit his cigarette.

'And then Mr Fleming's proposed recordings will not seem too ambitious a project after all,' continued Molly. 'This is the best news I have heard all year.'

'Indeed! What we have all been hoping for!' endorsed Boldoni, but another look at Pickering cautioned him to rein in his enthusiasm. 'Are we being premature?'

'Recordings?' said Rocco, and he drew on the cigarette. 'I think not.'

'You don't have to think about it today,' Molly said, clapping her palms together. 'But perhaps tomorrow. Or next week. Will you not work towards the recordings, dear?'

Rocco looked at her as he might look at an over-excited niece, sternly, but without wanting to flatten her enthusiasm. 'I think we should see what happens, shall we?' he said, and put out an arm to her, which she joyously took, and they walked towards the open window. After a couple of paces, he paused where he stood and looked back over his shoulder at Boldoni. 'Perhaps I might record one or two *canzoni napoletane*, you know, local ballads. It might be a nice tribute to Naples.' He grunted a laugh, 'My parting shot.'

Boldoni's quick mind leapt on the throwaway remark and he began to imagine how the Grazianis might respond to it. They had in mind to precipitate a comprehensive new Campobello record catalogue with the Jupiter Company, under their own auspices, and Boldoni doubted whether a few Neapolitan songs would satisfy their ambitions. But it was a start, and surely better than nothing. It might be enough to stall their monstrous threats. Once more he looked at Pickering. The pianist was shaking his head, and Boldoni's heart sank.

'Maestro,' called Boldoni. He tried to disguise the urgency of his plea. 'Would you like me to contact the Jupiter Company? If you are to work with Walter Fleming again, we will have to review your contracts and make overtures. I must inform Columbia of the news, and – and of course there will be complications, but—'

'Yes,' said Rocco. 'If I ever record again, it must be with Walter.'

'The right decision, in the circumstances, I think,' said Boldoni, feeling the weight of his own problems lifting.

'Will it be difficult to arrange?' asked Rocco.

'Not really,' Boldoni replied quickly. 'I'll get on to it right away. Would you like to tell Don Graziani the good news personally, or shall I?'

'Codswallop.' The single softly spoken word from Pickering landed with quiet but angular awkwardness in their midst.

'Wallace?' said Boldoni gently in the silence that followed.

'Oh, don't listen to me. Just carry on,' said Pickering, flicking his fingers at them as if to dust them all away.

'What do you mean?' asked Boldoni.

'I mean you're all talking codswallop. He can't sing. Not like that. It will take more than just a few weeks to get him into shape. Maybe more than months. Maybe he was right before, maybe he should stop while he's on top.'

'How? Why?' said Boldoni.

'I'll tell you why,' answered Pickering, without pausing, 'because the voice isn't there. It's not locked in. It's not—' He opened wide the fingers of both hands and jammed them together. 'The teeth aren't in the gear, however you want to describe it. If he sings now, it will be like, like forcing the wrong screw into the thread. It'll damage and wear it out in no time.'

'But it sounded wonderful,' countered Boldoni.

'To you!' snapped Pickering.

'It is just my opinion.'

'What would you know about it?'

'A little. Not much, I suppose.'

'Exactly. Don't choose now to start questioning my judgement. Now, when it really matters.'

He stood up from the piano and backed away like a

hounded animal, clutching his briefcase. 'If you want to go ahead with your madcap plan, that's fine, but don't expect me to have anything to do with it.' He fumbled with his spectacles and stuffed them into his jacket pocket. 'The Grazianis will be pleased with your decision.'

'Is that so bad?' ventured Boldoni.

Pickering whipped round on him. 'Since when did you start defending the Grazianis?'

'I'm not. It's just . . . we must admit that Don Graziani has been helpful. He has kept the public away, protected all of us from the newspapers. And there's the house, the staff.'

Pickering shot back, 'And meanwhile he'll be rubbing his hands, of course. The return of Campobello will line his pocket very nicely. And it'll help Bruno Graziani's bid to be the next director of the San Carlo.'

'What on earth do you mean?' asked Boldoni, almost smiling at the suggestion, but a look at Pickering showed it was no laughing matter.

'Oh, you haven't heard,' murmured Pickering airily as he headed for the door. 'No I don't suppose you would have. But I've been at the opera house nearly every day, and it's official. Bruno has plans. He wants to take over the San Carlo when the present director retires in a couple of months.'

Rocco drew on his cigarette, but said nothing, while Boldoni looked flabbergasted. 'But that's completely preposterous!' he said. 'What qualification does he think he has for the job?'

'What does he need?' answered Pickering. 'He's got his father's muscle, plenty of money, they're well-known benefactors of the San Carlo – and now,' he darted a finger in the direction of Rocco, 'and now he's got his old friend planning an imminent return. What better prize for the new director than to come swanning in with the Great Campobello at his heels?'

'Did I ever say anything about an imminent return?' said Rocco quietly.

Boldoni was shaking his head, still incredulous. 'One of the greatest opera companies in Italy, in the world, even, directed by a – by a gangster.'

Molly laughed nervously and fumbled to find words to ease the tension. 'Oh, we mustn't exaggerate. Bruno can be a charming man at times.' She added limply, 'He might make a fine director.'

Pickering took little notice, but turned to Campobello. 'I don't give a penny whistle about Bruno Graziani. But if you don't take my advice about your voice, you'll be finished before the year is out. I'll put money on it.'

For a moment all three of them stood in silence until Molly asked Rocco for one of his cigarettes, whereupon Pickering, looking at his watch, muttered, 'Well, if you'll excuse me I have other things to do. I'll be back at eleven to see Amedeo.' He left the room and paced silently away down the corridor. One could never hear Pickering coming or going; he habitually wore rather inelegant soft-soled shoes and took small, furtive steps that were almost inaudible.

Boldoni raised his chin, taking the situation in hand and moving on. 'Maestro, there is the matter of Signora Tomassini and her son. They will be moved to the Vomero apartment later this afternoon. Everything is arranged. I should mention the expense.'

'Never mind the expense.'

'It may have been a rather hasty decision. In the long

term this arrangement will prove very costly. The apartment—'

'I like hasty decisions,' interrupted Rocco. 'See that they have everything they need.'

Pietro nodded.

'Why, that is so charming,' said Molly, making an effort to lift the pall cast by Pickering's exit. 'I think you've done a wonderful thing to rescue that poor woman and her son. Perhaps she might like to come here for tea one day. Or join the staff picnic outing to the Posillipo headland next week. There are some sweet girls who work in the kitchen. She might enjoy that very much, the poor dear. She could make some new friends, a new life for herself away from the slums.'

A deflating silence followed Molly's suggestion. She took it as a hint that she should leave the men to finish their morning meeting in peace. Putting out her cigarette, and holding on to her smile until she was out of the room, she left them to their business.

Boldoni waited until the sound of her footsteps had disappeared before asking his question.

'Are you serious about the recordings?'

Rocco sucked deeply on his cigarette, frowned for a moment, and then sucked again, finishing it. Letting out a cloud of smoke, he replied, 'Wallace doesn't understand. If I do it, it'll be for my own reasons. Not for the sake of the great career, not for the great public, and certainly not for the great Don Graziani.' He stubbed his cigarette firmly into an ashtray. 'I'm home now, in every sense. And I'm going nowhere. Yes, I'll make some recordings, a few local songs, for my people and for Naples, and that will be an end to it.'

'Even if you make light of it, you must be aware that

this will cause a sensation. The potential earnings will be huge.'

'There you are, then. If you're worried about Signora Tomassini's expenses, put all the money from the recordings towards her and Amedeo.'

Boldoni received the suggestion in silence, and after a suitable pause asked, 'And what about Pickering?'

'He'll get over it. I just hope it won't make your life too uncomfortable in the meantime. He seemed quite annoyed with you.'

Pietro bristled inwardly at this slight incursion into his private life. There were certain matters he never discussed with the Maestro. 'No matter,' he said. 'You can be sure of my support, in any event.'

'So we are of one mind?'

'As ever, Maestro.'

'Excellent, *capitano*. Any other business this morning?'

Boldoni paused to consult his notebook, and began to blink repeatedly – a habit which indicated that he was clearing the clutter from his thoughts. 'I have confirmed the arrangements for our trip to Rome.' He adjusted his pince-nez, checking the notes in his book. 'We sail on the fifteenth to Civitavecchia, where a private train carriage will be waiting to take us direct to Rome. A car will meet us at the station. It's all arranged.'

'How long will it take?'

'We'll spend the first night in the hotel and go straight to the clinic the next morning. We sail out of Civitavecchia that same night, and by the following morning we'll be back in Naples. I'm assured the ship's first-class cabins are comfortable.'

'And the X-rays?'

'They'll arrive within the week. But they'll be sent straight to the Florio brothers. Unless you say otherwise.' He looked at Rocco expectantly.

'Don't be so concerned. For all their shortcomings, the Florios don't want to see me drop dead.'

'It's not that. They are just so completely in Graziani's pocket. Perhaps we should try a new doctor.'

'You're fussing unnecessarily. The pains are not getting any worse.'

'Nor any better.'

'The X-rays are precautionary. It's in no one's interest to hide whatever shows up.'

Their affairs complete, Boldoni put away his notebook and folded up the hinged pince-nez.

'Before you go,' Rocco called across the room, with a slightly uncertain smile. 'Did you pass my letter to Signora Tomassini?'

'Yes. I thought I might have to read it to her, but she seemed able to do it herself.'

'Did she say anything?'

'She expressed thanks, that's all. I imagine she is a little overawed by all the fuss, which is understandable. Such a sudden change for her.'

'Will you be seeing her again soon?'

Boldoni's nose twitched slightly and he said, 'Well, I thought I might drop by at the Vomero apartment this evening. Just to make sure everything is in order.'

'Very good,' said Rocco. 'While you are there, I'd like you to pass on an invitation to her and the boy.'

'For the staff picnic?'

'Certainly not. For the gala performance at the Teatro San Carlo, on the seventh. I'd like them to be my personal guests.'

Boldoni was taken aback. 'But that will be a very important occasion indeed,' he finally said. He chose his words carefully, because he had already sensed that the issue of Signora Tomassini and her son had grown large in the mind of his employer. 'The royal box. The most eminent citizens, and, of course, your first public appearance in months.'

'I am aware of that.'

'But do you think it is suitable? She and the boy – they are simple people.'

Rocco smiled once more. 'I might remind you, Pietro, that I too am a simple person. They are no different. She is my closest friend's widow. By rights I should be like the boy's uncle, his guardian.'

Boldoni was far from convinced, and the tight set of his jaw and mouth expressed as much, but he nodded his assent. 'I'll inform the appropriate people.'

'And make sure the signora has the right clothes for the occasion. I want her to look wonderful. I want her to feel that her husband would be proud.'

'Yes, Maestro.'

In a few moments Boldoni had stepped out of the house and into the garden again. He was hot, and felt pressed upon. A welcome breeze met his face, and he pulled at his unforgivingly stiff collar to allow the fresh air a greater reach. The high palms that were planted along the terrace were swaying back and forth into the territory of capacious mushroom-shaped cedars. The mist had risen and members of staff were hurrying this way and that. A mass of birds and insects hummed restlessly in the trees, playing, sparring. His own vigour had drained away somewhat since the morning walk, but everything else had sprung to life around him. He allowed himself to pause for a moment, to observe it all, before a host of spectral worries swooped down to intercept his pleasant ruminations, like mawkish crows, and compelled him back to work.

Chapter 15

Rocco knew that the luxury of his present anonymity was coming to an end, but while there was still time, he felt compelled to undertake a small pilgrimage. The object he wished to venerate lay within the walls of the Castel dell'Ovo, which was visible in the distance across the water from the Villa Rosalba, and the sight of it, daily, had been eating away at him these past weeks. It was time to face this thing and deal with it. As far as he knew, it was all that remained of his father's life and labour in the city. He had to see it close to, once again.

Pozzo drove him the short distance from Posillipo, and Rocco got out of the car just at the point where the causeway led off at a right angle from the riviera, over the water to the castle. The smell of fresh fish was strong. Bucketfuls of sardines – slender, silver and curling in the sunshine – waited to be collected by market stall holders. Close to where Rocco was dropped off, groups of young men squatted around piles of nets edged with cork floats. Their shaved heads were bowed as they picked at the threads on their laps. Cleaning out weed and repairing, they worked through the mountainous heaps on the quayside.

When Rocco was a child, the Castel dell'Ovo had been a military prison and barracks. His father had been commissioned to remove the rusting remnants of medieval ironmongery from one of its ancient stone arches, and replace it with something that would stand the test of time, defy the shoreline tempests and the breaking waves, stave off invaders, repel sieges, cope with whatever cataclysm fate decided to hurl at this war-battered city in the uncertain decades ahead. But by the late 1920s the fear of traditional warfare had diminished. The castle was now a telegraph station and a historical curiosity for tourists, and it was therefore in the company of a few ambling, well-intentioned foreigners that Rocco Campobello made his way across the causeway towards the fortified entrance, his face shaded by a wide-brimmed felt hat.

The bleak, thick walls of the castle barely made allowance for windows; indeed, the whole structure was little more than a titanic angular rock, crudely fashioned to accommodate a basic degree of human occupation. Rocco remembered his way around it with relative ease, and it took no more than a couple of minutes to find the grille, much the same as when he and his father had fitted it, around the time of his thirteenth birthday. He leant his cane against the pitted brickwork of an adjacent wall, removed a glove, and slipped a thick finger delicately around the base of a vertical steel bar, the furthest one over to the left. He found what he was searching for, even though it was hidden from view and despite the many layers of paint that had been applied over the intervening years. It was still there, tiny but engraved deep into the otherwise smooth steel surface: the letters RC.

'Your first work as a blacksmith,' his father had said, straight after Rocco removed the red-hot bar from the furnace, 'so we must mark it, for all time,' and while the metal was still hot enough, Enrico carved his son's initials into the bar with the sharp tip of a chisel. 'No one will ever see it, I'll make sure of that. It'll be our secret.' Rocco then had the privilege of plunging the rod, hissing and steaming, into the water butt, the most thrilling part of the whole procedure.

He had been allowed to work alongside his father as a special treat to mark the occasion of his treble voice breaking: his transition, in a sense, to manhood. He could remember the feel of Enrico hovering close in behind like a great bear, arms enfolding him as he worked, and the quiet security of the deep-spoken words of advice. Rocco liked the feel of the oil and heat on his fingers; it was crude, manly work. 'God has blessed you with the right hands for the job,' his father commented, and they both smiled because it was something he always said and had become a standing joke between them. 'It's not only muscle you'll need, though,' he went on. 'You have to focus, cut out everything else.' He demonstrated his hammer swing while he spoke, eyes fixed madly on a single spot. His fingers shone silver blue, like polished gun barrels. 'Only by blocking out every other thought in the world can you hit the place at the right angle', *slam*, 'at the right moment', *slam*, 'with the right force', *slam*.

Now, well dressed and forty-nine years old, Rocco gripped his fingers around the upright steel. He could remember vividly the tangy scent of the molten lead which they had poured into drilled holes to secure the bars to the wall. The stonemason had been here as well, a thickset ogre of a man with a heart of gold, and Rocco had felt fiercely virile at the end of a day working alongside these two master artisans. It had not been easy, and a salty wind had whipped in from the sea, stinging their cheeks as they toiled; but the job was well done, and the three of them stood back to observe it at the end. Rocco had never felt closer to his father. Enrico sensed the closeness, too, and put an arm around the boy's shoulder, scrunching him in tight.

The blacksmith and stonemason walked away from the Castel dell'Ovo that day and barely gave another thought to the job they had done there; it was one of many, after all. But that grille meant the world to Rocco. The image of it was locked in his mind as squarely as it was lodged in the old castle's masonry, and the accomplishment of it would underpin a good deal of what he was to achieve in years to come. The grandeur of its simple, unyielding geometry represented for him all that was inviolable and resolute. This was the meaning of work, this was dependability, nobility – qualities that perfectly matched the methods and character of his father.

It was clear as daylight to Rocco now, while the soft tissue of his index finger stroked back and forth across the burrs raised by those engraved initials. But a ghost from the past still remained, which neither this pilgrimage nor the benefit of hindsight could lay to rest. Why, in the name of all that was good and holy, had he allowed the magnificent influence of his father to slip from his life on so limp a pretext? It was surely not just because Enrico might have wanted him to carry on the family smithy?

Looking beyond the grille towards the calm blue of the bay, and hearing the little waves breaking against the rocky outcrop beneath him, he could dimly appreciate what had happened. The Voice had swallowed up everything in his life, the roles of mother and father, children; even lover. Was it so surprising, then, that, as he grew older, he became so distant from everyone in his orbit, so wrapped up in himself? There was never to be room for anything or anyone else. His father had been an early casualty, and others would follow; that was all there was to it.

PART TWO

Chapter 16

Naples, 1896

After Rocco had been singing in the church choir of
Santa Maria Regina Coeli and living at the Ospedale for
about two years, he saw his father for the last time. They
met apparently by accident in the piazza just outside the
Ospedale. Months had passed since their last meeting,
when Rocco had gone back home for a meal, a visit that
had been stilted because they found so little to say to
each other. He decided not to return after that. It seemed
best to avoid enduring a similar ordeal again.

Enrico smiled at his son almost shyly, indicating what
a happy surprise it was that they should run into each
other like this after so long, but Rocco guessed that he
had been hiding somewhere nearby, waiting for him to
come out. His father's persistence was annoying.

Rocco tried to smile but it didn't look very convincing. The contrast between them was striking. Although
Enrico would surely have washed before leaving home,
he looked unkempt, nowadays, beside his son. Perhaps
it was the months of regular baths and freshly laundered
clothes at the Ospedale. His father could never escape
the smoke and grime of the forge; his hands were filthy,
Rocco thought, tarnished dark as a Negro's, right up to

the wrists and beyond, and dirt lined the edges of his shrunken shirt cuffs.

'You look well,' said Enrico, his spontaneous flood of feeling and hunger for information stunted by Rocco's obvious unease. 'Is everything all right with you?'

'Yes, good,' replied Rocco. His voice was artificially high because he was making an effort to sound friendly, but he couldn't think of anything else to say and so started to look around the square.

'And your singing? Is everyone pleased with you?'

'I think so. I can read and write well now.'

'Really?' Enrico was delighted at the volunteered fragment and nodded encouragingly, but his son did not add any more. 'Signor de Luca is making the choir better all the time, they say.'

'Yes.'

'Well, that's good.'

'Why do you come so much?' Rocco suddenly asked, giving way to his irritation as if scratching at an itch.

'Does it bother you if I sit and listen to the choir? I don't disturb you.'

'It's embarrassing,' said Rocco. 'You're there almost every Sunday. The other guys tease me about it.'

'Is that why you try not to look at me?'

'You always sit so close.'

'I'm proud of you.'

'They call me a sissy, a little daddy's boy. And they say you're the scruffiest person in the church.'

Enrico looked down, but only for a moment. 'Are they orphans?' he asked.

'Most of them.'

'They're probably jealous, then.'

Rocco said nothing more. He felt a slight sting of shame

214

at what he had said, but was unable to do anything about it, and just looked away.

'I'm glad they're looking after you, my boy,' Enrico finally said and put a hand on Rocco's shoulder. 'I won't keep you now. I'm sure you're busy.'

'I'm on my way to Signor de Luca. He wants to see me about—'

'Off you go, now.'

'I'm sorry, Papa.'

'No, no.' He patted the air between them soothingly. 'I'll come by another time.' And with that Enrico spared his son any further awkwardness by walking away quickly. It was a run-down part of town, and the tall, dilapidated tenement blocks that lined the piazza were festooned with strings of laundry, beside which the unblemished marble masonry of Santa Maria's façade seemed almost imperial. Enrico was heading for a dark, narrow alley on the other side of the road. He had to wait for a couple of carriages to pass before he could cross, and took advantage of the pause to turn around and wave a last goodbye to his son, but he let his hand drop quickly when he noticed the boy had gone.

Rocco was relieved to have it over with so quickly, and hurried across the piazza towards the church. A young woman with a pretty shawl across her shoulders was selling pieces of mismatched porcelain on the cobbles, directly in his path, and she sat heaped and slumbering in the warmth of the sun. Until a few months ago Rocco would have spared a glance for a girl like this and caught her eye, if only because of her thick rope of hair and high bosom, but nowadays he was too preoccupied. In his mind he was already in the choirmaster's study, elevated to a world of high art and excellence.

Gabriele was waiting for him just inside the church door, and grinning. 'You're late.' He delighted in the admonition because there were so few occasions when Rocco stepped out of line.

'I got held up,' replied Rocco, hurrying on so as not to lose any more time. The difference in the boys' appearance had become more pronounced over the two years, partly because Gabriele, unlike his friend, had hardly gained any height, but largely because Rocco was compelled, by some ancient statute of the Ospedale, to wear his hair long, like a Renaissance prince. However, it was still Gabriele, with his sharp, humorous eyes and angelic face, who stole the girls' glances.

'Do you know what this is about?' asked Rocco. 'Have we done something to upset him?' Gabriele tried to answer but his words were swallowed up by a sudden attack of coughing. 'That doesn't sound too good,' commented Rocco as they skipped across the marble floor inside.

'I don't think he's cross,' said Gabriele, ignoring the remark about the cough. 'Quite the opposite, actually.'

'How do you know?'

'Because when he's angry he stops patting me on the bum when he walks past. And this morning he gave me a double pit-pat, so I think everything's all right.'

'Thank God for your bum,' said Rocco and they both laughed, much to the disgust of the sacristan who was mopping the floor of a side chapel. For all the hoo-ha about these boys' singing and the increasing reputation of the choir, the old sacristan disapproved of cocky young men thinking they knew everything and prancing all over his church as if they owned it.

They arrived at de Luca's door, knocked and, without waiting for an answer, entered.

'Ah, the legendary Tomassini,' teased de Luca as Gabriele came in first. 'What an honour and privilege for a humble choirmaster like me to have two such budding starlets here at the same time.' The friends looked at each other but it was Gabriele, as ever, who caved in to giggling. '*Basta, basta,*' chided de Luca gently, and bid the boys sit down opposite his desk.

'Well,' he began, and picked up a small glass paper-weight to play with as he talked – he always availed himself of some prop or other to occupy the irrepressible energy of his fingers, and the floor of the room was littered with the remains of pencils snapped at moments of intense agitation. 'I won't deny that it hasn't been good for the choir that you're doing so well. But you!' he pointed a pencil at Gabriele. 'You, with your Donizetti escapades at Avellino.' Gabriele looked dumbfounded. 'Doing lead roles in operas in your spare time! You must be getting quite rich.'

'No, sir. They don't pay much.'

'Cheeky swine. Did you think for a minute that I wouldn't find out about it? When was your last perform-ance?'

'Last night, sir.'

'Last night!' roared de Luca, flinging the pencil into the air and raising both elbows as if to haul himself from his chair in order to strike the boy. 'With a cold in the throat like that! How are you going to sing in church tomorrow?'

'I've known worse. I'll be all right.'

De Luca tutted and fell back in his chair. 'The utter

idiocy of the young. And you!' He now pointed at Rocco. 'What about you? Tell me how much warbling *you've* been up to outside the choir this year.' Whereas Gabriele, caught between a guilty conscience and an irresistible sense of fun, had blustered almost charmingly, Rocco looked straight into de Luca's eyes without smiling and answered, 'Very little, sir. And at a word from you I will stop altogether. The choir is my whole life.' His sincerity was as cool as a moonlit stone and it instantly flattened the humour in the air.

'Yes, yes, I know,' answered the choirmaster, his smile wilting. 'And I do appreciate it, Signor Campobello, I do.' Rocco looked at him expectantly, longing for something more, perhaps a compliment or an endorsement of his indispensability, or, better still, a spark of the same affectionate wit that spiced the choirmaster's interactions with Gabriele; but nothing of the sort was forthcoming.

'Now! To the matter in hand.' De Luca smacked his palms together and leapt out of his chair, but then paused and eyed the boys for a moment. 'What I am about to say,' he continued, 'is contrary to the interests of the choir and therefore probably against my own better judgement. I'm not entirely convinced I should be saying it at all, but, beneath this dusty old cassock – well, you don't really want to know what's beneath this dusty old cassock, but let me say that you sit before a man who has not entirely forgotten how exciting it is to be young, talented and ambitious.' Gabriele looked puzzled, but Rocco's eyes had lit up with intrigue.

De Luca, frowning, as if suddenly stalled by doubts, walked over to the window of his room. There was not much of a view; the street outside was narrow and the brickwork of the old building opposite heavy and windowless. A bronze church bell, housed behind Romanesque pillars high up in the adjacent campanile, began to clang loudly, and its resonance buzzed through the thick stone walls of the choirmaster's study as it had done for centuries. It was a sound so familiar to de Luca that he did not even blink. He had occupied this room for nearly three decades, and for him its dark, faintly scholarly, sepia-edged ambience held none of the mystique that proved so intoxicating for the young choristers who came to visit.

'You may have heard me speak of a certain Signor Graziani,' he said, still looking out at the grey rusticated wall on the other side of the street. Gabriele looked blank and shook his head, but Rocco's brows tightened. 'He is a kind man,' added de Luca with untypical sincerity. 'He has given generously to the Ospedale these past few years. Yes, he is a kind – and wealthy – man. But more importantly for you, he is a man with connections.' He eyed the boys closely. 'It could be an opportunity for you, gentlemen.'

'What sort of opportunity?' asked Rocco.

De Luca hesitated before continuing. 'You may have heard something about the government's plans to – how do they describe it? – to "elevate" the southern states, economically, culturally, socially. All part of their grand scheme to bring the north and south together, to heal the scars of unification. They plan to tear down this, rebuild that. And . . .' he returned to his chair with a sigh, 'they plan to give us a taste of their great munificence by hosting a festival here. An opera festival, at the Teatro Mercadante. They are sending a man from Milan – a well-connected man; apparently his brother is on the

219

board of directors at La Scala opera house.' Both boys'
eyes opened wide. 'Yes, I thought you'd be impressed.
Well, this man is here in Naples right now, and in touch
with our benefactor, Signor Graziani. The search is on
to find local singers to fill the ranks of this new festival
company. Graziani sent word to me at the Ospedale, and
I, though I may live to regret it to my dying day, sent
word back with the names of my two most promising
tenors.'

The boys looked at each other before Gabriele fell to
his knees with a characteristically overblown display of
feeling. He grabbed the end of de Luca's cassock with
both fists in a manner that betrayed a shade too much
humour. 'Maestro,' he cried, but was prevented from saying anything else by a sharp clip across the hair from de
Luca.

'Stop it, you idiot,' snapped the choirmaster. Rocco
sat still and said nothing, but kept his eyes pinned on
de Luca, waiting for him to continue. 'So the situation
is this: tomorrow, as we all know, is the feast of San
Gennaro. Our church will be almost empty because
everyone will troop off to the Duomo yet again to
hear the priests declare that, yes, the old saint's blood
has miraculously liquefied itself on the right day once
more. Very obliging of him, I'm sure.' Even Gabriele was
shocked by the undisguised blasphemy, and drew breath
sharply. 'I'm sorry,' said de Luca, 'but as I was saying, our
church will be empty, and we can manage without you.
I've arranged instead for the two of you to go and sing
for this big cheese up at the San Martino monastery. A
sort of private service, though a few of the monks will be
there as well. Our guest from Milan and Signor Graziani
will send word to you afterwards. I don't know, they may

want to hear you sing something operatic as well.' He turned to Rocco. 'I know opera is not really your thing, and if you don't want to go—'

'No, sir – that is – I'll find something, sir. I do some opera with Signora Signorelli from time to time.' On hearing what he knew to be a grand understatement on the part of his friend, Gabriele could not help raising his eyebrows.

'Good, good,' de Luca muttered with resignation, and gave them each a celebratory little glass of amaretto liqueur before sending them on their way. As they left, he caught Gabriele by the arm and pulled him over. 'Mind that cough,' he said quietly. 'If it gets any worse we can arrange for you to sing to this man another time.' But Gabriele gave him one of his disarmingly warm smiles and brushed off the suggestion. 'Just don't over-sing,' added de Luca with a whisper of seriousness in his voice. 'You've plenty of time.'

The boys walked around the cloister to the west of the church in order to get out by a side exit. They were silent while they digested this latest news.

In the end, Gabriele spoke. 'De Luca doesn't even know how good you really are. No one does. You're hiding yourself away. He's never heard you sing any opera! Why don't you go and talk to all the local theatre companies, like me?'

'Well, this is my chance, isn't it?'

'I bet you won't sing out properly, just like you never sing out properly in church.'

'Church is hardly the place to show off how big your voice is.'

'Why not? I do.'

'We're not the same.'

'You have to get yourself heard. How else will you ever get to New York with me?'

Rocco tutted impatiently. 'Maybe my voice isn't as strong as yours, all right? I don't want to wear myself out. The serenades are enough for me. In fact I've got one tonight I could do without. I've been giving singing lessons to the Ospedale boys all morning and I'd prefer a good night's sleep.'

'What's the money like?'

'For the serenade? Good this time, actually.'

'How much? I'll do it,' said Gabriele eagerly. Serenading back-street belles on behalf of eager young Romeos – who would step out of the shadows at the moment of conquest – was a safe and lucrative little earner.

'Twenty lire.'

'Serious? Who's the millionaire? Or is the pussy he's after worth that bit extra?'

'Haven't seen her. Don't worry, I'll manage. You shouldn't sing with that cold. Especially if we've got this thing tomorrow morning.'

'You must be joking,' laughed Gabriele, who never turned down the opportunity of easy money. He sometimes sang himself hoarse to fill his pockets, but no sooner was the cash earned than he had spent it all. 'I'll be fine. Let me do it.'

'Sure?'

'Dead sure.' The deal was struck. Rocco, who was actually being paid fifteen lire for the serenade but knew that the extra five would secure Gabriele's interest, handed over the fee and kissed his friend on the cheek. 'And don't forget about going to see your Papa,' Gabriele added predictably before they parted. He would cajole

Rocco about this almost every time they met.

'I saw him today. He was lying in wait for me in the piazza.'

'Serious? Good. Did you have a coffee together? Catch up a bit?'

'Not enough time.'

Gabriele pursed his lips. It was against his nature to be confrontational, but his disapproval was clear.

'Don't go on at me about it,' Rocco said. 'You don't understand. I can't be half this and half that. I'm a musician now. I've moved on.'

'No one's asking you to be a blacksmith, and he's not asking you to, either. All he wants is to see you from time to time. Just because you're a musician doesn't mean you have to be heartless.'

'I'll see more of him when I'm really on my feet as a singer.'

Gabriele stopped walking and stood still for a moment, looking down at the paving stones. His face was uncharacteristically solemn.

'What is it?' asked Rocco.

'It's you.'

'Me? What?'

Gabriele laughed at having to state the obvious. 'You must have noticed.'

'Noticed what?'

'The difference.'

'I'm different? Is that what you're saying?'

'It's not fun any more, is it? The singing, our plans for the future, all of it. We used to have a laugh, but it's become something heavy.'

Rocco thought for a moment. 'Is that how you feel?' he said.

'Me? I'm still having a good time, but I don't think you are.'

'Come on,' said Rocco. 'I'm just beginning to really enjoy it.'

'Really? Honestly?'

Rocco hid his impatience. He always had to stoop down mentally in order to meet Gabriele's primitive perspective of things face to face. Gabriele never saw the bigger picture, and it was beginning to get a little annoying. 'Truly,' he said. 'I've never been so happy in my life.'

'OK, then,' said Gabriele, smiling again. 'I'm glad for you. Just let your Papa know. Explain it all to him. He'll understand, he's a good man.'

They walked out into the street, and tossed a few cents at the beggar who always bided his time at the church cloister's side entrance. The wretch would squat on a step for most of the day, scraping a razor across his marble-smooth chin while observing the result of his labours from different angles in a little girl's hand-held mirror. His cheeks had turned deep pink with the interminable attention over the years, and no one had fathomed why he was never quite satisfied with the shave, but he seemed happy enough to carry on and on, and would catch the eye of passers-by with a beady look reflected in the glass of his pretty little mirror. The sight of him always amused Rocco and Gabriele, and they liked to give him something when they walked by. It made them feel like young men of consequence and prospects; it put distance between themselves and the very bottom rung of the ladder. This latest opportunity proposed by de Luca promised to widen the gap still further, perhaps irreversibly.

Flush with the notion that a degree of eminence now lay within their reach, they decided there and then to go and buy a pair of bowler hats for themselves, and perhaps a cigarette holder each. It would add swagger to their manner and impress the man from Milan.

Rocco had never been much of an athlete, but the following morning he skipped energetically up the long stairway that zigzagged from the heart of the old city up to the Vomero, the mount on which the monastery of San Martino was precipitously constructed. He emerged exhilarated, sweating and breathless on to the celebrated terrace esplanade at the summit, and pulled off his bowler hat. His hair was plastered wet across his forehead and he gripped a bunch of rolled up sheet music between hot, swollen fingers. He would have to wait for Gabriele, who was decidedly sluggish this morning. Slumping on to a nearby bench – one of several invariably occupied by courting couples after sunset – he looked out across Naples, taking in the vast curve of the bay and, further away, the pale blue rise of Mount Vesuvius. He had started to despise his fellow Neapolitans for taking such pride in their homeland. He shared none of their affection for it, nor had he anything but contempt for the shiploads of touring foreigners who wandered around, gazing open-mouthed, when they disembarked down at the docks. All Rocco could think about, as he looked out across the domes, rooftops and streets of his throbbing home city, was how best and quickest he could escape the place.

Gabriele had found the climb an ordeal and stopped to catch his breath several times on the way. After a particularly bad fit of coughing, he looked up and saw that Rocco had disappeared around a corner up ahead, and so decided to slow his pace. It was unlike him to trail behind but he did not feel great. His cold had deteriorated and he had barely got any sleep the night before, thanks to the tireless antics of his romantic patron, whose attempts at seduction had been met with nothing but closed shutters and sliding bolts.

Rocco suggested Gabriele should reconsider singing today, but Gabriele cut him short rather sharply, and so Rocco shrugged and let it pass. Very occasionally, there were times when a danger seemed to light up Gabriele's eyes, and it was best then just to leave him be. Besides, Rocco wasn't feeling talkative either; he was wrapped up in his own thoughts.

The boys were allowed into the monastery in good time and were offered some fruit and water, which made them feel like celebrities already. The huge and well-endowed *certosa* of San Martino, with its elegant courtyards, formal gardens and dazzling clear light, was a refuge of peace and order after the turmoil of the city below. It was Rocco's first visit here and he liked what he saw, especially the glimpse of monastic life. The disciplined routine that underlay the monks' activities made the Ospedale's daily schedule seem almost flabby by comparison.

The two friends were robed in cleanly pressed surplices with lace edging, then led to the interior of the church and installed in a pair of choir pews half hidden behind the main altar. Incense wafted through the chancel to the sound of the monks quietly shuffling to their places in the nave. Rocco felt comfortably calm in the confines of his box pew. His hands rested on his thighs, and his feet were neatly parallel within the black and white squared patterning of the marble flagstones.

226

Gabriele, however, seemed unable to sit still for an instant. He was directly opposite Rocco, and forever fiddling and sniffing; he leafed anxiously through his music, and strained to get a view, past the altar, of the two men in the congregation that they were seeking to impress.

Rocco did not see the men, nor did he attempt to, but when his moment approached, rose quietly to his feet. There were three bars of organ prelude to be played; his neck was relaxed, the muscles within toned and poised. He looked up, drew breath, tipped his brow forward, and allowed his voice to pierce the air. His eyes were peculiarly sightless, and, as the phrase grew, they narrowed with the intensity of expression and arced slowly around the area of the chancel. He lowered the sheet of music out of sight; it was unnecessary, because his memory was watertight; and not once did he entertain the smallest doubt that he would get through without a blemish. That was the key, as Signora Signorelli forever carped, because even a small grain of doubt could crack the edifice from the foundations upwards. He gave a delivery of consummate control and poise, and as he neared the final notes, he glanced across the aisle to make sure Gabriele was ready to take over the line, on cue.

Gabriele stood up as Rocco took his seat. A similar prelude of a few bars paved the way for his first entry, but something was wrong. Rocco could see that he was struggling – either a trace of phlegm that he could not dislodge in his throat, or some other hidden impediment. Rocco sensed that it might be a sudden collapse of confidence, but whatever the cause, it was clear Gabriele was not going to make it. The colour drained from his face and a look of blind panic took hold of him. With just a couple of crotchet beats to go before he was supposed to float in on a gentle high F, his eyes flashed across the aisle at Rocco in a desperate appeal. Rocco stood up quickly and took over the vocal line seamlessly, but he could see that Gabriele had turned to one side and was stifling coughs into a clenched fist, his shoulders rounded and his head hanging.

It was over within fifteen minutes and the two boys, along with the clergy and assorted acolytes, processed away to one of the elegant vestry rooms behind the church.

For once in his life, Gabriele had nothing to say, and they changed their clothes in silence. Gabriele's complexion was ashen, and every now and then he closed his eyes tight and seemed to shake his head. Rocco, holding his own elation in check, wondered what he could say to help, but before he had the chance, Gabriele's mouth tightened and he looked up sharply. 'I'm off,' he said.

'Right away? Don't you want to explain to these guys about your cold, or something? Maybe they could hear you another time.'

'No. I can't face them.'

'What is it?'

'I don't know,' Gabriele faltered, pulling on his jacket. 'I . . . I just have to go now. I suppose you'd like me to thank you for saving the day.' Rocco held his hands open and puffed into the air.

'Was it your cold?' he asked.

'Maybe. Maybe not.' He was fumbling with his collar and fighting to get his tie straight. He wanted out and away without more ado. 'I just couldn't do it, all right? Why should I explain myself to you?'

228

'You don't have to explain yourself,' returned Rocco, slightly needled. Didn't he deserve a little credit for stopping the performance falling apart completely? 'But you've sung much more difficult things, in front of lots more people. And with terrible hangovers.' He hoped the lighter note might ease the atmosphere.

'What would you know about it? Eh? Always so careful and perfect.'

'This isn't about me.' Rocco was stung. 'It's not me who cocked up.'

'What's that supposed to mean?' said Gabriele turning on him.

'You know what it means. You're reckless with your voice. A man can't spend all his money and still expect to find something in the bank when he needs it.'

'Oh. A philosopher now as well, are we? You always think you're so bloody clever.'

'You're just not usually as feeble as this. Grow up. Stay here for a minute and explain things to these men.'

Gabriele looked at him with a sudden fury.

'Let's see who the feeble one is, shall we?' he said, advancing on Rocco. 'Shall we do it here or go outside?'

'Don't be stupid. You could mess up the biggest chance we've ever had. Everything we've dreamt about.'

'Stupid, eh?' said Gabriele, and shot a fist out straight towards his friend, just beneath the heart; but Rocco was stronger and much bigger. He twisted aside, raised a hand and caught Gabriele's fist in his palm, as if catching a hard-thrown ball. While Gabriele was reeling with surprise, Rocco quickly brought up his other hand and slapped him around the cheek. 'Get a grip,' he said.

Gabriele stifled a roar and wheeled away from Rocco, who stood rooted to the spot, his size and solidity hiding the sense of shock he felt. Grabbing his hat and music, Gabriele ran for the door. He glanced at Rocco for an instant before going. There was a tempest in his eyes that could have been a desperate cry for help or the start of a blood feud, it was impossible to say which. Neither of them said anything else, and Gabriele ran out.

Minutes passed by, and Rocco waited alone in the sacristy, as he'd been instructed. He sat in one of the richly inlaid and partitioned pew seats that lined the walls of the long room. His thumping heart made his hands judder and his head nod minutely. Above him, on the vaulting, opulent frescos, opened up a celestial paradise populated by luxuriating cherubs and voluptuous semi-divines. Rocco felt small indeed in the midst of such grandeur.

There was a piano positioned on one side of the sacred chamber, and he wondered whether it had been brought in for the audition, though, as time dragged on, he convinced himself that the gentlemen had heard enough and were not interested. He looked at the new bowler hat on the seat next to him, and it seemed a ludicrous thing lying there, puffed up and cocky.

Just at that moment an ornate door at the far end of the room opened. Three men came in, together with a boy of about ten years old. First through the door was one of the resident monks, a middle-aged cleric who possessed a face of Gothic horror severity and was dressed in a monochrome habit with a plain wooden cross hanging at his neck. Next was the short, bespectacled Emilio Graziani, whom Rocco now vaguely recognized, having seen him once or twice at the Ospedale. He was holding the hand of the boy, who seemed earnest but comfortable in adult company and observed the proceedings

230

without saying a word. Graziani's face was moulded in an expression of weary surprise, and could not have contrasted more strongly with that of the final person to come in. Tall, fair and wreathed in smiles, the man from Milan pushed past the others and made straight for Rocco, hand outstretched. He was younger than Rocco expected and spoke with an educated, north Italian accent. The effervescent stream of compliments that flowed from him took the young singer by surprise, and he stared back, lost for words. The man said he was particularly impressed by the way Rocco had shouldered the burden of his colleague's unexpected incapacity.

'What did happen to the other lad, by the way?' he asked

'I'm not sure.'

'Has he gone?'

'Yes, sir.'

'Well, you showed great professionalism.'

'And friendship,' interjected Graziani, leaning forward and waving an index finger. 'You saved your friend an embarrassment. A man who stands by his friends in moments of need is a man to trust.'

Rocco was then asked to sing something operatic, as expected, and he chose Alfredo's pleasantly lyrical and unchallenging aria from *La Traviata*. 'Ah!' the Milanese gentleman exclaimed with delight at the choice, but did not yet explain why, and leant back in his chair to listen. The aria went reasonably well, Rocco thought, but was followed by a long silence. He smiled rather nervously at the blank faces of the people in front of him, and, assuming that he was way off the mark, now longed for the ordeal to be over. It was the man from Milan who broke the silence.

'My God,' he said quietly, which made the monk blink. Graziani was nodding slowly. The man from Milan looked sideways at him. 'Where did you find this boy?' Graziani did not reply, but raised his eyebrows slightly and kept his gaze fixed on the singer.

Rocco was asked if he would like to try something bigger, perhaps the famous aria from the new opera by Puccini, but he declined the offer, saying that he didn't think his voice was sufficiently developed – an answer that seemed to please the man from Milan greatly. One could tell an intelligent artist, he said, by the degree of his restraint and self-knowledge.

Rocco's choice of the *La Traviata* aria as an audition piece proved to be astonishingly fortuitous. The young Milanese impresario leant forward in his chair, eyes ablaze. He was a man who liked to follow his heart and take a gamble if the potential rewards were great. The matter of next year's festival in Naples was shelved for the moment as he put forward another proposal. 'I have a production of *La Traviata*, as it happens, on hold in Milan right at this moment. We were due to open in –' he counted fingers – 'in eight days' time. But, as fate would have it, our lead tenor has walked out and the understudy is in hospital. Appendicitis. It's not a major production, but it would be a shame for everyone if it didn't open on time. Would you be interested? Could you learn it in time?'

Rocco did not even pause to consider, or smile, or give any indication of the massive swell he felt within at the man's words. 'Of course,' he replied calmly; and then, as if by some instinct knowing that Signor Graziani's role in this business was going to be more than that of mere conduit or observer, he turned to him and said, 'There's

232

just the matter of the church, and Choirmaster de Luca.'

Graziani eyed him closely through his thick lenses, as if trying to catch the scent of what lay hidden beneath the surface of this young man. 'Would you like to be released from your duties at the church, then?'

'Of course, sir.'

'You wouldn't feel guilty about leaving the choir with so little warning? Letting down the choirmaster?'

'Not for an opportunity like this.'

'And do you feel able to handle the challenge?'

'Without question. Alfredo is the least demanding of Maestro Verdi's tenor roles.'

'Oh! So you know the repertoire?' asked the man from Milan gleefully.

'Yes, sir. I spend all my spare time studying the great operas and singing what I can. I know *La Traviata* pretty much already.' It was not true, but he could make it true in a couple of days, even if it meant staying up all night to memorize the words. 'I won't let you down.' The man clapped, clenched both fists heartily and looked to the heavens with delight. The monk, sitting behind, blinked again at the noise of the clapping, but otherwise remained motionless and did not take his eyes off Rocco.

'This choirmaster,' the impresario now began.

'Don't you worry about him,' cut in Graziani. 'There will be no complications as regards Signor de Luca. I'll see to it personally.' He looked at Rocco and the corners of his mouth almost formed a smile.

'And the other boy? Your friend. Should I listen to him before I go back to Milan? If he can't make it today, it will have to be tomorrow. After that I'm gone.'

'What do you think, Signor Campobello?' added Graziani, and the tone of his question implied that

233

Rocco's answer would be weighed with as much scrutiny as the quality of his singing. The three men, and the child, now waited for Rocco's reply, and this time he did hesitate a fraction before answering. A tumultuous battle was pitched, fought out and resolved in his mind during that moment, but the steadiness of his gaze did not flicker. When he spoke his voice was clear and sure.

'I think you'd be wasting your time,' he said.

'You don't think he has the right voice, or what?' asked the man from Milan.

'He sings too hard and does not know his limitations. He's on a disaster course.'

'But I hear he has already made a good impression in some provincial theatres. I mean, I'm hardly asking for the new Tamagno. I just want some reliable soloists for a little festival.'

'Gabriele Tomassini can't be relied on.' Rocco's words came quickly, his tone almost impertinently direct for a young man in such eminent company. 'He fell apart in the church just now. I don't like to say it but it's my honest opinion. You can take it or leave it.'

'I agree,' chipped in Graziani. 'The man had his chance to sing for us today. If he can't even clear that little hurdle, what would he be like when he's really under pressure?' Turning to Rocco, he added, 'And you're a brave lad to tell the truth like that. It's not easy to turn one's back on a friend.' Rocco just looked down at his lap.

'We do have to find good singers for the festival,' persisted the man from Milan in a last-ditch attempt, 'and the choirmaster definitely gave us reason to believe—'

'With respect,' interrupted Rocco, looking up again, 'there is a difference between being a good choirboy and singing opera.' The words were out. It was done. There was no going back.

'I see,' replied the man, clearly a little disappointed, but then he looked up and smiled. 'Well, never mind. It's good to know. We have a number of others to hear, but sadly all too few tenors, as usual.' For the second time in his life, Rocco heard, as if from a distant locked chamber in his mind, the sound of cackled rejoicing; but in reality a rather peculiar silence had descended on the sacristy. The monk, sitting behind, continued to watch Rocco closely. His eyes were a wasteland of pity and regret.

In a few moments it was over. Hands were shaken, thanks exchanged and arrangements made to pick Rocco up from the Ospedale early the next morning. He must pack and make himself ready with everything he would need for a three-month spell in Milan. All expenses would be taken care of, and a generous salary offered; but first, it was proposed that a haircut would be appropriate, a matter which Signor Graziani said could be arranged within the hour.

Before they parted, Graziani wanted a few private words with Rocco, and he told his son to remain seated where he was until given permission to move. The child watched without blinking from his chair, though he could not hear what was being said. He saw his father place a hand lightly on Rocco's shoulder and nod his head as he spoke. Then the hand was lifted and cupped around the young man's cheek for a moment before Graziani turned and walked back, stone-faced, to collect his son.

In the event, the promised opera festival in Naples never materialised; the munificence of the national government, despite its best intentions, proved more idealistic than practical; but it did not affect Rocco, who achieved immediate notoriety following his stunning debut in *La Traviata* at one of Milan's lesser houses. He did not return to Naples for another twelve years, and by then he was already a national celebrity, well-dressed and slightly portly, with a fashionable hairstyle and a waxed moustache. He was never seen in ordinary life without a cane, which he would sport rather elegantly, while giving the impression in public, rightly or wrongly, that it helped him overcome the inconvenience of an unspecific injury.

Chapter 17

1926

It was to be no ordinary opening night at Naples' Teatro San Carlo. The huge old auditorium was filled to capacity with an assemblage of rare social distinction; only those of sufficient nobility and influence had qualified for an invitation. Some might have said that the scheduled opera, Girodano's *Andrea Chénier*, was a little too modern for the taste of the elderly patrician element in the audience, but this made no difference to the atmosphere of excitement which fizzed through the air of the great theatre's cavity that night as if bubbling from the top of a giant champagne glass. The treat that lay in store was unparalleled in anyone's memory, and it had little to do with the evening's musical programme – though this, in itself, promised great riches, because it featured the dazzling American soprano, Josephine Carter, and the no less celebrated Irish tenor, Donal Mulligan. But the principal attraction of this evening, and also the reason why an enormous crowd had gathered outside, choking the city centre all the way from the Castel Nuovo to the far reaches of the Piazza del Plebiscito, was the promised attendance in person, as a fellow audience member, of the world's foremost opera star, Naples' own son, the stupendous Maestro Rocco Campobello, his first official public appearance since the incident that threatened his life six months earlier.

According to the dictates of a printed sheet that accompanied every crested invitation, the audience of grandees should be assembled and have taken their seats a full fifteen minutes before the curtain was due to go up. Uniformed stewards were under strict instructions to close all doors after this deadline and bar access to any latecomers, regardless of rank.

The buzz of anticipation settled of its own accord to an excited burble by the time the orchestra took its place in the pit. This was followed by the arrival of the entire company's chorus in front of the scarlet curtains, together with the evening's conductor, who was greeted with a respectable statement of applause but no more; spectators were saving their palms for better things to come.

The curtains then parted slightly to allow the prima donna herself, Miss Carter, through to the front of the stage. This was an unexpected treat, and a whirr of approval rose from the stalls. She was in full costume, ready for the role she would shortly assume, but her business right now was ceremonial. With all the grace and poise for which she was beloved by opera-goers from Buenos Aires to Moscow, she smiled and delivered a few well-chosen words in tribute to the colossus who was about to join them in the theatre, whom she counted, she said, amongst her dearest friends. On cue, at the close of her short speech, the conductor raised his baton and brought the chorus in *en masse* with a first *fortissimo* bar of unaccompanied ensemble. It was the final section of Verdi's grand march from *Aida*, chosen specially to honour the entrance of the great Campobello; and it was a glitteringly appropriate choice for the occasion, most people in the audience agreed.

As the first crashing orchestral chord followed the chorus' opening phrase, every person in the auditorium, elderly aristocrats, rich industrialists and thrusting young politicians alike, rose from their seats and turned to face the rear of the great horseshoe curve of galleries. Six extravagantly gilded tiers looked down on the bowl of the stalls, plum in the middle of which, topped with a gargantuan crown, rich with ornate plaster-work and canopied with golden drapes, was the as yet unpeopled royal box, a sumptuous blaze of crimson velvet and gilt.

Meanwhile, hidden from the audience, at the top of the marble stairway that led straight from the theatre's front entrance, a small party of formally attired people waited quietly outside the door of the royal box for their cue to move. They could hear the music, muffled though it was by partition doors. Leading the group was the retiring director of the San Carlo Opera, Don Fabrizzi, an eminent and courtly figure, with a gold and enamel cross hanging by a silk ribbon just beneath his bow tie. In his role as a bastion of southern Italian culture for more than four decades, Don Fabrizzi had entertained and befriended many of Europe's princes and rulers, and carried himself with the refinement of one accustomed to mixing in the highest circles. His wife, Signora Fabrizzi was also there, standing with the Conte and Contessa di Postillo, an ancient couple who belonged to one of the most distinguished aristocratic families in Naples. Alongside them was the tall and moustached Pompeo Tedeschi, local secretary of the Fascist party, whom Molly had last seen in the great glazed arcade when he took the salute of the blackshirted children's platoon.

Next to Tedeschi, and standing with Molly, were father and son, Emilio and Bruno Graziani. Molly had at one time rather liked Bruno, whom she saw as a kind of efficient, well-dressed business executive, someone capable of handling personnel with cool discipline and commanding their respect. But, ever since hearing the news that he had returned to Naples to take over running the family's affairs so that his father could retire, and particularly in the light of her recent encounter with Don Graziani in the Galleria, she regarded Bruno with caution. When she compared him to the aristocratic Don Fabrizzi, whose directorship of the San Carlo Bruno had set his sights on attaining, she could not help but think that it would be a travesty if he got the job. Even if Bruno proved to be less sinister than his father, an institution like this opera house needed a man of breeding and distinction at its head, such as Don Fabrizzi; someone who could shroud his expertise in elegant conversational flippancy and give the impression – though everyone knew otherwise – that he was a gentleman amateur. Bruno Graziani, for all his organizational competence, was just not cut from the right cloth.

Standing on his own to one side of Molly was young Amedeo Tomassini, his handsomeness amplified by the tail suit and starched white shirt, a form of dress to which he looked born. He had recently been introduced to the party as Maestro Campobello's pupil, and was every inch the promising young gentleman, head held high, hands tucked behind his back, pleasantly modest and remarkably at ease despite the eminent company. Few present, other than Molly and her husband, knew that the credit for Amedeo's princely bearing belonged largely to Pietro Boldoni, who had been giving him daily lessons in deportment and etiquette. The results were impressive to the untrained eye. Amedeo had adapted comfortably to his new life, and demonstrated that he was not merely a gifted singer, but sharp of wit, a fast learner, and surprisingly charismatic. All who came into his orbit were charmed, though Molly thought privately that the rags to riches experience for the lad was a sham and would probably end in tears for all concerned; but it offered amusing sport while it lasted, and certainly seemed the right medicine for Rocco at the moment, which was all that mattered.

Near to Amedeo, but standing back a little now in order to exchange what appeared to be urgent words with his assistant, was the Maestro himself. Boldoni was somewhat out of breath, having moments before pushed his way through the mass of photographers and spectators outside and skipped nimbly up the carpeted stairway of the opera house straight to the side of his employer with the news.

'Did she give a reason?' whispered Campobello. 'Was the dress not right?'

'It had nothing to do with the dress,' responded Boldoni, eyes darting around as he checked the others were not listening in. His instinct told him there was already a need for discretion about this business. Tedeschi glanced across at him rather tersely and looked at his watch. 'She wouldn't budge. And I don't blame her. She can't be expected to want to mix with people like this. The boy might be young enough to change himself, but she must feel—' The opera chorus could be heard at full roar, beyond the doors.

'Perhaps I should go to her. I might persuade her otherwise,' mused Rocco.

'With all respect,' fired back Boldoni under his breath, 'that would be inappropriate.'

Don Graziani looked at them with one of his forced smiles. 'Is everything all right?' he asked languorously.

'Perfectly, *zio*,' said Rocco.

'Thirty seconds,' said a house official and signalled to two liveried attendants who stood on either side of the double doors of the royal box. They made themselves ready by placing gloved hands on the bronze doorknobs ready to swing them open.

'I'll see to it that the seating arrangement for dinner is put right,' Boldoni said quietly, and Rocco nodded, allowing him to go. Boldoni was not included in the director's august party but would watch the performance from an adjacent box.

'Fifteen seconds.'

They all stood in silence and Pompeo Tedeschi raised his chin imperiously in preparation.

The doors were opened and the immense music flooded through to them. Rocco held out a hand for Molly to lead the way, and she, smiling broadly, walked smoothly forward into the box. The subsequent eruption from the audience quite blocked out the sound of the orchestra and chorus. It was followed immediately by a great arc of animal sound, like a rainbow, as every voice let out a whoop of surprise at the transformation in Rocco's looks, but this evaporated quickly in the ensuing cheers of delight. The conductor laid down his baton and turned to join in the applause.

Campobello stood at the centre of it all, surrounded by the gorgeous display of colour and wealth. His head was shaven smooth, his beard close-cropped and white. From where he looked out, the great space ballooned away on either side as if encircled by him personally, bound within his own embrace. He was the hub, and they were looking to him with humble gratitude and devotion. He gazed out at the ocean of faces. This was the meaning of success, he pondered, and the novelty of it, after six months of reclusiveness, startled him. This was his great reward, everything he had supposedly yearned for when he had stood, all those years ago, young and defiant, before the openness of the bay, while the sun sank in the sky and the *mozzonari* searched the ground at his feet for cigarette ends.

The audience continued to applaud, hands raised high for emphasis. There was something unnervingly devotional about their faces, a kind of expectant rapture, like that of pilgrims arrived at their destination, but Rocco neither asked for their supplication nor wanted it. Were the Church's great acts of pageantry likewise founded on so empty a premise: little more than the pumped-up aspirations of the hordes who filled the pews, nothing to do with God at all? These people, like the faithful, hungered for some message, a sign or gift of grace in return for their devotion. But whatever entity they were willing forth from him was absent, had never been more than a grand invention in the first place. Like their notion of God himself, the recipient of their grandest displays: a figure dreamt up to provide them with their own answer to their own problems.

They would have clapped on and on. He nodded to them, turning his gaze slowly from left to right, feeling their goodwill like a breeze on his face. He was not so parsimonious as to deprive them of a morsel of what they yearned for, and so, tapping a small grain of showmanship that lingered within, he translated it, as it were, to plentiful food for the masses, and in messianic fashion raised both hands in the air to satisfy their hunger. It was a gesture that brought a renewed and tremendous eruption of cheering. Tears flowed freely, and the frail felt their knees weaken with emotion as they fell back to their seats.

It was left to the conductor to move the evening on, and, resuming his professional pose, he brought the orchestra in with a new tune. It was 'Giovinezza', the bouncing, jaunty march that had become the Fascist party's unofficial anthem. In the royal box Pompeo Tedeschi stood to attention and gazed towards distant imaginary vistas, while a few elderly members of the audience sat down in silent protest that this song was more often than not nowadays played in preference to the 'Marcia Reale'.

Lighter applause followed the final chord of 'Giovinezza', at which point Tedeschi leant across to Rocco and added quietly, 'We all hope you might record that marvellous song when you return to the studio shortly.'

'Indeed?'

'Let me just say, I've heard it mentioned in high circles. The highest circle, in actual fact.' He hoped this last, almost conspiratorial remark would ignite a show of enthusiasm in Campobello, but the tenor did not respond. 'You have a natural gift with the public,' continued Tedeschi. 'I am reminded of the joy and affection that greets our Prime Minister's speeches.' Again, Rocco made no reply, but nodded to the others in the box that it was time to sit down, and took his own seat between Molly and Amedeo. The audience simmered down at last, and after a few moments of silence the performance proper began.

They were not long into the opera before Molly leant over to whisper something to her husband in the darkness.

'So, your signora has not come.'

'Apparently not.'

'Is that why you were looking so upset with Pietro before we entered? We all thought some catastrophe had happened.'

Rocco did not answer.

'I am disappointed,' Molly added after a pause, not taking her eyes off the stage. 'I wondered when I might be given the opportunity of meeting her. It appears I am to be deprived once again.'

'No one is depriving you of anything,' muttered Rocco. 'She had reasons of her own for not coming. The world does not entirely revolve around you at all times.'

'Hah!' laughed Molly. That was rich – her expletive was supposed to imply – coming from so stellar a figure as her husband. But her exasperation at his apparent hypocrisy felt hollow, because it wasn't really true any more. It fitted more closely the Rocco of former times, in the days when he was egocentric and oblivious of others. She had not quite abandoned the habit of using the old accusation if the need arose, because it had always been a trump card, but she realized it was irrelevant nowadays. She would have to devise new weapons if she wanted to defend her lines effectively.

But, if truth were told, weaponry against her husband was the last thing on her mind at the moment. In fact, one word from him and she would happily call a truce on all former grudges and let animosity dissolve. Indeed, she was prepared to go much further, as far as it was possible to go, but he seemed uninterested, and this was at the heart of her restlessness right now. Rocco had changed, for sure, but she felt no more welcome in his territory than before. He was no longer unkind or confrontational, but the chemistry she had hoped would spring to life as she witnessed his spirits rise from the ashes, remained utterly inert. It was doubly galling because of the spark of carnal desire that had ignited within her in the wake of his recovery. She had tried to ignore it, but it had a peculiar energy of its own, and refused to be masked. It brought to mind, with a kind of bitter-sweet nostalgia, their first weeks together, when they had played out quite well the part of passionate newly-weds and persuaded themselves that their marriage was going to be a normal one. Within a year, the deterioration beneath the surface had been impossible to ignore, and their behaviour towards one another likewise soured. The charade of decorum gave way to harsh words and quick tempers which became too prevalent to allow a continuance of physical intimacy. It suited them both, at the time, to move to separate bedrooms.

But the illness this year, together with Rocco's enforced period of rest and their move to Naples, had brought another change of climate between them. She did not want to flatter her husband with an overstatement of warmth, of course, but would have liked him at least to notice her taking every opportunity to touch his hand or kiss him on the cheek when they greeted. It followed that he had not, as she had hoped, suggested a thawing of their long-standing domestic arrangement whereby they cohabited entirely independently of one another; neither had he once invited her into his private apartment in the east wing of the villa, let alone raised the subject of their sharing a bed from time to time. It shamed her to admit that the latter had now become her most pressing and daily preoccupation.

Molly returned her full attention to the stage and pursed her lips at the sight of the soprano, Josephine Carter, indulging herself in her role. Molly had never particularly liked Miss Carter. Yes, the woman was a passably good singer, but the fashionable antics of her acting style were ridiculously overcooked. All that gasping and screaming and tearing of hair – supposedly in the name of realism! There was also the woman's dubious reputation with men. Miss Carter had set the pattern of a lifetime while a mere seventeen-year-old debutante by raising a storm of scandal after a three-day jaunt alone with the Crown Prince of Germany at his hunting lodge. She had weathered that storm as she did all the others, each one more outrageous than the last, so that her recent dabbling with a married Hollywood idol hardly seemed worthy of a mention in the newspapers. Molly thought it undignified and would have preferred this queen of the flappers not to have beached herself in Naples just now. Most irritating of all for Molly was the fact that the public perceived herself and Josephine Carter in a rather similar light; and the crowning annoyance was that in this unwarranted pairing Molly was cast at a disadvantage, because Miss Carter's status in the worlds of glamour, fashion and society was afforded her by dint of a supreme talent, whereas Mrs Campobello's came through her affiliation with stardom, nothing more.

*   *   *

As he watched the opera, Rocco pondered on Molly's barbed remark about the woman she described as 'his signora'. So, this business was no longer confined to the dark realms of his own thoughts, he reflected. It was spreading; perhaps the river was even about to burst its banks. If truth were told, it was not inconvenient for Rocco, sitting in that darkened auditorium, that Molly had unwittingly encouraged his thoughts back to the subject of Chiara Tomassini; because the reality was: he wanted to think of little else. The unhappy fact was that he had wasted so many years waiting for something like this to occur.

He had seen Chiara twice since their first meeting after the tavern incident. The first time had been quick and rather awkward. He had dropped by unannounced on a dull and foggy day to see if the new apartment was all right and that she was happy. There hadn't been much to say as he looked around, with her walking a respectable distance behind him. Her reticence, together with the resigned compliance of her manner and a kind of mournful tenderness that characterized her face, squeezed his heart and filled him with pity; but secretly it also inflamed him, though he did not realize until the moment came to say goodbye. He was barely out of the apartment building before he was trying to work out how and on what pretext he could return. It was to be provided by Amedeo.

The young singer had been spending most of every day at the Villa Rosalba, studying in one form or another, until it was decided by all that it would be more practical if he were to move in altogether, during the working week. A room was made available for him next to Campobello's own apartment, and a wardrobe of clothes acquired. He took to his new life like a bird to flight, was utterly dedicated and seemed to grow daily in confidence and accomplishment. He was also bright and amusing, and in no time had the measure of Pickering, gleefully holding his own against the pianist's acerbic humour. He was tempted to tease Boldoni as well, but understood early that this was more dangerous territory, and that he would have to earn his stripes before getting too familiar with the Maestro's aloof and quasi-military assistant. An intriguing adventure was unfolding daily at the Villa Rosalba, and it was in order to provide a personal report on the achievements of her son that Rocco was able to justify a second visit to Chiara Tomassini in her pleasantly elevated apartment, with its sea view, up on the Vomero.

This time the weather was glorious, and she met him at the door in a pretty floral dress. The windows were wide open and a warm breeze blew in from the west, lifting the tablecloth gently and loosening a strand of her hair.

To begin with, again, they spoke little but communicated much through silent smiles. He told her the good tidings about Amedeo, and a sparkle in her dark eyes betrayed her excitement but she did not go so far as to voice it; instead, she asked tentatively if her son was behaving himself.

'Perfectly,' said Rocco. 'I mean, he likes to push Mr Pickering and Boldoni a little, but they deserve it. The boy has character, and that's a good thing.' She smiled. 'Did you have a concern, then?'

'Only that he might be saying stupid things or upsetting someone.'

'Does he make a habit of it?'

'People get so excited about politics nowadays, and Amedeo sometimes likes to show off.'

'I've heard him spout off about the newspapers being shut down, that sort of thing,' answered Rocco, 'but we just laugh and he takes it well.'

Chiara frowned. 'Tell him to keep his opinions to himself. If the wrong person were to hear . . .'

'There's not much interest in politics in my house.'

'But the servants might hear him, or visitors. It's dangerous for him to talk like that.'

'I'll keep an eye on it,' he replied.

She made some soup which they ate together at the table in the kitchen, and they spent the afternoon talking of life as it used to be in the district of San Lorenzo when they were young. Names were mentioned, people and faces long forgotten by Rocco, their quirks and tragedies, great and small, peculiar incidents that spiked through the blanket of time and memory.

And they talked of Gabriele: how he had never let go of his dreams, the imaginary world of glamour and wealth that awaited them across the ocean in America; how he'd felt sure his singing would one day take him there, where they would enjoy unending luxury, a palatial home, wonderful food prepared by a legion of servants. Chiara recalled that she would smile sympathetically at his starry-eyed ramblings, but would never let him know the hopeless reality. Was Gabriele the only one left, she would wonder, who had not noticed the utter and irreversible deterioration in his voice? By the age of twenty-one he was struggling; five years later no one wanted to hire him, and by thirty he was a joke. There wasn't even anyone who could remember the time when he'd been considered promising. The men who worked alongside him at the theatre and his mates at the tavern would encourage his fantasies because they enjoyed the poetry of his descriptions. His talk of a heaven-scented future gave them a kind of warmth and faith, in the same way that a madonna's soulful smile gives hope and puts all things right in the heart of a devotee, and they would say quick prayers at street shrines for Gabriele Tomassini's dream to come true one day.

'So he never gave in to despair?' Rocco asked.

She thought about the question. 'Perhaps despair overwhelmed him at the end,' she said. 'But none of us ever saw it. I don't remember one day when he wasn't sure of a happy ending.' She added quietly, 'It didn't always make life easy.'

Rocco hungered for her to elaborate the story, and had to rein in the temptation to ask too many questions or appear invasive. But he was also happy just to sit there and watch her talk – her dimpled half-smiles and frowns as she stumbled her way through fading recollections; the shy way she would look askance to spare herself embarrassment if she seemed to be straying into personal territory; and the forthright edge that came into her voice as she gained confidence and wanted to put a point across. Rocco felt relaxed in her company, able to shed all the affectation and posturing usually demanded of him. He was spellbound by the intimate charm of the afternoon in her apartment, and assumed at the time it was because he was at last on the path towards a kind of absolution. But there was an alternative hypothesis, which he hardly dared contemplate: perhaps the warmth he felt in the widow's company had nothing to do with his past history with Gabriele Tomassini. Perhaps it was just about her; about himself and Chiara.

*   *   *

The opera concluded with the splendid duet between Miss Carter and Mr Mulligan, and the fall of the curtain was greeted with predictably rousing applause.

'Well,' Pompeo Tedeschi said to Don Fabrizzi, the company's director, as he ceased clapping after a respectable show of appreciation, 'so much for revolutionary hotheads. I've said it before and I'll say it again: stick your neck out and you'll lose your head!' He laughed heartily at his own joke which he had been rehearsing to himself all the way through the last act. It was a reference to the opera's hero, a liberal poet, ultimately guillotined during the Reign of Terror. 'But not a bad piece, all in all, I'll give you that.' Tedeschi would interpret everything he encountered according to the degree it endorsed or disputed his own political ethics.

'Yes, yes, quite right.' Don Fabrizzi smiled. He was too old and nervous to risk causing any bother for himself on the eve of his retirement, even though he felt secretly appalled at the muscular philistinism of the regime represented by the man beside him. For his part, Tedeschi regarded the old man's meek compliance, and the absence of contradiction generally in Naples, as a sign of the party's growing popularity. The Duce's ever increasing measures to tighten control of this ramshackle province were clearly a welcome relief for these ignorant and backward people.

After a short reception in the Teatro's grand foyer, the party was joined by the two principal singers of the evening. The tenor Donal Mulligan was first in. He was about forty years old, meaty, with an untidy mop of chestnut-brown hair and an irresistible smile. He came bounding across the marble to greet Rocco, a long

252

overcoat flapping around his ankles and his arms out-stretched. One or two people in the hall clapped at his entrance.

'And so,' his high voice bellowed through a Donegal accent as he grabbed Rocco's hand tightly in both of his own. 'What did the world's greatest tenor think of that performance, then?' Mulligan, accustomed to the Campobello of former times, expected a sharp and witty reply, but instead Rocco just smiled, lost for words. 'Oh, away with you,' said the Irishman, and embraced Campobello, a gesture that brought more applause from bystanders. Don Mulligan belonged to the slightly younger generation of tenors who had reached mastery of their art often in imitation of Campobello. In spite of this he had forged a particular niche for himself in Irish ballad repertoire, and had recorded dozens of them with immense success. It was perhaps for this reason, rather than for his achievements in opera, that he was adored not only by his countrymen but by a huge portion of Americans, for whom Ireland represented a twinkling hearth at the heart of their cultural identity. Mulligan's expansive personality and natural wit merely compounded their romantic devotion to the myth of Irish homeliness.

Some way behind, carrying a huge bouquet, and delayed by her stately progress through lines of hungry devotees, came the diva, Josephine Carter, even more winsome and delicious in evening dress than she had been in the Bourbon splendour of her stage costume; and, by the breadth of her smile and gracious acknowledgement of compliments on all sides, it seemed as if she rather suspected as much. Arriving before the gathering of special guests, she held out her hand for the taking, and Pompeo Tedeschi, not one to miss an opportunity, stepped forward.

'May I offer my congratulations, signorina, on a wonderful performance,' he said, bowing low, 'and on behalf of our Prime Minister, Signor Mussolini, who has asked me to send his personal greetings, may I also welcome you to Italy.'

'Why, thank you,' said Miss Carter, and then pointed her finger teasingly at the chest of Tedeschi, who towered a good twelve inches above her, 'and please tell your handsome Mr Mussolini that I very much hope to meet with him when I come to Rome. All my friends tell me what a wonderful host he is.' This was music to Tedeschi's ears and he all but blushed as he bowed once more.

She was now free to turn her attention to Rocco, whom she looked at with the informal warmth and affection of an old school pal. Pouting her lips and frowning with disapproval, she said, 'Oh, Rocco, what have they been doing to you?'

Again, Rocco seemed incapable of an appropriate reply, but took her hand and kissed it. Despite her reputation as a *femme fatale* and an artist of supreme, occasionally histrionic panache, Josephine Carter was, beneath it all, rather mystified by her own success, and consequently shy of it. She took refuge in men rather than seeking to devour them. Rocco had never been a lover, but was a special friend who had sung opposite her scores of times and shared the strains of their profession; he was one of the few who understood the woman beneath the diva. Molly was less convinced, but deigned to greet her with fitting grace.

They progressed from the opera house to the adjacent royal palace, where a celebratory banquet awaited them.

They were to expect nothing more than a trifle, an intimate tête à tête, Tedeschi warned, though he clearly wanted to score credit by the false modesty of his understatement. He had appropriated the role of host for the evening, despite the presence of the Conte di Postillo, the King's official representative, without whose permission there could be no reception held at the palace.

They entered the palace vestibule, an ostentatiously vast space decorated to its far-reaching heights in shades of grey and white and adorned with marbled reliefs and statues. A broad stairway led to an upper storey ambulatory, built around the palace's inner courtyard, which gave access to the sumptuous state apartments.

Servants in gilded livery stood to attention on either side of each step as the party made its way upstairs, led – for form's sake – by the Conte and Contessa di Postillo. They progressed to a chamber lined with crimson silk, where a gigantic crystal chandelier hung from the centre of a frescoed ceiling, and the walls were hung with rococo tapestries.

For all Molly's experience of state apartments and royal hospitality, she was pleasantly impressed, perhaps because she had not expected to find such opulence so close to the heart of this squalid city; but she was distracted from looking at her surroundings by Don Graziani, who was trying to engage her in a private word. His subject cast a cloud across her regal smile.

'Walter Fleming of the Jupiter Company is already in Rome as we speak,' Graziani said. 'He comes to Naples in two weeks' time because we told him that your husband could be persuaded to record. Boldoni has at last seen fit to sort out the contracts, but we have heard that Wallace Pickering has taken it on himself to contact Mr Fleming independently. Our own sources inform us that Fleming is extremely concerned about what he has heard.'

'What does Pickering think he's up to?' said Molly. 'I knew he was reluctant, but I didn't think he'd try to disrupt our plans. Will Fleming refuse to make the recordings, just because of what Mr Pickering says?'

Bruno Graziani cut in. 'That petulant piano player must change his tune, or be silenced.' Molly glanced at him with alarm, but his expression revealed none of the menace that was implicit in his words. The problem seemed for him to be like a disturbance on the shop floor which required prompt managerial intervention.

'Come now, gentlemen,' said Molly. 'I'm sure this is just a little misunderstanding.'

'Of course, my dear,' said Bruno with a shade more familiarity than Molly thought appropriate, 'you are probably right. Just a misunderstanding. Which is why we would appreciate it if your husband could make his intentions plain. So we all know where we stand.'

'I can mention something to him, if that's what you'd like,' she said.

Nearby, Donal Mulligan was laughing heartily, his arm slung around Rocco's shoulders.

'With that drunkard dog sniffing around,' Graziani said in a viper's whisper, flicking his hand in the direction of the Irishman, 'we may find Campobello's crown finally usurped, once and for all.' Molly stiffened at the coarse jibe. She was well capable of flinging the dirt when the need arose, but there was a time and a place.

Rocco, meanwhile, had introduced a dazzled but euphoric Amedeo to the two opera stars, both of whom immediately and generously took the boy to their hearts. Miss Carter, who spoke Italian rather well, was intrigued that the great Campobello, notorious in the past for his reluctance to take on pupils, should have singled out this young tenor. Amedeo responded enthusiastically to her interest and answered her questions without inhibition. In no time it was agreed that the two stars should get to know him better while they were in Naples, and Mulligan proposed that he should accompany them on their trip to the Roman remains at Pompeii in a few days' time. Miss Carter then took Amedeo by the arm and started to tell him whom she would introduce him to when he came to California, because come he surely must. 'We'll tell everyone you're my nephew and they won't believe it for a minute.' She giggled at the thought. 'I know lots of people in the Hollywood studios,' she teased, 'we might even get you a little part in a film.'

Molly overheard the remark, and said, 'Don't give the boy ideas, now, Josie.'

'Why not?' laughed Miss Carter, leading Amedeo away. 'Every young man wants to go to Hollywood. They'd adore you there. They're always on the lookout for dark handsome young men.'

'Tell her to pipe down if it gets too much,' quipped Mulligan at Amedeo with a wink, and then held up his hands in mock defence against Miss Carter, in case she chose to swipe at him.

There was an uncomfortable sense during dinner of an agenda awaiting its opportunity to be aired, so conversation was rather stunted. The only guests who seemed entirely unconcerned were Miss Carter (who demonstrated that she had officially adopted Amedeo as her pet for the evening by audaciously rearranging the place cards to seat herself next to him) and her co-star, the ever ebullient Mr Mulligan. Amedeo's own enjoyment of the evening rose as quickly as his memory of Boldoni's etiquette lessons diminished, and both were linked to his ever more rapid appreciation of the fine wine. Donal Mulligan's unrestrained attachment to the decanter did not help to slow the boy's intake.

Tedeschi, seated between Molly and the Contessa di Postillo, seemed permanently awaiting his opportunity to engage the attention of Campobello, who was directly opposite him; but any attempts to draw him in, such as an invitation for him to appear at a forthcoming convention of industrialists, or a suggestion that the Campobellos might like to spend a week at Tedeschi's palatial villa on Capri, were intercepted and neutralized by Graziani.

'Come now, Don Graziani,' said Tedeschi, stiffening but attempting to sound affable, 'you surely do not own Maestro Campobello, to make decisions and answer on his behalf?' Molly laughed to soften the coldness that this remark prompted in Graziani's eyes.

The veteran director of the opera, Don Fabrizzi, now changed the subject with a little statement of his own, delivered to the table as a whole. 'It is wonderful for us all to see our old friend Rocco Campobello back amongst us again,' he said. Turning to Rocco, he continued, 'In all your splendid career, sir, it is well known that circumstances have prevented you from performing at our illustrious opera house, and though I say this without the slightest grudge' (one or two chortled at his light-hearted dig), 'I have to confess that it would be the crowning joy of my life's work to see you perform on the San Carlo stage. If not during my tenancy as director, then during that of my successor. But I should warn you: time is running short.' More laughter, and Rocco nodded his acknowledgement of the sentiment. Don Graziani took the opportunity to interject.

'And of course it would be the first priority of the next director,' he looked towards his son, 'to ensure that your wishes, Don Fabrizzi, come to fruition.'

'Hear, hear,' called Donal Mulligan from the far end of the table.

'Indeed,' added Tedeschi: 'whoever that director might be.' His tone implied that the selection was far from decided. It was well known that the fascists favoured a candidate of their own, an aristocrat from northern Italy.

'Let us return our attentions to the lovely Signorina Carter,' cut in the tactful Don Fabrizzi, 'and her triumphs of this evening,' and, once again, everyone clapped gently.

'Don't waste your time talking about me,' began Miss Carter, and then, as if tickled by a sudden wheeze, pointed to Tedeschi's plate and said, 'But, Signor Tedeschi, what on earth are you eating?' Her bald comment was acceptable only by dint of her femininity, fame, and beauty, but even so Tedeschi looked nettled. Unlike everyone else around the table, he had been served no meat at all, nor potatoes, but a portion of boiled spinach, some walnuts and a large spoonful of yoghurt.

He countered his embarrassment by raising his chin and announcing so all could hear, 'Signorina, I observe strict rules concerning matters of diet. They are rules decreed by our leader, no less, who is an example to us all. He will allow nothing to enter his body except that which promotes health, vigour and mental industry.'

'Quite right,' said the elderly Don Fabrizzi lightly.

'But do you people copy *everything* he does?' said Miss Carter, smiling irresistibly.

'As much as possible, yes,' replied Tedeschi. 'And what better model could a man want? Mussolini is not only a great leader and intellectual, he is one of the finest sportsmen in Italy. And a consummate musician.'

'Musician?' said Mulligan, speaking through a mouthful of food. 'What kind of musician would that be?'

'He is expert at the violin,' replied Tedeschi.

'It's true,' chimed Miss Carter. 'I'll swear I've seen photographs of him playing the violin. And swimming, riding, fencing, boxing, even cutting corn in the fields and laying bricks, more often than not with his shirt removed.' There was a slight but quickly suppressed titter around the table. 'Is there anything he cannot do?'

'I have heard,' came in Fabrizzi again, his seriousness of voice ironing away any threat of disrespect, 'that he possesses considerable classical scholarship. Did he not recently cast his eye over some hitherto indecipherable Etruscan tablets, and suggest a translation, on the spot?'

'I believe he did baffle some of our leading classicists with his expertise,' said Tedeschi approvingly.

'Good heavens!' It was Molly. 'The way you speak of him, you would have us believe he was sent from God!' Though Molly believed in social hierarchy, she was naturally democratic in her leanings, and felt faint outrage at the extent of the plaudits being heaped on a mere politician. But her outburst earned her a raised index finger from her neighbour, Don Fabrizzi, and she refrained from saying anything more.

'From God? Perhaps not,' said Tedeschi, though his tone suggested he did not entirely discount the possibility. 'But I will say one thing. Mussolini has given this country a sense of nationhood. And people are no longer idle. They are standing up and helping to achieve the greater good. We have discipline and pride. Look at this city! It has never looked so clean.' At this comment a laugh was heard, and everyone turned; it was Amedeo at the other end of the table.

'I agree,' Miss Carter interjected firmly. 'It's some years since I was last here and there is a noticeable difference. The public gardens are just lovely.'

'Thank you, signorina,' said Tedeschi, taking credit personally and bowing his head. 'Our Duce has great plans for Naples. Housing, sanitation, schools, industry. I tell you, we will build and renovate on a scale that has not been seen in Europe since the time of our ancestors, the Roman emperors.'

'Did you know?' piped the elderly Contessa di Postillo next to him, raising a pale bony finger to make her point, 'that I am descended directly from the Empress Poppaea?'

'They had the grace to warn me before I married her,' chipped in her husband, and there was general mirth. He wore his fingernails long, which was traditional amongst noblemen, to show that manual work was alien to them. 'But I managed to persuade her to give up bathing in asses' milk on a daily basis.' More laughter – it was clearly a gag he had dined out on many times. 'She only does it at weekends now!' The Contessa's face creased up with delight at her husband's humour. She never tired of the joke.

'What about the workers?' It was Amedeo who spoke, and the smiles faded. Amedeo took another sip of wine and looked down the table to Tedeschi for a reply.

'I'm sorry?' asked Tedeschi.

'The workers, or anyone who wants to make themselves heard. Is Mussolini going to listen to their problems, or will he just send in his *squadristi* to sort them out? It's happening more and more.'

'And a good thing too,' chirped the Contessa. 'All we hear about nowadays is workers and peasants moaning. In my father's time . . .' but a flash of her husband's eyes caused her to trail off into silence.

'Shame on you, young man,' muttered Don Fabrizzi at Amedeo without much conviction. Rocco stopped eating and placed his knife and fork together.

'No, no,' said Tedeschi with magnanimous patience, 'it's a good question the boy has asked. Remind me of your name again?'

Bolstered by the wine and his sense that the foreign celebrities were behind him, Amedeo perhaps sounded more provocative than he would normally have allowed himself, as he leant back in his chair. 'My name is Tomassini. Would you like me to write it down for you?' There was the smallest gasp of shock at the table as Tedeschi looked briefly down towards him, but after a moment turned away and smiled.

'No, I think I can spell that, thank you. As for your question: you are deluded, of course, but I don't blame you for it. There is much misinformation available for those who wish to hear it.' He spoke to the table as a whole. 'The facts are these: the Fascist party has captured the imagination of the people of Naples and brought them to its cause without firing a single shot or striking a blow. And it was the same when our leader marched to Rome four years ago. We have power because it is the people's will.'

'No doubt about it,' endorsed the Conte quietly.

'You probably say that about Nocera, too,' Amedeo came back. 'There were no Fascists there until right before the elections three years ago. And then on election day – surprise, surprise – the Fascists were voted in overwhelmingly. Rumour has it something changed people's minds overnight.'

'Nocera was an isolated incident,' cut in Tedeschi. 'The troubles there were provoked by socialist agitators. Perhaps you would like to come to my office.' He smiled again at Amedeo. 'We'll go through the evidence together.'

'The blackshirts came in firing guns and burning down houses,' persisted Amedeo. 'Is that what you call the people's will?'

'Amedeo!' Campobello's powerful voice cut through, and all eyes turned to him. 'Enough,' he said.

'Yes,' added Miss Carter, noticing the forced restraint in Tedeschi's face. 'Let us talk of more pleasant things. Pompeii, for example. What am I going to see there?'

'I like best the Villa of the Mysteries,' said the Contessa airily, but Tedeschi cut her off.

'The Fascist party has saved Italy from Bolshevism. Young man, you would be advised to learn humility and obedience. That is the Italian way, and we are the envy of the world. You should forget about pursuing petty, selfish interests and think more about the good of the state.'

'Was Matteotti thinking about petty selfish interests when your leader had him murdered?' said Amedeo. There was a more pronounced gasp around the table, but no one tried to say anything; everyone looked towards Tedeschi, awaiting his answer; everyone but Campobello, who stared thunderously into space.

Tedeschi held still and blinked down at his plate. His courtly dignity remained intact, though a chill entered his tone as he replied quietly. 'Another socialist lie. The police are still hunting for Matteotti's killers.'

'One of the most respected politicians in Italy,' Amedeo turned to explain to Mulligan (who nodded, but did not speak Italian well enough to understand fully), 'bludgeoned to death because he dared to tell the truth. And since then—'

'Be silent!' came Rocco's voice, powerfully, and for a moment no one dared to utter a word. He looked down the table at Amedeo, who averted his eyes. 'It is time we left.'

Even Miss Carter was now shocked into silence, though Donal Mulligan, who did not seem to have grasped the import of what had occurred, reached for the decanter. A servant glided in to assist him. 'Is something the matter?' he asked and raised his face to Miss Carter opposite him, but a flash of her eyes cut him short.

'An outspoken young man,' Don Graziani muttered to Rocco.

Tedeschi was back in his chair, but could not stop himself cutting in again. 'Excuse me, but I wish to make our position plain on this matter.'

Campobello was on his feet. He turned to Tedeschi, and looking down at him said with quiet sternness, 'I think you've made yourself plain enough already. We must be going.'

'Oh,' trailed the voice of the Contessa, who was aware that something was up but had not grasped the details. Tedeschi raised his eyebrows, but accepted Rocco's admonition without protest.

Molly, Amedeo and Rocco now took their leave, while

the others filed through to an adjacent apartment. The awkwardness had been eased by the suggestion that the two stars might sing around the piano, and even as the Campobellos made their way down the great marble staircase they could hear Don Mulligan's sweet tenor raised in a rendition of 'I'll take you home again, Kathleen'.

Rocco said nothing to Amedeo as they passed through the great entrance, but pointed to the front passenger seat when they arrived at the car, an instruction which Amedeo meekly and wordlessly obeyed.

Molly was sitting beside her husband in the back seat as Pozzo drove away from the palace, and she looked at him askance. She thoroughly approved Rocco's having stood up to Tedeschi like that. Amedeo had behaved badly of course (what could one expect from so plebeian a child?), but it was hardly blasphemy! Molly's cheeks went pink with pride as she looked at her husband.

'You were wonderful,' she purred, and rested her hand on top of his. 'How dare that man steer every conversation towards his strutting little leader? Tonight was supposed to be a celebration of music and artistry, things that are eternal. Everyone knows politicians are here today and gone tomorrow. His insistence was in poor taste.'

'This lot think they are different. They talk of empire.'

'The only emperor in that room tonight was you, my dear,' she said, and felt a rush of warmth when Rocco responded with a slight smile. Recklessly, she seized the moment. 'Don Graziani fears you may have changed your plans about doing a little recording work with Mr Fleming.'

'I wish he would voice his fears to me rather than bothering you.'

Molly looked at him pleadingly and gave his hand a slight squeeze. 'Oh, but it's only because he and I share the same concern. We're partners in crime, you might say,' she added teasingly.

He smiled again and closed his eyes. 'I hope not.'

'Well? Can you set my mind at rest?'

Rocco's eyes were still closed as she waited on tenter-hooks for a reply. She eased the pressure of her hand, passing her fingertips through the coarse hair on the top of his wrist.

She was about to give up hope of a response, when he answered. 'I will do those recordings.'

Molly's fingers stilled their circling stroke and she looked out of the car window. Tears of joy formed in her eyes, and she found she had no words to say.

When they arrived back at the Villa Rosalba, Amedeo was instructed to go straight to his room. He had been rehearsing an apology all the way home, and now began falteringly to deliver it, but Rocco would not permit him the indulgence and, in a low voice, told him to go to bed.

Rocco then turned to bid his wife goodnight.

She hesitated. 'Are you going up as well?' she asked, and crossed her legs as she reached for her cigarettes.

'I have one or two things to do, but I'll go soon.'

As she raised a hand to light her cigarette, a bracelet snagged on one of the giant pearls in her necklace – a gift from the Maharajah of Jaipur some years before – but she released it with an elegant little flick of the finger. Her every action seemed lifted from a textbook on deportment. She took a step towards him.

Despite the long evening, her perfume was fresh and pungent.

'Would you like one?' she asked, indicating the cigarettes.

'Perhaps. But I'll wait until I get to my rooms.'

'May I not wait up with you?'

'What would be the point?' he replied. 'You must be exhausted.'

'Oh no,' she scorned. 'An old party girl like me! I thought you and I might have a drink together.'

'At this hour?'

'Why not?' she said, cigarette in hand and throwing back her head with abandonment. When he offered no response, she looked at him emphatically from beneath her long lashes. 'It's been a while since you and I played together. I'll order champagne.' She was about to pick up a bell, when Rocco sighed, pursing his lips with something like a tired smile, and she knew instantly the utter impossibility of her proposal. The flurry of sexual excitement that had overwhelmed her a moment before quickly drained away. 'Very well, then,' she said in a new voice, and drew breath deeply. 'I'll see you in the morning.'

'Molly,' said Rocco, but she had turned away, and raised a palm to silence him. She walked through a door at the far side of the hall and closed it quietly behind her.

Chapter 18

A while later Rocco was sitting alone at his desk, still in evening dress, elbows resting in front of him. Everyone in the house had gone to bed.

Suddenly, he clenched both fists on the desk and pushed himself to his feet. He walked quickly downstairs in the darkness and went to the room where the night porter sat. The light in there blinded him momentarily, but he explained to the porter that he would need the car immediately, though Pozzo was not to be disturbed; he would drive himself. The night porter's look of surprise was softened by a banknote placed into his hand, and Rocco asked him kindly to keep quiet about this.

The guards on night shift at the gates roused themselves sleepily from their chairs to open up, and Rocco edged the car out into the dark, abandoned street. Within ten minutes he had driven the length of the empty Corso Vittorio Emanuele, and begun to wind back steeply uphill towards the heights of the Vomero. On the right, stretching out below, he could see the lights of the city glowing, edged with the black abyss that marked the ingress of the bay at night.

He parked the car and walked straight to the apartment block. The night air was warm, but fresher here than down in the city, because of the altitude, and full of the sound of crickets. Rocco slipped a few lire to the night porter here as well, and trod lightly up the stairwell that led from the interior courtyard of the building. Arriving on the second floor, he stood in front of her door, and did not hesitate before knocking. When there was no reply, he rapped again, more urgently. Then he heard her voice.

'Who is it?'

'It is I.'

The prolonged pause that followed was testament to her moment of indecisiveness every bit as much as the door's eventual opening indicated her readiness to submit. And it was barely ajar before he pushed himself through with a forcefulness that drove her backwards, but only slightly, because he caught her in his arm to close off her retreat. She was dressed in a simple, sleeveless nightdress, and the soft skin of her shoulders brushed against him as she raised her forearms, instinctively defensive and trying to conceal the swell of her breasts; but she was overwhelmed, and arched her back, recoiling, almost, with shock at his advance. He took her face between his palms and brought it close to him, looking from eye to eye before he kissed her. Her thick dark hair was loose and bunched in his fingers. He felt it warm to the roots, its scent reminiscent of pine needles. 'My beautiful girl.' His accent had slipped into Neapolitan. 'I have thought of nothing but you all evening. Why did you not come?'

At the sound of these words, their roles reversed and she became the predator, pulling his head towards her and pressing herself against him. 'I could not come. How could I sit there and see you with your wife?'

Rocco smiled. 'She is my wife in name only, and has been for years. We are estranged. One word from you

269

and I will leave her.' Chiara mirrored his smile, and leant gently in, barely touching his lips with her own, brushing lightly from side to side. They breathed deeply into one another.

Rocco leant back now to slip the nightdress down as far as it would, and then pulled it over the ample rise of her bosom. It snagged briefly, but he released it and let it fall lightly around her ankles. She pressed her naked body against him. 'Beautiful Chiara,' Rocco whispered again, burying his nose in the hair around her temple, and tasting the soft down of her earlobe.

She pulled away slightly and looked at him. They remained like that for some moments, a smile rising on both their faces, before she took his hand and led him to her bed.

When Rocco arrived back at the Villa Rosalba later in the night, he had one of the guards put the car away for him and walked quickly indoors, bidding goodnight to the porter. He was half way up the staircase when he saw a figure standing in front of him, invisible until that moment because of the darkness. It was Amedeo, and he was still dressed as he had been at dinner.

'Why are you not in bed?' asked Rocco.

'I couldn't sleep. What happened tonight . . .'

'What do you mean?'

'At the dinner. I am ashamed about what I did.'

'Yes, well, we'll talk about it another time. Everything will be all right. Go to bed now.'

'Where have you been, Maestro?' A new tone had come into his voice.

'What concern is it of yours?'

Amedeo paused. He was three or four steps above

Rocco and looking down at him, though his eyes were obscured by shadow. 'I think it is my concern.'

'What do you mean by that?' said Rocco.

'You've been with her, haven't you?'

Rocco paused. 'Yes.'

Despite the darkness he saw Amedeo's head sink a little. 'I thought it would happen,' he said.

'You must understand,' began Rocco, 'Mrs Campobello and I—'

'You don't have to tell me.'

'I want to. I will not hurt your mother. I love her.'

'And is that the reason you chose to help me? So that you could get close to my mother?'

'Not at all.' Rocco frowned. 'I chose you before I had even met her. Don't you remember? When we spoke in the carriage on the way back from the tavern?'

Amedeo seemed to nod, and after a brief pause, turned and walked upstairs to his room. Rocco did not attempt to stop him.

Chapter 19

The New York policeman, Frank Crawley, was leaning against the rail on the top deck of the liner as it edged slowly in towards the docks. The sea far beneath him was being churned like the waters of hell to steady the pace of the ship's final approach. Gargantuan mooring ropes were tossed across a narrowing gap and caught by what looked like an army of shoeless dwarfs. Crawley chuckled as he watched them secure the ship's ropes around rusting piles on the quay. He'd seen some poor Italians in his time, in the streets of Lower Manhattan and Mulberry Bend, but Naples' dock workers were in a class of their own: comically small, faces like pecans, their feet grotesquely distended (he guessed) by years of labouring barefoot in corrosive salt water. Ah, there was a funny side to all this, he supposed.

It was a fine morning, and Crawley was encouraged by his first view of the city. There would be plenty here to tell his wife about in letters: castles, churches, a smoking volcano, all the kind of shit she liked to hear. More importantly, though, this place was a stinking dump, and that suited his professional needs. A town like this provided the perfect backcloth. Here he could hide, he could bribe, and he could work the local police like the nursery school amateurs they were. And hadn't the country's friendly new regime pledged to rid Italy of the old crime networks? Crawley would get all the help he needed. Within a few days, he bet himself, the most prized and sensitive police files in Naples would be sitting open in his hotel room. This job might prove a lot easier than he had thought.

A colleague of his from Chicago had recently travelled to Palermo on a similar jaunt: to hunt down an infamous North Side mobster who had fled America. After just two weeks the Bureau agent had his man in chains. Crawley was damned if he'd be outdone by the Chicago bunch. Yes, he did not mind admitting it: now that he was on the eve of retirement, it was a matter of pride as well as professionalism that he should come all the way to Naples to track down his adversary, Bruno Graziani.

For twenty-five years Frank Crawley had trawled filth in the streets of Brooklyn and the Bronx, from the back alleys of the foot soldiers to the urban palaces of the bosses. He had seen them all come and go, sometimes from the cradle to the cell – or the coffin – and had personally been responsible for sending down a few of the most notorious names in New York's bloodstained underworld. There had been some close shaves, but he had come through and liked to think that his in-destructibility struck fear into the hearts of his enemies – the same fear that had sent Bruno Graziani whimpering back across the ocean to his Papa in Naples. Back to this seedy shit-hole, Crawley mused as he walked down the gangway and on to Italian soil. The place sure stank; and the people stank, too. He did not just look down on Italians: he despised them as an under-race of crooks and beggars. The sooner he was back on the ship home, the better.

He had telegraphed the Naples police several times before coming, and specifically asked that no one should be sent to meet him at the port. He suspected they would be fool enough to send some sort of deputation – knowing Italians, even a brass band! – and, of course, the last thing he wanted was to be conspicuous. They must wait for *him* to approach *them*, he stressed in his telegrams, and he would be in touch as soon as he'd had a chance to settle in.

After clearing customs, he wrote a note at the porters' desk to have his bags sent direct to the hotel. He would take a walk along the seafront for an hour or so, to soak in the flavour of the place. After so long at sea it would be pleasant to stretch his legs with a stroll in the sun; and so he turned left, away from the dock, past the Castel Nuovo, and headed down towards the slight headland of Santa Lucia and the Via Partenope. He had done his research and studied maps of the city for much of the voyage. He felt satisfied he now knew the layout of the place pretty well, though the feel of it was different from what he'd been expecting. He'd read that this was one of the oldest cities in the world, and for much of history one of the biggest, too. He wondered what had happened to wipe out all the glory and leave it looking like this. Long live the New World and out with the old, he thought as he meandered along, following the low seafront wall and lighting a cigar. A succession of single horse carriages, with tassel-edged parasol canopies, clattered past him, some jangling bells on their harnesses. Their drivers seemed to be in a hurry and stood up with the reins in their hands, clucking and whipping the rumps of the horses to get them to trot faster.

Bruno Graziani had been high on Crawley's list for

274

several years. He was different from the run of the mill. He had no family other than his father back in the old country, no woman in his life, no children, and no sense of a community fiefdom. He didn't inspire affection in his men, but went about his business like an auditor for the tax revenue: the rules were clear, the landscape of operations either black or white, with no shades of grey. A ruthless bastard. He was also unusual in his tastes, preferring to mix with Anglo-Saxon Americans and the patrician class rather than fellow Italians. He would have his own private box at the opera and be seen at fashionable receptions in the company of judges and politicians – that was until recently, because his powerful friends had suddenly dropped him. Nailing this oily-haired, sharp-suited and, perhaps, sexually deviant society impostor would be a sweet finish to Crawley's illustrious career.

There was evidence enough now to put him away for years: forty-two truckloads of whiskey intercepted at the Canadian border last year, eight counts of tax evasion, involvement in multiple incidents of intimidation and mob war assaults, but, above everything else, the gunning down of a police officer in a hotel lobby just eight months previously. A teenage kid who was caught up in the gang had been persuaded to squeal, and now it had been proved pretty much beyond doubt that the shooting had been ordered by Bruno personally. Crawley was hot on the scent this time. He even carried a photograph of the young Graziani in his wallet, rather a flattering picture, he thought, taken some years ago. He had it with him at all times, and would take it out to look at occasionally. It fuelled the kind of hatred he needed to keep his mind on the job. He glanced at it now, as he approached the stretch of public gardens that edged the waterfront of the Chiaia district. Time's up, pretty boy, he silently communicated to the cold face of Bruno in the photograph. Get ready, because we're going to have our waltz at last.

Crawley cursed himself for having drunk such a jug-load of coffee at breakfast before docking. His wife would have said that he should know better at his age. As he approached the public gardens his bladder felt as if it would split, but then he noticed to his immense relief a *pissoir* next to the pavement. Or that's what he supposed and hoped to God it was. Either way, he would use it as a *pissoir*, he decided, smiling to himself, or he'd be risking an unfortunate accident in full view of all these ladies enjoying their morning promenade in the gardens.

A men's public convenience was a common enough sight in Naples: a small cylindrical pavilion, with wall panels allowing ventilation from above and beneath. The panels were plastered on the outside with notices, most of them municipal advertisements encouraging people to keep their city clean, but Crawley only saw them briefly, because the anticipation of relief had brought him to a point of no return, and he hurried inside.

He opened his flies and with a sigh of joy allowed the urine to flow freely. He had barely drawn breath again when he was aware that two men had joined him in the little pavilion and were standing behind, not taking their place at the urinal. He glanced sideways, uneasily, and noticed they were looking at him. Instinctively, he now looked towards the exit – and saw the trouser legs and shoes of two other men standing just outside. Instantly he understood what was happening, and closed his eyes. The idiocy of it. Looking up at the men again, he saw one of them indicate with a smile that he should finish his piss, and he knew now that the chances were his life would last only as long as it took to empty his bladder. He'd barely completed the task and had not had the chance to put himself away when the two men took him firmly by the arms. A third person then came in. It was Bruno Graziani himself, and he nodded a greeting. The others stuffed a sock into Crawley's mouth, while Bruno removed a long chef's skewer from an inside pocket of his coat. Briefly he glanced at Crawley's midriff, his open flies and the pale appendage shrinking in its bed of grey hair. He put a hand under Crawley's shirt and felt his way along the skin of his paunch to find the right place.

'This is not my style, I assure you,' Bruno explained as his fingers primed the exact spot for his incision. He spoke as if he were sitting at a dreary business meeting. 'I would have preferred to do this quietly in the countryside, but in this city a show is important. It is not enough just to execute an enemy. He must be seen to be humiliated as well. These people are primitive, you know.' Crawley grunted through the sock. There was someone new arriving outside the *pissoir* who wanted to come in and use the urinal, but Crawley heard Bruno's man, outside, explain that the facility was out of order, and so the person walked away without further question. Crawley grunted again, but it was too late. Bruno had pushed the long spike in up to its hilt, so that his thumb and forefinger pinched the soft flesh of Crawley's belly, and the policeman's life began to ebb away. 'Odd to think,' Bruno whispered into his foe's ear, 'there'll still be a warm drip of piss on the end of your dick when you're dead.' They were the last words Frank Crawley heard. He slumped to the floor, while one of the men held a rubberized bag – something like a child's

277

balloon – carefully against the wound. Bruno had a distaste for spillage and insisted that it was dealt with whenever possible. The other man was holding a second rubberized bag at the ready, but Bruno said to him, 'You don't need to bother with that one. We know that he emptied himself just a moment ago.'

Bruno replaced his kid gloves. He cut a fine figure in his neatly tailored suit; and the pale linen spats that he habitually wore, with their distinctive lapis lazuli buttons, set him apart in Naples as a particularly affluent and cosmopolitan citizen. 'Thank you, gentlemen,' he said to his associates. 'I must go now, as I have a lunch appointment which cannot be avoided. I trust I can leave you to tidy up?' The men nodded and Bruno walked out.

Within the hour, Crawley's body had been dropped into a long-forgotten well shaft in an eastern suburb. It was deep and the men counted five seconds before they heard the thud. They sealed the top of the well and that was that. As far as anyone was concerned, Crawley had signed his disembarkation papers and was never seen again.

Chapter 20

On the same morning that Rocco decided the conditions were right for him to tell Molly the truth about Chiara Tomassini, some news came through that was enough to delay the bombshell for the time being. It was reported that the tenor Donal Mulligan had been booed off the stage of the San Carlo opera house during the previous evening's curtain call, and word had it the Irishman was feeling deeply wounded. Molly, though a little stunned by the drama of the story, could not conceal the smallest hint of triumph when she related the incident to Rocco over a late breakfast.

'And there's more,' she said, holding a newspaper in one hand. Now her face shone unashamedly. 'The *New York Times* has made an announcement that you are about to return to singing.'

'Is that so?' answered Rocco flatly.

'Here it is,' she scanned the page. ' "The news the world has been waiting for . . ." more of that sort of thing, "after months of speculation . . ." blah blah blah – here we are: "News of Mr Campobello's intention to return to the recording studio was first aired in the Neapolitan press, and subsequently in Rome, after the tenor's triumphant appearance as a guest of the *king* –" well that part's not strictly accurate "– at a private performance in the city's San Carlo opera house last week. On stage that night were Mr Campobello's celebrated colleagues . . ." etcetera, etcetera . . . "Our correspondent in Naples has it on the highest authority that the great tenor's intention is to establish a recorded legacy that makes use of the finest scientific technology known to man, and –" this is the best part, "– and that the first series of recordings, to be completed with Mr Walter Fleming of the Jupiter Company within the month, will be followed by an announcement of Mr Campobello's imminent return to the opera stage. As yet there has been no word of which role or which—"'

'Where do these people find their lies?' Rocco roared.

For a moment Molly made no reply, but allowed her husband to sip at his coffee while his mood subsided.

'There has been a New York reporter in town,' she said chastely. 'Mr MacSweeney. Signor Graziani has been entertaining him.'

'Of course he has.'

'He only has your best interests at heart. After all, Rocco, you've been out of the stream for more than six months now. You can't just walk back in unannounced. Someone has to do some preparation work.'

'I have never, *ever* given the slightest indication that I will sing on stage again.'

'But the recordings,' faltered Molly, 'everyone assumes that is a step towards—'

'What do I have to do to stop people assuming? Do I have to shut my mouth for ever?' At that instant, a sharper annoyance than the conversation overtook Rocco, and his face flinched. Molly had turned away to rearrange some flowers on the sideboard, and did not notice how her husband had bent forward, holding a fist to the middle of his abdomen.

'We have to control speculation,' she continued, a lily stem in each hand. 'People will whisper that you are a spent force, rumours will spread, and before you know it, the world will be on our doorstep waving pitchforks. Mr MacSweeney's reports will serve to keep all that under control for the time being.'

'Have you met this Mr MacSweeney?' asked Rocco, recovering.

'Once or twice,' Molly confessed, still looking away.

'And what have you been telling him?'

'Not much. Only that you've been practising daily, which is true, and that you're on course to do two days of recordings, beginning on Monday, which is also true.'

'And I suppose he will now report about how badly Mr Mulligan is singing, and how fortunate it is for the world of opera that Rocco Campobello is returning to reclaim his crown as the king of tenors. Is that part of your plan?' Molly just stared at him, unable to articulate a denial. 'I know how Graziani does these things,' continued Rocco. 'I've seen it before, believe me. He will have personally arranged for a claque to lead the booing last night. It had nothing to do with Mulligan's singing. Graziani is clearing away the competition, can't you see that?'

Molly looked down into her lap and folded her hands. 'You can't be sure,' she said quietly. 'Mr Mulligan may have sung poorly. Look at the way he drinks. The people of Naples are known to be intolerant of mediocrity.'

'I do not need you to teach me about the people of Naples any more than I need to be told that Donal Mulligan is capable of mediocrity,' said Rocco, and when she made no answer he turned and left the room.

*   *   *

A few days later, news reached the Villa Rosalba that Mr Mulligan had decided, after a second disastrous reception and a string of biting reviews in the local press, not to proceed with the remaining performances of *Andrea Chénier*. He would shortly be departing for Rome, where he was due to make his own first series of electronic recordings later in the month. By coincidence, the ship on which he embarked for the journey up the coast to the capital passed quietly, during the night, the one on which Rocco Campobello and Pietro Boldoni were sleeping as they sailed back to Naples. They were returning from their brief visit to the Rome clinic where fresh X-rays of Campobello's abdomen had been made. Rocco had not realized Mulligan would be leaving Naples quite so soon and was surprised that the big-hearted Irishman had not left a message of farewell. On his return, he straight away telephoned Miss Carter to ask if she knew of any bad feeling in the air, and he sensed her denials were a little overstated.

When the much anticipated first day of recording arrived, Boldoni instructed Taddeo, the tenor's double, to be prepared early in the morning for what had now become a fairly routine piece of decoying. Taddeo had done well with his diet, but the strain of starving himself under the threat of possible redundancy had taken its toll on his confidence, and this showed in his demeanour. He had lost the hubristic swagger that formerly sat comfortably alongside his corpulence, and now carried something of a hunted look in his eyes, which other members of the household staff thought almost poetic. It was a fortunate side effect of the slimming regime,

Boldoni affirmed when he heard them chatting about it, because, in a way, it added authenticity to Taddeo's performance; after all, the Maestro himself had acquired a shade more vulnerability in his face since his crisis, and it would not do to impersonate him in the old bombastic way.

The chauffeur Pozzo swept a newly slender Taddeo away from the Villa Rosalba in the Lancia at ten o'clock precisely, while, unbeknown to anyone other than Boldoni himself, the great tenor was finishing dressing himself in the apartment of his mistress, on the Vomero. In the unlikely event that Mrs Campobello would emerge from her bedroom before ten o'clock, it would be the responsibility of Boldoni – who alone oversaw the complex comings and goings both of his employer and the double – to explain that the Maestro had already departed for the recording sessions. It was not a role he wished to undertake, but Rocco had assured him that he need only carry the responsibility for a few more days. Everything would shortly be changing, and what would happen thereafter Boldoni did not like to ask.

As they had lain in bed before rising that morning, Chiara asked Rocco why he was making these recordings, when all he ever talked about was leaving his career behind him. Her fingers toyed with the coral amulet that rested just beside the long scar on his chest while she waited for him to answer. He turned and looked at her. 'Have you not realized?' he asked.

'Realized what?'

He smiled. 'It's all about you.'

'Me?'

'And Gabriele.' At the mention of her husband's name she looked down. 'I honour him by singing here,' said

Rocco; 'here in my home, recording some of the songs we used to sing together. I see it as a tribute. My farewell. A small thing I can do.'

'And what has that to do with me?' she asked.

'I honour him and I honour you.'

'And do you honour him by making his wife your lover?'

Rocco lay back on the bed and stared at the ceiling. 'I honour us all. What we were in the old times, and what we will become, you and I. I think he would be happy. I think he would forgive me.' Chiara turned and rose from the bed. 'What is the matter?' said Rocco.

'You talk much about forgiveness, and blame. Like a sinner.'

'I am a sinner.'

She turned and looked at him. 'So that is why you have done all this?' She swept her hand to take in the apartment, its furnishings, pictures, ornaments. 'Is that why you dress me in fine clothes and come to my bed? To make good whatever sin you carry in your breast?'

'Chiara.' He spoke gently and held out a hand to her. After a splinter of hesitation she approached and took his hand. 'You are not my absolution. You are my salvation. When I make these recordings I will be celebrating that I am at last saved. That I have come home, where I belong.'

She sat on the bed once more, and he felt a stab of pain beneath his scar, but suppressed any show of it and put an arm around her shoulder.

Chapter 21

The monastery of San Martino had been chosen as the location for the recording because it was sufficiently quiet, above and away from the hubbub of the city. Boldoni had been told that microphones were very sensitive to extraneous noise, and even a distant burble of traffic could be picked up and reproduced clearly on the final disc. But Rocco wondered if this were the only reason for the choice. He suspected that Don Graziani might have had something to do with it. The old man relished symbolic gestures and sometimes went to great lengths to see them enacted. He probably had in mind a ceremonial relaunching of Rocco's career that would be reminiscent of that first break when the young tenor was paraded, on the very same turf, before the impresario from Milan. Such a shameless piece of theatre would be typical of Graziani. It would nourish his vanity and gratify the urge he always harboured to mix showmanship into his machinations.

Rocco was dropped off on the broad esplanade, high above Naples, with its celebrated view. Pietro Boldoni had arrived much earlier and was standing at the monastery's entrance gate, a case full of music in his arms.

'Mr Fleming is ready,' Boldoni said, 'and the orchestra is playing through the repertoire. The engineers set everything up yesterday. It was quite a business. Much more equipment than in the old days.'

'And Pickering?'

'He won't come. He says he's too busy with Amedeo.' They were walking through to the monastery's first courtyard, and passed a pair of uniformed guards who saluted. Boldoni added, 'You should know that Don Graziani is here.'

'I expected no less.' Rocco scanned the little courtyard that he had not set eyes on since the day he and Gabriele had arrived breathless from their climb, bowler hats in hand. Instruments could be heard fine-tuning and playing random fragments of melody. Boldoni pointed out the direction.

'Did you hear that he cannot walk?'

'Graziani?' said Rocco, stopping.

'His legs apparently gave way beneath him yesterday, but he still insists on being here.'

'Is it genuine?'

'Difficult to know.'

'I wouldn't put it past him to play for sympathy. He'll know how I feel about this business with Mulligan. He's probably worried I'll cancel everything.'

'I don't doubt,' said Boldoni. 'Forgive my saying, but he does stand to make a great deal of money from today's work. No matter what you sing or how you sing it, almost everyone who owns a gramophone will be buying a copy. It's no secret the Grazianis have been on the edge of their seats about this.'

They were making their way around behind the church basilica. Nothing at the monastery had changed; even the faces of the monks, who observed Rocco mournfully as he walked briskly past, seemed indistinguishable from those who had preceded them thirty years before.

'You have been here before,' said Boldoni, whose sharp powers of observation informed him that something in this place did not sit well with his employer.

'Just once.'

Boldoni did not pursue the subject, but ushered Rocco through to the sacristy. 'This was thought to be the most appropriate room.'

'Of course,' replied Rocco, sighing. It had been inevitable. The same room where he had sat and denounced Gabriele. A flood of images from the past threatened to assault him, but he repelled them, and brought the back of his hand up to his nose. He could still smell Chiara on his skin. The thought of her would insulate him against the whims of Don Graziani.

Boldoni continued, 'It is a little narrow for the orchestra, but the acoustic is good. The microphone is a most extraordinary device,' he went on, trying to conceal his almost boyish excitement about the innovation. 'They record the music like an ordinary performance, without the need for engineers in the room, while all the technical machinery and the technicians, including Mr Fleming himself, work next door, connected by cables. They listen to the performance simultaneously, but through loudspeakers. Most extraordinary.'

They entered the sacristy, and Campobello was welcomed by all present with an enthusiastic round of applause. String players tapped their bows against music stands, while woodwind and brass players laid down their instruments and rose clapping to their feet. Rocco acknowledged them with a raised hand while a small crowd of technicians in waistcoats and shirtsleeves began to gather round him. He held them at bay with an outstretched hand. 'One moment, gentlemen,' he said, passing his hat and coat to Boldoni. He had spotted Graziani on the other side of the room.

Stepping through a mayhem of cables, tripods, assorted stands and busy personnel, Rocco walked over to where the old man sat in an upholstered wicker wheelchair, a blanket across his knees. He seemed to have shrunk, or perhaps it was that the angle of the chair hunched him slightly. He had not shaved and the boundary between his cheeks and the goatee beard was less well defined than usual.

'Zio,' said Rocco, holding out both hands to the old man. 'What has happened to you?'

Graziani looked up at him, and after a moment's delay allowed a huge smile to thaw the empty wasteland of his face. 'Do you remember?' he said, taking hold of Rocco's hands. His voice seemed a little thinner, and the slightest of slurs took the edge off his consonants. 'Do you remember this room? Where it all began?' He looked almost childishly euphoric, as if he had pulled off a difficult feat against the odds and was reaping the reward.

'How could I forget?' said Rocco, smiling back. 'Though who would believe it, eh? All these people? So much fuss. How different!' He squeezed Graziani's fingers with his gloved hands.

'Oh yes,' came the reply, 'everything is different,' and then the old man's eyes strayed away across the room and grew cold again.

Boldoni, next to Rocco, checked his watch, leant over

and murmured, 'Mr Fleming is waiting next door,' to which Rocco nodded an acknowledgement and lowered Graziani's hands to his lap.

As they walked away Rocco said to Boldoni, 'It's not an act. Something has happened to him.'

They approached a small side door where serpentine trails of cables led the way through to a neighbouring chamber that was being used as the control room.

Sitting behind a panel of electronic meters, steel dials and switches, and surrounded by a gaggle of busy, earnest young men, was an elderly gentleman in a pale grey suit. He had the air of a professor, a look enhanced by his crimson bow tie and spectacles, and he rose elegantly to his feet as Campobello entered. He smiled an old, wily, experienced kind of smile – the sort that curls one side of the mouth but does not allow the lips to part. This was the veteran sound engineer and impresario Walter Fleming, doyen of the recording industry, whose astute ear and musical instinct had led to the discovery, on a global scale, of almost every musical star of the past quarter of a century, amongst whom Rocco Campobello ranked high.

It was only when Fleming had unfurled himself fully from his chair, and was holding out an arm that almost defied nature with its tendril-like reach, that it became apparent how extraordinarily tall and thin he was. A man of his frame would have to have had his suits hand made, but even so, the sleeves seemed to ride halfway up his forearm, as though his tailors could not bring themselves to admit the abnormality of his physique. Rocco took hold of the long hand and clasped it firmly.

'Good to see you, Rocco,' said Fleming quietly.

'You too,' replied Campobello. The look in their eyes spoke of a warmth and mutual admiration that required no bigger display.

Fleming's mouth held its curved smile. 'Here we are again, then,' he said.

'The two of us. Everything else has changed, though,' replied Rocco.

'You bet,' said Fleming, releasing hands eventually. 'Let me introduce you to my boys. I tell you, these guys are all so clever, they make me feel like an ape at the zoo,' and one by one he presented to the tenor all five of the young men standing there. They nodded in turn, muttering subdued words of greeting and regarding Campobello with cautious awe.

'Can we talk?' asked Fleming, and Rocco followed his lead to another room on the far side, now being used as a cloakroom.

'Boldoni was good enough to have the orchestral parts sent up yesterday,' Fleming said as they walked through. 'Nice arrangements, by the way. I think we'll try and get four done today and four tomorrow.'

'We have twelve prepared, though.'

'I know, I know,' said Fleming in a soothing singsong. 'But I think eight will suffice for the time being.' Rocco knew better than to question Walter Fleming's reasoning. No one in the industry could remember the last time he had made a serious blunder.

The door closed behind them and they were alone.

'So,' said Fleming, 'you've come back home to mother Jupiter. Columbia didn't suit?' Something had to be said about it to clear the air, but he was smiling because he knew the answer.

'I never doubted you were the best, Walter,' said Rocco.

'And I told you at the time. I went over to Columbia for different reasons.'

'I know, I know,' replied Fleming. 'It pains me to say it, but Boldoni was probably right to move you on. Brave decision, though. He must've known it would upset Graziani. How many years had the old man been helping himself to your earnings? I mean, I know you owed him a lot, but maybe not *that* much.' Fleming was perhaps the only person who could talk to Rocco about such things.

Rocco nodded. 'It was time to make a stand.'

Fleming looked straight at him. 'But you're back.'

'You know why? Because none of it matters any more,' said Rocco. 'Money is the least of my concerns nowadays.'

'Couldn't agree more.' Fleming's own fortune was reputed to rival that of the company's chairman.

'I've missed you all,' said Rocco. 'Carmichael, Abe Feldman, Harry – what was his surname? – you know, the one who could tell the success of a recording just by looking at the wax negative.'

'Harry Clarke. A sixth sense that guy had. No room for that kind of approach nowadays. They've all gone, to a man. Made way for the new generation. For better or worse.'

'That's sad. Those men were masters of what they did, with years of expertise.'

'Yesterday's expertise. Acoustic recording is ancient history. It's a different game now, Rocco. I stand back myself. These kids,' he waved towards the room they'd come from, 'they're so sharp, scientific. Technology is paramount. The human ear is considered a blunt instrument. But I think it's going to turn out well. There are some great voices coming through. We're in for a good spell, like before the war.'

'What do all the old engineers think about it?'

'I still see them from time to time. They listen to the latest pressings, the electronics, the wizardry, and a few of them say something's been lost along the way.'

'And you?'

Fleming smiled. 'Well, I'll do my best to keep a bit of the old magic going for as long as they'll have me. Or as long as the Lord tells me I should. But I stay away from the controls now. I just listen to the end result, talk to the artists, try to get the best from them, you know the sort of thing.'

'I certainly do.'

After a pause Fleming looked up at Rocco again. 'So. You quite sure about this?'

Rocco immediately understood the implication. 'You're worried by what Pickering has been telling you.'

'Not just that. I'm asking you. You sure about this? Or are others pushing you?'

'Graziani?' Rocco smiled. 'I wouldn't let him make me do something I didn't want. If anything, I'd cancel to spite him. You heard about Mulligan?'

'That was unfortunate.' Fleming's face, habitually benign and avuncular, was also capable of a sternness that gave credibility to his reputation both as steely critic of mediocrity and as a sly fox of the marketplace. He bore that expression now. 'Mulligan is a fine artist and a good fellow,' he continued. 'This repertoire you're taking on – Neapolitan songs – I think Graziani hopes you're going to beat Mulligan at his own game. You may know that Mulligan's popular songs are outselling his opera now. We've got to hope that not too many people notice the coincidence of your entering the market of popular song records in the same week that Mulligan was booed off stage in the same city, your city.'

Rocco shook his head.

'And what's worse,' continued Fleming, 'is that some people in the company are worried that you're running scared, chasing behind the likes of Mulligan instead of leading from the front, which is where you were when you were at your best.'

Rocco digested the comment. 'You mean to say my best is over?'

'I'm not pronouncing here. I'm asking. Do you think you're ready for this? For a grand return?'

'Who said anything about grand?'

'That's what they're saying.'

'Well, they're mistaken.'

'So, you're stopping?'

'Yes.'

'Why?'

Rocco thought for a moment. 'Because I have seen heaven and hell. And I understand that a man can choose to invite either into his daily life.'

'Maybe,' replied Fleming, 'or maybe it's just this: your voice is telling you, "hey, buddy, wake up to this: our time working together is nearly up", and you're trying to get your head around the bad news as best you can.'

'Maybe. Perhaps the two are the same.'

'Exactly.'

'Is that what Pickering says?'

'Absolutely not.'

'What made you think it, then?'

Fleming hesitated. 'If I'm honest, I think there were signs, even before your collapse.'

'Signs of what?'

'Don't put me on the spot, Rocco.'

'You've never been shy of speaking plainly.'

'All right.' Fleming straightened his long back and stood tall. 'I believe there were signs of deterioration.'

'In my voice?'

'I'm afraid so.'

'You're the first to say so.'

'I'm sorry for that.'

'What sort of deterioration do you mean?'

Fleming frowned, looked away and scratched his ear for a moment before replying. 'You've been darkening the sound over the years, expanding the lower register, sounding more like a baritone down there. And, of course, at the same time you've been hitting the high notes with a lot of muscle. I think you may have been fighting nature in pursuit of your art. Something had to give eventually.'

Rocco pondered the apocalyptic judgement without changing his expression. 'But we are here,' he replied at last: 'the orchestra's through there and your army of clever young men is ready and waiting. Are you telling me I should leave by the back door?'

'Of course not.'

'What, then?'

'Give it a try,' Fleming said quickly. 'And if it's not right, walk away.'

Rocco thought again. 'As simple as that?' he said.

'Yep.'

'People tell me I'll be missing the opportunity to leave a proper legacy.'

'There's no ignominy in retiring after a rule as undisputed king for twenty-five years. King of a golden era, no less. Remember, in the really early days, how the great de Reszke, finest tenor in the second half of the nineteenth century, refused to let himself be recorded because he didn't want history to remember him past his best.'

Rocco smiled. 'What I do remember is you criticizing de Rezske for being a stubborn old goat.'

'The truth was that he'd heard this young kid from Naples, and knew that his time was over.' Fleming smiled. He linked arms with Rocco and they walked towards the door.

Rocco had begun to feel the chill of the sacristy, and opted to put his coat and scarf back on before progressing to the little stage that had been constructed for him. High above, and suspended centrally from a great steel boom, hung the microphone itself, the central point of everyone's focus. Until a moment before, an engineer had been tinkering with it, but he had finished now and it was being raised slowly and reverently into position. Its nondescript shape and bland, perforated surface belied the great significance it seemed to have in the room, which was like that of an ecclesiastical monstrance held aloft above the congregation at the high point of the eucharistic rite. Campobello glanced up at it as he took his place on the stage.

Don Graziani had been manoeuvred to the far end of the room, where he looked on vacantly as people hurried around getting everything ready for the start.

The players were fine-tuning their instruments for the last time when Fleming approached Rocco again and, leaning close in, said in a low voice, 'There's this reporter here, by the name of Brian MacSweeney.' He indicated a thickset man with thinning, swept-over ginger hair who was sitting against a wall to one side. 'He's here to cover the story for the *New York Times*. Says he met you once some years back.'

'What story?' asked Rocco.

'Look, if you'd rather not have him here, just say the word.'

'Graziani arranged this,' said Rocco. 'MacSweeney is the same one who told the world I was returning to the opera stage.'

'You may be right. All I know for sure is that what we're doing today is hot news and a lot of people are going to want to know about it. Sooner or later someone will tell the story, and I'd rather it was someone who saw it happen. But don't fret, I'll get rid of him if you like.'

'No,' said Rocco, 'just ask him to come over here.'

MacSweeney's pink complexion turned a darker ruby as he walked quickly across the carpet that had been laid to deaden the sacristy's acoustic. He extended a sweaty palm to shake hands with the singer.

Rocco was brief but not discourteous. 'You are welcome to sit and watch, but I want no exaggerations, no talk of a grand return, and suchlike. Understood?'

'Does that mean, sir,' ventured MacSweeney, laying his freckled head on the block, 'that you are not planning an imminent return to the stage?'

'Yes, Mr MacSweeney,' replied Rocco quietly, 'it means precisely that, and you can put it in your notebook straight away.' MacSweeney looked up nervously at Walter Fleming, appealing for some kind of elaboration, but none was forthcoming. Instead, Fleming stood up to his full height, and the rectangular bulge of the little bible he carried at all times was clearly visible in his breast pocket. 'There you have it,' he said. 'Now, let's proceed with the day's work,' and he ushered MacSweeney away from the stage.

The conductor hired for the occasion had a few words with Rocco before running through the first song with the orchestra. It was to be 'Tarantella Sincera', a quick-paced romp in six-eight, with few or no uncomfortable demands on the singer's capacities. The orchestra began its practice run-through, and Campobello marked his line in a suppressed half-voice, floating the higher notes in *falsetto*. There being no problems, the assembled musicians awaited the signal from the technicians that the machinery next door was set for them to begin. There was a neat oak box next to the conductor topped with two coloured glass domes, one of which now shone green, and the players silently picked up their instruments. Rocco rose to his feet, and the conductor held his baton aloft. A moment later the second dome shone red, and after two dummy beats, the orchestra was brought in with the first *forte* chord.

Rocco, who did not need a score for the song, tipped his brow forward and opened his mouth to sing. Every musician present, conductor included, fought the temptation to glance at him as the first notes emerged. From a musical point of view it was a fairly nondescript phrase, but it was a good, confident sound, and several of them smiled as they played – a sweet little piece of history was unfolding before them.

After a couple of minutes the unambitious song crunched to its end with a single firm chord and a fine brassy high G from Campobello. The violinists held their bows in the air and everyone remained stock still until the red light was switched off. The instrumentalists then shuffled their feet in the customary way to show their appreciation, and everyone else present in the room, save Graziani, rose to clap. Fleming appeared at the door connecting to the control room and smiled across the distance to Rocco, though he did not join in the applause.

The orchestra settled down, a burble of chatter began, and Rocco walked up to exchange a few words with the conductor. Meanwhile, Boldoni had hurried over to Fleming's side. 'Well,' he said, beaming. 'Doesn't that put your fears to rest? Was it not perfect?'

'Promising, I'd say,' said Fleming, noncommittally, 'but I'm not sure if we can use it.' He was renowned for his lack of enthusiasm about a work in progress, something which the more emotionally volatile Boldoni could never understand.

'Why not?' he asked. 'There was nothing wrong with it.'

'I think we should have a listen to it and maybe try it again,' asserted Fleming.

'Is that necessary?' asked Boldoni even as he realized the absurdity of questioning Fleming's judgement. An immediate playback was possible in the control room in order to ascertain the finer details of balance, but to do that meant destroying the wax disc on to which the recording had just been cut.

The young technicians were less convinced by Fleming's negative hunch than by the eager insistence of one of their number that a dog had been heard barking in a quieter section of the song, and therefore, after much discussion, it was agreed that, to be on the safe side, another take should be made. Rocco was invited into the control room to hear the playback. There was no evidence of canine interference, and a certain amount of tutting was directed at the blushing young claimant, but Fleming's grim expression confirmed he was still of the opinion that the first take could be improved on, though he did concede an appreciative nod in Rocco's direction.

A few minutes later a new performance was undertaken, at the close of which all held still once again for the red light to be extinguished. The wait seemed interminable this time, but finally a loud click cut through the breathless silence and the light switched off. Half a minute later, news came through that the take was considered satisfactory, and several players cheered. It was then announced that they were to pause for coffee.

Fleming, towering above the bustle of shifting chairs, resting instruments and people crossing the room, approached Rocco, and together they went over to where Graziani was sitting at the rear. An elderly monk had just come in and was exchanging a few words with the old man. Behind them stood Bruno Graziani, also recently arrived, dusting down the shoulders of his suit.

'I eat my words, Maestro,' said Fleming quietly as they meandered over. His lips curved into that wily old smile again. 'That was you at your best.'

Rocco reached a hand up and rested it on Fleming's shoulder. 'You're going soft with age,' he said, 'and don't get carried away. It was hardly "Pira"!' The reference was to one of Campobello's former signature tunes, a fiery, barnstorming extravaganza from the middle of Verdi's *Il Trovatore*, and Fleming laughed.

There was a general sense of relief in the room, as everyone tucked into their coffee and biscuits. Earlier, inevitably, the shadow of concern had hung over the proceedings, as if they all secretly acknowledged the possibility that things might not go well today, but now that two takes had been successfully accomplished everyone felt the tension dissolve.

'*Zio*,' said Rocco, squatting down to talk to Graziani and taking his hand. 'What a business, eh?'

Graziani removed his heavy spectacles and looked straight at Rocco. He could see almost nothing, of course, but his gaze seemed more natural and direct now that his eyes were not misshapen by the thickness of the lenses. Rocco noticed a redness in the whites of his eyes. 'It was wonderful to hear you, my boy,' said Graziani. 'I have never heard you sing better.'

Rocco guffawed. 'Now don't exaggerate, *zio*.'

'It's true,' Graziani added, thinly, and then held out a hand, indicating the cleric behind him. 'You remember Fra Rafaello, of course?'

Rocco looked up at the rather stooped figure standing at Graziani's shoulder. It was the same monk. The years had merely added to the desolation of his face and the tragedy in his eyes. At the same moment a young electrician tried to catch Rocco's attention so that he could pass him a steaming cup of coffee, but found that he could not get through to the tenor, and blushed with embarrassment before giving up. Rocco was oblivious to everything. He seemed to say something, but his words, perhaps intended for Graziani, were inaudible, barely whispered, and his lips hardly moved. Nevertheless, a faint smile seemed to touch Don Graziani's mouth, and he held out a shaking hand to accept his own coffee cup. '*Grazie*,' the old man murmured, bringing the cup to his lap. Rocco had turned his eyes aside, away from the monk.

'Is something wrong, Maestro?' It was Bruno's rather

bland voice that broke the silence, and Rocco looked up at him with a jerk.

'No, nothing at all.'

'Coffee, sir?' the young electrician tried his luck again.

'No. Thank you,' replied Rocco, before turning to Graziani. 'Excuse me, *zio*. I have to speak with the conductor.'

The orchestra had been called back and were tuning up again while the sacristy began to clear. Rocco was asked to return to the stage, and soon all musicians, engineers and technicians were at their stations ready to begin. The next song was to be 'Pecche', a well-known favourite.

The string players immediately behind Rocco were chatting to one another, and the lead violinist – who knew his wife would never forgive him if he did not at least make the attempt – now plucked up the courage to lean forward and share a word with the Maestro. He offered his congratulations in a rather florid, old-fashioned manner, emphasizing that God had granted the world of music a blessing beyond compare in allowing the great Campobello to make so glorious a return.

'*Molto gentile*,' Rocco replied politely, but his attention was being distracted by the three guests in the chamber, who were repositioning themselves in order to be able to observe the next session more closely. The three of them were, in fact, in roughly the same place they had sat to watch the audition thirty years before, and as Rocco waited for the red light to be switched on, he could not stop himself glancing up at them. He looked down at his score, and one or two members of the orchestra thought they saw him purse his lips and shake his head. They glanced at one another, wide-eyed, wondering what the problem might be.

There was a hitch in the control room, it was announced, and they were kept waiting longer than expected. Flutes were lowered from lips and bows were raised off strings. Rocco shifted uncomfortably in his chair, crossing his legs and turning slightly to one side so that he would not have to face straight out into the chamber. The conductor noticed him fidgeting and leant over to ask if everything was all right, to which Rocco nodded.

The red light eventually flicked on, and the orchestra launched into the next song's full-blooded introduction. Rocco stood up quietly and felt a familiar ache dig at him beneath the ribs. He began to sing the opening line and the pain dug deeper – not enough to derail him, but an impediment, to be sure. And then, as he looked up quickly between phrases, something caught his eye, and that was enough. He stopped singing, closed the score in his hands, and sat down. The orchestra went on for a couple of bars but petered out when the conductor lowered his baton with a quizzical look at Rocco. After some brief whispering between the two men, while everyone in the chamber remained nervously silent, the conductor climbed down from the podium, ashen faced, and went to have words with Boldoni. Walter Fleming soon came through and joined them.

Boldoni whispered to Fleming, 'The Maestro wants Don Graziani's party to leave.'

'What?'

'He told the conductor he will not continue until they've gone.'

'What happened?' said Fleming. 'He was fine a moment ago.' He glanced up at Rocco, whose gaze was meandering across the ceiling fresco. 'All right, I'll deal with this.'

Fleming had experienced dozens of crises with temperamental singers over the years, though never before with Campobello. He went across to the visitors and explained that these were early days, an experiment, in a way, and it would be best for the tenor to have as few distractions as possible. It was an explanation that seemed to satisfy Bruno, who straight away got up, tightened the knot of his tie and glanced at his watch. The old monk, too, rose to his feet, but Don Graziani did not share their compliance and made no attempt to conceal his protests. He would not have this special day ruined, he said, and continued to splutter objections all the way to the door, but Bruno wheeled him out of earshot.

Campobello now walked from the stage and sat down at the edge of the sacristy, in one of the old built-in pews. Fleming was about to go over to him, when Boldoni suggested it might be better if he could be left to have a quiet word with the Maestro himself. Fleming nodded and remained with the orchestra and technicians, mentioning quietly to them that they should not stare.

Boldoni walked over and pulled up a chair next to Rocco. He knew better than to ask for an explanation. Close as he was to his Maestro, he would not presume, and neither did he think it would be effective, to redraw the boundaries of their intimacy at a time like this. Better by far to treat it, as ever, like an item on the agenda between a junior officer and his commander.

'Now that they have gone,' he ventured in a matter-of-fact voice, 'are you ready to begin again, Maestro?'

'I think so, Pietro, yes,' replied Rocco, and gave a slight cough. 'Just give me a moment, will you?'

Boldoni sat up and looked around. The orchestra and technicians had relaxed slightly and there was a burble of subdued conversation in the air. After a few moments, Boldoni spoke again. 'Mr Fleming has recently been recording tribal music in Asia.'

'Oh, really?' said Rocco, his gaze still fixed on the floor.

'Quite different to what he's used to,' continued Boldoni. 'The Victor Company believes it has a responsibility to compile a kind of sound archive for future generations.'

'Aha.'

'Ethno-musicology, they're calling it. By travelling around the world—'

'I will not allow them to manipulate me, Pietro,' interrupted Rocco.

Boldoni blinked and looked down. 'I understand,' he said.

'You know what I mean?'

'Yes.'

'I am not a dog, to be brought to heel with whips and rewards.' Pietro opened his mouth to reply, but faltered, and Rocco went on, 'I tell you, they arranged it all. This room. That old monk. It's an old wound, Pietro, and they think by pouring salt into it they can get me to do as they please.'

Boldoni hesitated, and then said, 'But you do want to continue with the recordings. Now that they've gone, you surely would like to finish the excellent work that you've already begun? Everything was going so well.'

Walter Fleming was watching from a distance as the tenor and his secretary talked quietly at the edge of the chamber. When the conversation came to an end, Boldoni came over to Fleming and asked if they could go next door for a word. Once there, he rubbed his forehead, squeezed the bridge of his nose between thumb and forefinger, and said, through a heavy sigh, 'He's ready to continue.'

'Is he losing his grip?' asked Fleming, quietly.

'No. He's ready now.'

'Whatever this is,' Fleming went on, 'it's in the mind. The voice is in surprisingly reasonable shape, but if he can't sort himself out upstairs he won't be in a fit state to carry on.'

'He's also in a degree of pain. The operation—'

'Psychosomatic,' interrupted Fleming.

'What?'

'Most likely an illness of the mind expressing itself in physical symptoms.'

'How can you be sure?'

'I think we should call this off, perhaps tomorrow—'

Boldoni turned on him urgently. 'No. I beg you, by all that you hold sacred, no. This once, please listen to me. There's more at stake here than you can realize. These recordings are absolutely vital. We've got him this far, we must give it another try.'

Fleming hesitated and then sighed. 'All right, we'll give it another shot. But we should prepare ourselves for the worst.' He went back into the sacristy, looked down the room at Rocco, and winked.

'Shall we proceed now, Maestro?' he called out, lifting the tension with his grandfatherly ease of manner. He then explained to everybody that it would take a couple of minutes to load a fresh wax blank on to the recording machine; they should remain seated until everything was ready.

When all was set, the red light shone and a new take

was commenced. *'Canta l'auciello dinta' casa antica,'* Rocco began, and the build up to the *fortissimo* climactic section continued smoothly. He opened up the cavernous immensity of his voice on the word *'Car-mè'*, and as he reached the high G, he broadened the tone, closing his eyes and leaning back to give full, passionate expression to the note. It was then that his voice faltered, but only slightly, and he tried to conceal it. The lead violinist had noticed something and glanced up at him in alarm, but Rocco was carrying on, moving towards a fairly high phrase. It was as he eased back from it, in a gentle *diminuendo*, that something gave way. The foundation instantly crumbled from beneath the note and the body of sound collapsed. The voice cracked and the note became a toneless howl. Rocco doubled over and let out a tight gasp. He clutched both arms around his abdomen, then fell heavily back into his chair, his face white. An unearthly silence fell in the chamber, and the red light clicked off loudly. Brian MacSweeney, who had been permitted to remain watching from the side, rose to his feet, open-mouthed, and his chair scraped noisily across the ground. Moments later, the sacristy was a scene of frenzied activity as Campobello, still curled over and with his coat thrown across his shoulders, was led quickly away, leaning heavily on the arm of Boldoni.

Fleming could hear the noise from next door, the confusion of yells and shifted furniture. He sat down wearily in front of the control panel and stared at the resting dials. Around him, the Jupiter Company engineers, who had overseen the shipment of their precious equipment, with great difficulty and at considerable expense, all the way from New Jersey, looked at each other. One of Fleming's young technicians in the control room leant back in his chair and chucked a pencil into the air. It clattered behind him on the seventeenth-century marble floor. 'So much for yesterday's stars,' the boy said, with a yawn and a stretch, but the comment failed to elicit the snigger he had hoped for from his colleagues. Instead, Walter Fleming glared angrily at him as he rose to his feet. 'May the Lord forgive you your ignorance, you arrogant little shit,' he said.

Chapter 22

Brian MacSweeney had been raised by solid Catholic folk and liked to think of himself as a decent, Christian kind of fellow, but he had no illusions about the strength of his personality. In the last few years, especially, he had been tempted to stray in ways that would have made his uncle Desmond, a priest in Athlone, shake his head with disapproval. Which is not to say that Brian lived life in a merry haze of moral abandonment. Rather the contrary: he struggled periodically against the influence of his inner demon, and would often lie awake at night weighing out an acceptable balance between guilt and personal advancement. Above anything else – and this was the crux – Brian MacSweeney hungered for the approbation of his fellow man. Whether it was praise received for a good article or just a laugh in appreciation of one of his jokes, he wanted to be noticed and he wanted to be liked; and he would go to any length in pursuit of this need, even to the extent of transgressing his own moderately held standards of Christian charity. This was the heart of his weakness, and he was confronting it face to face on a giant scale this evening, sitting in his shabby Naples hotel room.

Signor Graziani had asked for a lot of journalistic favours over the years – a sentence slipped in here or there, sometimes an entire column with a particular slant – and he paid well; increasingly well, as the size and frequency of the favours escalated. The current project, however, was in a different league, both in terms of its profile and the promised fee. There had been mention of another kind of reward as well: a more formal tie with Graziani, based on a long-term friendship and mutual trust, all of which was flattering for a man of MacSweeney's limping self-esteem. But it only made his present dilemma all the more sticky. The events of today had turned the entire situation on its head.

He knew what he had to do, but needed to find ways to justify it; after all, it was going to be a pretty underhand act, by any standards. But then again, why should he be their puppet? He imagined the Grazianis dining on suckling pig and champagne; he pictured Campobello relaxing into the erotic caresses of his glamorous wife; all of it in contrast to himself, a hard-working, honest, respected man of letters, unable to afford more than a slum hotel with crumbling plaster walls and rattling water pipes. Should he not be allowed the opportunity to advance himself a notch, just as they must surely have done at various times in their careers? So what if it meant reneging on the agreement with Graziani? Masterminding a publicity campaign to relaunch a slumbering maestro was one thing; it was quite another to be the only journalist on the planet to witness the collapse of music's greatest colossus.

And as for the tenor himself? MacSweeney smiled as the light of righteous justification dawned on him. There was no need to carry the sack of guilt over this one. It was payback time for the newspaper industry. The so-called Great Campobello was a self-important, ostentatious bully, famous for his intolerant spats with the press; he had always gloried in his power and gave little consideration to the small man. Well, his time was past, and it would be the pen of Brian MacSweeney, son of an impoverished but God-fearing Irish immigrant, that would announce the fallen titan's demise. Gratifying, indeed, he thought with a satisfied smile, sweeping a ginger lock to one side and stretching for his notepad. The legend of David and Goliath was alive and well here in Naples.

Despite their seniority in the clan, Marco and Andrea Florio arrived at the Grazianis' house with trepidation. The family's affairs were near to crisis point. Much had been made recently of the American policeman's disappearance, particularly in one newspaper (owned by a loyal Fascist), which claimed that Crawley had come to Naples in order to secure Bruno Graziani's extradition to the United States. The New York Police Department had so far distanced themselves from the incident, partly, it was rumoured, because they did not want to offend Mussolini. The Italian government did not appreciate foreign interference and had sent an assurance to President Coolidge that a thorough investigation into the mystery of the missing agent was under way. At this stage, however, the matter seemed to be in the hands of the Naples police, and they had discounted any link with organized crime. But this did little to stop the spread of speculation.

The doctors immediately noticed the change at the Grazianis' house. They had been coming here for ten years, but Bruno Graziani's comfortable appropriation of his father's study heralded the arrival of a new era in which the Florios' long-standing service, and the many secrets they had shared within these same four walls, did not guarantee them any rank or status. It was disquieting, to say the least.

The study had been transformed, and many of the changes augured well. Cracks in the plaster had been filled, and the walls freshly painted. A large oriental rug had softened the formerly spartan ambience and dampened the classroom acoustic. New furniture and ornaments had been acquired, a large abstract bronze and a darkly enigmatic canvas in the style of Paul Klee. Don Graziani's forbidding study had not exactly become cosy, but was being turned into a functioning, modern bureau where the elite of working society, industrialists and politicians, could come and conduct business in an appropriate environment. The centrepiece was a huge contemporary desk, behind which, in a new leather armchair, Bruno Graziani now received them. His hands were caged and he was not smiling.

'What is your prognosis, gentlemen?' he asked, coming straight to the point.

For a moment the doctors hesitated, and then Marco Florio volunteered a reply. 'Don Graziani is stable, and safe for the time being. He needs complete rest, and should be protected from anything that might weigh heavily on him. We must be kept informed of any developments.'

'Particularly on the left side of his body,' added Andrea. 'His leg, arm or hand, or even the muscles in his cheek.'

Bruno allowed for a substantial pause, then moistened his lips. 'I was asking about Signor Campobello, rather than my father.'

Andrea Florio sat up slightly in his chair. 'We have his X-ray results, from Rome,' he said.

'In a moment,' interrupted Bruno, raising a finger. 'First of all, explain to me what went wrong at the recordings.'

The doctors felt as if they were in some way answerable for the calamity. 'The patient,' began Marco, depersonalizing Rocco and thereby distancing himself from blame, 'apparently suffered a breakdown, caused by a combination of factors: some related to his former illness, others brought on by the particular circumstances of the day.'

'He has spoken to you about it?'

'We have his confidence,' replied Marco discreetly. 'We believe the abdominal pain was due to pressure of the breathing mechanism pushing against the ribcage, in particular the area – not yet fully recovered – where the rib was removed.'

'The voice itself?'

'Unconnected to the incident,' replied Marco, 'but only relevant inasmuch as the bellows which support the flow of air to the vocal cords – his lungs – will not in future perform to the same capacity.'

Bruno did not move, nor did he ask for an explanation, but his silence, and the severity of his expression behind those caged hands seemed to demand one.

Andrea Florio took the hint. 'Which means that when the Maestro sings, he will just have to take breaths more often and not quite so deep.' He hoped this fragment of reassuring news would soften the gravity of Bruno's mood, because of what he needed to say next. He drew breath deeply and went on, 'The pain may also be related to the development of a further complication in his pulmonary condition. The X-rays have unfortunately given rise to the suggestion that,' he faltered slightly, '. . . that there may, perhaps, be a small new abscess forming beneath the diaphragm. A subphrenic abscess. Entirely treatable, and not in any sense . . .'

Bruno sighed and seemed to relax back slightly, as if the ill-tidings offered him a more satisfying kind of nourishment. He encouraged them to continue. 'Not in any sense . . . ?'

'Not in any sense life endangering. If it is treated within a reasonable period of time.'

'What about his state of mind?' asked Bruno. 'Will he be stable enough to work again, or do you think our great Maestro is finished at last?' His flippancy of manner made Andrea wonder which of the two prognoses he would prefer to hear.

'There is enough evidence in the Maestro's recent behaviour,' said Marco cautiously, 'to suggest that the mental strain has left him – how shall I say it? – vulnerable to delusions.'

'You are referring to the ridiculous obsession with his past life? Or the lady friend?'

The Florios looked at one another. 'We . . . we did not know about a lady friend,' muttered Marco awkwardly.

'No matter,' continued Bruno, sitting up and bringing the subject back to the table. 'I'll speak plainly. The man is in danger of going mad. Which is all the more reason to get him back to serious work as soon as possible. This new abscess. What would the treatment involve?'

'It would be best for him to undergo removal of accumulated deposits at the Baldassari clinic in Rome. The doctor there has suggested as much.'

'When?' asked Bruno.

'As soon as can be arranged. The surgeon predicts a good recovery.'

'How long can it be delayed?'

Marco Florio looked at Bruno with slight surprise. 'Is there a need to delay?'

'How long can it be delayed?'

'A month, perhaps, at the most.'

'I say six weeks.'

Marco swallowed. 'I would not like to recommend a delay of that long.'

Bruno stood up and walked around the desk, taking up position behind them. Marco stole a nervous glance over his shoulder as Bruno squatted down between them and spoke close to their ears, two words, slowly and clearly: 'Six. Weeks.'

After a pause, Marco drummed up the courage to say, 'May I ask why the treatment needs to be delayed that long?'

Bruno stood up, but remained out of view behind them. 'Simple,' he said. 'The plan to relaunch Campobello on record has been postponed. We must sidestep that now and go straight for the main prize.'

'What prize?'

'Put him back on stage. Here in Naples. And soon.'

'Would that be wise?' began Marco, 'in view of recent events?'

'A gamble. All or nothing. We must play our cards once and for all, and see what happens.'

'The strain would be too much for him,' said Marco.

'I am suggesting just three performances. I heard him sing last week. It was splendid.'

'He broke down.'

Bruno ignored the remark. 'The San Carlo is putting on Boito's *Mefistofele* next month. Campobello knows the opera backwards. I can arrange for him to replace

314

the tenor scheduled to sing the part of Faust for three performances only. It will be enough to re-establish his reputation and secure my own nomination as the company's new director.'

'Even three performances would be – I think, with all respect – excessive,' said Marco.

'Two, then,' said Bruno.

Marco looked around the room uncomfortably and blurted out, 'Must we be compelled to gamble with the Maestro's health? His life might be at stake. This is not a game of dice.' A sharp look from Andrea silenced him.

'Very well,' said Bruno. 'A single appearance. One night. The opening night. After a huge campaign of publicity. Campobello's great comeback. Don't you see, gentlemen? The very precariousness of the outcome will work to our advantage. All ears will be turned to the San Carlo. Will he make it, won't he make it? People across the world will be on the edge of their seats.'

Andrea Florio continued to remain calm as stone, and said nothing.

'When would this be?' asked Marco.

'In just over five weeks' time.'

'It is one matter to use your own doctors to justify a plan,' said Marco, still agitated, 'but quite another to persuade a singer against his will.'

'I'll take care of any persuading that needs to be done,' replied Bruno.

Andrea's eyes were set and steady. 'I think, perhaps,' he said calmly, 'a single performance might be feasible. If he were willing to cooperate.' Marco shot a look at his brother but thought better than to intervene. 'As long as he could leave for Rome immediately afterwards. The very next morning.'

315

'That can be arranged,' replied Bruno.

'We would have to medicate to keep the pain and fever at bay,' added Andrea.

'I will be relying on you to keep him fit enough for the great night. So. We are in agreement?'

'We will still have to persuade Signor Boldoni, and Pickering.'

'Ah yes, Boldoni and Pickering,' said Bruno. 'Boldoni, I think, will not present a problem if we deal with Mr Pickering effectively. The fat little Englishman presents a special kind of obstacle. He exerts too much influence over the Maestro, and always has done. Right now that influence is contrary to our interests. I had him over the other day. For tea. He's still stubbornly opposed to Campobello singing, at least for another eight months, perhaps longer. In fact,' and now Bruno came round in front of the doctors again, smiling, as if having seen a neat way to move on to the next item on his agenda, 'in fact, I would like to enlist your help in dealing with the little pest.'

He sat down at the desk and began in a new and more friendly tone, rubbing his hands together gleefully. 'Gentlemen, I have been educating myself.' He opened a drawer and pulled out a large, illustrated book of human anatomy. 'I think you will approve.' Turning to a bookmarked page, he said, 'I have become quite expert in the internal workings of the forearm. Have a look at this.' He turned the book around to them and pointed his pencil at various points on the diagrams. 'I have given particular attention to the *flexors digitorum sublimis*, here, and the *carpi ulnaris*, not to mention the *palmaris longus*, here, and I would like a little bit of practical advice.'

316

The brothers looked at him, at a loss for words, until Andrea asked, 'What is your particular interest in those tendons?'

'Isn't it obvious, in view of what we were saying? They are the ones that control the mechanics of finger movement.'

Half an hour later, the doctors were leaning against the railings that overlooked the sea near to the city's old fortified arsenal. Their faces were pale. It was chilly, though a fine day, and the light was exceptionally clear, but the beauty of the view was far from their thoughts. They were silenced by the prospect of the task that had been passed into their hands.

It was Marco who eventually spoke. 'He still harps on about being director of the San Carlo. Does he imagine they'll consider him when this scandal of the New York cop is hanging in the air? He doesn't stand a chance! We're risking Campobello's life, and getting ourselves into . . . into this horror to help him chase after a crazy dream!'

'Steady, brother,' said Andrea. 'Not so loud.' He looked around in all directions. 'This isn't just about becoming director of the opera. He's desperate, like a cornered dog.'

'He doesn't give that impression. He seems to think he's got it all worked out.'

'Don't you believe it,' replied Andrea. 'The anatomy book, for God's sake! He's cracking. He's being hounded and there's nowhere left to turn. Everything's coming out – his hatred, his anger, his . . . peculiar methods.'

'That doesn't help us. He won't go down until long after he's pushed us under first. And I get the strange feeling he's enjoying it all. He seems to like the idea of nudging Campobello over the edge.'

'He's always secretly loathed him,' murmured Andrea.

'Why should he, though? His father worships the ground Campobello walks on.'

'Maybe that's something to do with it,' said Andrea with a sigh. 'What I do know is that he's out of control. It's going to be a dangerous time for us, no question. But it might just be the moment we've been waiting for.'

'What do you mean?'

Andrea looked him in the face. 'The chance to get out, *fratello*. The old man's finished, it seems. And Bruno's cracking up. If we play our cards right, wait for the opportunity, we could walk away and watch the whole thing go under, right before our eyes.'

'You're playing with fire.'

'I know, I know,' muttered Andrea.

'This business with the pianist,' said Marco and shook his head. 'I just don't know if I can go through with it.'

Andrea put an arm around his brother's shoulders and they began to walk along the seafront. 'I was thinking,' he said, 'I'll handle this from now on. You stay out of it altogether.'

'On your own?' said Marco, stopping and looking at him with surprise. 'Why should you do it on your own? It's too horrible. We should share it.'

'No, no,' replied Andrea gently, and gave Marco a kiss on the cheek. 'All those years ago I got us into this. Remember? When I did the first job for the old man? Well, I want to do this for you now. You leave it to me.'

Marco tried to protest, but Andrea would not hear of

it, and changed the subject as they turned inland to find their car, which was parked in the Rione Santa Lucia.

Marco's nervous relief at his brother's offer found expression in a stream of light-hearted chatter, and he barely noticed that Andrea was not listening very carefully to him; he had little idea of the dark plague that had settled on his brother's thoughts, nor the scheme that was taking shape behind his nods and smiles.

Chapter 23

They decided to talk this through on the west terrace, overlooking the sea, even though it was a cold and grey morning. Mount Vesuvius was hidden by cloud, the sea was a dull green and in the distance merged into the pale sky because the horizon had been smudged away by mist. However, Molly was not of a mind to notice either the view or the chill this morning. She wore a cape, but rebellious goose pimples stood up the length of her pale arms, up to her shoulders, more from shock than cold.

Ten minutes before, a solemn-faced Rocco had suggested that it was time they had a chat. At his words, a febrile shock had pulsed through her abdomen, and a few moments later, the sentences were spoken that would change her life.

Her husband now sat opposite her in a wicker chair. He was wrapped in his coat and took a long drag on his cigarette while he waited for her to digest the news.

'Do you love her?' Molly said at length. She raised her chin and looked out at the sea.

'Yes. I do.' Molly's mouth tightened and she suppressed the smallest whimper. She kept her gaze firmly fixed on the distance but her eyes were filling. After a long silence, she dabbed at them with a handkerchief. No one ever saw a tear fall on to Molly's cheek.

'And what do you propose to do?' she asked.

'I have no proposal. I could not keep it from you any longer. I had to tell you.'

'Rather late in the day.'

There was another silence before Rocco spoke again, his voice unusually high, stripped bare. 'You must tell me what you want me to do. You can have anything you want.'

'I've never been able to have what I want. It's always been you, you, you. Who am I? What have I got? Everything has always been about you.'

'That's not true, Molly. You sometimes had what you wanted. Including a lover. More than one lover, in fact.'

'Now you're blaming me for everything, I suppose. Blaming me for your misdemeanours.'

'My misdemeanour, as you call it, is no worse than what you yourself did, twice, and both times you kept it secret until I found out myself. Maybe there were more that I never knew about.'

'Oh! Here we go. You were telling me about your affair, and yet you can turn it around to make it sound as if I've brought this on myself.'

Rocco sighed. He had heard this kind of defensive deflection a thousand times. Molly was as quick and agile as an eel in the art of self-justification. 'I have done no more or no worse than you have done to me, more than once.'

'I never loved those men!' Molly screamed, and buried her face in her palms. Recovering, and after staring into space for a minute or so, she went on, 'I looked for lovers because you so obviously didn't need me, didn't want me.'

'Now you're blaming me for *your* misdemeanours.'

'What did you expect?' she spat. 'You never let me anywhere near you. You never let anyone get close to you. You and your precious voice. It's only now, now since—' she broke off and began to weep quietly into her handkerchief. 'It's only now, since your . . . illness, that you need someone all of a sudden. And, for some reason, you've decided that person has to be someone other than me.' Her head was bowed, her slender shoulders hunched and shaking beneath the cape. Strangely, Rocco did not pity her. It was too late in the day for that. At last she looked up, blew her nose lightly and turned to him again. 'So. What are we going to do?'

'I will leave, if you want. I probably should.'

'With her?'

'We have not discussed it.'

'And your career?'

Rocco looked mystified by the question. It was the last thing he had considered. 'Finished.'

Again, Molly tried to hide a high-pitched sob, and then breathed deeply to calm herself. 'Where would you go?'

'I don't know. I thought about Switzerland.'

'Why Switzerland?'

Rocco shook his head. 'As good a place as any. I've never sung there. And I've been told there is a doctor there who could help me with my illness.'

'Your emphysema? Shouldn't you go back to New York?'

'I've never had emphysema,' he said quietly, 'but I'm not talking about my chest, I mean the illness in my mind. People are saying I've had some kind of breakdown.'

'Oh,' Molly looked for a shred of solace in mockery, 'so you're abandoning your life and career and you're taking off with your dumpling-shaped fantasy of simple Italian womanhood, and you're going to hand yourself over to the care of some Swiss quack. Is that the measure of it?'

Rocco sighed. 'If that's how you want to see it.'

'Tell me how else I should see it!' she yelled back at him. But he did not answer. 'Have you given one thought about what the future might hold for me?' She beat her wrist against her chest. 'A woman of . . . of my age. Publicly humiliated, discarded, like so much . . . trash!'

Only after the air had subsided and Molly had returned to the succour of her handkerchief, which she held close against her mouth, did he venture another comment. 'I will do whatever you want,' he said, rising to his feet. His breath clouded the cold morning air. 'And I am sorry. I can only hope that you will be happier in the long term without me. I believe it will be so.' He turned to go, but stopped when Molly called out for him to wait a moment. Her voice had regained a relatively stable composure.

'I would ask that you do nothing and tell no one for the time being,' she said. 'At least until I have had time to plan what I should do next.'

'Of course.'

'And if you must see this woman,' her voice wavered, 'I beg you to be as discreet as possible. Do not suffer me the indignity of a public scandal just now. I need to prepare myself.'

Rocco nodded and looked at the ground for a moment before turning and leaving Molly alone on the terrace.

She pulled the cape close around her shoulders and gazed emptily out to sea. The distant outline of Ischia was rising above the bed of pale grey mist. It gained definition by the second and it fascinated her; momentarily her thoughts were diverted, like capillary rivulets that are drawn to a deviant but stronger flow. She could have sworn that just ten minutes ago the island had been completely shrouded. She watched the peculiar meteorological transformation of the distant view for some time, and as she did so, an idea emerged from the devastation in her mind. It grew steadily in shape and form and it was not long before her native resourcefulness had used it to frame the bones of a scheme.

The island of Ischia was where Don Graziani was convalescing at the moment. It occurred to her that her alliance with the old man might yet prove useful, in ways she had not previously envisaged.

Chapter 24

Wallace Pickering and Pietro Boldoni had taken supper together in the staff kitchen of the Villa Rosalba. It was quite rare that their schedules allowed them time to relax together, and so they decided to enjoy a glass of Madeira before retiring upstairs. Eventually, Boldoni felt overwhelmed by a great tiredness, probably exacerbated by the weight of his worries, and, yawning into his palm, said that he was going to bed. Pickering quickly drained another half-glass and said that he, too, would come up.

Their accommodation was on the third storey of the Villa Rosalba, and formed something of a separate apartment in which they could live together while still retaining the appearance of respectable independence. They had their own bedrooms, which connected to a shared bathroom, and there was an adjacent sitting room for their private use, together with a small office for Pietro. They did not always choose to share the same bed at night because Pickering would often stay out until late at the opera house, where his expertise was being gratefully put to use by the music staff; and Boldoni frequently liked to work at his desk until the early hours, which meant that their bedtimes rarely coincided. Occasionally, if he was feeling in particular need of quiet reassurance,

Pietro would creep into Wallace's room in the middle of the night and curl close into him, but as a rule they would occupy the same bed only if they happened to have spent a quiet evening together and were retiring at the same time, as was happening tonight.

They stood side by side at the twin basins of their shared bathroom, wearing blue pyjamas that differed only slightly in the thickness of their stripes. Unusually, Pickering was decidedly the more upbeat and talkative of the two, while Boldoni's face looked drawn. He needed cheering up, Pickering decided.

'I know he's a cheeky lad an' all,' said Pickering, 'but the boy can sing, I'll give him that. You should hear his "Je crois entendre".'

'"Mi par d'udir", you mean?' said Boldoni with a weary smile.

'Excuse me,' replied Pickering immediately falling for the bait, 'it was written by a Frenchman in French, and so I'll give it its proper title. You Italians! Think you own every good tune that's ever been written.'

'I'm glad Amedeo's doing so well. The Maestro's proud of him.'

'We're not there yet, not by a long shot, and there's some things only nature can do. Give him ten years and he'll shape up into a useful tenor.' By Pickering's standards, this was praise indeed. 'Still, I think it would do the lad good to give a little recital,' he added. 'Nothing fancy and just a small salon or something. Get him used to the feel of an audience, see how he holds up in public. I've got a funny feeling the performance bit might be his strongest card.'

'Could he manage a whole recital on his own? Or are you suggesting he share the programme with—'

'Oh, don't start that again,' interrupted Pickering stretching for a hand towel. 'I thought the *ill-advised* recording session put paid to any idea of you-know-who singing again for the time being.' Boldoni was brushing his teeth now, and did not answer. Pickering went on, 'I said as much to Bruno Graziani the other day.' At this, Boldoni paused from brushing and stared, dead still, into the basin in front of him. Pickering continued, looking into the mirror and gently wiping a flannel beneath each of his eyes. 'He asked me if I had changed my mind about the condition of the Maestro's voice. Cheek of it! I laughed him out of court, of course. How could I change my opinion when the facts are the facts? Campobello can't take a decent breath, so he's got no support, so the voice has got nothing to keep it up. Quite aside from the slack muscles of his neck and throat. Quite aside from him being all topsy-turvy at the moment, though I didn't say that bit to Bruno, of course.'

Boldoni spat his mouthful into the sink, rinsed out with a tumbler of fresh water, and turned to look at Pickering. 'You didn't tell me you'd been to see Bruno.'

'Didn't I? Well it's not that important. I was only there for less than half an hour. He was quite friendly.'

'So,' Boldoni said quietly, 'what did you say exactly?'

Pickering looked back at him, slightly chastened by the sudden serious tone. 'I told him I'd do my damnedest to protect the Maestro's voice from being injured any more than it has been already, and if that meant him stopping singing for six months, a year or two years, so be it, end of story. I was quite firm, actually. Why? Did I say something wrong?'

Boldoni held Pickering's gaze in silence. He felt like

weeping with pity, but also with pride for the stubborn, well-meaning little Yorkshireman, his lover of two decades; but he controlled himself, and put a hand on his shoulder. 'No, Wallace,' he said, and squeezed the shoulder hard. 'You've done the right thing.'

'I'm glad you think so,' continued Pickering, not registering the emotional turmoil behind Boldoni's eyes. He stretched for his own toothbrush. 'And I think you've been very good about this as well. So has Rocco. I'm proud of you both. It hasn't been easy, but you've seen sense. Walking out of that ridiculous recording session was the best thing that could've happened.' The tap was running and he had the toothbrush in his mouth now so that his final sentence came out as an unintelligible burble.

Boldoni folded his towel neatly over the bath rail and made his way to Pickering's room. He took off his slippers, placed them side by side under a chair, and climbed into the large bed. He lay there, warm, and curled, on his side, head resting comfortably on the downy pillow, and gazed across the room without blinking. He could hear Pickering gurgling and spitting in the bathroom. Dear, innocent Wallace. He had no idea what he'd done, of course, about the consequences of his defiance; but Boldoni knew. As surely as tomorrow's sun would rise, even though it might be veiled by rain clouds, Boldoni knew that their fate was now sealed.

Every Tuesday evening Pickering would come home late from the San Carlo opera house, having stayed to help the young and rather inexperienced chorusmaster with his weekly full chorus rehearsal. The company was working on Boito's *Mefistofele*, and with the show opening in less than five weeks, Pickering felt that they were pitifully under-prepared. He had done his share of chorus coaching over the years, and so volunteered his services to whip the idle bunch into shape a bit. He thoroughly enjoyed every minute of it and the chorus members had become immensely fond of him, even if his standards of ensemble and intonation were higher than anything they had ever come across before.

This Tuesday's session had been particularly productive and cheery, and it was therefore in a positive and quietly self-satisfied frame of mind that Pickering now left the theatre. As usual, he walked over to the adjacent Piazza Trieste e Trento to find a taxi that would take him back to the Villa Rosalba. Some weeks ago he had abandoned his preferred horse cabs in favour of motorized taxis, because of the cooler spell.

Still glowing from the convivial camaraderie of the rehearsal, he hardly noticed the cold air in the dark, abandoned piazza. He flapped his pudgy hand at the nearest taxi driver – it was his lucky night: there was one just there, waiting, as if ordered in advance. He gave his destination, received a wordless nod in reply, and climbed into the back. Relaxing into the comfortable leather seat, he sighed contentedly. This spell in Naples might not be so bad after all. Age and – dare he say it? – venerability had sprung upon him unawares. It seemed like only yesterday that he was just another staff pianist and *répétiteur* at Covent Garden, and then all those years working so hard with the Maestro, closeted from the larger world of music; and now here he was, out of the ivory tower, with time on his hands, and suddenly being treated like a grand sage, a fount of wisdom and encyclopaedic musical knowledge. Yes, he would be very happy in this city while he waited for Campobello's gradual recovery.

So lost was he in this uncharacteristic flutter of conceit, he neglected to take much notice of the world that raced by beyond the taxi's windows. Only now that the vehicle was slowing down to turn a tight corner did he realize that he was in unfamiliar surroundings. He leant forward – which was a struggle, because of the deeply yielding springs of the back seat – to tap on the partition glass. He had to tap twice before the driver took any notice, by which time they had advanced some way into the bowels of the city, to an area he did not recognize at all. The driver slid back the glass, turned his head and raised his chin. Pickering addressed him in indifferent Italian, repeating the address and saying that he didn't think this was the right way. The driver replied with a nod and slid the glass to again. Pickering leant back with a sigh, supposing that it must be some kind of back-street route. There wasn't much else he could do.

He did not have long to contemplate an alternative hypothesis. The car pulled over rather abruptly and came to a standstill. Everything then happened so quickly that Pickering could barely understand what was being done to him. The door was opened by a complete stranger who indicated with a curt gesture that Pickering should get out. For a moment he was too surprised and flustered to move. The stranger was joined by the taxi driver, and together they pulled him roughly from the car, so that he caught his foot on the running board and almost fell into the street. He put out a hand to save himself but was yanked to his feet by one of the men, who now put a cloth bag over his head. The other ripped at his jacket to get it off his back. He felt a violent tug on the arm of his shirt, and the sleeve tore free from the shoulder seam, leaving his pale-skinned arm naked to the night air. He tried to protest in broken Italian, but felt a knife blade under the hem of the bag, touching against his throat.

'You make noise, you die,' said a voice close to his ear. He was being gripped tight around the armpits, and he became aware of another car pulling up and a third person arriving on the scene, who quickly addressed the two men holding him, asking them some brief questions to which they replied in monosyllables. The new arrival then leant close to the bag and spoke to Pickering in English. His voice was gentler.

'Listen to me. You must stay still if you wish to live. If you struggle or make a noise, these men will not hesitate to kill you. Do you understand?'

'Yes,' replied Pickering, panting heavily under the bag and shaking. He felt a band being tied around his arm, above the elbow.

'This will hurt a little,' the man warned, and began to turn a device that constricted the band, tightening Pickering's flesh until it pinched. He let out a muffled yelp of pain.

The men now appeared to be discussing something. The new arrival was speaking to the other two in a commanding way, and they seemed surprised and a little resentful, though Pickering understood little of the content.

The terse interaction ended with what sounded like a concession on the part of the original two men, and a few moments later Pickering heard one of the cars start up and drive away. He was jostled towards the second car, its engine still running. He clumsily found his way into the passenger seat, the door was closed after him, and they drove off at speed.

'I know you,' said Pickering, his hands trembling. 'You're the doctor. What's this about? What are you going to do to me?'

Andrea Florio did not answer.

'Can you take me home, please?' asked Pickering.

'I'm afraid not.'

'Where are you taking me, then?'

'Out of town.'

'Why?'

'Because that's the best place. Believe me: I wish with all my heart I did not have to do this.'

'Who's making you do it, then? Why me? What's this about?' Then Pickering closed his eyes as the realization dawned on him. 'It's Bruno Graziani, isn't it?'

Andrea's silence confirmed his suspicion. The doctor leant over and pulled the bag off his head. Pickering said no more. The shock of the back-street assault gave way to an overwhelming release of tension that left him shuddering in the seat, which in its turn yielded to an unfathomable grief. His eyes were sealed but the tears streamed through, and his body convulsed with sobs.

Andrea Florio did not attempt to calm him or explain any further. The poor man would know everything soon enough.

PART THREE

Chapter 25

Milan, 1899

By the time Rocco's name reached the billboards of La Scala, Milan – Italy's foremost opera house – he had carved himself a notable reputation in the city's minor theatres; but to the regulars of La Scala (who would not stoop to watch opera at another house), he was still something of an unknown, and, at a mere twenty-one years of age, a pipsqueak whose head it would do no good to inflate. Their reticence made the impact of his opening night at the prime house even more spectacular: the commanding presence, the power of the upper register, the sheer elasticity of the voice. Three times during the course of the evening, a member of the theatre staff had to come on stage to calm the applause so that the show could carry on. Emilio Graziani, who had travelled up from Naples specially for the occasion, had taken care to organize a favourable claque (no mean expense at La Scala) but it proved an unnecessary precaution.

By now, all thoughts of the Ospedale, his father, and the entire world he had known before coming to Milan, were unwelcome intrusions for Rocco. They had been dwarfed into irrelevance by the scale of his recent opportunities and their memory all but incinerated by the furnace that now raged continuously inside him.

This inner fire, and the maintenance of its steady, white heat, had become the core of Rocco's being. It was fanned and regulated through the discipline of a punishing daily schedule, a routine which allowed for no outside interests or distractions. He worked single-mindedly in the cause of self-improvement, and had done so for three years, ever since leaving Naples. When not exercising his voice or studying, he would sit in on opera company rehearsals, observing, learning, and filling notebooks with jottings. He made a point of introducing himself to influential people, and had no real friends other than an infatuated young soprano from the chorus at the Teatro Rossini, whom he would fuck when it pleased him; but he kept her presence in his life a secret, and rather loathed himself for the entanglement. The profile that he preferred to cultivate – and the gentlemen grandees he sought to impress thoroughly approved of it – was one of clear-cut commitment and ambition.

There was a peculiar calm in the dressing room to which Rocco returned after the final curtain call of his debut at La Scala, and he locked the door behind him. The distant sound of applause was at last petering out, and it finally stopped. Sweating and breathing heavily, he allowed himself the luxury of a moment to recover. He rested a hand against the wall, hung his head, eyes closed, and clenched a fist tight. It was the high point of his life to date, but he would not dwell on it for long. There was even more important business yet to come this evening, and he had to be ready.

He got to work removing his make-up and changed

back into normal clothes. He had bought himself a fine new frock coat – with black silk lapels and a fashionably tailored waist – so that he would look his best for all the well-wishers. Theatre staff had been instructed, however, that no one should be allowed through to his dressing room before Don Graziani had paid his visit, and it was not long before Rocco heard the knock on the door and Emilio Graziani was there, arms open to embrace his young protégé.

'This day,' Graziani said, 'will be written about in the history books.' He took Rocco's face between his palms and drew it towards his own. Rocco flinched fractionally as he thought he was about to be kissed on the lips, but at the last moment Graziani tilted his head slightly so that his cheek squeezed against the young man's. 'Would that I had had a son like you,' he said in Rocco's ear.

Rocco stiffened. 'Don't be harsh on Bruno, *zio*,' he said. 'He's only a boy.'

'He shows no talent in any department,' said Graziani, releasing Rocco. 'Like his mother.'

'He is clever.'

'That's no good on its own. I don't need a university professor for a son. I want a boy with balls. But him? He cries at night because he's frightened of the dark. He says he sees devils, and he howls in his bed.'

'Devils?'

'Red devils, with big horns. "Wah, wah, wah!"' Graziani mockingly imitated a child's screams, and then leant towards Rocco. 'How can you find your way in the underworld if you're so scared of the dark, know what I mean?'

'Maybe he misses his mother.'

'No matter! Tonight is your night. You were magnificent. From tonight you join the ranks of the great.'

'It was acceptable,' said Rocco, 'nothing more. Thank you for coming all this way.' He allowed himself a smile. 'I owe you everything, *zio*.' Don Graziani waved the pleasantry away with a flick of the wrist, like an unwelcome scent. He was intolerant of flattery.

Rocco now sat down and crossed his legs. Ponderously, he lit himself a cigarette, and regarded his patron with cool poise.

'So?' he asked, when Graziani had taken his seat. 'Did our visitor make it on time?'

'Indeed he did. Mr Fleming sat beside me for the entire performance.'

Rocco glanced away and flicked some ash into a little silver tray. 'And?'

'He was impressed. He wants to record you straight away. Here in Milan. The day after tomorrow.'

Even a year ago, Rocco might have leapt to his feet and flung his arms around Graziani at this news, but he had been schooling himself in the art of restraint. 'That's good. Very good,' he said and took another drag. 'Again I must thank you, *zio*.'

'No, my boy,' said Graziani. 'I thank *you* for your wonderful voice. Mr Fleming says he cannot remember having heard such promise in a male singer.'

'And the terms?' cut in Rocco, putting a stop to any extended hyperbole.

'I have secured a good price. Mr Fleming was shocked by the figure, but I managed to persuade him.' Graziani's eyes narrowed slightly in a reptilian fashion behind the bottle lenses of his spectacles. 'There is the matter of our own agreement to sort out first, of course,' he said, and laid his hand on Rocco's thigh. 'You know I have never asked for a single *centesimo* for all the help I have given you.'

'I know, *zio*,' said Rocco straight out. He had thought the issue through in advance and prepared himself for it. 'I am aware of everything you have done and will be in your debt for as long as I am able to sing.'

'No, no, no,' said Graziani, as though the idea disgusted him. 'There is no question of debt. Let us call it friendship, a family arrangement. We look after each other, in small ways.'

'We don't need to go through it all again, *zio*. You don't have to ask. I'm happy to sign the agreement for you, as a way of saying thank you.'

Graziani seemed pleased and patted his boy on the knee. They agreed on a time to meet in the lobby of the Hotel Rossini, where they could complete all the formalities in front of a public notary and witness. They would then proceed straight to Mr Fleming's rooms on the third floor, which, Graziani had been told, were an appropriate size for a temporary recording studio.

Graziani made ready to leave. Before opening the door, he added quietly, as if in passing, 'Your father has been coming to my house, asking for news of you.'

'What do you tell him?'

'That you are well and happy. And that your singing jobs are paying for all your needs. That seems to be what he wants to know. Should I say anything else?'

'Does he know about tonight, about my debut here?'

Don Graziani turned down the corners of his mouth. 'It did not occur to me to tell him. I thought—'

'You did right,' interrupted Rocco. 'He would only

have tried to come, and his presence would have been a distraction.'

'Good boy,' said Graziani, and cupped his cheek one last time, 'good boy.'

Shortly after Graziani's departure, Rocco got ready to meet the public and checked himself in the large mirror of his dressing room. Two great lamp pans shone full on him from either side of the glass. He raised his chin to adjust the black silk necktie so that it sat in line with his collar stud, and drew a comb through the moustache he had begun to grow. He tried to twist its ends into points, but it wasn't quite thick enough yet. Placing his new top hat at a tilt on his head, he slung his greatcoat over one arm, reached for his silver-topped cane, and gave one last glance in the mirror before going to greet the crowd of admirers who were assembling outside the dressing room.

Released, eventually, from their attentions, the new star emerged from the stage door of the theatre, raised his cane to acknowledge the small crowd outside, and got into the carriage that awaited him. He was going straight to the apartment of Sofia, the chorus singer he had been seeing these past few months.

Sofia Bosetti hailed from a large farming family in the far north, and her yeoman father had scratched together every cent he could manage in order to send his talented young daughter to try her luck as a singer in Milan. Her meetings with Rocco were brief and fervid, but when the opportunity arose she would talk at length about the livestock and mountain scenery at home, which she clearly missed. Rocco seemed to listen, but he was not so much interested in the rural idyll as in the flicker of

Sofia's accent, which he found erotic, and guessed must be due to the Austrian influence. What he liked best about her, of course, had nothing to do with her conversation: it was her unquestioning acceptance of his needs; and tonight, of all nights, that simple acquiescence was an urgent requirement.

Whether by prior arrangement or habit, she seemed to know what was expected of her and was leaning against the door frame of the bedroom as he let himself in at the far end of the corridor. Some of her clothes were already discarded, but she still had on the single-piece calico undergarment which she knew he liked, and her black stockings, which were gartered at the knee. She made no move towards him, and the audacity of her smiling restraint triggered a pulse of desire in Rocco's loins before he had closed the door behind him. His eyes travelled the length and breadth of her, dwelling as much on the pale, bare skin as the hidden coombs that vanished beneath silk and ribbons. She was fair haired, with pink apple cheeks, unlike any girl he had known in Naples, and he felt like eating her whole.

There was something bestial in the manner of his lovemaking, a disregard for restraint of any kind, and she willingly submitted to every angle of it. Not once did she suggest, in word or gesture, an agenda of her own, but gave him the freedom to serve himself, an opportunity he snatched greedily. Spurred on by her stooping compliance he did not attempt to hold himself back, but, tensing and uncurling his neck like a cobra, released himself utterly into her.

Sofia's breathing quickened only in an attempt to mirror Rocco's, and now that he had slumped on top of her, she allowed it to calm, just as his quickly slowed.

341

He remained there for no longer than it took to recover himself, and then got up to wash. She followed him into the bathroom.

In the aftermath, as he groomed and dressed himself, he felt compelled to answer her endless questions about the performance at La Scala, and managed to do so politely enough, but was in a hurry to get going. He felt a little irritated at her padding around the apartment after him, asking this and that, and eventually shut her up by placing a finger on her lips with a smile of contrived affection, which seemed to please her, so they were both happy.

Two days later, and five minutes in advance of the appointed time, Rocco swept into the lobby of the Hotel Rossini. Two young men followed close at his heels, neither of them older than nineteen. They had volunteered to attend to the rising star's every need; Rocco was therefore able to use them to good cosmetic effect but at little cost to his pocket. Today they were fulfilling the role of supportive seconds, and Rocco rather ceremoniously handed them his coat, hat and cane. Out of the side of his eye he had already clocked Don Graziani in the hall, together with young Bruno, but pretended not to have seen them until after he had dismissed his minions; only then did he turn to greet his patron. They embraced briefly and went straight over to a pair of smartly dressed men – an independent witness and a public notary – who stood behind a table to one side of the lobby.

The matter was agreed, signed and sealed within minutes, though the public notary, who was a kind, fatherly man and too long in the tooth to be impressed by Rocco's entrance charade, took it upon himself to read out the particulars of the contract to the young man twice over. It was only after Rocco persuaded him that he understood exactly what he was signing, the percentages and the nature of the agreement, that the formalities were completed, and they proceeded to the upstairs suite where the recording was due to take place.

Rocco was beside Bruno as they climbed the stairs. He looked down at the boy, now about thirteen, with a trace of dark downy hair on his upper lip. Rocco winked at him but received nothing more than a perplexed frown in return. 'This has got to be better than school, eh?' he asked in a chummy way, but Bruno did not answer.

Having been brought up in a city of diminutive inhabitants, it was unusual for Rocco to feel dwarfed when he entered a room, and yet that is what happened when he was met at the suite door by the immensely tall and serious-faced man with sandy hair, who was introduced to him as Walter Fleming.

Rocco was immediately impressed with Fleming's calm management of time and people. His manner was reassuring and kindly, but his methods clear from the outset: they were here to do a job within a short but adequate window of opportunity. If they cut the flab and got down to it they could get this thing done, and done well. He led by example, dispensing with unnecessary chat, commanding the attention of the grand and humble alike without having to smooth his words with diplomatic polish. Rocco happily acquiesced in the face of such lucid professionalism.

An upright piano stood on a rough piece of staging about four feet off the ground, and Rocco was invited to take his position next to it on a slightly lower stage. He stubbed out his cigarette and discarded his jacket. Straight in front of him, and adjusted to an appropriate height, was a large conical horn, the narrow point of which disappeared behind a curtain screen. The technical apparatus had been set up behind this crude partition, including, on a side table, the case of unused wax discs. They were a delicate enough commodity in their present blank condition, but by the end of the day were to become considerably more precious, and their preservation, in immaculate condition, for the long journey to the processing plant, was the heavy responsibility of the technician who now briefed Rocco on what he had to do.

The repertoire of ten songs had been agreed in advance, and the appointed pianist – a local man – was introduced to Rocco. Fleming explained how the time limit of three minutes per disc would mean omitting certain repeats from the original scores and abbreviating some of the accompaniments to give maximum time to the voice. 'The composers might turn in their graves,' he said, before taking his place behind the curtain, 'but they would forgive us if they understood the technical limitations of a ten-inch shellac disc.'

A dummy run was undertaken and immediately played back. For all Rocco's iron restraint, he could not suppress a smile of pleasure on first hearing his own voice reproduced, and turned towards the wall to hide it. He then became aware of a slight consternation behind the curtain and heard the technician's whispers grow more urgent. Fleming, who would not stoop to the discourtesy of whispering when there were other people present, spoke up at last. 'Well, that's got to be good,

Alfred. Good for you, for me, for the company, but most of all for the young lad over there.'

'What is the matter?' Rocco asked the pianist, who seemed to understand English and was listening to the conversation. 'They're saying they've never heard a voice transfer so well to the wax, son,' the man said. 'Whatever you've got, it shows the machinery off to its best effect. They think you're going to be a sensation.'

The ten records were made at remarkable speed, one after the other. A single failed take was caused by part of the stage cracking beneath a piano castor, but otherwise the session went smoothly. Rocco shook hands heartily with the men from the Jupiter Company, and accepted their praise with a modest tilt of the head. Donning his coat and bowler hat, he then lit a cigarette, gripped his cane, and stalked briskly from the hotel lobby into the sunshine of the street, his twin acolytes hurrying along behind him. The whole affair had taken less than three hours.

The enormous success of those first records led to Campobello being invited to the Metropolitan Opera in New York, where he was to become the company's mainstay. In time he defined the Met's choice of repertoire and almost single-handedly turned it into a temple of operatic excellence. London's Covent Garden followed soon after, where he worked with Wallace Pickering for the first time, and he went on to score successes in almost every other major opera house in the world, but it was the Met that was to become his artistic home. It was there that he felt most comfortable in experimenting with his radical new methods of stagecraft. Brutal realism became his credo and though he did not set out to shock, he certainly never shied from upsetting the quietude of the more sedate members of New York's affluent audience.

As his career progressed and bore ever more bountiful fruit, Rocco grew increasingly intolerant of mediocrity, especially in those who worked alongside him, and it was not unknown for him to storm out of the theatre during rehearsals at signs of incompetence in colleagues. By the same token, there were times when he could drum up a magic that would infect the entire company, raising everyone's game with a single touch of genius. It happened once when he was rehearsing with a famous English soprano. The plot demanded at one point that she reproach him for a suspected act of infidelity, and when the moment came, the soprano, an experienced performer of the old school, turned away from her errant lover with woeful elegance, lowering her large beautiful eyes to the ground and clutching a hand to her breast.

'No, no, no, for God's sake!' shouted Rocco, interrupting her aria, and the pianist accompanying them ground to a halt. 'I've just broken your heart! You should want to kill me! Come on!' The soprano looked with an embarrassed smile to the wings, hoping someone would come to rescue her, but Rocco grabbed her by the shoulders and started shaking her. 'Come on, woman. I've humiliated you!' He stared furiously into her eyes and she recoiled. 'I loved you once, but I'm bored now, and I've found a more beautiful woman.'

'Mr Campobello, please,' she murmured, pulling her head away. He was almost spitting into her face.

'A better woman,' he continued, 'who excites me more. Now. What are you going to do about it?'

'I . . . I—'

'Slap me.'

'What?'

'Slap me.' She raised a delicate hand and quickly patted the tips of her fingers on his cheek. 'That's not a slap.' He was still shaking her by the shoulders. 'Slap me.' She tried again. 'Harder.' She tried one more time, beginning to panic, and by now a small crowd had gathered to gloat in the wings. 'Slap me, woman!' he yelled, and then, with a sudden shriek of fury, something in her snapped and she walloped him hard, right across the face. With the speed of lightning, and a white heat in his eyes, Rocco raised his own hand to strike her back, and there was an audible gasp from the people watching; but he held his hand in the air, staring at the soprano, holding her gaze, transfixed. He let out a tremendous high G in full voice and held on to it for several seconds, while the soprano covered her ears with both palms, in terror at the huge noise. Then it was over, and he took one of her hands. 'You see?' he said. 'That was theatre. Let's carry on now,' and he gestured to the nervous accompanist to resume.

Theatre staff were continually intimidated by Rocco's iron discipline and austerity, but they took comfort in a single thread of vulnerability that seemed to link the unbending perfectionist to a man of flesh and blood within: his constant requirement for cigarettes, both in private and professional life. It was a regular, if incongruous sight, backstage, to see the great tenor, dressed in full and extravagant costume, drawing again and again on a dwindling cigarette and pacing back and forth with a thunderous expression, while the orchestra raged in anticipation of his entrance on the other side of the scenery. He would smoke up to the last moment before walking on stage, handing the smouldering remnants to an assistant and occasionally exhaling a grey cloud in view of the audience as he emerged from the wings. Ultimately, he would hand-pick stage assistants for his productions, who understood and catered for his chain-smoking.

Within two years of those first Milan recordings, Rocco was lodging at the Waldorf Astoria and negotiating for himself the sort of fees previously reserved for the greatest singers on earth. Not only Naples seemed distant, but Italy as a whole, and all the people he had formerly been close to. Sofia Bosetti wrote irritatingly often during his first few months in America; her letters were full of woes about her life and pleas that she be allowed to come and join him. His replies became briefer and less regular as her letters grew ever more desperate. He believed she was playing him for sympathy, stretching the truth, at times deceiving him outright for effect. First she talked of poverty, then sickness, and sometimes suicide. It was when at last he received a letter in shaky handwriting, claiming she was about to give birth to his child, that he decided enough was enough and never wrote back again. Several more letters arrived over the course of the next few months but he put them straight in the fire. Eventually they stopped.

It was largely Sofia's lovesickness that made him resolve never to commit to a woman, a decision he would stick to for a decade, up until his unexpected engagement to society belle, Molly Whittaker. Colleagues assumed he was too consumed with work to be bothered with the distraction of a wife, and there was speculation in some quarters that he might be homosexual. In truth, Rocco was repelled by the cancerous attachments that burdened his married colleagues, and he would not allow the crystal purity of his own work to be impaired

348

by the petty demands of a female. What no one in his orbit ever knew, however, was that, paradoxically, his sexual urge towards women was uncontainable, and that the solution he found was to frequent many and varied brothels in the cities he travelled to. He made a point never to visit the same whore too often, lest she, like the legions of women who threw themselves at him, grew to expect more from him than he was prepared to offer. His one companion, partner, tyrant and lover, was his voice, and he spared not a minute of his day, nor a penny from his purse in ensuring its development, its protection, and future prospects.

His own high standards were matched by those of the outstandingly spruce and orderly young secretary he employed, in the person of Pietro Boldoni. The two young men treated each other like brother officers in an elite corps who were surrounded by a following of inept native spear-carriers. They liked to conduct their business with quasi-military precision, and would begin every day with a meeting at ten-thirty precisely, when plain words were spoken and meticulous plans conceived. It was an unlikely meeting of minds. Boldoni, a highly educated, God-fearing aesthete from Tuscany, had hitherto been rather disdainful of southerners, not to mention those of low birth. He clearly made an exception for Rocco, who had left behind all traces of his humble origins and refined his public image by the time Boldoni joined his staff. The waxed points of his moustache were turned upwards and sharpened like thorns. His handmade suits and shirts were jaunty, bordering on flamboyant, and he had developed a penchant for checked British tweeds, replenishing his stock every year or so to accommodate his gradual increase in girth.

Six years after arriving in New York for the first time, with two more recording series to his name and his reputation booming, Rocco noticed amongst the letters he was handed one morning by Boldoni, one from Naples. It was from Gabriele Tomassini. He glanced through its contents without any show of feeling, while, in the background, Boldoni was continuing his recitation of the day's administrative matters.

To my dear old friend,

You see, I can write. Someone has been teaching me, and he checks for mistakes when I finish. I learn so I can write to my old friend. Everyone in Naples is proud of you, Rocco. Your father is proud as well, and he talks about you all the time, but he knows you are busy. I am married now. I think you are not married yet. Maybe I can find you a good wife!

I am writing to you, my old friend, to ask if you can help me. I have been singing all these years but I cannot find a really good job yet. Signor de Luca wants young men in his choir. Maybe if I come to New York you can ask someone in an opera house to listen to me singing. I just need one chance. You said that everybody needs just one chance.

Please come to Naples soon. Everyone at home misses you.

I send you my warmest wishes, and I hope this day finds you healthy.

Gabriele Tomassini

Boldoni stopped speaking and looked up at his employer. 'Is everything all right?' he asked.

Rocco blinked. 'Absolutely,' he said, and folded up the letter. 'Carry on with what you were saying.'

He would have liked to forget about the letter during the busy days that followed, but it had a buoyancy of its own and kept bobbing to the surface of his thoughts at inconvenient moments. He tried, inwardly, to deride it: it was presumptuous, childish and opportunistic, therefore contemptible on several counts; but still it refused to sink quietly out of reach. At one point, a valiant fragment of himself, like a lone survivor clutching a raft in stormy seas, questioned if he shouldn't just help the poor man a little; but the idea, and the despairing voice behind it, was quickly snuffed out, never to return. There could be no journeys backward, no meanderings into sentiment. His former life had been an unfortunate blemish that he had successfully navigated around and left far behind. Any remnant of it served only to muddy the water of his present adventure and distract his clear forward gaze. On one matter alone did he yield some ground: he decided for the first time that he would send some money to his father. He had Boldoni arrange it, and set up quarterly transfers from then on, although no message was ever attached with the payments.

A few years later, while he was taking a late summer holiday at Lake Como in the north of Italy, word reached Rocco that his father had been taken seriously ill. For a day or so he considered making the trip to Naples to see the old man, but for once in his life found himself unable to make a decision. He was released from the quandary a couple of days later, when a telegram was delivered to the hotel saying that Enrico had died peacefully in hospital the previous night. Boldoni intercepted the telegram when it arrived, and took it upon himself to break the news to the Maestro at the start of their regular morning meeting. He thought he had the measure of Rocco by now, and imagined the news would be greeted with a solemn nod, followed by a respectful pause, and then some quietly voiced, but clear instructions outlining the changes that would have to be made to their schedule for the next fortnight or so. But he could not have been more mistaken.

When Campobello heard mention of his father's passing, he neither blinked nor reacted at all, but began to talk at a tangent, first, about the poor lighting backstage at Buenos Aires' Teatro Colon, and then about the mechanics of the light bulb in general, and what a near miracle it represented to mankind. Boldoni's attempts to interrupt and bring him back to the immediate issue of what he planned to do about his father, were ignored. For the rest of the day, Campobello remained in his room, working incessantly, and answered all enquiries from the other side of a locked door. It was only on the morning of the third day after Enrico's death that Boldoni managed to persuade Rocco to unlock the door and let him in. The windows and curtains were closed, the bed linen strewn around the floor, and the Maestro unshaven and naked. He had not been working at all.

Boldoni spent three hours quietly talking to him, or at him, because there was no dialogue, while Rocco lay curled on his side in the middle of the gigantic mattress of his bed. He was persuaded at last to rally, shave and dress, and later that day he and Boldoni boarded a train, leaving Wallace Pickering (now an integral part of the

352

household) behind at the hotel. By the following evening the two men had arrived in Naples.

They took up temporary residence at the resplendent Hotel Vesuvio, overlooking the sea on the Via Partenope, where Boldoni succeeded in making Campobello agree that it would be tactful to receive city dignitaries and well-wishers in moderate numbers. A comfortable suite was therefore booked, with a drawing room large enough to entertain visitors.

Rocco appeared to recover from his initial catatonic reaction to his father's death and began to work on his role in Donizetti's *Lucrezia Borgia*, a new production which was due to open at the Berlin Opera in just over a month. He had never performed this opera before and, although he already had the music and text prepared to perfection, there was a great deal of background research that he wanted to have done by the time rehearsals began. So he did not spend his time in Naples ruminating on the peculiarity of being back home for the first time in twelve years, but worked quietly in his hotel room, and handed over the organization of his father's funeral to Boldoni, who fulfilled the task without having to burden his employer with the detail.

A modest private service was arranged at Enrico's local church – the same church in which he had been married, and where Rocco and his sisters had been baptized. The funeral cortège then processed a short distance through the lanes and into the piazza of the splendid San Domenico Maggiore, a much larger church. Here, a public requiem mass was conducted, with full choir, as was considered appropriate for the father of an internationally renowned public figure. A suggestion that Rocco might perhaps like to sing something for the mourners was snuffed out by Boldoni before it properly saw the light of day.

Rocco walked beside the coffin during the procession, cutting a fine, if slightly corpulent, figure in his black morning suit and gleaming top hat. His presence attracted far more attention from onlookers than the business of the funeral or the open casket in which the dead blacksmith lay. He made a point of greeting as many people as came to shake his gloved hand, and pretended to recognize those who claimed friendship and kinship, though the truth was he had forgotten almost all of them, which was peculiar for such an organized thinker. The one person he had not forgotten, and whom he expected to appear before him at any moment, was Gabriele Tomassini; but in the event his former friend did not materialize, which was something of a relief.

In the days that followed the funeral, Boldoni ordered work to start on the construction of a family mausoleum, into which the body would be placed as soon as building was complete. He also arranged for Maria Anna, Enrico's ancient, feeble-minded sister, who spent her days muttering endless one-sided dialogues, to be moved to a special home where she would be cared for, at Rocco's expense, for the remainder of her life.

Enrico's tiny, lower ground apartment, where the family had been raised, was sold straight away; his possessions, which were of no particular value, were either given away to neighbours or incinerated. Likewise the sum remnants of his redundant smithy. Within days, all trace of Enrico Campobello, that resolute tower of industry, who had persevered through the trauma of the cholera epidemic to give his son a fighting chance, had vanished from the district. His memory, of course, was enshrined, but only because he was the father of an eminent son. In years to come, few in the parish, if any, ever remarked that the Great Rocco Campobello's legendary commitment and indestructibility reminded them of qualities possessed by the powerful old blacksmith they had laid to rest; and no one commented that perhaps more credit for the illustrious son's natural gifts should be laid at the feet of his humble father.

As soon as Enrico's affairs were settled, Rocco left Naples and returned to the salubrious comfort of the Italian lakes, where he could work in peace.

Over the years that followed, and under the good influence of his canny secretary, Campobello quarried out of himself a rather less austere public profile. He accepted invitations, attended receptions and entertained regularly. He would host interminable open-air summer lunches, and sit in splendour at the head of a long, vine-shaded table, every inch the Italian patriarch, bountifully generous and genial. But looks were deceiving, because as the years went by, and as his reputation swelled, he grew more private and withdrawn. He learnt to get along superficially with people because it was a skill he was expected to possess, but socializing remained a cheerless ordeal. Occasionally he would let his guard slip and a fellow guest at dinner might glimpse a wilderness in his eyes; but the Maestro would be quick to patch it over with a smile or humorous set piece.

Boldoni was wise to the furies that plagued his employer's inner world, because in darker moments Rocco would offer glimpses of anguish and occasionally of vitriol. He would confide to Pietro how much he despised most other people, especially his colleagues, lesser men, he would say, whose careers had turned flabby through self-satisfaction. They were not called to the higher service, because they had allowed themselves the distraction of so-called happiness. These bitter confessions would occur late at night, with Rocco, more often than not, clutching a tumbler of cognac. He would stare at the glass, bleakly, between sips, as if his whole world were tuned to the lamentable tragedy of its diminishing measure. For sure, he would say, in a dialogue with himself, the old days were more carefree, but it was no good looking back. There was no alternative for him any more, and if the road held straight like this all the way to the grave, so be it. He had carved a deep and lonely chamber for himself years ago, and bricked up all routes of escape. But it wasn't all bad; at least it was warm down there; he made sure the furnace was kept ablaze, a steady, white heat; a constant, contained roar. He and his voice were lonely companions in that hidden world, but, together, they fed the fire.

Chapter 26

Naples, October 1926

The night that Wallace Pickering failed to return home from the chorus rehearsal, Pietro Boldoni lay in bed imagining the worst. He was under no illusion about the ruthlessness of Bruno Graziani, but the question that swayed in and out of his thoughts, like a razor-edged pendulum all night long, was whether anything might have worked in favour of Pickering to lessen the extent of the brutality. Perhaps the years of dedicated service to the Maestro would work in his favour; or his hopeless, fumbling innocence; or his age, and nationality: it would not do to upset the British. But every glint of optimism was stifled by a blanket of despair when Boldoni remembered the merciless track record of these people.

By six-thirty he was up, dressed and ready to confront the situation in an even and practical frame of mind. He made some perfunctory enquiries at the villa's gatehouse, then at the Teatro San Carlo, and finally with the city's police department, and in each case he took care not to disclose his own personal dread and vested interest, lest he make matters worse for himself. When, as expected, there were no leads from any of these channels, he returned to the Villa Rosalba to confront the Maestro. It was by now ten-thirty, and time for their regular morning meeting. He knocked on the door of Campobello's study and entered to see his employer standing behind his desk, a small sheet of paper in his hand. Even from this distance Pietro could see that it was a telegram.

'It's from Wallace,' said Rocco. 'He says he has no place here any longer if my career is finished. He has decided to leave.' He passed the telegram to Boldoni. 'I'm sorry, Pietro.'

Boldoni breathed deep, caught between seismic relief and cynicism. He took the paper. 'Where was it sent?'

'Salerno.'

Boldoni let out a bitter laugh. 'How on earth would someone like Wallace find his way to Salerno in the middle of the night? Unless he was helped.'

Rocco sighed. 'What are you suggesting?'

Boldoni sidestepped the question. 'Do you think the telegram is genuine, that it's definitely from Wallace?'

'Is there any reason to suppose it is not?'

Boldoni pursed his lips. 'There are other possibilities.'

'Pietro,' said Rocco and placed a hand on his assistant's forearm. 'You know as well as I do that Wallace has been feeling uneasy. And he is awkward; clumsy, even. This might have been the only way he could handle leaving.'

'You don't know what I know,' Boldoni cried out, despite himself.

Rocco paused for a moment while Boldoni got the better of his feelings.

'You must go after him,' said Rocco, moving his hand to Pietro's shoulder and lowering his head to engage his eyes. 'You must go to him straight away, don't delay.

He must have gone to England, don't you think?' For a moment Boldoni contemplated protesting, but only for a moment, because it was clearly the correct course of action. He nodded and looked down, visibly ashamed. 'Don't give it a second thought,' Rocco reassured him. 'I can manage on my own for a while. I mean to simplify my life, anyway.'

'I will return shortly,' said Boldoni, stiffening. 'I will find out what has happened, and, with or without Pickering, I will return.'

They spent the remainder of the morning together, working through outstanding business. Even at this most critical of times, Boldoni did not spare the smallest detail but made sure every last matter was tied up. 'Oh yes,' he said, finding a note he had jotted to himself the day before. 'You should be aware of a rather persistent young man who insists on meeting you. If he tries too hard, it might be a good idea to alert the police. I was about to do so, as a matter of fact.'

'The police? Is that necessary? Who is he?'

'No one I have heard of.' He looked down at his note. 'Calls himself Benedetto Figlietti. He lives in Rome and has written here several times, begging for an interview, in the way that some people do. He now talks of coming to the gates of the house to accost you in person. Says he wants to tell you something important.'

'Is he a singer?'

'He doesn't say. He just wants to meet you. You know what these fans are like. Anyway,' Pietro scribbled on a piece of paper, 'this is his name, just so you know, if he starts becoming a nuisance.'

Rocco put the slip in his waistcoat pocket, while Boldoni arranged the files and papers on his desk in such a way as to make them comprehensible to a temporary secretary. Anything remotely confidential he took care to conceal in locked drawers to which only he and Campobello had keys. By one o'clock he had bid his employer farewell and hurried, suitcase in hand, from the house. Pozzo was waiting for him, with the Lancia, under the entrance portico.

The following day was beautifully clear and fine for the time of year. The sea was as still as glass, and Rocco decided that he would take Chiara on a trip to Sorrento in his private launch. Dispensing with the services of his own boatman, and dressed in a blue blazer with flannels and a white sailing cap, he steered the gleamingly varnished vessel gently up to the pier at Mergellina, where he had arranged to pick up Chiara. He spotted her from some way off, standing alone, waiting for him. He held out his hand to help her aboard, then reversed the launch out into the deeper water, steering a course south, in the direction of the Castel dell'Ovo promontory. They sat beside each other on cream leather seats, Rocco's hand lightly clasping the lacquered wheel, their faces protected from the breeze by a shallow, chrome-edged windscreen. It was early in the day, and they were gloriously free and alone.

The launch's engine purred, and Rocco pulled the throttle back so that the propeller's distant gurgling turned to a roar, but still not loud enough to drown out the sound of the water breaking against the hull.

Chiara leant back and turned her face up to the sun, closing her eyes. Rocco looked at her and smiled to himself. He had to speak up to be heard over the engine. 'I have two good pieces of news,' he said.

'Anything about poor Mr Pickering yet? Amedeo is so sad.'

'Not much. I received a telegram from Boldoni this morning saying that Pickering may have embarked on a ship at Messina. Don't worry about Amedeo. I will carry on with his lessons on my own. You must tell him to come back to the house tomorrow. He's the most important person in the world to me right now.' At this she opened her eyes and pouted at him with mock resentment. He smiled again. 'Apart from you. I don't have children, but with Amedeo I feel I have a chance to make up for it.' This seemed to satisfy Chiara. 'Now, let me tell you my good news.' She leant against him and pulled his arm around her shoulder. 'First: the Florio brothers have my X-rays back from Rome, and they say everything is clear. There's nothing to worry about.'

Chiara drew aside some locks of hair that were being drawn across her face by the breeze. 'What about the pains?'

'My broken rib, apparently, and the strain of a singer's deep breaths.'

'That's wonderful news,' she said. 'What else?'

'I've told her,' he replied without hesitation. Now Chiara sat bolt upright and looked at him with wide eyes. 'I've told her everything,' he repeated.

'How was it?'

'Terrible, of course.'

'I feel ashamed,' said Chiara.

'You mustn't. I should have broken from her a long time ago.'

'Why did you marry her? You say you never loved her.'

'It seemed to be the right thing to do when I did it.' He

361

smiled rather glibly at his former folly, belittling the immensity of the decision he had made at the time and the consequences of the error. 'It seemed right for someone in my position to marry a woman like Molly. That's all I can say.'

'What is she going to do now?'

'She hasn't decided. I'll give her whatever she wants. It's the scandal she dreads more than anything. She'll do her best to be seen to rise above it, while making me look like the devil incarnate. But I don't care.'

'It will be horrible.'

'No. It will be wonderful. I'll retire. We'll go with Amedeo and live somewhere new. In the countryside, in the mountains maybe, a long way from anyone.'

'Amedeo would hate that. He likes cities and newspapers and things.'

'We'll make his dreams come true, whatever they are.'

Chiara settled back in the seat and turned her face to the sky again. They moved smoothly across the water without saying any more for a while. They were now some way from the coast, and because of the unusually calm sea, Rocco chose to take a straight course across the bay, distancing them even further from the shore, to hasten the journey. Far off to their left they could see the rooftops of Ercolano, and behind, the great and gradual upward sweep of Vesuvius. They were probably halfway across the open stretch, at the furthest point from the coast, when Chiara at last spoke again.

'So, now will you leave your troubles behind you?'

Rocco frowned and smiled at the same time. 'Troubles? What troubles?'

'All this searching. For something in the past, for forgiveness.' He made no answer, and for a while she seemed to be content with this, but then persisted, 'Well?' Now Rocco pushed in the throttle so that the boat's prow sank down, and turned off the motor. They glided on for a few yards and then came to a halt, the water lapping gently against the launch's sides. Chiara did not question why they had stopped but waited until Rocco was ready to speak. He lit himself a cigarette and looked out at the horizon.

'He would have crossed about here, you know. Gabriele. On his way out.' Rocco raised his hand and pointed out his approximation of the route. Chiara did not respond.

There was another long pause before he began again. 'I'd like to tell you about something peculiar that happened to me during the operation. I think I may have died for a moment.'

Again she did not reply, but her eyebrows came together in a slight frown.

'And in that tiny moment when I was dead – it seemed like years – in that moment, I could see my body lying there, so sad, so fragile. Then I met someone, or something. Actually no thing, a non entity, that's the only way I can describe it. It, he, seemed to be in charge. It was his decision whether I should live or die.'

'Like God?'

'You could call it that. But it was different from anything you imagine as God. We had a conversation, but it was like talking to myself. Whoever this was – God, if you like – seemed to be part of me at the same time as being separate, deciding my fate. And although we were arguing a point for hours or years, it was clear from the start that the decision had already been made.'

'That you would be spared?'

'That I would live, yes. But by then I didn't want to.'

363

'Why not?'

'At first I was terrified and begged to be allowed back. But after I had seen it, or him, it was like . . . I just wanted to be released. It was too wonderful for words.'

Chiara sat up and the heavy timber hull rocked gently in the water before stilling itself again. 'What happened?' she asked.

Rocco pursed his lips. 'Against my will I was sent back.'

'For a reason?'

'He told me I could not be released until I had set my house in order.' Rocco smiled, almost with embarrassment. Then he turned to look across the water at the distant spread of Naples: the ochre regularity of the massed housing blocks, topped by church domes and bell towers; the two old fortresses, their weather-beaten walls eternally defiant against the sea; the steep rise behind the city, crowned by the jutting heights of the Castel Sant' Elmo and the monastery of San Martino.

Chiara asked, 'What does that mean, set your house in order?'

'I knew what it meant at the time,' answered Rocco. 'It was as clear as day; though the longer I am back, the more difficult . . .' He paused and lowered his eyes before continuing. 'For too long I had forgotten who I was. I had sacrificed everything for my voice, my success. I had forgotten,' his chin sank against his chest, 'I had forgotten how to love.'

For some time Chiara let him be, because he seemed to want silence. His head remained bowed, nodding very slightly, eyes fixed on some dark recess of the hull's interior. It was the first time he had articulated his plight to her, and, now that it was spoken, like a spirit let free from a locked box, he was having to face it as an entity in the world.

She touched his hand. 'And now you have found love again,' she said gently.

He turned to face her and there were tears in his eyes. 'I went astray so long ago,' he said, struggling with himself. 'When I think of my father, but more than anything, when I think of *him* . . .'

'Of who?'

Rocco turned his face westwards, towards the open horizon.

'Gabriele,' he said quietly. Because he was facing out to sea, he could not see that Chiara, too, had turned away at the mention of her husband's name. 'Gabriele Tomassini,' he repeated again, as if the words formed part of a revered inscription. 'My old friend.' He shook his head and tears spilt from his eyes. 'My whole career,' he continued, voice cracking, 'everything, all of it. It's nothing! It's ugly, filthy. Compared to the friendship I threw away. He trusted me. He loved me. And so did my father. And . . . there were others. I threw them away. I didn't just throw them away, I spat on them. You've no idea what I did.' He tightened a fist and bit his knuckles to calm himself, eventually raising his head to drag on his cigarette. Chiara neither spoke nor moved. 'He wrote to me, you know. Gabriele wrote to me in New York, asking for help, and I never replied. I've worked it out: he must have gone missing soon after that. He wasn't around when I came back to bury my father. I was expecting him to come calling, but he never came because he was already dead. I know for sure,' he buried his face in his hands, unable to look across the sea any longer, 'I know in my heart that he rowed out here and killed himself in his despair. And I know I could have saved him, if I'd written back, if I'd held out a hope, given him a chance.' The tears ran down his cheeks. 'Can you ever forgive me?'

Chiara was still looking out across the water, eyes half closed because of the brightness. She said nothing. Rocco at last turned to her, confused by her silence. 'Chiara?'

'Yes,' she sighed. 'I am here.'

'Did you hear what I was saying?'

'Yes, I heard.'

'Well? Do you forgive me? Can you look me in the face and still love me when you know what I did to Gabriele?'

She sighed again, as if compelled at last to speak the inevitable words, even though, in her folly, she had always hoped the need to say them would never arise. 'You've made up a nice story,' she said. 'And it is kind of you, because in your heart you are a kind and good man. But it has nothing to do with the truth.'

Rocco turned to look at her, confused. 'What do you mean?'

'When you turned your back on Gabriele, it was the best thing you could have done.'

'How can you say that?'

'All these years you've been torturing yourself because you think you betrayed Gabriele in order to help yourself. But that's not what happened,' she said, and now smiled faintly. 'He told me about that audition, you know.' Rocco looked up at her and his mouth fell open, but he found no words to say. 'Yes, he told me how he couldn't manage to sing in the chapel, that he got too tense and later had a fight with you.'

Rocco stuttered. 'Did he . . . did he . . . ?'

'He knew you did the right thing in leaving. And at the time you knew him well enough to understand that he could never become the sort of man you would become. He never had that drive, that discipline. And later,' she went on, 'when he wrote to you in New York. You did him a favour by not replying to that letter. I remember when he wrote it. I did everything I could to stop him.'

'Why?'

She paused to consider before going on. When she began again, her voice carried an edge. She had an agenda of her own to air here, and as she looked across the sea, squinting, almost fiercely, into the glare, it was as if she was calling an old foe into the ring. A trace of bitterness entered her tone. 'Gabriele was a sweet man in many ways, a charmer in his day, and a dreamer, but he was a hopeless buffoon.'

'How can you be so heartless?'

She ignored Rocco. 'He failed at everything he did. If you'd invited him to New York and given him a chance to sing, he'd have fallen flat on his face, embarrassed you and completely humiliated himself. He couldn't sing. And even if he could, even if by some miracle he'd done well in America, do you think for one moment he'd have given a second thought to his wife and child back in Naples? He would have left us behind for ever, that was the sort of man Gabriele Tomassini was.' She turned to face Rocco and there was a slight fire in her eyes. 'You know what I mean. You know in your heart he was no different when he was a boy.' She turned away again. 'I put up with his idiocy for too many years. I married him when I was just eighteen. I should have known better, because my father was a worthless drunk as well, but I was too young to think for myself. Every cent Gabriele earned he spent on booze and whores. You've made up a beautiful, romantic memory of him, but it's nothing like the truth. He didn't kill himself because of you. He did it because it dawned on him he was a hopeless loser, a failure, as a husband, as a father and as a man.'

Rocco knew better than to contradict her. The depth of pity he had felt for himself was subsumed by the tidal outpouring of feeling that was flowing from Chiara.

'If anyone should be full of regrets today,' she said, 'it should be me. I've wasted my life because of a stupid, stupid decision I made when I was still a girl.'

After some time, Rocco said gently, 'Why didn't you say anything about this before? You always spoke tenderly about him.'

'Because that was what you wanted to hear,' she answered. 'Did you expect me to complain when you talk about him with something like hushed religion in your voice? I didn't lie to you. I just didn't tell you the whole story, but now you know. You can leave the ghost of Gabriele to rest in the miserable pit where it belongs.'

She was no longer upset, or even defiant, but had somehow imploded, and sat slumped in her seat, staring into space. She picked up a rope that was dangling from a cleat on the side, and began to play with it between her fingers. Rocco put an arm around her shoulder, but she did not respond, so he let his hand drop, threw his cigarette end into the sea, and started up the motor. They progressed onwards in silence towards the cliff-faced shoreline of Sorrento.

Rocco got back to the Villa Rosalba at twilight and as he approached he extinguished the headlamp on the launch's deck. One of the household staff had been alerted when the Maestro's boat was spotted heading home from the south, and stood there rather formally, waiting for Campobello to toss him the painter to secure the mooring.

As Rocco walked up the steps to the terrace he was greeted by his valet, and the sight reminded him with a jar that Boldoni was no longer at the house.

'A gentleman has been waiting at the gates for most of the day,' said the valet. 'He says he has something urgent to tell you and has written several times. He begs for a short interview.'

'What is his name?'

'Benedetto Figlietti.'

'Oh yes,' said Rocco, remembering that Boldoni had mentioned the man earlier. 'Is he still here?'

'Yes, sir.'

For a moment Rocco considered having a quick meeting, but then sighed. 'I've had a long day,' he said. 'Tell the gentleman that I promise to make an appointment, but I am too tired right now. He should come again some time.'

The valet nodded and departed while Rocco made his way briskly through the house to the door of his east wing apartment. He wanted to retire to bed, to rest the weight of sadness and relief that had simultaneously taken root within him. Chiara had struck at the heart of his affliction, and by a peculiar metaphysical chemistry the grief that had subtly burdened him for decades was turning to vapour. He could feel it lifting, vanishing into the ether and leaving fresh lightness in its place, as he lay motionless on his bed, staring at the ceiling above him. The labyrinthine antics of Don Graziani suddenly seemed like so much piffle. None of it, none of them, mattered any more. The evaporation of Gabriele's ghost had freed him from them all. He almost felt pity for the poor old man, so twisted and hunted, and now a spent force. He silently resolved to confront his old patron, in a spirit of filial fondness, and explain that the charade was over at last. Would it not be a relief for them all? Was it not time to step away from the toil, and rest?

Chapter 27

Don Graziani was residing temporarily at his small holiday villa on Ischia, where he could convalesce in an atmosphere of calm and benefit daily from the waters of the island's hot mineral springs. He had begun to feel a little better by the time Bruno, who had already ignored two summonses from his ailing father, at last came to visit.

The coastal villa was designed primarily for summer use, and whilst it enjoyed a generous acreage of terraces overlooking the sea, its interior rooms were rather small. However, it was too cold today for the two men to chat in the open air, so they sat in the neat but dark little drawing room where a fire had been lit for them.

If Don Graziani's recent ill health had caused him to reflect on his mortality and given him a reason to attempt a closer bond with his only child he did not show it this morning. He was sitting hunched in his wheelchair with a blanket over his knees, but he made a point of demonstrating from the start that the physical impairment did not extend to any weakening of his mental faculties. Never one to cushion his agenda with small talk, he began even more bluntly than usual. 'It seems you are bent on your own destruction.' Bruno made no reply but waited for an elaboration. 'This policeman from New York,' continued Don Graziani. 'A sloppy business. Once again, I've had to rescue you. I will not be able to do so for ever.'

Bruno blinked but contained his response. 'Could you please explain?'

'You dress like a peacock. Do you know why peacocks have all those beautiful feathers? Do you know why they strut around trying to impress?'

'I would ask you to get to the point.'

'I will,' said his father leaning forward and holding out a pale index finger. 'Peacocks have those feathers because they want to be noticed, because they want to get fucked. Look at you! Did you never think, when you chose to kill the American in that place, that you might be recognized?'

'I had guards at the door. Nobody saw it happen.'

'Someone tried to get in. When you were doing it, somebody tried to come in for a piss.'

'Roberto got rid of him.'

'Look at what you wear,' Don Graziani said contemptuously, indicating his son's elegant spats with their distinctive lapis buttons. 'No one else wears anything like that here. People whisper, word gets around and you begin to get a reputation. The walls of that public urinal did not reach the ground, you idiot. That man who wanted to have a piss noticed your ridiculous feet in there. He also noticed quite a few others in there scuffling around and knew perfectly well that he was being fobbed off by Roberto. And so, like the responsible fascist he was, he went straight to the police and reported what he had seen. The police, of course, suspected something straight away.' He sneered at Bruno. 'It seems your footwear is famous. Luckily for you I still have influence with the police. I've had the matter buried, but it can't carry on like this. I've told you a thousand times,' his voice was rising and he wagged his finger, 'it is not like the old days.' He added, apocalyptically, though in hardly more than a murmur, 'We should begin to wind down some of our interests.'

Bruno opened his mouth to answer but stopped himself.

'And now there's this,' Don Graziani continued, with revulsion in his voice, waving a sheet of paper that he produced from under his blanket. 'It arrived yesterday.'

Bruno took the paper and began to read. It was a telegram from one of their associates in America, telling, in brief, about the publication in the *New York Times* of an article about Campobello. The piece, entitled 'The End of a Legend' was by one Brian MacSweeney, reporting from Naples, who claimed to have been present at a recording session during which the Great Campobello not only failed to find his voice, but suffered some kind of emotional breakdown. Bruno folded the paper and put it in his pocket.

'MacSweeney has proved himself an opportunist and a worm,' said Don Graziani. 'He must be silenced, of course, but no mess this time.'

'You can leave it with me,' said Bruno.

'Well, I would hope so. And one last matter: Rocco has told his wife about the mistress. She has come to me asking for help.'

'What do you want me to do about it?'

Graziani sighed and shook his head at his son's meat-headedness. 'It clearly will not do to have Rocco involved in a marital scandal on the eve of his comeback, will it?

Molly's position as his wife must appear to be secure, for the moment at least.'

'You're suggesting we get rid of the mistress as well?'

'Of course not!' spat Don Graziani. 'We'd lose Rocco for ever and open a hornet's nest.'

'What, then?'

'Our friend must be made to sing on the required date and he must be made to relinquish the woman. You will have to devise a watertight strategy. It will not be easy because his mental health is fragile enough, as we have seen, but you will have to find a way.' Bruno looked at his father without blinking, and the corner of his mouth suggested the slightest of smiles. 'I don't know what you think is so amusing,' continued Graziani. 'Our very survival may depend on whether or not you can get him on to the stage.'

'But, Papa,' said Bruno patronizingly. 'Do you not remember? We've talked about my plan to get him on stage.'

Don Graziani jerked fractionally in his chair. 'What? Yes. I know.'

'You gave my plan your approval. Remember now?'

Don Graziani shot him a vicious look. 'Of course I remember.'

Bruno's tone was quietly triumphant. 'I think you should be resting more. You seem distracted. It's not good for your health to work yourself into a frenzy. I will manage everything.'

'I am still the head of this family,' snapped Don Graziani, but Bruno just nodded.

'What have you done about the queers?'

'Both have gone.'

'I trust you handled that without upsetting things

374

too much. The men are worried, you know.'

'What are you saying? Who has been telling you things?'

Don Graziani eyed his son coldly. It was his turn to twist the knife. 'It's not for you to ask me to explain myself. It is enough for me to tell you that there have been grumblings in the ranks. Nothing serious yet, but you will have to work to earn the men's trust. This is not New York.'

Bruno's face set hard as stone at the implication of his father's reprimand. For a moment he was lost to everything, until he saw Don Graziani gesturing furiously for help to heave himself on to his sticks.

Bruno supported his father by the arm all the way to the door, but said little else. At the entrance to the villa, Don Graziani let go of him and called for his manservant. His voice was thin and weak, which seemed to infuriate him, and he twisted around, muttering curses and asking where the hell the idiot had gone. Then the servant appeared, and Bruno said goodbye. Don Graziani looked up at his son as though he had almost forgotten he was still there, and gave him a light kiss on each cheek before turning away, now holding tightly to the arm of the servant.

The few friends that Brian MacSweeney had – and none of them was particularly close – were continually surprised at how innocent he was. Considering the incisiveness of his prose, which bore witness to an arch and lucid mind, he was capable of astonishing naïvety in his behaviour, and occasionally downright foolhardiness. He never seemed to learn by his mistakes, nor foresee the immediate consequences of some of his more reckless actions. In some ways, it was a quality that endeared him to his friends, because it added a dash of colour to an otherwise rather grey and dour man; but they also worried that one day he might slip up rather badly.

The bizarre fact about his present situation was that, unusually for him, he *had* tried to think quite hard about what might happen as a result of the Campobello article, but not once did he consider the matter of his own personal safety. There was a mean, citrus streak in MacSweeney that gloried, from time to time, in others' misfortunes, and right now he was rather relishing the prospect of causing the Grazianis a pinprick of grief. They had been good patrons, true, but he had grown to resent their complacent assumption of lordship over him, and he decided that it was time to redraw the ground rules a little.

Puffed with thoughts of his own capacity to flex some muscle, he concluded warmly that this article would stop them in their tracks and make them reconsider the degree of respect he should be shown in future. He rode the wave of this pleasing assessment for some days after the article had been published, and walked around Naples with his head held high. He was indeed a herald of earth-shattering events; future generations would remember him as a notable chronicler of his times.

Buoyed by reflections of this sort, MacSweeney set off up the busy Via Toledo one fine morning on one of his favourite missions: to visit the shop where he could replenish his waning stock of cheap local wine. Having accomplished the task, and with a rather heavy box in his arms, he began the long walk back down the street, happily whistling an Irish tune that had recently been made popular through one of Donal Mulligan's best-selling records.

It was while stepping off the pavement at the Largo del' Carita, close to the steps at the entrance of Sant' Anna dei Lombardi, that MacSweeney was struck by a car. It was quite a savage blow, catching him on the right side, instantly dislocating his pelvis and cracking a rib. He was thrown to the ground and the bottles of wine shattered on the cobbles. Ruby rivulets oozed from the splintered shards and found their way circuitously to the gutter.

The street was crowded and people were shouting different instructions to the driver of the vehicle that had hit him. Cars and carriages choked up the street behind while MacSweeney, gasping with shock and pain, tried to drag himself clear. A man advanced to help him amidst the confusion, but stopped when he heard the offending car's engine roar and its gear being jammed. Again, there were contradictory shouts directed at the driver, who appeared flustered but had made the decision that he should reverse. Some witnesses later said that he looked backwards out of his window and must certainly have seen where he was heading; others maintained that he was blameless because the whole scene was such a muddle. They did nothing to stop him, however, and while MacSweeney inched his way to the kerb, powerless from the waist down, the car's back wheel swerved to one side and humped itself directly over his head. There was a double cracking sound and a small explosion. The car then shifted out of reverse, and, meeting with less resistance this time, eased its way forward through the mess. Very quickly, the driver was out of his car and had hurried round to MacSweeney's motionless body.

Horrified onlookers tried to help, but the driver shouted at them angrily to stand clear. He was a doctor, he said, and would take the poor fellow straight to hospital – though everyone could see that it was too late for that. Without more ado, he dragged MacSweeney into his car and headed down a side street away from the scene.

Police reports later confirmed that no traffic accident victim had been admitted to hospital that morning, and that it would be difficult to trace the identity of the alleged victim. None of the many witnesses felt confident enough to describe the driver accurately. Perhaps they smelt a rat and decided to observe the old law of *omertà* – self-preservation and honour through silence. The police claimed they would keep the file open, but their official assessment was that it should be regarded as a hit and run accident.

Chapter 28

Amedeo felt exhilarated at the end of his day of coaching with Rocco. The departure of Pickering and Boldoni had cast a shadow over life at the Villa Rosalba, as had Mrs Campobello's recent tight-lipped hostility, but Amedeo's buoyant nature would not be held down. The positive side to the new state of affairs was that he had found a real friend and soulmate in Alberto, the talented young pianist they had engaged to replace Pickering. The two shared a cheeky sense of humour, and their combined enthusiasm for work spurred an appetite for excellence that was all but insatiable. By the end of the day Rocco had to insist that they stop practising. He warned that too much work at this stage might roughen the edges of Amedeo's still fragile instrument. The two young men acquiesced chastely, but as soon as he had left the room began to pick at fragments of song again, trying this and that at the piano, experimenting with varying nuances and tempos. Rocco heard them and came storming back into the music room, which made them pack their bags and exit without another word.

Amedeo now sat contentedly beside his mentor in the back of the Lancia for the ride back to his mother's apartment on the Vomero. Rocco liked to drop him off personally when the boy went back to stay with Chiara, but he was tactful enough not to dally, and rarely even walked across the threshold – a courtesy that Amedeo appreciated. Indeed, the young student could not fault his illustrious mentor in any department. If the Maestro seemed occasionally taciturn or withdrawn, Amedeo would consider such gravitas appropriate in a colossus, and would look at him admiringly, wondering what weighty concerns occupied the thoughts of great men.

Amedeo's own life at the moment was progressing as if in an enchantment. Until recently he had been floating through life like a twig on a river, spinning downstream without particular direction, occasionally snagged by reeds; but since meeting Rocco he had been drawn by a strong directional current, and happily submitted himself to its tugging flow.

His former preoccupations had paled. It had been a month since he had attended a meeting of his Struggle Committee – a group of earnest youths who met weekly at the tavern to thrash out the woes of shipyard workers. He barely gave a second thought to the government's recent industrial (so-called) reforms, the damaging injustice of which would formerly have set his heart ablaze; and he ignored a furtive rally that was being organized to protest about democrats being muscled out of parliament in Rome. His passions were channelled elsewhere because a new world had opened for him, and with it, the last traces of petulant adolescence seemed to have melted away, all of which was a great relief for his mother.

Amedeo looked sideways at Rocco in the back seat of the car as they drove along. The great man was smoking, as usual, and lost in thought, gazing out of the window at the passing streets. A burdened look was engraved on his brow today, and there was a sense of suppressed agitation in his eyes. It was as if his awareness of time slipping past was at odds with a herculean task that weighed upon his shoulders. For all his warmth and kindly disposition towards Amedeo, Campobello sometimes seemed like a man standing precipitously on the threshold of his own Hades.

It was while Amedeo was thus observing Rocco and contentedly wondering about the underlying heart of his malaise that he noticed the tenor's eyes drawn to a more immediate, external focus. He was leaning forward slightly and looking around Pozzo to get a better view ahead. The car had begun to slow down.

They had not quite reached the summit of the Vomero hill and were being waved down by a group of four men in the road ahead. The men were in quasi-military black shirts with epaulettes, and wore riding boots and jodhpurs. Two of them held batons, and all had revolvers holstered to their belts. The foremost man saluted them formally and indicated that the car should take a left-hand turn out of the traffic into a side street.

Campobello slid open the glass partition and said wearily to Pozzo that they had better do as they were told. The car came to a halt and Rocco opened his window. One of the uniformed men stood to attention, saluted again and, bending down, he said, 'I'm sorry to delay you, Maestro.' Flicking aside the whistle that hung by a plaited leather lanyard around his neck, he took a folded paper from his breast pocket. He was a handsome young man, and well groomed. Another tall and polished trooper took up position behind him. 'I have orders to detain citizen Amedeo Tomassini,' he said in clipped tones. His eyes darted towards the young man sitting next to Campobello, and the timbre of his voice turned a shade harder. 'Get out of the car and come with us, please, sir,' he said to Amedeo.

'Wait, wait,' interjected Rocco. 'Orders? Whose orders?'

The man waved the piece of paper. 'Orders from the Central Municipal Bureau of Civil Jurisdiction,' he began.

'The *what*?' said Rocco.

The trooper sighed. 'Sir, it would be best for everyone if you allow us to carry out our orders without impediment, because if we—'

'You can spare me your strutting arrogance,' said Rocco. 'Tell me who has issued this order and why.'

The man closed his eyes for a moment and then put his hand on the car door. 'Maestro, if you don't want to get into trouble, you'll do as I say and let me carry out my orders.'

'Do you know who you're talking to?' said Pozzo in disbelief from the front seat.

'Silence,' commanded the other black-shirted men standing behind.

'Give me the name of the person who ordered this,' insisted Rocco.

The trooper in front now stood tall and called to the other two members of his squad, indicating that that they should go around the car and take Amedeo by force. He then leant down to Campobello again. 'Citizen Amedeo Tomassini has been participating in subversive activities that threaten to undermine the peace and stability of the Municipality of Naples, and as such he is required to remain in custody to answer some questions, without delay.'

The other two had reached Amedeo's door by now, opened it and were trying to drag him from the car.

'It's all right,' said Amedeo, his hands shaking, 'you don't need to pull me. I will come.' He turned to Rocco. 'It's all right, *zio*. They'll ask me some questions and then they'll let me go. I have nothing to hide.'

'Don't be ridiculous!' said Rocco, and turned back to the trooper in charge. 'You will desist from this assault. What is your name?' The man standing behind the chief trooper took out his oak baton and began slapping it into his palm.

'Look, sir,' said the trooper to Rocco, as if conceding a point, off the record, as a gesture of good intent, 'if you have any concerns about this I suggest you take them to Prefect Tedeschi.'

'Pompeo Tedeschi?' said Campobello. 'Is he behind this?'

'Let's just say that he, or someone in his office, might be able to give you more information than us.' With that, he saluted once more and joined the other two in bustling Amedeo from the scene. Rocco did not see what they did with him next, whether they took him to a car or into a building, because one of the squad waved Pozzo forwards, glaring at him threateningly and holding up the traffic on the main Corso to allow the Lancia back into the stream.

An hour later, having quickly visited and torn himself away from a distraught Chiara, Rocco Campobello was standing in front of Pompeo Tedeschi's large plain desk on the first floor of the imposing Municipio building. The uniformed secretary who had led the way through to the office told Rocco that 'the Prefect' (as Tedeschi had begun to style himself) was committed to a very busy schedule this morning, but that he had agreed, in these special circumstances, to a brief meeting with the Maestro. 'The Prefect is in the habit of making sacrifices to look after the interests of his friends, and as his friends are many, his daily sacrifice is great,' said the secretary. Rocco was not of a mind either to be stalled or impressed by propagandist hyperbole, and without replying to the secretary, walked briskly up to Tedeschi's desk. Two framed photographs hung on the wall behind: one, a stern but surprisingly sensitive full-face portrait of Mussolini, and beside it a handsome profile of the nation's moustached monarch, the small and dapper Vittorio Emanuele III. The desk was clear, but for two neatly stacked piles of papers, one face up, the other down, between which rested a fountain pen, its lid removed.

'Maestro Campobello,' said Tedeschi, smiling broadly and rising to his feet. 'An honour, indeed.'

Rocco allowed his hand to be shaken, but wasted no time in pleasantries. 'I wish to know who has ordered the detention of Amedeo Tomassini, and why,' he said.

Tedeschi looked completely baffled by the opening remark but quickly disguised his uncertainty. 'Detention of who?' he asked.

Rocco repeated the name. 'My pupil,' he explained: 'the young man who accompanied our party to the opera last month, and whose impertinence towards you at dinner I had thought was a settled matter. He wrote to apologize, as did I myself.'

'Of course,' replied Tedeschi, 'and I have forgotten the incident altogether. The boy needs to watch his tongue, of course, but I'm sure time, and your own good influence, will smooth down his rougher edges.'

'In which case would you be kind enough to explain why he was dragged from my car this morning by a squad of men,' he gestured at Tedeschi's black shirt, tie and jodhpurs, 'dressed in the same manner as yourself? Do you call these men soldiers, police or something else? And on whose authority do they act?'

'I assure you I know nothing of this.'

'The men's leader referred to you by name,' Rocco replied.

This time, Tedeschi worded his defence more carefully. He was genuinely nonplussed by the accusation, and knew nothing whatever of the incident's provenance, but did not wish to appear ignorant. If someone else were ordering the activities of the Party's *squadristi* in the city, he was either being undermined locally or sidelined by central government in Rome. As it happened, for various reasons, both possibilities had been preying on his mind recently and were the cause of great anxiety to him as he lay sleepless in bed at night, but he was shrewd enough to realize that it would only make matters worse if he were seen to be losing control; and so he decided to qualify his denial of involvement by appearing noncommittal.

'Signor,' he said in measured tones, 'I occupy this office in a physical sense, but the office of Prefect is one to which an entire organization of individuals contributes, yes, with myself at its head, but that does not mean that I am constantly in touch with everyone in the department, nor am I personally responsible for every decision that is undertaken in this building.' He smiled, attempting to lighten the air. 'After all, Maestro, you would not count yourself responsible for an entire opera's performance. There is the chorus, the orchestra, the, the . . .' His inspiration dried up, and Campobello went on without a pause.

'Do you or do you not answer for the actions of your party's *squadristi* in this city?' he asked.

The bluntness of the question riled Tedeschi, but in a fluster he managed to misinterpret it. 'I answer only to my leader, to our Prime Minister, and to none other, no matter how celebrated he may be.'

'I am wasting my time here,' said Rocco. 'I must take my complaint to Rome.'

'However,' replied Tedeschi quickly, 'I shall of course look into the matter right away and see what has been done and why. It is possible, perhaps even likely, that the boy has been involved in some unlawful or seditious activity. It wouldn't be the first time.'

'What else has he done?'

'There have been reports. We have good reason to believe them.'

'You keep a file on him, then?'

'You don't expect me to discuss that.'

'I want answers, signor,' said Rocco, coldly. 'The boy has become more than a pupil to me. He has no father. Whatever you do to him, you do as if to a member of my own family.'

'Yes,' said Tedeschi, looking away, airily. 'I had heard that you were – how shall we say? – becoming close to that poor, unfortunate family.'

Rocco looked back at him coldly. 'I will await illumination on what has occurred,' he added, before turning to leave. 'By noon tomorrow, if you would be so kind.'

'I assure you, Maestro,' Tedeschi concluded, 'that I

shall do everything in my power to find out what has happened.'

Shortly afterwards, Rocco's car swept up to the entrance of the Villa Rosalba and waited while the guards jumped to their feet to open the gates. Rocco, sitting in the back, was too consumed in dark thought to notice the young man who had approached his window, and who now tapped lightly against it. Pozzo leant out to shoo the fellow away, but Rocco stopped him. 'What can I do for you?' he asked, and the young man took off his hat. He was tall and fair haired, with an open, rather star-struck smile, the sort that Rocco had seen a thousand or more times before on the faces of breathless devotees. But this young man had a kind of familiarity about him. 'Have we met before?' Rocco asked him.

'No, Maestro, never. My name is Benedetto Figlietti.'

'Ah, yes,' said Rocco, recalling. 'The one who's been trying to see me.'

'Yes, Maestro. I would like very much to talk to you. Just a few minutes of your time.'

'Very well,' said Rocco, 'but now is not a good time for me.' The young man's face fell. 'There's a problem I need to sort out right now, so we'll have to make it some other time.'

'Tomorrow?'

'Very well, tomorrow,' replied Rocco, distracted. 'Ten o'clock prompt.' Turning to Pozzo, he added, 'Inform the guards, will you?' Pozzo nodded and the young man stepped back, waving his hat as the car drove past and through the gates.

Chapter 29

As it happened, at ten o'clock the following morning the guards refused to allow Figlietti through the gates. When he protested that he had an appointment with Signor Campobello, and that the chauffeur would vouch for him, they told him that the Maestro was busy with a far more important meeting, and that he should not be so impertinent, a comment that made Figlietti bark an insult at them and walk away fuming – which amused the guards greatly.

They had been telling the truth, however. Rocco was indeed in the middle of another meeting, one which demanded his complete attention. He had entirely forgotten about the young man at the gates because half an hour earlier the Grazianis, father and son, had called by unexpectedly, and what they had came to discuss caused all other considerations to evaporate.

Upon arrival, Don Graziani had inched his way, step by shuffled step, into the house, supported by a stick in each hand and with a member of staff hovering tactfully on either side in case his legs should give way. His head quivered and his eyes fixed themselves on the immediate landscape to be negotiated with each step. When at last he lowered himself into the chair that had been fetched for him, he exhaled with the relief of one who has come through a long and perilous voyage. Noting the deterioration, Rocco glanced once or twice at Bruno but failed to get a response.

As soon as they were settled, Bruno took charge of proceedings. His hair was oiled neatly flat, and a golden collar pin pushed the knot of his tie out from his silk shirt front. He held several sheets of typed paper and did not hesitate to make clear the purpose of their visit. He was well prepared with facts and statistics, but, as ever, his manner allowed for not the slenderest glint of personal chemistry, not even at the point when he first let drop the substance of his proposal. It took Rocco a moment or two to digest the implication of it.

At last he replied. 'How can you be so sure you will be able to find him?'

'As you know, our connections are extensive, to say the least.'

'But this is a political matter. Tedeschi, or one of his fascist friends, is behind it. You won't be able to help. If they suspect you're taking the side of a socialist subversive, it'll be just the excuse they need to come down on you.'

'On the side of a socialist!' Don Graziani chuckled from his chair, but Bruno's expression did not change.

Rocco lit a cigarette. 'The ridiculous thing about all this,' he continued, 'is that the boy has turned a new leaf. He is interested in nothing but his studies. Politics, all that juvenile anger, is behind him.'

'Tedeschi obviously wants to make an example of him,' said Bruno. 'Perhaps because he is connected to you.'

'Are you trying to say this is my fault?'

'They would like to demonstrate that no one is immune to their laws, even those with the highest connections. I know the boy is not related to you, but,' a less than

389

wholesome look flitted across Bruno's eyes, 'your feelings towards his family are not entirely unknown. The point is this: by one means or another we can sort this out. We will deliver the boy safely back. It will not be easy and it will require a degree of expense and planning, but it can be done.' The offer was not delivered in a tone of comradeship or even sympathy, but as the prelude to a bilateral arrangement, the second part of which would balance or outweigh the good news of the first. 'And because of the great inconvenience that it would cause,' Bruno continued, 'I make no apology for telling you that we will have our terms. Terms which might be regarded as steep, but which I assure you must be met, if you would see Amedeo Tomassini returned to . . . his mother's arms.'

Rocco held Bruno's gaze in silence before nodding. 'Well, I suppose you'd better let me know your terms.'

He was looking out of the window as Bruno proceeded to recite his prepared statement in a businesslike manner. Reading, in part, from a typed sheet, he outlined his demand for Rocco's participation in the production, the solitary performance at the San Carlo, and delineated the basic statistics and timescale involved. Through the window, over to the left, Rocco could see a stretch of the northward shore, and in the far distance a line of small fishing boats being strung out to net off the little bay at the Capo di Posillipo. 'The X-rays have confirmed that you are fit enough to cope with the strain,' Bruno was continuing. Still Rocco looked out of the window, now glancing across to the garden side, where the spreading tops of the cedars billowed like a verdant cumulus against the blue sky. A small ache began to announce itself in his ribs. 'And we have every confidence, as do the doctors, that the unfortunate incident at the recording session was a one-off. They recommend shallower breathing, and—'

At this, Don Graziani raised his hand to interrupt his son, 'I think the Maestro knows best on matters of singing.'

Bruno blinked his assent. 'Your singing on the day of the recordings – other than that single unfortunate moment – demonstrated to everyone that your voice is in first-class order. We have every confidence that this performance, of an opera you know very well, will be a triumph, and—'

'You don't need to go on.' It was Rocco now who spoke, his voice pleasantly mellow. 'I agree to your terms. Without hesitation.' Bruno managed a slight smile. 'I will start straight away,' continued Rocco. 'I have a new pianist – as you doubtless know.' He waved a hand in the air. 'So you can tell your people to alert the press, tell the San Carlo, do whatever you want. As long as the boy is released.'

'He will be,' replied Bruno. 'But . . .' and he paused, 'I am afraid there is more. There is another condition which must be met.'

'Yes?'

'We will have the boy released into your care on the day of the performance, not before, and—'

'Not before? You mean you don't trust me? You think I'll back out?'

Bruno ignored the interruption: 'and it is our condition that, after he is released, he and his mother must leave Naples, leave Italy.'

Rocco looked into empty space for a moment, and then turned to Don Graziani. 'Why this, *zio*?'

'The triumph cannot be undermined by a scandal,'

answered the old man simply, without looking back at him. 'If the world must hear about your broken marriage, it will be done with dignity: a proper announcement from lawyers to the press, before rumours and filth have a chance to spread. It will be better for the woman and her son, as well.'

Rocco asked, 'What if Amedeo is released quickly? When they find he has done nothing wrong, they might just let him go.'

Bruno replied, 'These people do not admit mistakes. It will be all we can do to make sure he does not disappear for ever without trace.'

In the light of one or two other instances he had read about, this was a possibility Rocco could not contest. 'After the release, where do you suggest I send the two of them?'

'Wherever you like,' replied Bruno. 'I'm told Switzerland is very pleasant.' The unwholesome filter spread once again across his eyes.

Rocco looked at him for a moment, and then said quietly, 'You know everything, don't you?'

'That is our only defence in these difficult times,' answered Bruno, putting away his pen and gathering the papers. 'Are we all agreed, then?'

'One thing,' replied Rocco. 'I will agree to everything you have proposed, but at the end of this business, when we have both kept our side of the bargain, my account is settled.' At this, Graziani turned to face him with a look of shocked surprise. 'This will be the last service either of us performs for the other,' continued Rocco. 'The ground will be level, all debts clear. Our association will be at an end.'

Don Graziani looked down at his lap and shook his

head. 'It saddens me to hear you speak like this,' he said.

'You have brought it on yourself. These are my terms,' replied Rocco.

After another pause, Don Graziani nodded his assent. 'I think you should have a look at this, though,' he added, and took a folded newspaper cutting out of his breast pocket. He laid it on the table beside him and patted it a couple of times. 'Read it in your own time. You may decide you need our help more than you think.'

There was something funereal in the atmosphere of the group as they laboured their way towards the entrance portico, where the Grazianis' car awaited them. Their progress was slow because of the old man's minute steps, and nobody spoke. Rocco leant forward to kiss Don Graziani's hand at the point of departure, and in return he received the briefest of pats on his close-cropped scalp, but there was a sense of affection turned stale, and a weary disappointment in the air.

After the car had pulled away, Rocco returned to the hall. Molly had appeared. She was standing on the stairway, looking down at him, and there was more colour in her cheeks than there had been of late.

'Well?' she said. 'Have they gone?'

'I take it you know exactly what they were here to discuss.'

'I have to keep abreast. What do you expect? Did you think I would quietly allow myself to sink beneath the waves and drown?'

'My only concern is for the safety of Amedeo.'

'You can hardly be surprised at what has happened,' she said, coming down the stairs.

Rocco had turned to walk away, but paused now and looked back at her. 'What is that supposed to mean?'

'Oh, come on, Rocco. You may be infatuated, but I don't believe you've lost your senses altogether. How could a boy from the slums expect to gentrify himself overnight? He was bound to slip up sooner or later. You should never have encouraged him in the first place.'

'The intention was to foster the boy's talent, not to "gentrify" him as you say.'

'Nevertheless.'

'And we will continue to work with him as soon as this business is cleared up.'

'Don't you think it might be best . . . ?'

'Molly!' Rocco turned on her, not with anger, but with a decisiveness that cleared the nonsense from the air. 'Molly,' he went on more gently, and approached her. 'This is not about you and me. Not even about me and Chiara Tomassini. This is about the life of a young man, a brilliant, beautiful young man with a great future, whose only hope rests with me. This is not a game. Do you understand?'

For a moment Molly was speechless. 'Of course,' she said at last. They stood facing one another without speaking for an instant, and all other agendas seemed to recede.

Rocco broke the silence. 'I'm sorry, Molly,' he said quietly. 'Sorry for everything.'

He looked down and then turned to go, but she called out to him. 'Rocco!' It sounded almost like a plea, and she raised a hand to her neck.

'What is it?'

'Are you sure you can go through with this? This

scheme, it's so precarious. Maybe there's another way. Could we not try to work something out? Together.'

Once again, he observed her. Momentarily, though hopelessly, they were united. 'I will be all right. You don't need to worry.'

'The Grazianis—'

'Leave the Grazianis to me. I know how they think.'

Molly was not convinced, and watched, perplexed, as he turned and left the room, closing the door behind him.

He was alone on the seaward terrace when he turned his attention to the newspaper clipping that Graziani had left, and the pain at his side had begun to tug insistently. He unfolded the paper. It was quite a long article. He closed his eyes when he read the bold print of the title, because he understood instantly the gist of the piece. A small slip of paper was appended with a clip behind the cutting, and he flipped it out to see what was on it. There was a short message, written in Graziani's distinctive, though now shaky, hand:

We gather the author has had the sense to return to America, where I do not think he will decide to bother us further.

Rocco screwed the note tightly in his fist, and tossed it into the sea.

Chapter 30

At this time of year, because of the cold, Pozzo and Taddeo preferred to spend their idle moments in the porter's room, off the entrance hall of the villa, where there was a wood stove burning all day long. They sat there now, huddled close to the fire, palms splayed for warmth, like mountain shepherds. Taddeo watched an oily drip inch its descent from a joint in the stove's long flue until it was joined by a heavier, faster drip from behind; together, they tumbled downwards at speed and eventually fell hissing on to the stove, where they boiled away and vanished, leaving a worm of black smoke as their memorial.

Pozzo and Taddeo could hear the sound of energetic piano playing from upstairs, occasionally interrupted, paused, with sections repeated, or abandoned, or re-started at a different place. Sometimes the house would be filled with a great resonant flood of tenor singing, but mostly the Maestro would conserve his larynx and employ a *mezza voce* because of the hefty workload he had prescribed himself daily in the run-up to the performance.

Two weeks had gone by since the public announcement of his much-awaited return to the stage, and since then everything had changed at the Villa Rosalba. Pozzo said that he had heard this was what it used to be like when Campobello lived in New York: an unbending domestic routine, the day divided and subdivided into compartments of time that were announced across the villa by a pre-set code of whistle blows. The servants went about their duties with clipped precision, as if under the threat of instant dismissal, and every member of staff, including Pozzo and Taddeo, carried with him the anxiety of a military operative in a theatre of war.

'He's put on a bit of weight, I'd say,' remarked Pozzo, glancing quickly at Taddeo's midriff, 'which will be good news for you.' Taddeo's lips tightened at the implied insult, but he did not respond. For better or worse he had been thrown together with the pesky chauffeur and just had to put up with his little jibes from time to time.

'On balance,' said Taddeo, 'I'd say things are better now than they were. At least we all know where we stand. The two of them don't argue so much, not so many slammed doors or shouting from her, and at last he's actually doing something, rather than moping around like a lost schoolboy.'

'*Aspetta, aspetta*. Not so fast,' reprimanded Pozzo, rubbing his hands to warm them up. Pozzo had assumed a slight seniority over Taddeo and become a little haughty, because he considered himself part of an elite inner circle; after all, he was privy to the Maestro's secret comings and goings to the Vomero apartment. Taddeo had an inkling that the chauffeur possessed knowledge of some intriguing snippets, and he was quietly curious and envious, but as far as specifics were concerned, he and the rest of the staff at the Villa Rosalba remained in the dark.

As it happened, Pozzo had not had cause to drive

Campobello to Signora Tomassini's flat now for nearly a fortnight. He had had words with the building's porter – who was by now something of a chum – and it was confirmed: the Maestro and the signora were not seeing one another any more. Whether they had quarrelled, or whether it was to do with the boy's disappearance, or the imminence of the performance at the San Carlo, neither Pozzo nor the porter had a clue.

'He's definitely looking more like himself, nowadays,' continued Taddeo. 'He walks with the cane in just the way I learnt to do, and he's even taken up that funny limp again. What's that about, by the way?'

'Even if I did know, do you think I'd tell you?' replied Pozzo, stretching his conceit a little too far. 'It's just one of his ways.'

Taddeo stood up. 'As you say, he is a little more plump. Which means I can ease off the diet a bit, thank God. I'd say we're about the same size now, wouldn't you?' He patted himself with both hands on the ribs. 'In fact, I'd say we've never looked so alike. Veritable twins.' This, of course, was the trump card in Taddeo's pack, and no one could deny the truth of it.

'Enjoy it while you can,' concluded Pozzo, checking his watch and getting up to go. It was lunchtime. 'Because I doubt he'll be needing you for much longer.'

The smile dropped from Taddeo's cheeks. 'What do you mean?'

'Have you heard his singing? It's getting better by the day. He's on top form again, they say. He'll be back as he used to be in no time.'

'And?'

'He never had need of a double in the old days, did he? This business of decoys and hiding himself away was just something to do with his illness. Now that he's over it, he'll take up his public life again.'

This was one taunt too many, and Taddeo decided to fight his corner for once. 'Well, if the Maestro's going back to the way things were, he'll probably move back to New York soon enough. Then all the staff here will have to start looking for new jobs!'

Pozzo raised his eyebrows but made no further response. Let the oafish mimic lose sleep over it, he thought. He would keep his own counsel and give the impression of private intelligence. Silence was always a more powerful weapon.

Inside the music room, the polished brass carriage clock that stood on the mantelpiece struck one o'clock, and Alberto, the young pianist, looked up from the keyboard to where Campobello stood. The tenor stroked the white stubble of his beard while he stared hard at the open vocal score on the stand in front of him. Alberto's eyes were ringed with dark circles. He was exhausted, having worked a punishing schedule with Rocco from morning till night for nearly two weeks. He waited hopefully for the nod that it was time to break for lunch.

It had been challenging, but it had also been immensely stimulating. Alberto had been warned by his musical elders that the great tenor was a legendary pedant, but nothing had prepared him for the staggering attention to detail with which the Maestro attacked his task. Campobello was a perfectionist to the last hair on his head, and, as far as Alberto was concerned, his style was never less than princely. The complete absence of humour in their long sessions was certainly wearing, but it lent a high-caste, spotless solemnity to the atmosphere, so that their place of work felt like consecrated ground and their artistic goals seemed chaste, touched with a grace, imperceptible to commonplace musicians. Despite his tiredness, therefore, Alberto felt privileged beyond words to be working here.

The highlights for Alberto were when the Maestro would take him to the opera house so that he could sit beside him in all the production meetings, not only with the director and conductor, but with the scenery and prop builders, lighting technicians, costumiers and make-up artists, as well as fellow singers. Staff at the San Carlo were more accustomed to the big stars arriving just a few days before the opening night, when they would be briefed on the basic movements of their character; but Campobello wanted knowledge of every aspect of the production, its background, inspiration, its structure and intentions, together with the positions of each character on the stage, including chorus members and walk-on actors. He would ask questions that the producer had not even asked himself, and thereby work with the whole team to raise the production's dramatic efficacy.

The most striking meeting that Alberto witnessed was Campobello's first encounter with the production designer, a young artist from Bologna whose previous two productions were reported to have been outstandingly daring. As soon as the bright-eyed young man was introduced to Campobello it was clear they would get on. The designer bubbled with enthusiasm for his project, spreading out a huge portfolio of drawings with an incessant stream of explanation. Rocco was impressed by all the plans, scene-sets, and the two detailed stage models that the designer had built. They were cutting-edge concepts, which combined practicality with dramatic punch. But the tenor's interest in the scenery was nothing compared to his fascination with the costume drawings, which he stared at open-mouthed. It was the design for the costume of Mefistofele, the bass role, that consumed Campobello's attention. 'It is the Prince of Darkness himself,' he muttered, looking up and down at the cloaked fiery figure, with its leering black and scarlet face, and its gargantuan bull's horns. He continued to look in silence for quite some while.

The clock's single chime faded away, the morning session was complete, and Alberto waited quietly at the keyboard for a sign from the Maestro, who was usually very punctual; but this time, it seemed, Campobello had something on his mind. He looked up from the score on his stand and fixed his sombre eyes on Alberto.

'In one sentence, what would you say is the weakness in the character of Faust?'

Alberto was a highly accomplished pianist and possessed a wisdom for music beyond his years, but he was certainly no Pickering when it came to a wider understanding of the repertoire. He was compelled to think quickly, because Arrigo Boito's *Mefistofele* was not a work he knew well, and he hadn't given much thought to the background psychology of the characters. Hungry for lunch and with aching fingers, he improvised. 'Faust's weakness, as I see it, is that after a lifetime of philosophical confusion and tying his thoughts in knots, he sees the chance of a short cut to enlightenment, a quick way to have all his worries and questions about the world put to rest, and he takes it. Without thinking about the price.'

Campobello thought about the answer for a while,

and then said, 'Well, yes. But why? We have here a wise old man, a decent man at heart, visited by the devil and tempted to sell himself *for all eternity* in return for just a short and fleeting vision of peace. And he falls for it?'

'Maybe he knows that a Christian God will step in at the end and save him when the time comes, if he repents. Which is exactly what happens.'

'That's the soft ending that Boito chose, and he got it from the poet Goethe. In the older version of the story, by Marlowe, God is merciless and sends old Faust to the fire, which some would say he deserves.'

'It depends what the storyteller is trying to teach: a message of forgiveness or a caution against selfish greed,' said Alberto.

Rocco pondered this for a moment. 'The storyteller is like God, then, with the power to punish or forgive, as the whim takes him. Just a flip of a coin.' He shook his head. 'Perhaps. But that doesn't help us. We have been dished the outline of a character, like a diagram, and our job is to turn him into a living, breathing person. So we need to search the material closely to help us build our picture.' He looked around the room for his cigarette case. 'In the old play, Faust is already dark. He invites the devil, as someone he can do business with. You see, he's already damned in a sense. But in Boito's piece, this opera, the devil creeps up on the poor old man in disguise. Dressed as a monk! At this point, Faust, yes, is scholarly and the holder of many secrets, but he knows little of the dark side. He is drawn into it, tempted by visions, promises, and because of the sort of work that he does – ' here Rocco turned and walked towards the window, drawing on his cigarette – 'he makes the perfect victim. Easy pickings.' He seemed to contemplate the view before turning around and looking at Alberto again. 'You see, many – you included – would say that his weakness is his short-sightedness, his greed, but it's not that at all. His weakness is the part of his character that makes him an easy target for the devil.'

'Which is?'

Rocco opened his palms. 'His brilliance, of course. His accomplishment. The devil wouldn't have wasted his time with a nobody.'

Alberto was quite a shy boy in company and had a polite smile permanently fixed to his mouth, particularly when he talked to his superiors. It was fixed there now, as he nodded, not entirely following Campobello's drift; but he could see the Maestro was wrapped up in his own thoughts, and decided to observe a respectful pause before asking, 'Are we going to have our lunch, Maestro?'

Rocco nodded and they walked in silence from the room. Making their way to the dining room, Alberto enquired if there had been any more word of Amedeo.

'Prefect Tedeschi seems to know more than he's letting on,' replied Rocco, 'but still denies responsibility.' He said no more. The matter of the Grazianis' deal had not been mentioned in the villa since their visit, two weeks before. Bruno had sent word that plans were taking shape but that the success of the operation would depend on surprise and secrecy. The less it was talked about the better.

As usual, Alberto helped himself to food laid out on the dining room sideboard, but preferred to take it to the staff kitchen to eat rather than sit down with Rocco and Molly. Husband and wife therefore sat down alone at the table today, as they did most days.

Considering the weight of the circumstances that

pressed upon Molly, she made a valiant attempt to sound upbeat about life and chatted away rather blithely during lunch. In truth, she was deeply torn about the decision she had recently made, but felt it was a necessary course of action in order to protect herself against the worst eventuality. Don Graziani had played the whole affair down. He told her that Rocco's folly was probably just a symptom of his illness, and that it would pass in good time; but Molly's outrage and pragmatism were beginning to outweigh the lingering hope she had entertained that her husband was capable of reform; and so she had set her own plan in motion.

Rocco still had no idea about the airmail letters she had been receiving in her private box at the central post office – letters from her father's lawyer in America, who had been preparing the ground for divorce proceedings. He recommended initiating action shortly after Rocco's San Carlo appearance. The signs and sums were promising, and her father, delighted that his beloved daughter might at last be released from the clutches of the Italian peasant, was gearing his considerable influence to help in any way he could. There would be some unpleasantness, Molly realized, but at last she sensed the possibility of a life waiting beyond; and her situation, as blameless victim of an adulterous husband, would be beyond public reproach.

'I've read that there's quite a war raging in the New York press about you,' she said across the table. 'They're calling it the Battle of the Maestro's Voice, would you believe? Will he manage it, won't he manage it? That kind of thing. Opinions are running high.' Rocco swallowed a spoonful of soup in silence. 'Nice Mr Fleming is standing by you. He's told everyone that MacSweeney's article was full of half-truths and didn't paint the whole picture. He says he's prepared to release that one electronic recording – the one you *did* manage to complete successfully – to prove it. Wouldn't that be exciting? The whole world would buy it, even if just to see if it's true.' Rocco tipped forward his bowl to collect the last of the soup. 'Mr MacSweeney has been very restrained, it seems,' Molly went on. 'While the rest of them have taken sides for or against him, he's been mysteriously silent. They say he embarked for America from Naples nearly three weeks ago, but no one's heard from him since. Perhaps he jumped ship half way across the ocean! Either way, he's in deep water now. I don't blame him for keeping his head down.'

Having finished his soup, Rocco broke off a hunk of bread from a loaf on the table, cut a large wedge of cheese, and left the table without a word to Molly, taking his food with him.

He had become expert at hiding the sharpness and frequency of the pains in his side. He did not want anyone to know, in case the production were jeopardized, which might have devastating implications for Amedeo. He put a hand to his flank now as he went upstairs, rubbing at the flesh through the cotton of his shirt. The pain eased as he reached the landing, which was good because every time it faded, he would hold out a small belief that it might not return.

He was on his way back to his study to have a look again at the letter that had arrived this morning. It was dangerous to keep it longer than absolutely necessary. The sooner it was destroyed the better. Munching the bread and cheese as he locked the door of his apartment behind him, he took the letter from his jacket pocket and unfolded it. It was from Boldoni, and posted from London a week ago. A messenger boy, whom Rocco had never seen before, had brought it to the Villa Rosalba, and insisted, despite the guards' threats, that he should hand it personally to the Maestro, and none other.

Pietro wrote in the letter that, after much investigation, he had tracked Pickering down to a rented room in a house in Bradford, Yorkshire, and that, although the pianist had at first refused to see him, he was eventually persuaded to meet up. Boldoni did not want to say too much in the letter. He concluded,

There is much to tell. Matters demand action. Within the week I shall begin my return journey to Naples, but I ask that you keep this information to yourself. I will book into a hotel and contact you privately. I cannot be specific about anything at this stage, because the danger is immense. Please expect to hear from me in a week. In the meantime, I advise you to arrange a private meeting with the doctor, Andrea Florio. Tell him that I have seen Pickering, and that you need to know everything.

Rocco folded the letter and placed it carefully into the embers that still glowed in his study fireplace. He waited, staring at it until it popped into flame, and did not leave the room until he was quite sure the resulting ashes had crumbled to dust. If the dark suspicions that were beginning to take shape in his thoughts were true, he would have to cover his tracks with great care at every move. There was no room for error with these people.

Chapter 31

Don Graziani was lying face down on a couch at his holiday villa on Ischia. He was stripped naked, and a towel was draped over his hips. Above him stood Andrea Florio, with his sleeves rolled up. He was massaging oil into Graziani's back, and hiding his distaste. The role of masseur was not one that a doctor of his calibre and status liked to be asked to fulfil, but the old man trusted so few people, and would have felt vulnerable to be thus stripped bare and manipulated by anyone other than one of his inner circle. Andrea and Marco Florio were the only members of that select bunch who were qualified, or, indeed, sensitive enough, to do the job.

Don Graziani was trying to chuckle, but his muscles were not responding obediently, and the laughs came out as pained, regular little grunts. It was a peculiar side effect of the old man's condition that he had begun to develop a sense of humour. How ironic, thought Andrea, that it should be now, at this advanced stage of decrepitude, that he should feel the inclination to laugh, just when the state of his muscular and nervous system no longer allowed him to express the mirth convincingly. Still, it allowed for a degree of intimacy between them that was previously unthinkable. It might be helpful for Andrea when the moment came.

'What are you laughing about, you wicked old man?' asked Florio, rubbing the scented lavender oil gently between his shoulder blades.

Graziani allowed his grunts to subside before he made the effort to speak. He was relaxed, which made his words slur into one another even more than usual. 'It's that oaf, Tedeschi,' he eventually enunciated. 'He hasn't got a clue what's happened to Rocco's boy, and yet, and yet – ' he grunted again, 'and yet he believes so much that no one else could have done it, he's started to brag.'

'You mean he's claimed responsibility?'

'Not quite. But he drops hints. Tells people to watch their step or they might find themselves picked up one day, like you-know-who. Or warns people who get too uppity that all men are equal beneath the state, even great opera stars. That sort of thing. I think he's persuaded himself that he's done it, and he's proud about it. The emperor's new clothes, heh, heh.'

'Does anyone know what did happen to the boy?'

'It's no good asking me. I never know what's going on any more. Look at me! It's pathetic.'

Andrea smiled to himself. He knew better than to ask, of course. If the Grazianis had anything to do with Amedeo's disappearance they would have given it 'special red' status; which meant that its details would be known only to the old man, Bruno and the operational personnel involved, whose discretion was guaranteed with their lives. Fear underpinned the system, and a fear that was so great, it was watertight. The thought of it made Andrea's stomach lurch, because he remembered what he had come here today to accomplish. For all his history with these people and familiarity with their methods, there was no refuge from the facts: the gamble he was about to take was as dangerous as it was irreversible. The last time an inside conspiracy had been unearthed, the perpetrator had been found drowned in a bath full of blood; and he had been told, before being pushed under, that the blood in the bath belonged to his children and grandchildren.

Andrea decided to begin before he lost his nerve. It was as good a moment as any, and the old man was in a pleasant mood. He would make it sound like a conversation piece between two practical men. That was how the Don liked to operate. No fuss, no frills. If he tried too hard it could backfire, and his fate would be sealed.

'I am your doctor, first and foremost,' he began, 'and I have been ever since that night at the hospital.'

'My friend, as well my as doctor.' The words came from Don Graziani with such slow sonority that Florio was taken aback and wondered if the old man had seen through him already. But he had to go on.

'I do not wish my loyalty to you to be in any way . . . compromised.'

Don Graziani did not move but his eyes shifted quickly sideways. He was not wearing spectacles and his sight would have been cloudy, but the movement of those eyeballs spoke of a serpentine reflex within. 'Someone is trying to swing you. Is that it?'

Florio's hands hesitated, but then began again, working oil into the greyish flesh. The skin was slack and had to be eased back flat after every kneading movement. 'Yes,' he answered simply.

'Someone close to us?' For all his fragility, Graziani's mind was sharp as a desert cactus.

'Yes.'

'I thought the time would come.' His voice rasped dry

and flat. For a moment nothing more was said, and then Graziani spoke again. 'How bad is it?'

'Am I speaking out of place?'

'How bad is it? What has he asked you to do?'

'Change your medication.'

'Kill me?'

'No. Just sedate you. So that he can get on and run the family without interference.'

Graziani sighed. 'He will finish us all,' he murmured.

'I am at your service,' said Andrea, quietly. 'I will always remain loyal.'

There was now a long pause, and Don Graziani closed his eyes. When he spoke at last, it was as if their earlier conversation, with all its devastating implications, had not taken place. 'My grandfather,' began Graziani, 'I remember him well, a kind old man, lame, with one of those swollen feet, like an elephant. He could never wear a shoe on it.' Florio's heart was racing after the effort of his earlier revelation, and he had to work to keep his hands steady, but he did not interrupt. 'He farmed olives and oranges in the fields outside Sorrento, and he married the schoolteacher's daughter, who everyone said was too good for him. They had fourteen children. Eight lived. My mother was the sixth. Good family people. The most delicious oranges I've ever eaten. It's a different kind of sunshine in Sorrento. The fruit is the best in the world.' He fell silent and began to breathe heavily, eyes still closed.

Andrea eventually finished his task, rubbed clean the Don's pale, wasted torso with a clean towel and then asked quietly, 'Are you awake, Signor?' There was no reply, and so Florio placed a little bell on a table within reach of the couch. 'If you need the servants,' he whispered close to the Don's ear, 'just ring this.' He was about to leave, when Graziani began to speak again, now even more slowly and weakly than before.

'I always said that Rocco's soul was shaped of cold grey stone,' he said. 'Stone that is soft to the pick, like the rock beneath Naples. It crumbles at the mere brush of a finger. That's why our city has so many tunnels and caverns underground. It's the same with Rocco. A labyrinth of hidden chambers. Drop a bucket too deep into one of the wells and something nasty could be brought up. Or worse. The whole lot could start to collapse, chamber after dark chamber. Imploding, one upon the other, bringing down the whole grand city above. The man and his art in ruins.'

Andrea approached the couch again. 'You think he is unstable, then? That he won't be up to the performance?' he asked.

Don Graziani seemed to be sleeping, and again Andrea thought he should tiptoe away, but at last an answer of sorts emerged. 'Bruno is a fool. Our chances of success or failure, with Rocco like this, I'd say, are even. My idiot son is gambling with our entire future.'

'That is all too clear,' ventured Andrea, 'which, I confess, has made me think that—'

'That he must be stopped before he brings disaster on us all,' interrupted Graziani. 'Perhaps.' He opened one of his unusually dilated, sad brown eyes. 'If I need your help in this matter, can I rely on you?''

Andrea leant down to the couch for the last time. He kissed Don Graziani's hand. 'I am at your service,' he said quietly. 'Always.'

*   *   *

Andrea felt drained as he crossed the grey waters on his way back to the city. Dread left a kind of weariness in its wake.

The seed of suspicion between father and son was already there, then, and had grown healthy small roots. All Andrea need do was nurture it. He knew the form, and it was frighteningly simple. If, by the end of the week, he was still alive, it would mean that the first stage of his strategy had succeeded.

As it happened, he did not have to wait that long. He was precipitated into the second stage before the same day was out. There was a note waiting for him at his surgery, hand-delivered by a member of Rocco Campobello's household staff, and it requested that he go to the tenor's house as a matter of urgency, preferably before the end of the day. Andrea thought at first it might be a medical emergency, but this notion was dispelled when the tenor received him at the front door of the Villa Rosalba, apparently fit and well.

Campobello led the way silently to his upstairs study and locked the door behind them, before asking Andrea to sit. Without preamble he said, 'It is time we talked about what happened to Mr Pickering.' For a moment Andrea did not know what to say, and his eyes darted around the room as he searched for a way to evade the question, but there was no way out, and he drew a deep breath before looking up at Campobello. 'It is a matter of deciding where to begin,' he said.

Chapter 32

Bruno Graziani judged that it would be safer if the men he had hired to masquerade as Fascist party *squadristi* were to disappear into the woodwork as soon as possible after they had fulfilled their role in the operation. Amedeo, in fact, never set eyes on them from the moment he was taken from Rocco's car, nor did he have a clue that they were anything other than what they purported to be. They put a cloth bag over his head and drove him, without speaking, for several hours inland, to an isolated farm deep in the countryside. There, they handed him over into the care of four different men, local toughs, whose discretion – handsomely paid for by Bruno – was as immutable as the rocky hillock beside which their ancient farmstead was tucked.

For all their coarse manners and rough ways, the men were not unfriendly to Amedeo. They teased him that he was an urban softy who'd had life too easy, and Amedeo struck up a rapport with them. His particular friend was the dwarfed, heavily moustached hunchback, whom the others called the Beast. Four foot tall, with a shortened left leg and a distended chest, the Beast possessed a deep, rasping voice and spoke in a local patois that was almost unintelligible to Amedeo. But the two of them formed an alliance early on when Amedeo discovered the Beast was a decent clarinettist and had mastered the extraordinary art of circular breathing, so that he could play tunes continuously, without pausing to take a breath. The others warned Amedeo, jokingly, that he should beware of the Beast. 'He may be small, but he's dangerous,' they said, and nodded at him, knowingly. '*Come un' napolitano*,' replied Amedeo, joining in the humour, which made them all laugh. What he did not know, however, and what would certainly have tarnished his enjoyment of the dwarf's company, was that the Beast had twice before, and without hesitation, undertaken the role of hostage executioner when given the nod by his superiors. It was not a job he particularly relished, but someone had to do it, he would say.

Amedeo was confused about why he was being held, when no questions had been put to him; neither had he been visited by a single party or police official. He began soon to suspect that this whole affair had more to do with Campobello than his own political subversiveness, and he wondered if there might be some connection with Pickering's disappearance; he half expected to be joined at any time by the tubby pianist. As his imagination ran wild, he speculated that this was a kidnapping, staged in order to raise a ransom from the great singer; in which case, why the apparent show of fascist muscle? One fact was clear: the men holding him were being paid to do the job and had nothing to do with politics, nor had they the first idea what their prisoner might or might not have done. They had heard of Mussolini but knew little about what he stood for, because life in the countryside always seemed to go on the same, no matter who held power in Rome. Even the name Rocco Campobello was only dimly recognizable to them.

Amedeo got on with life at the farm as if he were one of them. They took it in turns to chop logs, cook meals, bake the bread, wash the clothes, and feed the livestock that had been herded into pens for the winter months. Fetching the water from the mountain spring, in great basket-clad glass flasks, was an especially tedious task, as it involved negotiating the volatile temper of the resident donkey, on whose tired old back the jars were transported up and down the mountain path. After ten days of established trust, it was decided that the townie weakling would not hazard a flight through the hostile surrounding landscape, especially as the weather was cold and wet, and Amedeo was granted the questionable privilege of being included on the water collection rota.

However, the captors made it clear from the start that, for all their comradely spirit and their appreciation of his singing, any notion Amedeo might entertain of freeing himself would result in a swift evaporation of the pleasant atmosphere. It would be better for everyone, they told him, if they could just trust each other to do what they were supposed to do while they were here together. After that, they would go their separate ways and everyone would be happy. The good news, the Beast told Amedeo, was that they were sure he would be released eventually. It was just a matter of patience. But this did not reassure Amedeo; he asked them how they could possibly know what fate awaited him if they didn't even know why he'd been detained. They shrugged off the question, and a cold fear would descend on Amedeo; especially at night, or when he heard a creak on the floorboards outside the room where he slept.

The rest of the time, Amedeo tried as best he could to get on with his studies. The sophisticated patterns of scales and vocal exercises he had been taught by Pickering sounded incongruous within the walls of the rustic farmhouse, but delighted his captors; as did the operatic arias he would work his way through, as many and varied as he could remember by heart. For want of other reading material, he began to pore over the ancient bible that he found covered in dust on a high shelf at the farm. In the evenings he and the men would decant copious quantities of wine from one of eight gargantuan barrels in an outhouse and pickle themselves pleasantly around the hearth, while sharing bread, cheese and jarfuls of tomatoes. He was a prisoner, no question, but he began to enjoy the simple, eucharistic quality of those evenings, eating and drinking in the company of his unlikely peasant wardens. Halfway through his incarceration, he discovered a tiny slip of paper hidden deep within the leaves of the bible, with someone's name on it, together with the name of a village, Sant' Angelo dei Lombardi. He had never heard of the place, and quickly put the piece of paper in the fire. Apart from that one slender clue he came across nothing else that might indicate where they were.

Chiara Tomassini's only mooring in the maelstrom of despair that threatened every moment to overwhelm her was the daily letter she received from Rocco. At the start, he was warmly positive and reassuring, exactly the pillar of strength and resourcefulness she needed. He did not spell out the details of the arrangement whereby Amedeo's safe return was guaranteed; but he did go so far as to make clear that his agreeing to undertake this single performance at the Teatro San Carlo was, in a manner of speaking, the leverage required to activate the machinery of his release. Chiara did not question the plausibility of his claim, nor demand to know the mechanics involved. Having been brought up in the back alleys of Naples, where so many aspects of life were subject to subtle networks of loyalty and the exchange of favours large and small, she knew that effective solutions were often achieved not through the machinations of the law, but by barter, or other means best kept concealed. She comforted herself that her plight was in the hands of a giant amongst men, and invested all her hope and trust in Rocco's judgement.

However, as the days went by, the tone of his letters seemed to change. She had accepted his advice that it would be better and safer for them not to meet until the situation was resolved; but whereas in the first days his letters brimmed with optimism and news of hope, after a fortnight of separation they became shorter, tautly unemotional, and carried little or no mention of Amedeo. He seemed to have become completely preoccupied with his work on the opera. He would agonize over its smallest details, and refer again and again to complexities of singing and interpretation, a subject about which Chiara understood nothing at all – nor did she care to learn about it at a time like this.

She wrote back once to ask if he could refrain from being so technical, and remind him that she had not had news of developments in Prefect Tedeschi's bureau for several days. The result was that for the first time Rocco let a day go by without writing to her. When he resumed, the tone of his letter was dark and self-absorbed. He did not address Chiara's concerns, but complained that he couldn't sleep a full eight hours each night because his curtains were too thin; he fumed about the noise of the staff clinking plates downstairs and the ignorance of his accompanist; the opera's producer had begun to grate with him, and even Arrigo Boito, its long-deceased composer, came in for abuse because of the way he had crafted the score. *It has never ceased to amaze me how little understanding some of our most cherished opera composers have of the mechanics of singing*, was typical of how he would begin a vituperative outpouring, when all the while Chiara wanted to skip to the part that told her what had become of Amedeo.

Reading between the lines, she could sense the strain in Rocco's letters, and wrote back begging him to meet her in person. He had come too far into the world of light and love, she said, to be drawn back into the misery that had shadowed his life before the illness. Rocco denied her absolutely, but in abstract, meandering prose. His reply was not unkind, but he seemed unable to express himself plainly, which made her think he was confused in himself, and that squeezed her heart all the more. She wanted to be close to him more than ever because of it; but his refusal was absolute. He wrote that she did not and could not understand his method of working, but it was the only way he knew how, and he would not be distracted. He signed off with a final affectionate promise that there would one day be an end to this nightmare, but thereafter refrained from writing altogether, and Chiara was cast adrift in her despair.

As the day of the performance approached, posters announcing the event were pasted all over the city. Every Neapolitan newspaper carried a mention or photograph of the Maestro on its front page, and the city hummed with speculation and gossip. Meanwhile, Chiara watched and waited alone, at the mercy of the worst imaginings.

Then, with just a few days left before the great night, she heard a knock on the door of her apartment, and opened it to a most unexpected visitor. Pietro Boldoni was standing there, though it took her a little while to recognize him because he had grown a full beard. He smiled almost apologetically, as he took her hand and planted a light kiss on her knuckles. 'Signora,' he said with warmth and comfort in his tone, so that she knew, even before he said anything else, that there might at last be cause for hope.

Chapter 33

It was an anxious few days for Andrea Florio. The apparent progress of his plan so far gave no cause for complacency, because he knew that its success might be overturned in an instant – perhaps when he was least expecting it, and in horrific circumstances. The sight and smell of death were familiar enough to Andrea, but that did not dilute the terror he felt at the utterly black notion of his own non-existence. Consequently, he slept little during this week, which meant that his days, when he needed to perform with vigilance and a clear head, were even more of a challenge.

Nevertheless, two days after having been summoned to meet and explain himself to Campobello, Andrea made sure that he was in a calm and composed frame of mind before going to see Bruno Graziani. He had set himself an agenda, and would carefully choose a moment to pitch the remark that would advance his cause; but the opportunity proved elusive, because Bruno had an agenda of his own, and its slant was unsettling.

They were walking slowly along the recreational avenue that cut its way straight down the centre of the Chiaia public gardens. Behind the rows of leafless plane trees, tall green palms swayed in the strong sea breeze. When the weather was good, especially in the early evening, this long promenade would be full of ladies, gentlemen and children, taking the air and stopping to talk to friends, but today it was cold and overcast and everyone out on the avenue was hurrying along purposefully. Andrea and Bruno were wrapped up against the chill, with heavy black coats, scarves and fedora hats.

Bruno spoke first. 'I have not had a chance to hear in detail about your encounter with Mr Pickering.'

'What exactly would you like to know?' asked Andrea.

'The details,' answered Bruno in an uncharacteristically jaunty tone, as if preparing himself for a little treat. Andrea could not dismiss the suspicion that it might be a trap. 'Did he make much noise, for example? Cry? Squeal?'

'A little. I . . . I gave him something to bite against, because of the pain.'

'Very considerate. Of course, no one saw you do the deed. You sent Roberto away.'

'This happened nearly a month ago,' said Andrea.

'Twenty-four days. But we have not had the opportunity to chat about it alone together. What about spillage?'

'You mean . . .'

'Blood, urine. It isn't good professional conduct, you know, to leave fluid evidence on the scene.'

Andrea could never understand Bruno's obsession with this. In a city rife with effluence and gutter filth, a little more would hardly be noticeable. 'He . . . I . . . Roberto wanted me to do it there, in the street, over a drain.'

'That was my intention. Well?' The pleasantness of his tone was disconcerting.

'With respect, there was a great deal of blood. I thought it would be better to take the patient somewhere quiet. I explained this to Roberto – but he has a limited understanding of medical matters.'

'The patient. That's a nice description.'

'I am a doctor.'

'Did you think to take spare trousers and underpants?'

'There was no need. He contained himself.'

'Unusual in such circumstances.'

'Perhaps.'

'Was he *very* distressed? On a scale of one to ten.'

'Well, ten, of course.'

'Hmm. And he'll never play the piano again, you think?'

'I should imagine a certain amount of facility will return, in time. But it will not be the same.'

'Which side?'

'I'm sorry?'

'Right or left arm?'

'The . . .' he was thinking quickly, 'it was the left.'

'You must have been feeling generous. He would surely have been more disabled if you had chosen the right.'

'Actually, Mr Pickering is left-handed.'

'Aha, good thinking, then.'

'But it would have made no difference. A pianist has to be ambidextrous.'

'Perhaps you should have done both, then, while you were at it.' He chuckled at his own joke.

Andrea knew that Bruno regarded every encounter, even one with a supposed close colleague, as a trial of loyalty, and that beneath his words there lurked a subtext of questioning doubt. Too long a pause, a slip of any kind, might cripple Andrea's credibility, and so he quickly nudged the conversation back into Bruno's court. 'He did whimper most of the way to Salerno.'

'Ah,' sighed Bruno with what sounded like relief.

'But he got the message that he was lucky to escape with his life. By the time he boarded the train I was convinced we would never be troubled by him again. It was a well-conceived plan.'

'I'm glad you approve.' Bruno had stopped beside the plinth of a bronze statue to one side of the avenue. It was a male athlete, muscular, of a classical genre, and Bruno glanced over it from top to bottom. 'An indulgent piece, don't you think?'

Andrea was preoccupied with other thoughts. 'The statue, you mean?'

Bruno was staring at it with a kind of wonder. 'You would not find something like this in New York. Only a profoundly Catholic culture could produce a public monument of such . . . unashamed sensuousness.'

Andrea was at a loss. 'I . . . I had not thought.'

Turning away from the statue with a kind of satisfied smile, Bruno continued his walk along the avenue. Andrea decided the moment had come, and, as he spoke, his heart leapt. 'There is something . . .'

'Yes?'

'I hesitate to talk about this.'

'In some cases it is more of a crime to remain silent. You can speak freely.'

'Of course I must tell you. You are the head of the family now.'

Bruno exhaled heavily through his nose and scratched his eyebrow. 'Is this about my father, then?'

'I visited him three days ago,' said Andrea, 'just to check on him, give him more medication and . . .

423

massage him. I was concerned by what I found. His conversation meandered. Talking about his childhood, his grandfather's farm, that sort of thing. I suppose he was perhaps less careful than usual about what he was saying. Because of the medication, most likely.'

'He said something indiscreet, you mean?'

Andrea stopped in his tracks, to add an authentic sobriety to what he was about to say. 'I would be failing in my duty were I not to bring it to your attention.' Bruno turned his eyes on him. They were flat and drained of expression, like a pair of dry beach pebbles, pummelled dull and bleached by the sun. He waited for the doctor to illuminate him. 'I believe,' ventured Andrea, and having come so far could not turn back, 'I believe Don Graziani may have become delusional, specifically in relation to you.'

'In what manner?'

'He asked me if I'd had orders from you to kill him.' At this, Bruno raised his chin sharply and began to glance around, as if surveying the urban skyline, but said nothing. 'He believes you are beginning to resent his interference,' continued Andrea, 'in family affairs.'

'Business is business.'

'And he . . .'

Bruno looked at him again. 'Say whatever you have to say.'

'He thinks you are envious of his fondness for Campobello. That it would not unduly concern you if Campobello came to harm.'

Bruno clenched his teeth, which visibly tightened the muscles in his cheeks. 'He told you this?' he said.

'Some of it openly, other parts . . . by intimation.' Andrea was watching him carefully, to gauge how he

424

should proceed, but other than that reflex flinching of his cheek, Bruno gave no further response.

'And Campobello himself?' Bruno asked, changing the subject and starting to walk again. 'Will he be fit enough, in your opinion? Will he rise to the occasion?'

'There's little to suggest otherwise,' answered Andrea. 'He is singing well, and completely committed to the task.'

'Mrs Campobello telephones me every day,' said Bruno. 'She is most observant and helpful. I had thought to put one of our people on the household staff, but there is no need. She says her husband is quite his old self again. Working every moment of the day, bossing people around, wrapped up in himself. It all sounds promising.'

'We must remember,' began Andrea, 'that he is doing all this only for the sake of the boy. Is there any news of him?'

'How should I know?' replied Bruno curtly.

'I presumed you were at least in touch with his captors, in order to negotiate the release, when the time comes.'

Bruno let out a puff of a laugh. 'Whatever made you think there would be any negotiation involved?'

'You mean,' Andrea continued, hesitantly, 'you have not yet had dealings with the captors?'

'Our side of the deal – which, incidentally, is not your business,' Bruno said, 'is to ensure the boy's release. Not to "negotiate" with his captors.'

'I understand,' replied Andrea. He had no doubt at all that Bruno was behind the abduction, but had to give the opposite impression. At the same time, he harboured a fear that Bruno might renege on the deal in order to keep Campobello at heel for a while longer. He was a loose cannon, capable of anything nowadays, and might even have the lad slain on a whim. 'Obviously, Campobello will only cooperate on the day if he is convinced that the boy has been delivered safely. Before he is required to go on stage,' added Andrea.

Bruno answered sharply. 'Campobello will know that if he doesn't do exactly what is required of him, the boy is as good as dead.' Aware that he was in danger of over-stepping the mark, Andrea said no more.

Before they parted, Bruno – who avoided shaking hands whenever possible – stopped and looked directly at Andrea; but instead of making some brief acknowledgement of their going separate ways, he dropped a remark which the doctor did not at first know how to interpret, because it came so quickly and lightly. 'I do not wish my father to be present on the night of the performance. Do I make myself clear?'

'His health may prevent him attending, in any case,' replied Andrea.

'I don't mean that. I don't want him present in any sense. At the opera house, or anywhere else.' Andrea did not know what to say, and after a pause, Bruno continued. 'My father is going soft. It's clear to me that thoughts of retirement have blurred his thinking. He no longer knows what needs to be done if we are to survive, as a family and as a business. By the time Campobello walks on to that stage, I want you to have arranged for my father to have gone. In the most final sense. Can you do this for me, yes, or no?'

'I see.'

'Can it be done? Some kind of medical procedure, impossible to trace?'

'Yes, yes,' said Andrea, looking towards the ground

with a frown. 'If that is your wish, I can go to Ischia on the morning of the performance, and . . . put everything in place.'

'I'm glad I can rely on you.'

'Of course.'

'You will not regret it.'

They had arrived at the far end of the promenade, where Bruno's car awaited him, engine running. The bodyguard, Roberto, was waiting there, smoking and talking to a street merchant who had hold of an ostrich by a bridle. The bird was harnessed to a cart which carried a large upright advertisement board. 'What will they think of next?' muttered Bruno, climbing into his car, and Andrea raised his hat to him. The chauffeur closed the door after Bruno and gave the doctor a look of weary exasperation, which had a faintly mutinous trace in it.

Andrea remained where he stood until well after the car had vanished from view along the seafront road. In a moment he would have to begin the walk back down the avenue, but right now he could not bring himself to move at all. Although the utterance of that fatal order from Bruno had been the best possible outcome he could have hoped for, indicating, as it did, the complete rift he sought, and although, as an educated man, Andrea had read his history and knew that the greatest dynasties known to mankind were littered with instances of patricide in the pursuit of power, he could not help but stand there, frozen with shock, for some while, staggered beyond reason at being witness to the ease with which a son could give the order for his own father's murder.

*   *   *

427

Pietro Boldoni had a sensitive nature, prone to romance, artistic flights of fancy and ponderings on divinity. He experienced fear more acutely than most people, because his imagination was agile enough to fathom the depths and possibilities of man's natural enemies, such as pain, death and cruelty. This made his courage – which was an acquired discipline rather than a natural talent – all the more outstanding. The fact that he could sense great fear, face it without blinking, and advance towards it unflinchingly, meant that there was something of the hero about him, though few had seen him tested or knew he possessed the quality. He quietly acknowledged it in himself, however, and it bolstered his warrior's spirit in these darker, lonely times.

He had returned to Naples secretly, in the knowledge that the merest whisper of his presence there would invoke the wrath of an organization against which his resistance would be as feeble as grass to the scythe. If discovered, he predicted, his end would be a neat and quick affair, with none of the trappings of a traditional honour killing, largely because the political climate nowadays did not allow for too much ostentation. Despite this ever present threat, he comforted himself that he was not without weaponry of his own, albeit of a metaphorical kind: truth and justice were on his side, and he was thus God's soldier, loyally defending his Maestro, embodying, surely, the nobler leanings of human enterprise. His other motive – that of an avenging lover whose heart was on fire with a private fury – he kept in abeyance.

His first meeting with Campobello after his return was an emotional occasion. They stood opposite one another, in a seedy hotel bedroom near the city's central station, and did not speak, until Boldoni, despite his earlier resolve, could hold back no longer and fell into an embrace against the broad chest of his beloved Maestro. The moment passed, and he pulled himself together as quickly as he had at first dissolved, and began straight away to relate his tale.

He described how his search for Pickering had taken him to a lonely moorland village on the edge of the Pennines, in West Yorkshire, to seek out members of the Pickering family and ask if anyone had news of Wallace. Of the immediate family, only the mother remained in the village, a hardy old widow, from a bygone era, it seemed, with leathery skin and thin white hair that she tied in a bun. She lived in a tiny dark-stone terraced cottage with a garden that backed on to heather-clad moors. He had met Mrs Pickering once, many years before, when Wallace had managed to tempt her (but not her sceptical husband) down to watch Campobello perform at Covent Garden. She had seemed a kind and tolerant lady, who probably recognized the intimacy between Pietro and Wallace, but never referred to it.

As they sat in her comfortable little sitting room, Boldoni noticed an old upright piano in the corner. Its lid was closed, covered with an embroidered doily and several framed photographs. He imagined Wallace, as a boy, discovering the first secrets of his spectacular musical instinct here in this room, unprompted by his family, at that very keyboard, while the fire blazed in the hearth and the rain lashed horizontal against the windowpanes, even as it did now.

Pietro gently stated his business to Mrs Pickering between sips of tea, and then put his question: had she any idea what had befallen her son? After some feeble attempts at evasion, he scented her weakening and enhanced his plea by sinking to one knee beside her chair, and taking her hand.

At this passionate display, Mrs Pickering's resistance dissolved. Wallace was indeed in Yorkshire, but had taken a room in the nearby city of Bradford so as to remain in hiding. As tears welled in her old eyes, she related how her son had not even been to visit her yet and seemed to be in a nervous state of near collapse, terrified for his life; she was only letting Pietro in on the secret because she feared Wallace might do something desperate. The following day, Boldoni travelled to the address he had been given and at last found his friend. Pickering had been reluctant to let him in, and whispered madly from the other side of the door that Pietro should go away and not come back, because there was no escaping these people, they would find him, they would kill him, they'd kill them all. Boldoni had to threaten to break down the door before he was let in at last, and then, only after he had managed to calm Pickering down so that he could talk sensibly, did the truth begin to emerge.

After Pickering had been abducted, that night in Naples, he was driven out of the city by Andrea Florio. The doctor was under orders from Bruno Graziani to perform a piece of surgery on the pianist's forearm: avoiding the main arteries, he was to ensure the tendons and muscle systems within the soft tissue, between wrist and elbow, were thoroughly and irreparably severed, thereby disabling the effective workings of Pickering's hand and fingers, perhaps permanently. It was to be interpreted as a punishment, the doctor explained, but more importantly as a warning: Pickering must refrain from interfering with Campobello's career, and remove himself from the scene altogether, or face the consequences. In the event, Florio had put his own life in jeopardy by failing to carry out the orders. Instead, he put Pickering on a train to Messina, where he was to board a ship for Marseilles. There were train tickets to take him from there to Paris, and thence on a flight to London's Croydon airport. The Grazianis had spies everywhere, Florio had warned as he bandaged Pickering's arm to make it look as if the planned injury had been inflicted. 'We can take no chances, or we are both dead men,' Andrea had said. 'They must never know that you are unhurt, no one can know, not even those closest to you. They will find you wherever you are, however long it takes – that is the way with these people. I have seen it happen before. You must get away, tonight, away from Naples and then away from Italy, and most importantly, away from Rocco Campobello. For ever.'

Boldoni remained with Pickering for just a few hours. Having listened in horror to what had happened, he knew that the Maestro himself was now in peril, and that the time had come for immediate action.

As soon as he arrived back in Naples he sent word to Campobello, and the hotel meeting was arranged. They had some time alone together to discuss what should be done, before they were joined by their new, unexpected ally, Andrea Florio. The three men then settled down to explore an idea based on the outline of a strategy Pietro had been pondering on his journey all the way from London.

Before they could proceed any further, however, they had to secure the participation of two other men, whose role in the plan would be critical to its outcome. Boldoni did not want to risk a second meeting at the same hotel, but instead arranged to see Campobello, and the two men, a few days later at a nearby guest house. Pietro got to the room a few minutes early, and was watching from an upstairs window, parting the curtains by a finger's breadth, as Rocco's car pulled up in the street below. It had purple blinds drawn down across its windows for the privacy of its occupant. Campobello stepped out on to the pavement with a hat pulled low over his brow. His coat's fur collar was turned up and a heavy scarf wrapped around his neck, which concealed most of the rest of his face.

When Rocco arrived in the room, he said little to Boldoni, but sat, smoking, while they waited for the arrival of the other two men, neither of whom yet had any inkling of what this was about. A noise from the hall below and the sound of feet clumping heavily up the staircase announced that they had arrived.

'Well, here they come,' said Pietro. 'Do you think they will be up to it?'

'They will be fine,' replied Rocco reassuringly. 'Beneath all the nonsense they are good men, and strong.'

'They'll need to be,' said Boldoni quietly.

There was a knock on the door. Pietro looked up and cleared his throat; he called for them to enter. The door opened, and in walked Pozzo and Taddeo, both with rather puzzled expressions.

Chapter 34

An unlikely event took place the day before Campobello's much-vaunted return to the stage. It was so unlikely that it had not been foreseen – and therefore went unnoticed – by those who would most like to have known of its occurrence.

Don Emilio Graziani left his island villa on Ischia for the first time in some weeks in order to make a visit to the office of Prefect Pompeo Tedeschi. Graziani had been feeling a little stronger these past few days, though he still had no appetite. He could walk a little, but his left arm was almost defunct and his words were slurred to the point of incomprehension.

His launch was met at the quayside by a car, and, along with a small entourage of men, he was taken straight to the Palazzo Municipale, where advance notice had been given of his arrival. On the way there he asked his secretary, beside him, if his son, Bruno, had any knowledge of the visit. 'Not as far as I know,' the man replied. 'We have kept quiet about it, as you asked, though it hasn't been easy. He'll discover soon enough, and then my own position will be . . . uncomfortable.'

'Everyone is with us?' asked Graziani slowly. Speaking was an ordeal.

'To a man.'

'Then you need have no concerns.'

Tedeschi had been warned of Graziani's decrepitude, and, aware that it could only benefit him to be seen as compassionate, arranged to have an office on the ground floor prepared for the meeting. As the old man was wheeled in, Tedeschi remained seated behind his desk, pen in hand, with a cerebral expression fixed to his brow. He stayed like that for a fraction longer than he needed to, until Graziani and his men were well into the room, before permitting himself to look up; whereupon he closed his file ceremoniously, stood tall and strode from behind the desk, arms wide open in welcome. Beside the wizened old man, Pompeo Tedeschi, tall and athletic in his starched black shirt and gleaming leather belt, had the air of a man at the peak of his powers. His smile drew the pencil-thin moustache on his upper lip into a perfect horizontal line, and he embraced the old man, planting a kiss on either cheek. Various members of his staff were surprised that he should extend so extravagant a greeting to the man generally acknowledged to be his foe, but there was more than a little triumph in Tedeschi's blustering manner this morning.

'We are all looking forward to tomorrow night,' he said, fetching himself a heavy chair with easy vigour and placing it, for himself, beside Graziani's wheelchair. 'You must be very proud.'

'It will be a happy occasion,' said Graziani, 'though I may not be attending in person. I get so tired nowadays.' His secretary stepped forward discreetly to realign the spectacles that were hanging slightly askew on his nose.

'I am sorry to hear that,' boomed Tedeschi, rubbing his hands together. 'You deserve to be there. You are a part of the San Carlo theatre's history, as much as . . .'

he tossed a hand in the air in search of inspiration, but floundered, and added lamely, 'as much as the royal box itself.'

Graziani nodded. 'I have other demands on my attention at present.'

'More important than the great Campobello's return?'

'I refer to the future of our great nation: Italy herself.' At this, Tedeschi's back straightened, as if the bugle's reveille had sounded, and he all but rose to his feet. 'A man in my position and at my stage of life,' Graziani continued, pausing for breath after every few words, 'can see clearly the benefits being afforded our country and our people by the Fascist party, and above all, by our Prime Minister, our great leader.'

'I am delighted to hear you say so,' responded Tedeschi. He had suspected that this might be a mission of appeasement, but Graziani's statement had the scent of capitulation.

'I have neither the time nor the energy to relate how I have come to this conclusion.'

'And I do not ask for it.'

'But I would like you to accept this,' Graziani went on, without looking at Tedeschi, and beckoned his secretary with a flick of his index finger, 'on behalf of my family, in the hope that it will contribute to the party's well-deserved success in the next election.'

Tedeschi received the cheque, glanced at it and raised his eyebrows. 'This is more than generous, signor. I am speechless.'

'We must look after one another, must we not? I also would like you to know,' he continued, 'that I have withdrawn support for my son's bid to become director of the San Carlo Opera.' Tedeschi pursed his lips and nodded

435

sagely at this concession, as though to imply, not without a note of sympathy, that it was a foregone conclusion in any case, because of the recent turn of events. 'You will forgive the folly of an old man in supporting the dream of his only child thus far,' said Graziani, 'but it is now clear to me that my son's ambitions, and, I might add, his methods, are out of control. I tell you this in confidence: as soon as this business of Campobello's performance is over, I intend to distance myself from Bruno Graziani.' He spoke the surname dispassionately, as though it were mere coincidence that he shared it.

'I see,' said Tedeschi, his euphoria rather blunted by the severity of Don Graziani's pronouncement. The old villain, it seemed, was as ruthless in defeat as he had been in defence of his throne. 'What do you intend to do, yourself, might I ask?'

'I will retire quietly,' Graziani replied. 'Perhaps to the countryside. To live out what few days God has in mind to grant a tired old man.'

'No, no, no,' murmured Tedeschi politely, looking down, 'I'm sure you will outlive us all.'

'One would expect,' Graziani's voice changed tone and he looked sideways at Tedeschi, with a lizard glance. 'One would hope and expect that, in return for one's actions today, the police will see fit to close certain files of an unsettling nature. Vicious rumours, unfounded allegations.'

Tedeschi expected no less, but did not possess the tact to let the matter brush past unmarked. 'We must bear in mind,' he replied, stiffening, 'that two American citizens have vanished within three weeks of one another in this city, and that both of them, coincidentally or otherwise, appear to have been acquainted with the Graziani family. There will be a degree of speculation that will be difficult to suppress. It's not like the old days any more.'

'So we are continually reminded,' cut in Graziani drily. 'I need not tell you, however, that on the field of battle the victorious captain is remembered by posterity for his good treatment of the erstwhile enemy, not for glorying in the slaughter of unarmed prisoners.'

'A noble sentiment,' smiled Tedeschi, who easily succumbed to flattery of this kind, 'though not one to which you yourself have always subscribed. Let us say, I shall do what I can to make sure you enjoy a peaceful retirement. Needless to say, I have no jurisdiction over police matters. Were there to be any more activities of an unwholesome nature . . .'

'We are not children, signor,' concluded Graziani, and waved his hand feebly to summon his men for assistance. He bid farewell with the smallest of nods and pointed towards the door. Minutes later he was out in the crisp winter sunshine, a man at each wheel of his chair, lifting it carefully down the steps of the building. 'That man's destiny is written all over his face,' Graziani muttered to his secretary beside him. 'He'll swing by the neck one day with the public cheering on; and then they'll throw his maggot-ridden carcass to the dogs. Along with his repulsive leader. I only hope I live to see the day.' At precisely the same moment, Tedeschi, buoyed by conquest, was walking crisply up the grand stairway towards his office on the first floor. A black-shirted adjutant walked in step at his side. 'It was the only practical solution for him,' Tedeschi commented. 'Graziani has always been a practical man first and foremost. Given the slightest opportunity he would have us all knifed in our beds. We must close the lid on him and keep it firmly closed.'

'What about Bruno?' asked the adjutant.

'He'll be helpless without his father's support. We'll bring him in. See what he's made of. After the opera.'

'On what charge?'

Tedeschi stopped in his tracks and glared at the man. 'Do I need to spoon-feed you people all the time? There must be a hundred and one charges to choose from.' The adjutant nodded and branched off down a corridor towards a different office.

Chapter 35

Campobello had made it clear that he would accept no guests at the Villa Rosalba in the days leading up to his performance, even though Molly tried to insist that a number of friends and eminent visitors – including some who had travelled all the way from America for the occasion – might be offended not to have hospitality extended to them. Her solution was to reserve no fewer than eight apartment suites for her private guests at the Hotel Vesuvio, which was spectacularly positioned on the seafront, opposite the Castel dell'Ovo.

Three days before the performance, Molly grew impatient to join in the fizzing, cosmopolitan atmosphere at the hotel, and announced her intention to take up residency there herself. At the subsequent string of parties, she ran into all sorts of old friends, and explained her presence playfully by saying that Rocco had become insufferably dictatorial in the run-up to his great night, and that spoilt boys deserved to be left to stew in their own juice. This never failed to raise a laugh, and no one thought to pry further.

In reality, of course, the great tenor was beyond criticism in everyone's eyes. Indeed, he had never been regarded with such awe or admiration. Word had spread from the opera house – through members of the chorus, the coaching staff, and even the theatre's cleaners – that, on the occasions when the Maestro allowed himself to use his full voice, the results had been thrilling. A miracle had been promised to the world, and people waited breathlessly to be bathed in the wonder of it. No slur could dampen their expectation, and no slander tarnish the great man's halo. Molly was shrewd enough to realize this and therefore held her vitriol in check. The time to unveil her arsenal of weaponry would come soon enough.

Cocooned in his apartment at the Villa Rosalba, Rocco was immune to the swell of goodwill that churned around him. He had watched from his window as Molly left the house three days before. She had a clipped assurance of manner, a purpose in her step, which seemed to announce to anyone who cared to look that she had reached a decision, and reached it even-mindedly. Before climbing into the car, he thought he noticed her glance around at the façade of the villa one last time, nose aloft, in a rather theatrical moment of reflection. The whole display was entirely in tune with the nature of her departure: ostentatiously irreversible.

Now that she was gone, and because he wanted as little noise and distraction as possible, he cut down staff activity in the villa to a minimum. He was completely alone for most of the time, except for the porter and a butler, but they remained in their separate quarters unless specifically called.

It was therefore to a silent house and a rather desolate atmosphere that Chiara Tomassini arrived on that last evening, before the day of the performance. She had received Rocco's short note in the morning and had come, despite the pouring rain, because she was aware that this might be the last opportunity of seeing her lover for some while. His summons had been the answer to her prayers.

He met her at the front door and his face was grim, which made her own tentative smile wither in the bud. For a moment it occurred to her that she did not know this man very well after all, and she felt rather ashamed. In a flash of dread, she wondered if he had been put off her by her girlish infatuation, but he stepped forward and took her in his arms, and her anxiety eased. He then led her indoors, across the hall and into the drawing room, where he closed the door behind them.

'Chiara,' he said quietly, and took her hand. All at once, her feelings burst, and she began to weep. He tried to comfort her, but she pulled back, recovering herself. 'Why have you not written?' she asked. 'Didn't you think what I must be going through? What news is there?'

'Good news. They are releasing him tomorrow, as we thought.' She stepped back further.

'Can you be sure?'

'Yes.'

'What if something goes wrong? Who are these people? Do we know he is all right?'

Rocco looked down. A great burden seemed to press on him. 'I don't know everything,' he sighed. 'I can only tell you what I believe. All will be well.'

But she wanted more. 'Tomorrow, you say?' He nodded. 'Just as Boldoni told me, then? At the station?' He nodded again. 'We must pray to the Lord to help us,' she said. 'I will pray all night.' Rocco remained where he stood, head still bowed.

After a while she looked up at him. 'What has happened to you?' she asked.

It took him a moment to gather himself for an answer. There was something primitively noble in the pain of his expression. Chiara had seen it on the faces of the great beasts paraded in cages at the city carnival: resigned, but confused by the nature of the devilish trickery that had entrapped and served them this ghastly destiny.

'It has begun to claim me back,' Rocco said simply. 'I thought I could leave it behind, but that was my folly.'

'I don't understand you.'

'People think they can change their lives, but you can't fight your destiny. It will find you out in the end and pull you back where you belong. In my case, that is back to the bowels of hell.'

'It will pass,' she said, but, at the mention of hell, discreetly made the sign of the cross on her breast.

He shook his head. 'There's a tyrant in my soul, with his own laws and bullies, just like the men on the streets nowadays, pushing everyone around with truncheons, keeping order.' He smiled bitterly. 'Put my house in order! That was my mission. Well, I have order in my house now. It's not the kind of order he meant, though.'

'You've been on your own for too long. It's making you ill again.'

'I was idiot enough to think I could let it all pass away. And look what happens. You and Amedeo would have been safe and happy if it had not been for—'

'Don't—'

'I will never forgive myself.'

'There's no need for forgiveness if we are together,' she said, and looked pleadingly into his eyes, laying her hand on his. 'You can leave your misery behind. I will take care of you.'

'I am too far gone.'

'I can save you,' she whispered. She was gazing at him, into him, and holding both his hands now. Her face held comfort and gravity in equal measure, an expression which elevated her usual prettiness to a sepulchral, Marian beauty. Rocco floundered momentarily.

Looking into her eyes, as if spellbound, he said quietly, 'You've never asked about my mother.'

Chiara looked at him with surprise. 'I didn't think you could remember her,' she said. 'You were just a small boy when the cholera came.'

'I remember many things from that time. Like shadowy photographs in an old album. People say it only lasted three months, but it felt like a lifetime. Men and women dropping dead in the street, just falling where they stood. My mother was slower. I remember the blood in the bucket when she was sick. Staring into space, for days, without blinking, cold skin, mouth open. Papa checked her to see if she was still with us. In the end they collected her on a cart. They were a day late. I remember they went from house to house, thumping on the doors, all of them drunk, and singing. Otherwise they'd have been too frightened to do the job.'

'And the rats,' he continued, as if in a dream. 'The disinfectant in the sewers drove the rats crazy. Thousands of them came up from underground, bigger rats than anyone had ever seen. Bald, with red eyes and black teeth. Rats that had lived under the city since Roman times. They ate the corpses in the street. Bodies everywhere, waiting to be collected. We didn't even find out which pit they threw Mamma into. There were too many dead to register.' Chiara held his hand but said nothing.

'Papa and I never talked about the cholera afterwards. The only way to survive was to hide our pain and fight on. He was as strong in his mind as he was in his arm. I learnt it all from him, you see. He showed me that to win you must put your pain and your feeling to one side, and keep looking forwards. He talked about the purity of the steel, something that will never break, never corrode.'

'Did he know you were hurting so much after your mother died?' asked Chiara softly.

'It was all he could do to keep us alive.' Rocco paused, staring into nothingness. 'I tried to copy him, but he and I were different. He was master of his own soul. But me? My master was something else. I gave my life to the Voice, every ounce of me. And so my soul withered away, a hollow little hell inside. With its own rats, eating away, spreading poison.' He sank his face into his palms.

'You must let these terrible thoughts go,' she said.

'There's nothing left of me, Chiara.' He sat hunched and motionless. 'I have become an empty man. Hollow.' He sighed. 'I have nothing to say for myself.'

'You do not have to say anything to me,' she answered quietly. 'It is not your words I love.'

As he continued to look at her the burden seemed to ease fractionally. 'That is why I loved you from the moment I walked into your home,' he said.

'This is not the end.' She squeezed his hand.

'I only live now to make the two of you safe.'

'You speak as if I might never see you again. As if some disaster is going to happen.' When he made no reply,

444

she asked, 'Can you go through with this? Are you well enough to sing tomorrow?'

Rocco ran a hand across his prickly scalp, turning away from her and walking to the window. Looking out across the parkland, he could see that a few people were loitering on the far side of the gates despite the lateness and the rain. The excitement had drawn a trail of spectators all the way from the city out here to Posillipo, and some extra guards had had to be employed.

Rocco turned back to Chiara. 'You mustn't worry about me. You have your own challenge tomorrow.' He crouched down beside her and began to go through what she had to do, most of which she had already been told by Boldoni: Amedeo would be brought to the station at twelve noon precisely; they would meet her in a public place with tickets and instructions, after which she and the boy should board a train bound for Rome before travelling on to Milan. They were to proceed to Geneva, where they should take up temporary residence at a certain hotel and wait there until Rocco or his representative came to meet them. It might be days or even weeks, but it would happen. They would find all the money they needed in a private bank account that had been opened for them.

'The details are here,' he said, handing her an envelope.

'And after that? What sort of a life will I have in Switzerland?'

'All I can say is that you will be well provided for. Boldoni will see to it, if I myself cannot.'

'But—'

'Don't put your fears into words,' he chided, and put a finger to her lips. 'If you do not speak the words, they

445

remain hidden. Leave them in the shadows.'

Just for a moment, Chiara's fears got the better of her and she closed her eyes tight, fighting back tears. And because her eyes were shut, she did not register that, just then, Rocco's face twisted into a grimace. A wave of nauseous pain had flooded across him, and he counted to himself as he struggled to hide the ordeal. The old spasms and aches that had niggled at him for weeks had evolved into great tidal contractions, and when they came he could do nothing but hold his breath, measure time, and wait for them to recede. His face went ashen pale with the strain, before it began to lift.

Her eyes were still shut as he put an arm around her shoulder. She looked at him and a flicker of grateful relief eased the worry in her eyes. He pulled her close in against his chest and held her there for some while, until it was time for her to go. She asked no more about when they might meet next, because she feared the answer. Nor did she want to say anything that might deepen the wound of his own dark musing. Instead, they parted as they had met, in sad and rather shy silence. Pozzo was waiting to drive her home, and Rocco watched from the door as the car made its way down the gravel drive.

She glanced back after the gates had closed behind her, but he was no longer there. The front door was closed. Dusk had settled. The red glow of the horizon over the sea to the west was giving way to darkness. It seemed as if all lights at the Villa Rosalba had been put out.

Chapter 36

The next morning, Amedeo woke unusually early. It was still dark, but there were noises, indoors and outside, signs that something was going on. He could hear voices deliberately subdued, which was worrying, because his captors had never before had the grace to hush themselves on his account. Now they were talking urgently and didn't want him to know about it. He tensed as he lay stock still in bed, straining to hear and staring wide-eyed into the pre-dawn gloom.

He had been suspicious that something was up for a couple of days; ever since the Beast had been called away for a quiet meeting with the man who seemed to be the most senior in the group, a jovial oaf they called Toro. The Beast had come back an hour or so later and made a point of avoiding Amedeo for the rest of the day, which was unlike him. It made the boy think. If the worst were to happen, and they had been ordered to do away with him, this is how he would expect the Beast to behave: almost embarrassed, with a hint of uncharacteristic politeness. When Amedeo suggested, on the same day after lunch, that it was his turn to clean out the shit-house across the yard, they each volunteered themselves in his place. It was tantamount to a *coup de grâce*, Amedeo thought, and barely slept that night.

The light was beginning to edge around the shutters of his bedroom window when the door burst open and Toro was there, rifle in hand. 'Sorry, lad,' he said, and Amedeo felt his blood run cold. Toro pulled him, shaking, from his bed. 'We have to go right now,' he said. 'I've left you in peace for as long as I could.'

'What are you going to do to me?' asked Amedeo, hurriedly putting on some clothes, but Toro did not answer. Nor did he leave the room: he waited, watching until Amedeo was fully clothed, and then pulled a cloth bag from inside his jacket which he put over the boy's head. Amedeo cried out, but Toro hushed him, saying it would be better for everyone if he just did as he was told and they could get this over with as soon as possible.

He was bundled into a car, and they drove along bumpy tracks at a slow pace for about half an hour before coming to a stop, and Amedeo's stomach lurched. He was pulled from the car by the Beast, who patted him on the back and whispered in his ear, 'We're going to miss the singing, laddie.' He tied a string around the bottom of the bag, to secure it to Amedeo's neck, and the light was cut out altogether.

Amedeo stumbled forward across rough terrain for a few paces, his face sweltering from the heat of his breath within the bag. Convinced he was being led to an appropriate spot for execution, he was suddenly filled with terror at the thought that he would never be able to use his eyes again. He called out to the Beast to take the bag off, no matter what they had in mind to do to him, but received no answer. Then he felt himself being pushed down by the shoulders, and thought they wanted him on his knees, but they pushed him into another car. The engine started up. 'Where are we going now?' he called out, but there was no answer. 'Beast? Toro?' The silence was menacing, and continued for the three-hour car ride that followed.

When at last he felt the car's suspension graduate from a rough track to paved cobbles, he began to suspect that he was being brought back to Naples, which was confirmed by the sounds of street life outside. Amedeo asked tentatively if they could take the bag from his head, now that they were back in the city, and after a moment's hesitation it was removed. There were three men in the car with him, none of whom he had ever set eyes on before. 'Where are the others?' he asked, but the men did not answer, and looked away from him with something like disgust.

They parked by the railway station and were met by two other men in spruce blue suits, who unceremoniously now assumed care of Amedeo. The car, with the other three men in it, made off quickly, heading back into the choked traffic of the Corso Garibaldi.

'Where are you taking me?' asked Amedeo, as the two men – one holding him with an iron grip by the arm – escorted him into the station building. It was full of noise and bustle, and no one particularly noticed the three of them walking briskly through the crowds beneath the great expanse of the glass-roofed hall.

'You'll see soon enough,' was the response.

Pietro Boldoni witnessed it all from a distance. He had come, despite the risk of being spotted, in order to report back to Campobello that all had gone according to plan. Rocco had insisted that nothing less than an absolute confirmation from Boldoni personally would persuade him that he had not been double-crossed. Pietro therefore made sure to position himself so that he could see clearly as the three men approached the woman who stood alone beside the pillar to the left of the ticket office, as had been arranged. He also watched carefully as the young man fell into her arms and held her tightly before recovering himself at a word from one of his suited companions, presumably a warning not to make a spectacle of himself. Pietro saw the woman take a bundle of papers from the other man, and, wiping her eyes with a handkerchief, listen to his instructions. She nodded once or twice, and after a couple of minutes it was all over. The men checked their watches, pointed out a direction for the boy and the woman to go, and turned swiftly away from her. Chiara clutched her son's arm, paused a moment to look at him again, and he then stooped and picked up her single suitcase.

Boldoni followed them from a safe distance all the way to the platform; he watched them climb aboard, and waited until the whistle was blown. The train began to pull away, and still Boldoni did not leave his post, not until it had snaked its way from under the glass roof and disappeared from sight.

Chapter 37

The Strada San Carlo, immediately outside the opera house, and the east half of the Piazza Trieste e Trento were cordoned off for the whole day. Police were out in droves from early morning, deploying barriers and rearranging the flow of traffic to minimize congestion in the heart of the city. Hundreds of people, officials and curious observers, were already on the surrounding streets by ten o'clock, some putting up decorations, flags and wreaths, others cleaning the pavements, many just gawping open-mouthed at the preparations. A steady flow of pedestrians drifted towards the hub of activity during the course of the day, so that by late afternoon the Carabinieri militia, in their customary Napoleonic hats, were stretched to keep the crowds in check. However, there was never a sense that the situation could turn nasty. A carnival atmosphere prevailed, with people waving hand-held flags from the rooftops and balconies of the surrounding buildings; impromptu brass bands struck up famous tunes from opera, street vendors were out en masse, and delicious scents from hot food stalls worked to ease the wintry chill in the air. Even if they weren't to be granted a glimpse of the great man when the moment came, people felt that just by being there and joining in the festivity they were in some way taking part in a piece of history.

From about four o'clock onwards there were several false alarms. After five, every car that was allowed through to the theatre raised a cheer from the crowd, and the Carabinieri had to dart back and forth to secure potential breaches in the line of restraint. At last the city's populace was rewarded for its patience, when, a few minutes before six o'clock, the Lancia edged slowly under the theatre's rock grey, vaulted portico, and Rocco Campobello stepped out of the car, dressed in his hat and greatcoat with its thick fur collar. In one hand he carried a silver-topped ebony cane, in the other a pair of white gloves. A mother-of-pearl cigarette holder was set at an angle between his lips, from which came the smoke of a lighted cigarette.

The pillars of the portico were too thick to allow people much of a view of him, and so, while cameras flashed and onlookers clapped, Campobello stepped out from the arches into the open street and raised his cane in the air. This unleashed a tremendous roar of approval and a storm of applause from the crowds, who stamped their feet in rhythm, so that even the granite of the paving reverberated. The vast cisterns beneath the city had long been deserted, but had any of the little well-men of old been at work in the depths that night, they would have paused from their murky labour to wonder at the commotion that was making their underworld resonate like a drum. Rocco acknowledged the throng with a wave, before turning away and entering the opera house.

Bruno Graziani had arranged in advance that his car would pick up Molly from the Hotel Vesuvio and they would travel to the theatre together, arriving half an hour before the performance was due to begin at seven forty-five. Neither of them had been invited to join the party in the royal box this evening, that having been kept for the director and his wife, together with Prefect Tedeschi and an unnamed government dignitary from Rome. Molly and Bruno were ushered to a nearby box, reserved for the two of them, from which Bruno now surveyed the growing assemblage in the theatre with a rather proprietorial air. This would be a triumphant evening for him personally, he pondered, the fruit of much machination and planning. There would be no stopping his ascent to the director's chair in the wake of tonight's feat.

But the time for celebration was not yet upon him. He was looking around for Andrea Florio, who would bring news with him of a no less critical nature. Bruno checked his watch. The doctor was late.

They had barely settled into their box, when Molly announced that she would like to go and visit her husband in his dressing room. It was unconventional, especially given the formality of the occasion, but she said she had particular reasons for wanting to wish him good luck. Bruno regarded her with a whisper of suspicion but thought it might not be a bad idea to have news directly from Campobello that the evening was on course, with no potential hitches. He went over to the door of the box to ask his bodyguard, Roberto, if he would arrange an escort for the signora; but Roberto was not there, which vexed Bruno, so he called out for one of the theatre's liveried attendants to accompany her backstage.

The Maestro's dressing room was the first along a corridor of identical rooms, and just a few steps away from access to the stage itself. Molly attracted a deal of staring as she entered the corridor. It was a bedlam of activity, with people in costume, wardrobe and wig assistants weaving around each other, fragments of song cutting through the air, instruments being tuned, and the heavier distant burble of the excited audience on the far side of the scarlet proscenium curtains.

As Molly rapped on the Maestro's door, she heard a resonant voice from the room next door berating some poor assistant within: 'How can I possibly go on stage when half my costume is missing?' boomed the man. Molly could see from the name on the door that it was the lead bass, singer of the opera's eponymous role, the demonic Mefistofele.

She knocked again, and when there was still no answer, the shadow of a frown crossed her perfectly smooth brow and without more ado she entered. The room was empty, the lights switched off. She wheeled around in alarm and looked for someone to ask. A costume lady was standing nearby.

'Where is Signor Campobello?' asked Molly abruptly in Italian.

'Who wants to know?' the woman replied no less defiantly and crossed her arms.

'I am his wife.'

The woman's attitude was somewhat flattened by this, and she said that the Maestro had finished getting ready a little while ago, his make-up was complete, and he had gone to the *sala verde* at the far end of the corridor in order to warm up his voice. He had asked not to be disturbed.

'I see,' said Molly, and after a moment's hesitation she stalked purposefully along the corridor, forcing several people to sidestep out of her way, to the door at the far end. This time she did not knock, but walked straight in.

The *sala verde* was an elegant room, with green silk wall linings and an inlaid marble floor. A pair of French windows opened on to a neat courtyard garden, sandwiched between the opera house and the royal palace, where hopefuls would stand for hours on the night of an opera, especially in summer when all the dressing-room windows were thrown open, to hear the famous singers warming up for the performance.

Two full-sized grand pianos faced each other in the *sala*, and at one of them sat her husband, barely recognizable beneath his costume. He wore a full-length viridian velvet robe with matching hat, rather in the style of the anachronistic Renaissance garb donned by academics on university high days. Much of his face was hidden beneath a long white wig and beard, a convention for Faust in the opening scene of the opera, when he is portrayed as a tired old man, prior to his rejuvenation at the hands of Mefistofele.

Molly stared at him, slightly taken aback by his appearance, and a half-smile came to her lips.

'Rocco?' she ventured. 'I take it that's you underneath all that?'

'You'll have to take my word for it.'

'I thought I'd come to see how you are.'

'Or did they send you to check on me?'

'Of course not,' Molly answered, injured at the suggestion. She hesitated before continuing. 'I came to wish you good luck. I'm so happy for you. Everyone is. This is a wonderful day.'

He nodded.

She could think of nothing else to say. 'I'll leave you to get ready, then. How exciting. Barely twenty minutes to go!' An impulse urged her to give him a kiss on the cheek, but she had not taken a step before he looked up and his expression stopped her in her tracks. Beneath the wig and make-up he was looking at her rather intently. 'What's the matter?' she asked.

'It's nearly over,' he replied.

'What do you mean?'

'I think you know. In your heart.' She blinked and looked away. 'I have a simple question.'

'Don't.'

'Will you forgive me?'

'There's . . .' she faltered, 'there's no need for that. We've both made mistakes. I'm not too proud to claim that I've been blameless. Surely . . . Now's not the time—'

'Goodbye, Molly.'

At this, she felt a rush of heat that made her light-headed and almost overwhelmed her. She looked around for some kind of distraction. Her only refuge was to belittle the situation. 'Don't be silly, dear. We'll celebrate afterwards. There's a great triumph in the palm of your hand.' He did not respond. 'I'll see you at the reception, then,' she added in a deliberately light tone, and turned to leave the room.

On her return a few minutes later to her place in the box, Molly did not feel much like talking. When she did not volunteer a comment, Bruno asked, 'I trust the Maestro is in fine form?'

'Yes, I believe so,' she answered, and prevented any further discussion by turning away from him to scan the stalls below for familiar faces. She had sat in the audience for her husband's performances many scores of times in the past, but never before had she felt so terribly sad. It was as if a dark and final curtain was closing over her life. It made her want to cry, like a little girl, and she longed to turn the clock back to happier times.

Beside her, Bruno suddenly caught the eye of Andrea Florio, who had entered a box on the other side of the auditorium. The two men looked straight at each other for a moment, with no greeting or signal passing between them, until Bruno eventually raised his eyebrows, questioningly. Andrea's eyes were wide, almost startled. At last he jerked a little nod at Bruno, who responded by tilting his head graciously to one side, with the slightest of smiles.

The orchestra had begun to file into the pit, and the auditorium was almost full. Molly saw that the doors at the rear of the royal box had been swung open and that its occupants were beginning to take their seats. 'Oh look!' she said to Bruno, pointing to the box. 'How lovely! Your father has come, after all.'

Bruno's head whipped around, and for a long moment he sat stock still, staring at the figure of Don Graziani, dressed in tails, who was slowly making his way, with the aid of a pair of sticks, to a chair at the front of the box. Pompeo Tedeschi hovered close behind and lent an arm to help the old man lower himself to his chair, before taking his own place next to him. They began chatting to one another.

Bruno said nothing, but turned his attention from the royal box back to Andrea Florio, across the huge cavity of the auditorium. They met each other's eyes coldly, and the doctor looked uneasily away.

'Is something wrong?' asked Molly. Bruno blinked and turned to her with a smile.

'Not at all. The old devil said he was too unwell to come, but just look at him! I swear he'll outlive me!'

Molly laughed politely. 'Well, he seems to be getting along just swell with Signor Tedeschi. Who would have thought? How nice that they can behave like gentlemen and put all that unpleasantness behind them.'

Bruno gave her a quick look. 'What unpleasantness is that?'

'Why, the scene at the dinner table, in the Palazzo Reale, don't you recall? When that silly boy, Amedeo, had too much to drink. If you ask me, he was bound to get himself into trouble sooner or later. As my father would say: one cannot educate pork.'

Bruno did not answer, but checked his watch. It was time for the performance to begin. He looked back in the direction of his father, who was nodding at something that Tedeschi was saying; and then he responded, with brief hand gestures; and was that a smile? Who would have thought it, indeed? Bruno sat watching them for a while longer, wondering what on earth they could find to talk about with such agreement.

Don Graziani had been told that his son was already at the theatre, but he had no desire to tire his weak eyes searching the gilded auditorium.

'You are taking Bruno immediately after the performance, then?' he muttered to his neighbour.

'Signor!' spluttered Tedeschi, and a cloud of rotten breath accompanied the expletive.

'Spare me the affectations,' said Graziani, leaning away slightly. 'I make it my business to know what is happening. I wanted to reassure you that I shall not stand in your way.'

'Of course, I cannot make any comment,' replied Tedeschi, 'but I appreciate your support. All Italy applauds you.'

'I'm sure. I have already ordered my men to step down.'

'How many men have you here?'

'Seven or eight, including those assigned to Bruno. Don't worry. Even as we speak, Bruno is unattended. You can move in whenever you please.'

Tedeschi nodded and smiled; he was within inches of his old enemy's ear. 'We are so very glad that you decided to come.'

'We?'

'We, the city. The people of Naples. Tonight will be a landmark in our city's history.'

Graziani said no more, but allowed his attention to be drawn elsewhere, and Tedeschi sat back in his chair, gratified to the core.

As soon as Molly had departed the backstage corridor, Rocco emerged from the *sala verde* and met his young pianist, Alberto, who had arrived at the door on cue, as arranged. Alberto looked nervous, and nodded at his Maestro. Campobello checked up and down the bustling corridor for one of the production administrators. The lead bass, Signor Facelli, was still ranting about the missing parts of his costume, which was causing quite a commotion amongst backstage staff. They were having to improvise quickly to rectify the situation.

Rocco spotted the person he was looking for, and called out to him rather tersely that he could not possibly be expected to prepare himself for a performance of this magnitude with all the noise and continual interruptions. He required fifteen minutes of complete peace, he insisted, and to that end was requisitioning rehearsal room six, on the ground floor. He would go there immediately, with his pianist Alberto, and there should be absolutely no disturbance, nor was a single person even allowed to enter the stairwell that led down to the ground floor rehearsal rooms.

'Fifteen minutes?' the man faltered, looking at his watch, already exasperated with all the other problems. 'The curtain is due to go up in just over ten.'

'Are you clear? Not a whisper on the other side of that door.' Rocco pointed firmly to the entrance to the stairwell and began to make his way there, Alberto at his heels. Campobello's status, together with the great significance of the occasion, gave him the authority to demand whatever he pleased. After he had departed, the administrator felt compelled to guard the stairwell door personally, despite the several other jobs he needed to be doing at the same time.

Rocco and Alberto were already hurrying down the steps. 'Is everything ready?'

'Yes,' replied Alberto. 'He arrived a few minutes ago. Do you think he will have enough time?'

'Not really, but we'll manage. The face is done already?'

'Yes, Boldoni did it. It's not brilliant, but . . .'

'Never mind.' Rocco's calm tone reassured Alberto, who was feeling out of his depth.

Alberto opened the rehearsal room door and ushered Rocco inside. Neatly folded on a side table was a full set of ordinary clothes for Campobello, including hat, coat and scarf; and beside the table stood Boldoni, whose face flickered briefly into a smile as the Maestro entered.

Next to Boldoni, waiting in a bathrobe and looking wide-eyed, but resolute, was Taddeo. His face had been painted pale, and made up with lines to look like an old man. Alberto hesitated for a moment, before a flick of Boldoni's finger galvanized him into action and he got to work on Taddeo right away.

Shortly afterwards, Boldoni and Campobello, now in street clothes, left the room and headed towards a small door that was hardly ever used nowadays. Pickering had discovered it some months ago. It provided access from the theatre to a staff pantry in the next-door Royal Palace, a portion of which backed directly on to the San Carlo, and Boldoni had procured the key for it. They passed through the door, crossed an abandoned meat storage room with large rusting hooks screwed into its ceiling joists, and went out the far side, into a defunct staff kitchen. From here they walked through a courtyard and made their way to one of the Palace's several back doors which opened on to the Royal Gardens. It was a short walk from here down to the great iron gates flanked by their celebrated equestrian statues. The gatekeepers, who appeared to have some prior understanding with Boldoni, swung them slightly ajar to let the two men through, hardly sparing a glance for the taller man, who was wrapped up thoroughly against the cold. It was a dark night. They climbed into a waiting car and were driven away.

Taddeo, meanwhile, dressed in Campobello's costume as the elderly Faust, complete with beard and wig, had successfully got himself with Alberto to the Maestro's dressing room without attracting any suspicion. The performance was already five minutes late, and there was a knock on the door. Alberto went across to intercept the visitor. It was the senior stage manager, insisting that he be told immediately when they would be ready to begin. The possibility of Campobello failing to appear had been secretly taken into account by the production staff, and an alternative Faust – the tenor who had been booked to sing the remainder of the run – had agreed to remain on standby in the theatre.

'Signor Campobello needs a little more time to get ready,' replied Alberto, who knew this stage manager personally and was struggling to sound convincing. 'Just five minutes. Ten at the most. They can wait that long.' The manager nodded reluctantly and withdrew. Alberto locked the door.

Taddeo looked across at him through the reflection in his mirror. 'We have to hold out a little longer,' said Alberto. 'If he doesn't come by eight-fifteen, the whole thing's off and we're to get away as quickly as we can. That's what Boldoni said.'

Bruno Graziani checked his watch again. The noise from the auditorium had increased as the three-thousand-strong audience began to grow restless. No official announcement had been made, and the performance was now nearly half an hour late. For some while, Bruno had been tapping his fingertips animatedly, but now, in a sudden flash of impatience, he slammed his palm down on the velvet sill of the box and sprang to his feet. 'Excuse me,' he said to Molly, with a quick bow.

'Do you think something has gone wrong?' she asked, alarmed, but he had already left the box and closed the door behind him. He looked left and right for Roberto. He called out, but the curved corridor was empty and his voice echoed brutally between the marble floor and the shallow arc vaulting.

'Where is the man, for God's sake,' he muttered to himself, and walked briskly around to the service staircase at the stage end of the building. He hurried down the steps, two at a time.

Taddeo and Alberto were still in the dressing room, having stalled the management for as long as they felt able. The deadline had been reached, and Alberto left the room with the intention of telling the producer that Maestro Campobello had decided he was unable to proceed with the performance.

Taddeo was left alone in the dressing room to change into Rocco's street clothes, which were still hanging in the cupboard. He felt relieved that nothing worse had happened. All he needed to do now was hide his face as much as possible, hurry from the theatre, with Alberto clearing a path before him, and step into Pozzo's waiting car. There would be a grisly moment when the crowds caught sight of him at the stage door, but it would be over in a flash, and they would be on their way to Rome. Tomorrow's headlines would announce that Rocco Campobello had booked into a clinic in a new crisis, and Taddeo would hide himself in Rome, drawing the scent just long enough for the Maestro to make good his escape.

But no sooner had he opened the cupboard to retrieve his employer's clothes than the door of the dressing room opened and he was faced with a cold and expressionless Bruno Graziani.

'What's happening?' Bruno asked calmly, closing the door behind him. He noticed the key on the inside of the door, and turned it.

Taddeo stood his ground, leaning back against the dressing table, too terrified to speak. Bruno seemed almost to smile, before turning away and sitting down in a chair on the other side of the room.

'So this is how the Great Campobello ends his career?' he asked. 'A gibbering wreck, without the balls to come clean and tell the world he's not up to it. I thought it might come to this.'

Taddeo held still and kept his eyes fixed on Bruno.

'Or maybe you planned it this way from the start. You wanted to wait until the boy was released, and then you would renege on your side of the bargain. Did you really think you'd get away with it? Don't you know me better than that? We deal with treachery in the harshest manner.' He opened his jacket and removed a pistol from a holster at his ribs.

'When I think of all those years,' he continued, 'most of my life, really – when my father harped on about you. "Rocco this, Rocco that." The wonder boy. The son he never had. Instead he had me. With all my – ' he raised a hand in the air ' – abundant talents. You were the yardstick against which I was always to be measured, and found wanting. I spent my youth trying to be like you, to please him. And look at you now. Now when I need you. Look at you! Pathetic.' Bruno got to his feet and walked over to Taddeo. There was a sudden harsh rapping on the door.

'Signor Campobello! Signor Campobello!' It was Alberto.

'Tell him to go away. Now!' hissed Bruno through his teeth. Taddeo glanced up at the door. He knew his voice would give him away. 'Tell him!' Bruno brought the pistol up to Taddeo's chin, and then suddenly froze. He took a pace backwards, staring, speechlessly, at Taddeo.

Alberto was rattling the door handle. 'Signor Campobello! Are you all right in there?'

Taddeo looked into Bruno's eyes and knew the game was up. 'It's all right, Alberto,' he called. 'Just give me a few minutes to change.'

'All right. I'll be waiting. But don't take long. The other tenor is ready to go on, but they need the costume.' Alberto was heard to step away from the door.

With one hand Taddeo pulled the hat and wig from his head, and with the other ripped off the beard that had been pasted hurriedly to his chin shortly before. 'Please, signor,' he pleaded, locking his hands together in front of him. 'I am only obeying orders. I didn't know what I was getting into. I'm just a household servant.' There were tears in his eyes.

Bruno was blinking repeatedly and now held out a hand to silence Taddeo. 'Where is Campobello?' he asked.

'I'm sorry, signor, I'm sorry.' Taddeo fell to his knees, weeping openly.

'All right. Tell me where he is.'

'Signor, how can I do such a thing? I cannot betray the Maestro.'

Bruno walked up to the kneeling man and calmly placed the gun barrel to his head. 'You tell me now, or you die.'

Taddeo held out for one last appeal. 'Signor! Don't!'

Bruno cocked the gun.

'All right! All right!' cried Taddeo, clutching his palms over his ears in blind panic. 'I'll tell you everything I know. I can tell you where they've gone. They're hiding. Hiding until they can escape in a few days' time.'

'They?'

'The Maestro and Pietro Boldoni.'

'Boldoni? He's in Naples?'

'Yes, signor. They've been planning this.'

Bruno's eyes darted hither and thither around the room, ablaze with rage. 'They think they can outwit me? Where are they? Tell me now!' He raised the gun again.

'Let me write it down, signor. It is complicated, let me write it.'

Bruno stepped back and allowed him to go over to the dressing table, where, stooped and with a trembling hand, all the while whimpering, Taddeo began to write.

There was a knocking on the door again. 'Maestro. It's time to go.'

Bruno grabbed the scrap of paper. He indicated the door. 'Is he in on this as well?' Taddeo looked down, apologetically, without speaking. Bruno read what was written on the paper.

'Signor Campobello!' called Alberto.

'What the hell is this?' asked Bruno looking up from the paper to Taddeo. 'Do you take me for some kind of fool?'

Taddeo raised his hands in the air and backed away, blind terror in his eyes. 'It's where they're hiding, signor. I swear it. I swear it on my mother's grave.'

The door handle rattled. Bruno pointed the gun into Taddeo's face. 'If I find you have misled me I will oversee your death personally, and believe me, you will be begging me to pull the trigger by the time I've finished with you.'

'It's the truth! That's where they are.'

Bruno hesitated. The handle rattled once more. He

put the gun back in its holster and unlocked the door. When he appeared in the doorway, Alberto stood back in surprise. A small crowd had gathered there, and Bruno pushed his way through them, ran down the service staircase and out towards the stage door.

Back in the dressing room, Alberto locked the door from the inside once more. Taddeo was trying to undress, but shaking too much to do it effectively. Alberto put a hand on his shoulder. 'It's all right,' he said. 'It's over.'

'Yes,' replied Taddeo, whose tears were genuine. 'I did it, though. It worked.'

'You told him?'

'Yes,' said Taddeo, and looked up at Alberto, his euphoria and relief now getting the better of the shock.

'He'll be on his way, then,' said Alberto, smiling. 'Come. Let me help you get dressed. Pozzo's waiting. We'd better not delay any more. I'll come with you as far as the stage door.'

Taddeo nodded and began to dress more quickly.

Word spread fast after the announcement on stage that Maestro Campobello had suffered a setback. No one knew the details, but there were whisperings that it might be the same problem as before, come back to finish him off. So when Taddeo, clothed as Rocco and wrapped up well, appeared at the stage door, the crowd who had gathered to catch a glimpse of the departing tenor fell deathly silent. Many crossed themselves, one or two fell to their knees in prayer. The car was waiting there, engine running, just a few paces from the theatre, and Pozzo was holding open the door. Taddeo stepped across the pavement to the car, his footsteps audible in the hush. As he got into the back seat someone in the crowd called out

'God bless you, Maestro!' Another did the same, then another, and then more joined in, some calling him by his first name, others directing imprecations to God, so that by the time the car pulled away the street was filled with a cacophony as people cried their words of goodwill and prayer.

Pozzo sped away, out on to the Via Partenope, and headed along the coast. '*Urrà!* They've fallen for it,' he said, chuckling. 'They've all fallen for it. We've done it, lad, we've done it.'

Taddeo let his head rest back against the comfortable leather of the seat. 'Thank God,' he murmured. 'That was the worst experience of my life.'

'You can relax now, *paesano*. We'll have you on the early morning train from Caserta. This time tomorrow you'll be settled in your luxurious hotel in Rome. Can't be bad, eh? Ha, ha!' Taddeo, too, was smiling. '*Ecco!* Look what I've got for you here,' continued Pozzo, holding the steering wheel with one hand and rifling for something beside him with the other.

'Steady,' said Taddeo, leaning forward to see what he was doing.

'It's time to celebrate,' said Pozzo. He pulled out a champagne bottle from somewhere, placed two glasses on the flat walnut surface between the two front seats, and started to pour.

'Let me do that,' said Taddeo. 'I've got nothing to do here.' He took the bottle and added, 'Do you think anyone will try to follow us?'

'Maybe. You're right. Better put my foot down.' He accelerated along the road that climbed to the heights above Capo Posillipo. 'Cheers!' he said, raising his glass and drinking it in one. They rounded a corner but found themselves slowed by an old car in front. Taddeo was faintly relieved.

'Damn thing. Come on, come on,' said Pozzo, and hit the horn repeatedly.

'I don't think we need to hurry so much now,' said Taddeo. He looked over his shoulder. 'There's no one following us. We've got all the time in the world.'

'We're off!' cried Pozzo gleefully, seeing an empty stretch of road ahead and pulling out to overtake. 'Have another glass,' he said, reaching for the bottle. 'What?! Not finished your first one yet? Come on, man.' The bottle slipped through his fingers and ended up glugging its contents in the footwell of the front passenger seat. 'Damn it!' snapped Pozzo, and stretched over to retrieve it before it emptied itself completely.

'Careful!'

It was not even a particularly sharp bend, but it startled Pozzo as he came up triumphant with the bottle in his hand. He jerked the steering wheel too savagely to the right, over-compensated with a counter jerk to the left, and then lost control completely. The Lancia crashed at speed through a flimsy wooden fence to the side of the road, rolled over several times down the bank, and collided violently with the trunk of a great cedar tree beneath. The spreading mushroom top of the tree swayed for a moment after the impact; a nearby herd of goats looked up quizzically, and a sprinkling of dark green needles descended on to the crushed roof of the car.

As soon as the theatre manager had made his announcement on the stage of the San Carlo to the effect that Maestro Campobello had suddenly been taken ill and would be replaced by the evening's understudy, there was a great uproar in the auditorium. For the most part it was confined to cries of disappointment, shaking of heads and heated exchanges of concern, but one or two members of the audience were seen to stalk ostentatiously into the aisle and out of the theatre in protest at having been led a merry dance.

Pompeo Tedeschi glanced across to Bruno's box. Seeing that his bird had apparently flown without him noticing, he let out a vicious expletive and sprang to his feet.

'What is happening?' said Graziani, but Tedeschi was already at the door of the box, instructing a small platoon of Carabinieri who had appeared as if from nowhere.

'Get after him, wherever he's gone. And one of you stay with Signora Campobello. Find out what she knows and then have her escorted home.' Five troopers ran to do his bidding, while two others entered the royal box, much to the distress of the director and his wife. The two guards took their place either side of Don Graziani. Tedeschi now came up behind the old man, and tapped him rather abruptly on the shoulder.

'Signor, we have to talk outside, on a matter of urgency.' He handed him his sticks. Despite Graziani's protests, he was forcibly lifted out of his chair and on to his feet by two militiamen and escorted to the small reception area behind. Not a single one of his bodyguards was present, but policemen were everywhere.

'What the hell do you think you're doing? Fetch my doctor immediately,' Graziani said viperously to Tedeschi, who towered over him.

'We'll assign medical care at the appropriate time, have no fear,' replied Tedeschi. 'I am placing you under arrest, Signor Graziani. There's no need to go into details here, but in the first instance you have broken the law that prohibits civilians from carrying firearms. That will be enough to detain you for the time being.'

Graziani actually managed a smile. 'You buffoon,' he said straight at the Prefect. 'You'll have to do better than that. I haven't carried a weapon for more than ten years.'

But Tedeschi seemed to be ready and came back in a flash. 'Perhaps, yes, but you have been boasting to me all evening about the men you have deployed in the theatre. Well, while you've been sitting here, we've checked them out and have so far picked up six, all of them employees of yours, and all carrying handguns, apparently on your authorization. It won't do, sir, won't do at all.' He shook his head magisterially.

'Those men are here to help you, idiot! You wanted to take Bruno.'

'We'll start with the chief rat,' replied Tedeschi, indicating to his men that they should get Graziani out quickly, to save any further disruption. They all but lifted him, flapping his sticks in the air. 'In good time we'll deal with your pestilential son,' continued Tedeschi. 'And then we can talk more fully about the sorry matter of Inspector Crawley and Mr MacSweeney. Really, signor! Did you think we could just brush that under the carpet?'

'So you would take my money?' shrieked the old man, straining his neck to catch a last glimpse of Tedeschi over his shoulder. 'You accept a generous donation to your coffers and then put the blade in my back?'

At this, Tedeschi stepped in front of Graziani, who was lowered to his feet again. The Prefect was smiling triumphantly. 'Oh, you mean this?' he said, pulling out a paper, tearing it in two and placing the pieces into

Graziani's breast pocket. It was the cheque. 'Our party has no need of funding from the likes of you. I would no more accept it than feed my own mother with carrion. Take him away!'

'Carrion is what you *are*!' barked Graziani impotently as four of Tedeschi's men negotiated the lifting of him down the staircase. People were staring up from the entrance foyer below. 'You've no idea what you've taken on! Do you know who I am?' His cries went unheeded, and within minutes he was driven off, in full view of the crowds, in the official vehicle that was ready and waiting in the theatre's portico.

Chapter 38

A taxi would have been no good to Bruno because the lanes in that part of town were too narrow. He travelled there, instead, in a single-horse carriage.

As he got out of the carriage, he handed the driver a bunch of banknotes and demanded the man's coat. The driver had already spotted the holstered pistol, and did not argue, but nervously gave over the tatty old garment and took the cash. A moment later he was gone and Bruno stood alone in the dark alley. He checked Taddeo's scrawl on the piece of paper and looked up at the enamelled number to one side of the crumbling archway. The coat had been an unnecessary precaution. The area seemed to be derelict and completely abandoned; he had no need of disguise. He imagined it was one of the condemned quarters of the old town, the remains of an irreparably degenerate slum, soon to be cleared to make way for a new road or some other civic development. The Fascist government was promising great improvements for Naples.

He walked through the arch and into a deserted *cortile*. His hunch had been right. The windows of the high buildings, former tenement blocks, all around showed that the place had been gutted. Nothing but rotten splinters remained of the windows and shutters, and in some places the outside walls had been knocked through completely. Even the lowliest back-street scavengers, little more than sewer rats, had given up on the place, having long since scoured it stone by stone in search of anything of use or value.

It was dark, which made Bruno uncomfortable, but he walked on, across the *cortile*, following the instructions to the letter, into a tiny, derelict courtyard on the far side. There in the middle, exactly as Taddeo had said, was the square steel lid. A dim sliver of light could be seen where the metal plate did not quite fit the old aperture cut into the cobbles, and Bruno knew he had come to the right place. He slowly raised the heavy lid and saw, falling away beneath him, a deep shaft, sparsely lit by oil lamps which hung on rusty hooks every so often all the way down. There were niches cut into the wall of the shaft, for use as foot and hand grips, and, without hesitating, he holstered his gun and climbed over the lip of the well, quietly pulling the lid over his head behind him. It was a long and deep descent.

As soon as his feet reached the firm ground at the bottom, he drew his gun again and looked around. He paused to calm his breathing, because the sound of it was oppressive in the underground acoustic and would warn them of his approach. He then began to walk slowly along the only route open to him, a narrow passage illuminated by lighted wicks in small earthenware jars. His eyes were wide and alert, fixed on the way ahead as he edged forward. Finger poised on the trigger, he moved at a stuttering pace, inflamed by the proximity of his quarry yet hampered by a pathological dread of the dark – the same unmentionable affliction that had shamed him since earliest boyhood.

He was aware of several passages leading off on either side, some wide enough only for a child, others shallow, so that a man would be forced to lie flat against the damp ground, to crawl through. He approached and passed each one with caution, but his only way was forward: the way already lit by whoever had come before, and the disturbing thought dawned on him that his presence here might have been expected. His breathing became quicker and more shallow the deeper he progressed, and he gave up trying to suppress it.

His tunnel came to an abrupt end when it opened into a colossal chamber, half of which dropped away to form a great stagnant pool. He circled the edge of the large open space, back against the outer wall, until he saw the lights continuing down a narrow tunnel on the far side, and he quickly darted into the mouth of it. At one point he thought he was aware of a noise behind, and whipped around, raising his gun and nearly firing it; but he managed to control the impulse, and held his breath to listen. There was no sound other than the pronounced pulse in his temples.

His suspicion that there was someone behind made him shuffle quietly back the way he had come, but when he passed around the first bend in the passage he found to his horror that the oil lamps along the way he had come had been extinguished. There was no choice but to carry on, but with the threat of the unknown ahead and the dread of a malicious presence in the darkness behind, he felt compelled now to press his back against the wall and edge his way onwards in a sidestep, darting a look to left and right alternately. And he now had to stoop, for the roof of the tunnel was closing in as it progressed.

At the point where he was forced to bend over double if he intended to carry on, a stab of panic took hold of him. His purpose evaporated and he called out into the darkness. 'Rocco! Rocco! It's me, Bruno. I've come to find you. To see if you're all right. Are you all right, Rocco? Everyone's worried.' His voice echoed on for some while, until a hungry silence consumed and obliterated all trace of it. 'Rocco!' Still nothing, and Bruno cursed savagely under his breath. 'Rocco,' he screamed, 'I know you're here! Damn you all to hell!' and he fired his pistol into the darkness. The sound of the gunshot was cataclysmically deafening in the rocky confinement of the tunnel, and he cowered low, cradling his head in his arms. A smattering of loose stone fell from an unseen spot in the darkness above, but he barely noticed it for the ringing in his ears.

He had no choice but to continue along the passage. His heavy breathing now acquired an audible edge with every exhalation, slightly bestial in quality, something between a wheeze and a whimper.

'Rocco!' His voice was breaking. 'Can you hear me, Rocco? Help me!'

'Here.' It was barely a word, more like an aspirated sound, and it came from somewhere to Bruno's right, as if close at hand. He stopped, frozen with shock, and wondered if he was imagining things. He took a step back and looked sideways. Feeling for the wall of the tunnel with his hand, he became aware of an entrance to a side passage on the right, unilluminated, and tentatively edged his way forward into the blackness of it. He held a hand out in front, waving it back and forth in the damp air in case the tunnel came to an end. He let out a cry when his knuckles cracked against a rockface ahead, but found that he could continue if he turned off at a right angle. All light from his former tunnel had now vanished, and he was in pitch darkness. 'Rocco,' he called out again, now quietly, standing still for a moment. 'Is that you?' There was a slight hissing sound ahead, and he strained his neck towards the gloom. He took some more small steps forwards, on and on, now powerfully regretting having deviated, until the narrow walls on either side suddenly disappeared. He must have arrived in an open cavern.

'Rocco?' The name was barely spoken, but it resonated in there as if under the dome of a great church. Just at that moment, a small flame appeared to light itself in the gloom, about thirty yards ahead of him. 'Who are you?' called out Bruno, dazzled by the unexpected light. And then, emerging into faint definition from the absolute blackness beyond the flame, so that it was dimly illuminated, Bruno beheld a face. The horror of it was immediate. He barely took in the detail of its features before turning to flee, screaming with every breath, no longer concerned to feel his way but crashing into the tunnel's walls, grazing his scalp, face and shoulders, turning wherever he felt an opening deeper and deeper into the complex of passages. In his blind raving he was oblivious of an open well shaft that lay in his path, and stumbled over the lip of it, falling, bouncing off the side walls before hitting the water deep beneath.

Rocco and Boldoni clearly heard the sound of the impact, even from where they were, a hundred and fifty yards above and to the west. They could hear as he splashed around in the cholera-infested waters of the ancient cistern, and they were also aware that he eventually managed to haul himself out, groaning, on to some kind of a ledge in the darkness. Thereafter the noises became more feeble, as he must have crawled his way deeper into the underground labyrinth, wherever he could find an opening, deranged by terror and shivering with cold. After an hour or so of ever more pathetic crying there were no more sounds. Whether he had stumbled and fallen to his death down another shaft, or whether he had floundered, insane with fear, into some dark hole, to curl up and hide from his demons, no one would ever know.

Boldoni flicked on his torch and passed one to Rocco, who did likewise, before sitting down on a smooth rock. While Boldoni went around the cavern lighting the many candles and lamps he had earlier put in place, Rocco quietly began to remove the magnificent headdress he had arranged to have secretly taken from the Teatro San Carlo's costume department the day before. He held it by its broad horns for a moment before placing it to one side. In all his time as a stage performer, he had never seen quite so exquisitely conceived a piece of costumery.

Without speaking, Boldoni approached his employer, unbuttoned and removed his shirt, and with a combination of creams, soaps and water, began to remove the scarlet and black face make-up that had been so hurriedly applied less than half an hour before. When the task was complete, and Campobello had dressed, Boldoni spoke for the first time. 'You have plenty of food, water, cigarettes, light, wine, and even a comfortable bed.' He pointed to the side of the chamber, which he had been stocking by night for a week. As ever, he had anticipated the Maestro's every need. 'I will not re-light the passageway out, just in case some idiot tries his luck down here. I doubt anyone would find this place.'

Rocco looked around. Now that the candles were lit, they were dimly aware of the vast cavern around them. Its domed heights vanished into the gloom. 'I was last here thirty years ago,' said Rocco.

'It was an inspired choice.'

'More than just a hole to hide in,' continued Rocco. 'I have dreamt about this cave for most of my life. I feel as though it's part of me.'

'It's certainly haunting. And so very quiet. Though I don't know if I'd want to stay down here for too long.'

'There is something comforting about the confinement of it. I feel safe here,' said Rocco. 'Alone, but safe.'

Boldoni paused to join him in looking around the great dark space. 'If the bay is Naples' bosom, then this must surely be her womb,' he said quietly, to which Rocco made no reply. Boldoni raised his hand, and came close to resting it, comfortingly, on the Maestro's shoulder, but could not bring himself to take such a liberty.

'I'm going to leave you now, Maestro,' he said, 'and return tomorrow evening with a report. Three days should do it. Everyone's attention will be turned towards Rome – assuming Taddeo does his work; and then, when no one's looking, we'll get you out of here and away.'

Rocco looked up at his assistant and held his gaze for some while. Words were inadequate. He held out his hand, which Boldoni shook rather formally.

'Until tomorrow evening, then,' concluded Boldoni, and, flashlight in hand, turned to go.

It was something more pronounced than déjà vu that stopped him in his tracks after walking just twenty paces from the Maestro; but to have described it as prescience would have been counter to Boldoni's conviction that the inexplicable in this world – nay, the miraculous – was merely a demonstration of the divine hand at work. In later life, therefore, he would ascribe his deciding, for no apparent reason, to turn around and check on his employer, to the intervention of an angel. He would swear that he had even felt the gilded touch of some princely hand on his shoulder. What he did thereafter, however, and the success or otherwise of the decisions he was about to take, was all too human.

He turned and saw Campobello slumped on the cold rock, hand outstretched towards him, an apoplectic expression locked to his face, but absolutely incapable of sound. Stunned as much by the sight as by his foreknowledge of its occurrence, Boldoni froze for a split second before rushing back to help. He tried to pull Rocco up into a sitting position, but he seemed to have stopped breathing. His face was trapped in a spasm of agony, eyes bulging, and the colour of his skin was changing to a shade of purple.

'Maestro! cried Boldoni. A trickle of saliva was dripping from the side of Rocco's mouth, and his eyes began to roll back in their lids. Pietro wrapped his arms tightly around Campobello and heaved. 'Signor!' He felt powerless, and glanced in desperation heavenwards, but saw only the cold rock of the cavern walls disappearing into the blackness.

Suddenly, Rocco gasped, released from the worst intensity of the contraction, and he began to breathe. He stared at Pietro. 'I am dying.'

'No, sir, no,' said Pietro, and putting Rocco's arm around his own neck hauled with all his might until he had the big man on his feet. Pietro stumbled under the strain, but found his footing again. 'I've got to get you out of here. To the hospital. We'll get to the Florios. They'll make everything better.' Rocco was breathing heavily now, great heaving grunts. Pietro managed to get him to start walking. 'Is the pain under your ribs?' he asked, shining the torch ahead and already wondering how on earth he was going to manage to get this huge man up the length of the last shaft.

'My head,' gasped Rocco, 'my head is on fire.'

'All right, all right.' Pietro took faint encouragement from Campobello managing a response. The agony was receding slightly and he seemed able to support his own weight. They progressed slowly towards the exit.

*

It was nearly midnight, and Marco Florio was standing in the lobby of the hospital, still wearing his coat and hat. He had arrived a little earlier in response to a compelling summons from his brother, and was at the centre of his own pressing situation, busily ordering hospital staff off in different directions, when he saw Boldoni burst in from the street entrance. He had never seen the neat little secretary look so distraught and helpless. Boldoni called over to Marco, beckoning him urgently for a private word.

'Andrea is downstairs in the operating theatre,' began Marco. 'He has quarantined the entire wing, to keep everyone out and hush this dreadful business up. I'm glad you've come, because we're going to need some decisions. Thank God we can still call the shots in this place, even though the old man's gone down, I hear. Taken into custody by Tedeschi.'

481

'What? Wait! What did you say? Hush what business up?' said Boldoni.

Marco looked at him as though he were deranged. 'The business with Maestro Campobello, of course. Isn't that why you're here?'

'Of course it's why I'm here,' replied Boldoni. 'But what do you know about it? What did you say about cordoning off part of the hospital?'

'Andrea has ordered everyone out of the west wing since they brought him in, about half an hour ago,' said Marco.

'What on earth are you talking about?' said Pietro. This was no time for crossed wires. The Maestro's life hung in the balance while they quibbled.

Suddenly, it dawned on Marco Florio that Boldoni might not have heard. 'Oh my God,' he said. 'You don't know, do you?'

'Know what?'

'He's been killed. In a car accident. Pozzo as well, about five miles out of town. He didn't stand a chance. He was dead before the people in the car behind even managed to get the door open.'

Boldoni reeled at the implication of the news, but immediately came to his senses. 'That wasn't Campobello. It was Taddeo in the car. The double. The Maestro's outside in a carriage, and critically ill. We need to get him into surgery straight away.'

'What?'

'Where's Andrea?'

'I haven't even seen him yet. I've only just arrived myself. He must have gone down to look at the body. He'll be there now. You mean to say it's all a mistake? It's not the Maestro?'

482

'Clear this place!' ordered Boldoni, thinking fast. 'Every last person out. No one must know about this, is that understood? Absolutely nobody. And I need help to get Campobello down to the operating theatre right away. We'll need a surgeon we can trust.' Marco Florio nodded and quickly turned to pass word to a senior orderly.

In a moment, Marco was out in the street running towards the carriage, ready to help Boldoni. But when he saw Boldoni leaning over a slumped body on the pavement, weeping, and calling repeatedly into the inert face, he hesitated. Boldoni turned his tear-stained face to the doctor, who now stooped to one knee and nudged Boldoni aside. He tried for a pulse.

'I can't feel his breath,' Boldoni said. 'We are too late. We've lost him.'

Chapter 39

The city put on a state funeral for Rocco Campobello. No one had seen the like of it before. Shops were closed, flags lowered to half mast, and everywhere along the route that the cortège took, great swathes of black cloth were draped from the rooftops. It seemed as if the entire population of Naples had come out on to the streets, to watch in silence as the procession made its way from the Duomo, where the requiem mass was held, to the cemetery, where the coffin was entombed within the mausoleum that housed the remains of Enrico, the tenor's father.

Molly Campobello, looking austerely beautiful, attended the cathedral service but declined to join the long procession on foot, opting instead to travel to the cemetery by car. Pietro Boldoni therefore had the honour of leading the mourners who accompanied the coffin, amongst whom was an array of stellar musicians and politicians, together with ambassadors from many territories, members of the army, representatives of the King and the Pope, and a personal emissary from the Duce.

Don Graziani was granted a dispensation to attend the mass, but was discreetly attended by a circle of police-men dressed as fellow mourners, and taken back into custody directly afterwards. Boldoni stole a quick glance at him during the ceremony, but the old man seemed distracted and could not stop looking around the great heights of the cathedral.

Several large speakers had been installed near to the altar by Walter Fleming and staff from the Jupiter Company, and the congregation was treated to the first ever public playing of the final recording made by Campobello, his sole electronic legacy. When the Maestro's voice rose up in song, a huge sound, filling and resonating wondrously through the cavernous building, there was a gasp from the congregation; but their delight turned to melancholy at the recollection of their loss, and tears flowed freely from men and women alike. At the end of the recording, the Bishop of Naples commenced the liturgy, to the accompaniment of singing from the massed choirs of several of the city's great churches.

Boldoni managed the aftermath of Campobello's demise meticulously and made sure that all funeral arrangements were undertaken with a scrupulous observance of protocol. With Molly's consent, he took sole responsibility for the handling of the body, from the moment Andrea Florio officially pronounced death to the final sealing of the coffin lid. Molly had insisted on glancing at the corpse briefly in the hospital mortuary – much against the advice of everyone, because of the extent of the disfiguring injuries. She then endorsed Boldoni's opinion that the body should not lie in state on an open catafalque, as would have been traditional at such a high profile funeral. It would be too distressing for the public to see their beloved Maestro in such a condition.

Molly Campobello's final tribute to her husband,

inside the family mausoleum, was to lay a bunch of roses on the top of his casket. She then took a step back and contemplated the coffin for a full minute, her black lace veil raised to give a clearer view, before turning and walking out of the little building with great restraint, for which she was admired by reporters and public alike.

Molly seemed placidly reconciled to her future as a widow, and asked Boldoni kindly to begin the process of closing down the Villa Rosalba. She would be returning to New York immediately, where her long-estranged father was ready and waiting to accept her back into the family fold. She accepted Boldoni's resignation, though he reassured her that he would not abandon his post until all administrative matters relating to Campobello's estate – of which Molly was the major beneficiary – were complete. When she asked, without any great show of concern, what he intended to do with himself next, Boldoni smiled and said that he planned to build a new life in Los Angeles, and added that Mr Pickering had elected to move there with him. She asked why they had chosen Los Angeles, to which he replied, briefly, that he thought the west coast's more liberal society would suit the two of them, and that some of the Maestro's former colleagues, including Miss Josephine Carter, had offered their hospitality. Molly looked away, perhaps needled that Boldoni had confided his future plans and received offers of help from the likes of Miss Carter, while she herself had not been consulted. The dratted little man deserved whatever came to him, she concluded, and turned away from him without another word.

Chapter 40

Three years later, in the mountains of southern Switzerland

Signor and Signora Cavalli had a reputation for being pleasant and friendly folk, but they kept themselves very much to themselves in their old stone farmhouse. There were not many neighbours amongst whom to share this reputation, and the closest of them, cattle farmers near Olivone, rarely encountered the Cavallis more than once a month. The signora would always smile and wave at passers-by, though her husband, who had been an invalid for some time, was more reclusive. Rumour had it he was declining and might not even make it through the summer.

They seemed to be comfortably off and never had to work, and this was ascribed to the success of their son, who lived in America and came back from time to time on visits, looking more handsome and affluent on each occasion. Other visitors came, but very rarely, and they would arrive in large cars, which could barely negotiate the rough mountain tracks that led to the farm. It was easy to spot the Cavallis' visitors. They were always dressed in inappropriate metropolitan clothes, and would gawp at the views while taking walks to sniff the medicinal mountain air. More often than not, they would meet a herd of cows in the meadow and end up scurrying nervously back to the safety of their hosts' house.

One morning in early summer a young man arrived on foot in the village of Olivone and asked the way to the Cavallis' home. He was set on the right path, and after a bracing climb – which he seemed to enjoy, because he arrived at the farmhouse with a broad smile and rosy cheeks – he stood before the signora and removed his hat. He spun her a story that he was a local lad looking for work as a gardener or odd-job man, and he did the accent well enough for her not to doubt him for a moment. In fact, Signora Cavalli was charmed by his bright eyes and friendly manners, and she invited him indoors for some cake and coffee. It was the least she could do after his long hike, she said, though she doubted there would be any work for him. Her husband had become rather particular about not having strangers about the house.

'He has been ill for some years,' she said, and looked a little tired, 'and recently it has got worse. I'm afraid the doctors don't hold out much hope.'

The young man looked genuinely sympathetic and asked if he should leave right away; but she melted at his considerateness, gave him a conspiratorial smile and said that he should just walk down and have a chat with her husband; perhaps the signor might make an exception in this case; she could certainly do with the extra help.

She pointed the young man in the right direction: her husband was reclining in a wicker chaise on a lower terrace. It was a glorious day and he had asked to be left there in the sun, to look at the lovely mountain scenery. While Signora Cavalli got on with preparing lunch, the young man wandered slowly down to the reposing invalid.

He was motionless, a blanket across his lap, wearing a straw hat and some green tinted sunglasses. The young man observed him from behind for a moment. Cavalli's mouth was hanging open slightly. A bumblebee was moving from flower to flower close by, and a very slight breeze brought a flicker to the longer blades of grass at the garden's edge.

'Good morning, sir.'

Signor Cavalli turned his head with a slight jerk of surprise towards the young man, having not heard his approach. 'Yes?' he said.

The man knelt down beside him and looked into his face for a little while.

'What do you want?' asked Signor Cavalli. His voice was clear and quite high placed, though he wheezed and his breath was short.

'I'm going to be honest with you,' said the man, smiling. 'I told the signora I was looking for work, but I'm afraid the truth is: I just wanted to come and see you.'

'Who are you?'

'Don't you recognize me?'

'No. Should I?'

'Maybe not. I came to your house some years ago. You remember? When you lived in Posillipo?'

Signor Cavalli gave him a sharp look. 'Who are you?' he asked again.

'My name is Benedetto Figlietti. I called by several times at the Villa Rosalba but you were always too busy to see me. Once I managed to get an appointment, but you forgot all about it. I was very upset at the time, but it doesn't matter any more. It's taken me years to find you.

A lot of searching. But here I am. Here we are. Together at last.'

Signor Cavalli looked into his smiling face. 'Why did you want to meet me so badly?'

'For the best reasons.'

'Do I know you?'

'Not in an ordinary sense.'

'You have a familiar face.'

'Do I?' asked Figlietti, delighted. 'Well, I suppose it's possible you remember me from that one quick meeting we had outside your house. Or perhaps I'm familiar for another reason.'

'What other reason?' Signor Cavalli could only manage short sentences between each breath.

'Some people say that I look just like my mother's family, and they have a point, I suppose. The fair hair, the eyes. But there's something else I see in the mirror. Something in the jaw, the lips. I must get it from somewhere else. My father, I suppose.'

Signor Cavalli's eyes opened wider and he looked at the young man, without blinking. When he eventually spoke, his voice was more subdued and hoarse. 'What is your mother's name?'

'Sofia Bosetti. You knew her in Milan a long time ago, she—'

'You don't have to remind me. I remember.'

The young man waited for the shock of his revelation to dampen before continuing, all the while smiling. He took hold of the older man's hand. 'It bothered me a lot, for a long time. Not knowing you, not being acknowledged by you. And what happened to my mother. It burned me up. But now I don't mind so much. I have a lovely wife of my own, and a beautiful baby boy. I'm just here to close the circle, and to be your friend.'

'A baby, you say?' Cavalli said weakly. His eyes had reddened.

'Yes,' replied Figlietti, getting up off his knee for a moment to fetch something from inside his jacket pocket. 'Actually, he's not a baby any more, he's two. Walking, talking. I've brought a picture of him for you. You can keep it.' He slipped a small photograph of an infant between Signor Cavalli's unusually broad fingers, and laughed. 'I've got your hands,' he said, and held up his own muscular blacksmith's hands.

Signor Cavalli looked at the picture silently for some while. 'And your mother?' he asked quietly.

'Happy,' replied Figlietti. 'You don't have to worry about her now. I'm not saying it wasn't hard for her at first, with a baby, no money, no husband, her career finished. But she eventually went back home to my grandparents' farm and married my father. He's a farmer, too. She jokes nowadays that you leaving her was the best thing that could have happened. She said that if I ever found you I should send you her best wishes.'

Signora Cavalli stood some way off, next to the doorway of the house, drying her hands on a cloth. The sun dazzled her, and she raised a hand to shade her eyes. She could see the young man down on the lower terrace, on one knee, laughing and talking to her husband, and she smiled. He'd obviously charmed the poor old dear. She had a couple more jobs to do and so decided to leave them to it as they seemed to be getting on just fine. It was a while later that she heard a light tap on the open door behind her, and the man was there again.

'You had quite a chat,' she said.

491

'Yes. Your husband is a wonderful man.' The signora's smile fell instantly from her face and she turned to look straight at him. Though the lad's face was full of good-will, there was something about the way he had spoken the last sentence that told her he knew the truth. They looked at each other in silence.

'How did you find out?' she asked.

'Don't worry. Your secret is safe with me.'

'Why did you come?' she asked.

He raised his eyebrows. 'Let's just say that I wanted to see if I could help in any way. Anything. I mean it. But I don't think Signor Cavalli wants anything doing just now. He says – ' he hesitated and looked into the signora's eyes, 'he told me that his house is in order now.'

'He said that? Those very words?'

'Yes. And he's right,' Figlietti said, looking round the room. 'You keep a very tidy home, signora.'

'That's not what he meant,' she added quietly, but Figlietti did not respond. He took out a card from his wallet. 'I'll leave you with my details,' he said. 'If ever you need me. For anything at all.' He made the point emphatically and held the card pressed to her palm for longer than he needed to. He then bid her farewell and was gone, removing his jacket as he walked down the track away from the house. She watched him until he disappeared around the corner.

Within the year, Signor Cavalli had died of a tumour on his lung. There was a small private ceremony, with just a few neighbours attending, and the body was buried at the local church. The signora sent a telegram to the young man, and he managed to get to the church in time for the funeral service. He had his little boy with him, and also brought news that his wife had just given

492

birth to a second son, to whom they had given the name Rocco.

Before the man left, the signora handed him a gold chain with a little coral amulet hanging from it. Her husband had asked her to pass it on, she said.

Signora Cavalli remained in her mountain home for the rest of her life, but would spend a generous portion of every year, usually the winter months, in California. While there, she liked to stay the odd weekend with her old friends, Mr Boldoni and Mr Pickering, who were always delighted to have her and entertained her royally; but most of her time in America, of course, was spent with her marvellous son and his family, at their rambling Beverly Hills home, set in its own parkland. She never got into the habit of calling him Franco, even though he had left his old name behind on the day he signed his first Hollywood movie contract, and his own wife had never once addressed him as Amedeo. For all the glamour and success that Franco Steel was to enjoy, some of his happiest moments were the quiet evenings he would spend in the kitchen with Chiara on her visits, perhaps after everyone else had gone to bed, when they could reminisce together, in the old Neapolitan dialect, and still shake their heads in quiet disbelief at the extraordinary adventure of their lives.

Author's Note

Most of my groundwork research into the lives of celebrity singers of the 1920s was undertaken some years ago, when I was commissioned to write a series of monographs on ten great opera stars from that period. These biographies were subsequently produced in five limited edition volumes, though I doubt many copies remain in circulation, except in specialist libraries and on the dusty top shelves of my study at home.

I accumulated further knowledge of the subject, and learned about the early science and history of the recording industry, when I worked for Nimbus Records, helping to launch their technologically intriguing series of transfers from original 78rpm recordings of the great singers onto digital CD.

I suppose my own early experience as an over-worked neophyte tenor with Italianate ambitions must lend a note of authenticity to the narrative's observations regarding vocal mechanics. One or two of Rocco Campobello's difficulties (though not – I must stress – his accomplishment), I have shared to an extent first hand, which may explain the undercurrent of sympathy some might detect for his emotional leanings in the aftermath of his revelatory crisis. The career of an opera singer is not the paradise it might seem.

Finally, I should add that the discovery of Naples – through its literature, history, musical culture, and through wandering its streets endlessly from top to bottom on my research trips – has been wonderfully illuminating. I unashamedly endorse the clichés. Naples does indeed steal the heart of the open minded visitor. For all its tempestuous past and ragged edges, it retains – or, more likely, has recently rekindled – the magic that made dewy eyed travellers in days of yore wax breathlessly: see Naples, and die.

A Dark Enchantment
Roland Vernon

GODWIN TUDOR, a young English photographer recently arrived in Athens, is intrigued by the mysterious and maverick British landowner Edgar Brooke, whose vast estate dominates the island of Pyroxenia.

While visiting Brooke's remote home, Godwin is enchanted by the breathtaking landscape and captivated by his host's capricious young daughter. But all is not quite as idyllic as it seems.

Inadvertently drawn into a terrifying international incident, Godwin does his best to play the diplomat. But consequences prove more devastating than he can imagine.

A haunting tale of love, adventure and intrigue, *A Dark Enchantment* marks the début of an exciting new storyteller.

'A rousing, red-blooded tale with colourful
characters in an exotic setting'
Joanne Harris

9780552775007